BENCHMARK

BY THE SAME AUTHOR

CONTOUR
Hardback ISBN - 978-1906221-447
Paperback ISBN - 978-1906221-430

APPLE GIRL
Hardback ISBN - 978-1905886-715
Paperback ISBN - 978-1905886-623

TWELVE GIRLS
Hardback ISBN - 978-1906510-381
Paperback ISBN - 978-1906510-947

TRIG POINT
Hardback ISBN - 978-1848761-254
Paperback ISBN - 978-1848761-216

WINDBLOW
978-18487624-28

JON BEATTIEY

BENCHMARK

Matador
5 Weir Road
Kibworth Beauchamp
Leicester LE8 0LQ, UK
Tel: 0116 279 2299
Email: books@troubador.co.uk
Web: www.troubador.co.uk/matador

ISBN 978-1848765-283

A Cataloguing-in-Publication (CIP) catalogue record for this book
is available from the British Library.

Printed in the UK by TJ International Ltd, Padstow, Cornwall.

Matador is an imprint of Troubador Publishing Ltd

To Helen, for consistent encouragement, my thanks; and to Sue, for consistent tolerance, my love.

AUTHOR'S COMMENTS.

This story is far more 'Irish' than its predecessors - and the inspiration comes, not only from West Cork, but specifically from the Woodstock gardens at Inistioge - and though there is a rose garden, and you won't find '*Cadhla*' there, you will find someone very much like her elsewhere, demurely holding a book.

The Manor House(s), though the main literal placement is in Bedfordshire, have strong internal overtones of Polesden Lacey (NT) in Surrey, where the entrance hall gives exactly the same vibes as portrayed in the text. Well worth the visit. The bench also exists, (with thanks to the Harrison family) though not on a hillside. The original inspiration - where this all started - came from the girl on a horse (see 'Contour'), also from real life, and though I'm glad to say she didn't fall off, she did offer a charming smile one Sunday morning. . .

If you like this story, maybe you'll love the purely romantic novel 'Seeking' . . .

Jon Beattiey

www.jonbeattiey.info

... THE SCENE IS SET ...

Roberta is expecting her third child. Husband Andrew has come to terms with losing their former office assistant Andrea to the film world, compensated by the installation of Hazel, previously seen as a rather dull witted au pair, into the Manor's regime as a quasi daughter. His elder daughter June, now absorbed into the Interior Design business, is seeing her marriage dissolve as husband William has gone off to the States, and she wonders if he'll return. Peter, his son also from the earlier marriage to Samantha, has accepted a promotional position in London with the Charity he and his mother work for. Roberta and Andrew's twins Abby (Aubretia) and Chris (Christopher) are growing; Grandmother Mary is struggling to cope with the demands of looking after the establishment and her increasingly precarious state of health. June is about to go to Ireland on her first major commission as a Design Consultant.

PROLOGUE

'Are you sure you'll be alright?'

'Stop fussing, dad. I'll have to be. I'm your daughter.'

Andrew felt the pull of emotion. His daughter, his precious elder daughter, the epitome of all he'd wanted a daughter to be, and taking on a role as though she'd been doing it all her life. So proud, and at the same time, concerned.

'Roberta's briefed me well, Donald and Siobhán are such nice people, and I've got my mobile, what could go wrong?'

He took a deep breath. What indeed? Maybe he would be seen as worrying unnecessarily, but there were other factors in the equation. Roberta had become far more dependant on June of late, and with her pregnancy advancing, the demands of the business would increase the strain. June's marriage was as precarious as his had been four years ago; his subsequent divorce from Samantha so changed things and he wasn't sure how June would cope.

'I'll - we'll miss you.'

'Dad! Really, I'm not going for more than a few days, now am I? You've got Hazel.'

Which was true. Hazel. The girl who'd progressed from kitchen wimp to indispensable au pair to the nearest concept of another daughter. Who'd filled the gap in his life left by Andrea? No, impossible, no-one could fill that gap. Different. Taken into his life as a very precious extraordinary person, recalling that infinitely priceless moment on top of the Sheep's Head in West Cork, alongside an old trigonometrical point of all things, but so so symbolic at the time.

'Yes, I - we have Hazel.' Roberta wouldn't be without her either.

He hefted her suitcase. 'You said only a few days. From the weight it's two weeks!'

June laughed. 'Got to be prepared. From messy jeans to decorative dresses. It's not as if I have to carry it. Right. Let's go and face the fray.' She leant forward and kissed his cheek. 'Love you, dad.'

'And I you, my daughter.'

About to leave her bedroom, she held his hand for a moment. 'You're okay about Andrea?'

He knew what she meant. Andrea, his weakness, the girl who so pulled at the other side of his emotions, the girl who had proved irresistible and yet, incredibly, tolerated by his true love Roberta. Now set to go through this rite of passage, her leaving party, all mixed up with the cast 'n crew showing of the television programmes shot here a couple of months ago that may well result in an avalanche of curious interest in what they did; would they survive the onslaught?

Their eyes met. The memorable day, the 'Open Day', when she - June - had returned to his affection and when some scout for the film people had locked onto them. The conversation they'd had in the car that wet and soggy day. The time she'd looked for him the day his divorce from Samantha - her mother - had been finalised. Milestones. What a significant daughter she was.

'I'm okay about Andrea.' Indeed, he was. True, he'd flirted with the golden haired deliciousness ever since the Brewery's collapse, had sex with her before Roberta and he had properly got together, held her, comforted her; *loved* her even now, all as part of him and his make-up. And that Roberta knew helped him tremendously in his caring; he knowing she was unworried. Part of him. She'd not have it any other way but, the wry smile, maybe comforted in knowing that peculiar relationship was stabilised by the girl's moving to another world.

'So let's go, dad.' At the back door, she pushed him away. 'You go on, I'll check on Mary and the twins.'

In the small barn at the back of the house, the party was getting into its stride.

'Andrew, dear man. Thank you again for the use of the place. Come and meet . . .' Alain, silver grey mane of hair sleeked back, lightweight fawn chinos, deep maroon shirt, the guy who'd taken Andrea away from him into the world of film and fame, waved a champagne flute at him.

He was escorted round; one introduction after another, people he knew by name and reputation, people he'd probably never meet again, and the few who'd been part of the filming crew, including that willowy Sally producer girl, once seen in jeans and a bra-less blouse on Day One now looking like something out of the Times 'Style' supplement. Where was Roberta? And Andrea? And Hazel, come to that?

'Where are the girls?' he asked Alain.

'In your big Barn with Marilynn. Ten minutes or so, then we'll start. That okay?'

Marilynn, the glitzy presenter of these programmes. 'Sure. And thanks.'

'No problem. It's good.' The quizzical look suggested a comment might be appropriate.

'You'll take care of my girl?' Andrew had to ask, for she was so precious.

Alain nodded, aware of the significance. 'I know what you mean. She's her own person, Andrew. She'll take care of herself. But yes, I'll look after her. Promise. Go and find them, bring 'em back. I've got to check on the technicalities.'

June re-appeared from her temporary sojourn in the Manor's kitchen in time to take his hand once more.

'Mary's okay with the twins, dad.' His own precious two year olds. Dears, both of them.

'Good girl. We've got to fetch the others out of the big Barn.'

'Right.' She felt the tension still in him, the pressure of the changes now so close and virtually unavoidable. 'It's going to be fine, dad. Just relax and enjoy the moment of glory. Roberta will. Andrea will. And Hazel will love it.'

He turned to look at her. 'Yes. And you're right. I wonder what your mother would make of all this?'

June blinked. Dad was thinking about her mum, mum Samantha, all cuddled up with her new man down in Kent? A sure sign he was stressed. 'You need a drink, dad. Loosen up, please. Enjoy the evening. Take pride in it. You'll love it.'

Once the assemblage had taken seats and quiet established, the technical guy pushed a button on the recorder thing; what was his name, Tim? The credits rolled across the huge plasma screen especially installed for the occasion. Then the opening sequence and they watched as Roberta, his own darling wife and the once more mum-to-be Roberta, did her walk from the gate across the yard to look up at the Barn. The Barn, focus of their endeavours, home to the Smiley Interior Design business, her world. Then into the building and its wonderful array of bespoke designs, the pan around that showed how brilliant a designer she was. *Take pride in it*, June had said. So he should, so Roberta should. He squeezed her hand, held loosely in her lap. Her pregnant lap. The lovely smile from deep brown, amber flecked eyes. He loved her, the girl he'd rescued from her tumble off that horse and after which curious day they'd never looked back. Body and soul, especially soul. So much a part of him.

They were shown two entire half hour programmes. Then Alain stood up and expressed his thanks, his admiration, for the way the Manor's personnel had approached the filming in such a professional way; Roberta preened but Andrew's mind was elsewhere.

June was going to Ireland, tonight. On her own, well, other than with the couple with whom they'd contracted to re-design the décor of their main house overlooking the Suir river near Waterford and the small retreat somewhere hidden down the Borlinn valley. Nice people. How would she get on?

Andrea was going to become Alain's P. A. No longer to be his bête noir, *the girl whose presence in the Manor's office constantly kept him in tune with his emotional side. The girl who'd added so much to the drab days before his divorce, before he and Roberta became soul mates. Would she regret the move?*

Peter was going to London, albeit daily, to run the volunteer's office for the Charity; make life changing decisions for individuals who'd make such a difference to others in desperate straits and who in turn would become stronger people in their own way. Proud of him, the way he'd turned out - and he'd fallen for Hazel, bless her. Such a happy coincidental thing. He hoped it would blossom and last. She deserved any amount of love, that one. He'd never stop loving her either, in his own way.

Mary - blessed mum Mary - having brought Roberta up in true 'in loco parentis' because of the social stigma that would have otherwise been attached to her father and his infertile wife. A weird arrangement, given Roberta was Mary's love child with Henrietta's husband. All water under the bridge now. But she was showing her age, rather too obviously, wouldn't entertain any idea of seeing the doctor and Roberta was worried, not good news given Roberta's unplanned pregnancy. Though not regretted, the prospect of a family addition, no way.

So these were the benchmarks. June's success in Ireland, Andrea's at the film studio, Peter's in London, Hazel's in the office and her attachment to Peter, Mary's well-being, Roberta's successful pregnancy. Points of reference. Crtieria. And his - keeping it all together. He'd try.

'Andrew!'

'What? Oh, sorry.' Roberta was pulling at his sleeve. 'Miles away.'

'So it seems. What did you think? Worth all the hassle? Alain's coming our way.'

True, he and another smart suited guy were obviously targeting Roberta, for after all, it was her show. He brought his mind back to the reality of this evening's event.

'I think so, don't you? You were brilliant, love. And our girls. Did us proud. You happy?'

'Yes.' She switched on her smile as the approaching pair came within earshot. 'Alain. We loved it. Was it what you wanted?'

'Absolutely,' the other man spoke up. 'Alain's done a superb job, as always. Such an inspired choice of location. Sorry, let me introduce myself. Larry Suissman.' He held out a hand. 'Sorry I didn't get to properly greet you two people before. Great place you have here.'

'Larry's our Managing Director,' Alain explained. 'Pays our wages, so I'm glad he's impressed. Can I get you good folks another drink?'

The party rolled on. At a suitable moment, and after a few of the hierarchy from Inspired Productions had said their thanks and farewells, Andrew climbed on a chair, clapped hands together and managed to bring some quiet to the motley.

'This is the point where I have to do what I wish I didn't. A moment I've been dreading. This evening's screening has been great, I think we've all seen what a great series it will be, but it's a sad time for the Manor as well as a proud one, for we're losing one of our stars. Andrea - you've seen her tonight on screen, and she's here with us now - Andrea!' He beckoned her across.

'She's been the girl who's held the system together for the last couple of years or so, without whom I - we - would have been lost. And because she's been talent spotted as a result of this production we're losing her. Andrea,' he stepped down from the chair and put an arm round her, 'our thanks and all our love.'

Roberta, standing close, stepped forward. The imp in her would have wished to add a comment about the love bit, aware her husband knew Andrea a good more intimately than many might realise, but she had her role to play. The little box was in her hand and she popped the lid.

'This is a small token of our love and esteem, An, from us both. It comes with all the very best wishes for you in your new career.' She took the ring and reaching for Andrea's hand, slipped it on. The slim platinum and diamond ring sparkled. Maybe o.t.t., but a symbol. They could afford it.

'An eternity ring? Really?'

Roberta nodded. 'Andrew's choice, my thought. We both love you, Andrea, so this is something to remember us by.'

She, too, put an arm round, so the threesome were held together. Andrea said a few emotional words, photos were taken, and the hubbub broke out again. So brief an interlude, but a milestone. And now it was time for June to go as well. She'd seen Donald at the door.

ONE

He couldn't remember. It wasn't Monday, was it? No, Saturday. Fuzzy headed, eyelids glued together, whatever time had they eventually managed to get to bed? Oh, the party! She was still sound asleep, dear girl. Attempting to focus into reality was painful. However many glasses had he had? The thought brought on pressures and therefore with as much care and caution as he could muster, managed to reach the objective relief without cannoning into either door frame or loo.

Roberta felt him go, stretched, rolled over and reviewed the prospect of the day. An ordinary weekend, as far as it went, like many another. The party was behind them. Done and dusted, apart from dealing with whatever debris was left, but she didn't mind that. Just sad that there wasn't going to be any cheery repartee from June, and by now, she thought, looking at the bedside clock, she would nearly be in Ireland, if they'd managed to catch the ferry. Not leaving until nine last night hadn't given them very much lee-way, if any.

She'd enjoyed the evening. Seeing the results of the effort, talking to the hierarchy, lapping up the adulation. All worthwhile, despite the little tiffs she'd had with Alain during the filming. So when the programmes were out 'on air' as Alain had said, they'd really take off. The niggles of how they'd cope she pushed away. Hazel would remain with them, Peter would be around to give moral support, and dear mum Mary would look for another girl to boss around in the kitchen and nursery. June wouldn't be away above a week. Merely her growing tertiary womb-bound child to take care of, apart from the twins, that is, but they weren't a hassle. Lovable lusty chunks of family.

As Andrew came back from the bathroom, she swung herself out to sit on the edge. 'Morning, luv.'

He bent down and kissed her forehead. 'Morning. I hope you feel better than I do.'

She grinned at him. 'Teach you to drown your sorrows. I saw you.'

'What to do you mean, saw me?'

'When you thought I wasn't looking. Giving that paramour of yours a going over after we'd given her the ring. I wonder you didn't bring her up here for a quickie, the way you were snogging her. You know, the 'save the last dance for me' bit. Are you going red, dear?'

Well, he couldn't help it. The line betwixt sanity and sex was a fine one, but he'd stayed the right side, however tempting she'd been under that smooth red dress of hers he remembered too well. Two sides to Andrea. The ever so efficient, calm collected administrator orthodox side and the other, a demanding damsel in distress. Distress from not receiving the loving attention she craved. And he'd gone so far as to take risks with her . . . once upon a time.

'She wasn't wearing any . . . ' He stopped, aware of his thoughtless and sex inspired comment and Roberta smirked.

'Surprise surprise,' she said. 'But you didn't take advantage, at least not as far as I know and that's all that matters. Well done, boy. Go and rouse the twins while I use the shower. Then we'll have a decent breakfast before we sort last night's debris. Shame Peter missed it.'

Andrew nodded. 'True. Perhaps he wanted to. Not really his scene, maybe he'd have felt fish out of water. He'll be back before eleven, I have to meet the train. And June'll be in Ireland now.'

'Provided they caught the ferry.'

'Motorway, late at night, in that Jaguar? They'd catch it. I can't see Donald hanging about. She'll ring in once they've been breakfasted, I should think. Unless she waits until they get to their house. It's not all that far. Go and get your shower, dear. See you in a bit.'

The onus was on her to rationalise the change in the system, for it was her business, her house, her mother and, despite his involvement, which she'd never demean or deny in any way, her twins. And another embryonic infant coming. Had to be a boy, for Chris's sake.

Andrea had gone; Miss Temptation had moved on. To be fair, she'd added that tangy hint of spice to their lives, as well as being the super efficient office whizz and Andrew had loved her, in every which way. She'd no real quarrel with that, largely because no actual damage had happened to any of them - other than the broken wrist she'd suffered after castigating him over mis-mentioning the girl's name and fell over a chair in her haste to run away from his clutches. Stupid, that. And now that she'd gone there'd be no one for him to ogle or flirt with, other than Hazel, and he was too in love with that one as a daughter to move towards the danger zone. Then of course, he was also that much older now, so mebbe the hormones would quieten down.

She stood up and felt the unexpected twinge at the top of her thigh. Ouch. Not good.

'Andrew!' Would he hear? She took a couple of steps towards the bathroom door and the sharp stab of pain around her pelvic regions stopped her, brought on a sudden feeling of nausea and her vision blurred. 'Andrew! Andr . . .'

He came back through the bedroom doorway and saw her, on her knees, a face grey and twisted, a hand on her side, the other barely holding her upright, her mouth open, a soundless call for help.

'My love! What's happened?' He knelt at her side, attempted to lift her but she pushed at him.

'My side, the pain, oh ohhh, whatever have I done, call someone, Andrew, help oh oh ohh!' She leant forward and all but collapsed onto her side, her knees up into her stomach.

He left her briefly, went to the door and shouted, 'Hazel!

❧

Mary woke to the urgent knocking on her bedroom door, now thrust open in front of a wild eyed Hazel.

'Mary, Roberta's got something wrong with her. We can't get her up and Andrew's panicking. Please, please, can you come?' and without waiting, she'd gone, dressing gown cord trailing behind her.

Mary 's heart bounded and she felt the griping pain again. Her beloved daughter, in trouble. *She should never have fallen for another child, not at her age. Silly, silly girl.* With slow yet determined movements, she got herself dressed. No point in not, 'cos there's going to be work to be done. Twins, breakfasts, sort the place, all without the folk who'd gone gallivanting off. Whatever's the girl done to hersen?

She climbed the stairs, heavily, slowly, fearing for what she might find.

Somehow, between them, the pair had managed to get Roberta back onto the bed, where she lay on her side, Andrew gently massaging from waist to inner thigh. Hazel sat on the side of the bed, holding a hand.

'Ee, lass, whatever have you done to yoursen?'

Hazel rose and let Mary take her place. 'I'd best see to the twins,' she said, and fled.

Roberta managed a faint smile. 'I'm falling apart, mum. A most odd feeling.'

4

Andrew stood up. 'I'm going to try and raise Doc Mac. You stay put.'

'I'm not going anywhere, Andrew. Sorry if I frightened you.'

'It won't be the first time, but I'd rather you didn't make a habit of it, my love. Has the pain eased?'

She nodded, cautiously, and felt for her groin. 'Ouch! It's jolly sore. And round here. What do you think I've done, mum?'

Calling me mum rather than Mary shows how much she's worried, thought Mary, but it's something I've heard of, this pain down around there. Best let the Doctor fellow say.

'Got out of bed the wrong way, lass. Forgot you've got a young'un in there. You're not as young . . . '

'. . . as I used to be. I know. Tell me off, mum. Tell me I shouldn't have let myself be carried away.'

Andrew thought back to that day, and the few others afterwards. When she was as seductive as she'd ever been and he'd gone along with her mood; there was never any thought in either of them that they'd planned to add to the twins, but that's the way it was, and neither had been unhappy about the idea. Until now, when suddenly, complications had shown up, and fresh after they'd lost Andrea and June, and Peter was in London with the Charity's executive to talk over his new job. What could he say?

'I'll go and phone.'

When he'd gone, Mary stroked her daughter's hand and attempted some reassurance.

'I've heard tell o' this afore, my lass. Happen, you'll just have to get used to being less able to get about till the bairn's born. It'll sort itsen, ne're fret.'

'But the business, Mary. There's no one to show clients about if I'm stuck in bed or whatever. And you and Hazel can't deal with the twins all on your own all the time. Whatever will we do? Andrew'll manage some things, but you know what he's like!'

'We'll just have to cope. The bairn comes first. June won't be gone above a few days. And our Hazel's a grand help.'

Another faint smile. Just as well the girl had been brought out of her dull old state, and three cheers for Andrew's inspired idea of taking her into the family. That all too brief holiday in Ireland hadn't been wasted, and she thought back to the time when she'd played a silly trick on him, way up the hill, faking a faint in order to get him going. Serve her right, for this was no trick, but very much for real.

'Get me an orange juice or something, Mary, please. I'm parched.' With a slow delicacy beyond her belief, for she usually moved so sinuously, she eased herself up, legs splayed out in front of her, and itched backwards to lean on the bedhead. 'Not so bad now. And ask Hazel if she's alright with those two?'

'Don't fret, Roberta. You know she's fine with them. Just you stay still now.'

Despite her ache she had to chuckle. 'You think I'm going to leap off and follow you downstairs?' said before she realised where all this would lead and sobered up. 'I'm a pain, aren't I, mum? Bringing all this onto you all just when things were going so swimmingly?' Tears weren't far away. 'It's all so stupid. I must have wrenched something without knowing or it's the way I laid last night. So blooming annoying. Oh, damnation!'

'Aye, lass, annoying. But a cross you'll have to bear if you wants another little one. Better make sure it's the last 'un.'

'Oh I will, mum, never fear.' She remembered the thought she'd had when the possibility of pregnancy had arisen, a brief instantaneously abandoned abortion idea; the worry she might have produced twins again and her unspoken comment about sterilisation. A definite decision. 'Provided I get through this.'

Her mother looked at her. 'You're my daughter, lass. You'll survive. I'll go and get you some breakfast.'

Andrew had been lucky. Roberta's old-fashioned medical

6

man, Doctor Mac, had been at home. He'd listened to what Andrew had said, merely said 'hmmm' and 'ah', told him he'd be over within the hour. 'Keep her still, Andrew. I think I know what's the problem, but let me see her first. Shame it's happened to her, but happen it does to some women. She's not the first.' He wouldn't be drawn further and Andrew returned to the bedroom after checking Hazel was managing with the twins; how he blessed the decision to add her to the family.

Roberta lay back on the pillows. 'I'm sorry, love.'

'I'm sorry too, for you. Doc Mac's on his way. Says you're not the only one, whatever that means.' He sat on the bed edge and reached for a hand. 'And you're to keep still.'

A wan smile. 'Don't think I'm going to drag you up a hill today, love. Teach me to be sexy with you.' Then she became serious and added quietly, 'make sure mum doesn't do too much, please. I don't think she's all that great, and this won't help matters. You'd best look at the appointments diary and do what you need to. Pity, but can't be helped.'

They breakfasted together off a tray he'd fetched up, actually all rather cosy and nice, before repeating much the same exercise with Hazel and the twins in the nursery. He reassured the girl.

'Apparently, so the doc says, it's not an unknown thing. Not that it's any consolation, but at least it's happened to others. What are we going to do, Hazel? Shall I look after these two while you deal with the office, or shall we abandon the office today - given it's a Saturday? Just as well June's on her way, else she'd have aborted the trip. Peter'll be back later on, so that'll help.'

Hazel wiped Chris's mouth and returned the plastic car he'd dropped. Abby was quiet, sucking a thumb and looking at her father with wide brown eyes.

'Abandon the office, Andrew. I don't think there's too

7

much to hurt. Andrea made sure we were on top of things. And I'm sure she'd pop back for an hour or two of an evening if needs must. We need to make sure Mary doesn't overdo things as well.' She got up from her kneeling position by the children's small table and stood straight, flexing her shoulders. She grinned at him. 'How you're glad I'm here!'

He smiled back. 'Very true. No regrets?'

'Andrew, my only regret is that you weren't my biological father - not that I'm wishing my old mum on you! Never think for one moment I'm not very very conscious of my good fortune in where I am, what you've done. No, no regrets. Whatever needs doing, I'll do it, provided I can. You keep an eye on these two for a while, I'll go and sort things out with Mary, then we'll see what happens after the doctor's been. Okay?'

For a twenty year old who'd had such a problematic upbringing she was marvellous, and once more he thanked the depths of spiritual feelings they'd experienced over in Ireland only a couple of months ago. Almost like a conversion! If it hadn't have been for that fortnight, maybe she'd still be more of a domestic help than a daughter and a far lesser person than she was now.

'Okay. Well done you. This is where I say '*I don't know what I'd do without you!*', and I mean it.'

She nodded her head sideways and back, a Hazel trait, and grinned again.

'You can take me for another walk up a hill sometime,' and touched his cheek with her fingers as she left the room.

TWO

The Jaguar was warm and comfortable, the red leather seats absorbing her tired back. It had been such a hectic couple of days, not only sorting herself out for the trip and ensuring she had all the information she needed together with a case full of sample materials but doing the handover of her immediate clients to Roberta into the bargain. Then there'd been a few interesting hours with Andrea, as a sort of safety net for the office systems in case anything happened to Hazel, and the final bits of getting the cast 'n crew event into place. And the devious way in which she'd got the size of Andrea's finger for that eternity ring - her father's way of getting over the loss of the girl. Oh, yes, she knew all about what the relationship meant to them, and no, she wasn't too bothered about it either, for Roberta both knew and condoned it. Now a thing of the past, at least from what she could see.

The miles were zipping by. Siobhán was asleep, Donald holding the car at a steady seventy with one hand on the wheel, elbow on the door's window edge. Not a lot of traffic, Pembroke here we come. The ferry left just before three. Hope they'd make it!

She woke, suddenly. They'd stopped. Donald was opening his door, stepping out, and Siobhán stretched.

'Where are we?'

Siobhán turned her head. 'Newport Services. Want a pee?'

She thought. Hmmm. Not a bad idea. 'Are we on time?'

'Think so, dear. We can spare ten minutes or so. Go on, I'll wait till you get back. Don't want to leave the car unattended.'

She went. Motorway services at this time of night - she checked her watch, midnight, give or take - was like zombie land, and she was glad to get back to the car. Siobhán was gone barely three minutes. Donald changed places with his wife, and they pulled away. Sodium lighting gave way to the dark and the miles slipped away. Donald started to snore. She must have dozed again and for some time, a sure indicator of Siobhán's steady driving, for now they were off the motorway.

'A48,' said Donald, now awake, seeing her stir. 'Coming up to Carmarthen. Well on schedule. What comes of having a good car. Like it?'

'Comfortable. Quiet too. First time I've ridden in a Jaguar.'

'Eats up the miles. Been through a good few countries.'

She'd not fully understood what it was they'd done abroad, all she knew was they were 'retiring' and hence the need to spruce up their house, but was now a good time to ask any question?

'How old do you think she is?'

Obviously he meant the car; seemed like he was in chatty mood after his snooze. Siobhán briefly turned her head and June thought she'd smiled in the dark.

'The car's his pride and joy, June. I sometimes wonder if the house caught fire whether he'd drive off in it without worrying over whether his wife was in the passenger seat!'

Donald harrumphed.

'Twenty?' June offered, guessing as the seat leather was so creased.

'Not bad. Twenty-two this year. Adult. Hundred and eighty thousand on the clock. Good, eh?'

They'd come to a big roundabout and Siobhán swung the car away to the left onto the single carriageway road.

'Last lap. Another three quarters of an hour. Plenty of time. Be there before two. Ferry goes at quarter to three.' He turned back to watch the road and June relaxed back. She'd have another nap.

The next time she woke, they were pulling into a car park, where lines of vehicles were already on the move past a small ticket office. Beyond the offices or whatever they were, all lit up, she saw the ferry, a huge towering mass of a boat.

'It's big!'

'Twenty something thousand tonnes. Good boat. *Isle of Inishmore.* Does the round trip twice a day. We've never had a bad crossing yet. Timed it right. Can't abide waiting around.'

Siobhán slipped onto the end of the next moving line of cars; ticket details were checked at the little hut and they drove through the customs shed and into the loading area. Five minutes later wheels were drumming over the ramp and she was on board the ferry for Ireland.

Relaxing into one of the cosy settees on the top deck, June relived the day. Strenuous, exhilarating, and now, unbelievably, all behind her. Her father had coped quite well with Andrea's leaving, she thought, on top of the weird experience of seeing one's self on the screen. Though ever so slightly miffed at not being in the picture herself, she had to admit how well all three girls had acquitted themselves, her step-mum Roberta, then Andrea and Hazel. She also realised that if it hadn't been for the filming, Hazel's deception may not have been 'discovered'. Which would have been a crying shame for all concerned. Briefly she thought of Peter and his growing attachment to Hazel. Lucky her. Then logically, William came to mind and the way he'd treated her. She'd been so gullible as a youngster, thinking how a few kisses, an unbuttoned blouse, naked breasts and some careless fumbles under her skirt were then seen as the equivalent of love and a lifetime of partnership. Now she knew better.

11

He'd have to go.

The rumble of the engines far below increased, and looking out onto the eerily lit dockside, she could see they were under way. The tannoy sounded off, telling them it'd be a good crossing with a slight swell and four hours to Rosslare. Siobhán was already asleep, but then, she'd driven the last hundred miles or so. Donald had his head in a magazine. She cosied down as best she could and let the noise and vibration lull her asleep once more.

When she next surfaced, it was a dull grey morning, and below, an equally grey sea with icing sugar-capped wavelets was streaming past. Donald was asleep, untidily with his mouth open. Siobhán far more curled up, the blanket she'd brought up with her from the car draped across her legs. They were both friendly enough but deep down she'd felt some reserve, as though she wasn't quite accepted, not yet. Well, technically she was an employee, sort of. Perhaps seen as a 'contractor.' Whatever. She eased up from the cushions, gingerly put feet onto the floor, or was it 'the deck'? Stiff and muzzy headed, longing for a decent wash and fresh air, but, glancing at her watch, they'd been at sea for nigh on three hours so it wouldn't be long before docking. Most of the other passengers were still dozing. She attempted to walk across to the window, found the slight sway made her unsteady and had to reach for a table to stay upright.

She took a breath, tried again and this time balanced her gait. At the windows, damp and showing speckled raindrops, she saw a lighthouse on a rocky island. So they must be near land. She knelt on the seat and remained looking out. All a new experience, this, and though she'd never really considered seasickness, realised it wouldn't have been a problem. She rather liked the gentle movement, reminded her of a dance floor. Shame she'd be flying back.

A quarter of an hour passed and she'd got bored with looking at waves. A small fishing boat had crossed their stern and gone, then she noticed the dark line of land in the murk. Turning, she saw Siobhán coming across towards her.

'Good morning, June. Did you manage to sleep any? It's not easy in these seats, but we never bother with a cabin. Should be into Rosslare within half an hour. We'll have breakfast on the road.'

'I must have slept, thanks. I can sleep anywhere, never had a problem. The crossing's been quite smooth, hasn't it? Have you ever had it rough?'

'Only once. This boat's well stabilised, but occasionally you can get some pretty serious waves out here. Do you want a coffee to tide you over?'

June shook her head. 'No, I'm fine, thanks.'

'I'll get Donald one anyway. Sure?'

She nodded her head. 'Sure.'

Siobhán returned to her husband and June decided to explore, to make the most of the facilities while available. Five minutes later the tannoy went to call them down to the cars and within half an hour they were driving up the slope away from the dockside and into Ireland.

Twelve hours previously she'd been supping tea in the Manor's kitchen. Amazing!

It was so different. They'd called into a fuel station someplace, June had no idea where they were, and had a super breakfast from the deli hot counter - bacon, sausage, a goodly dollop of sauce all in a soft yummy roll, and a huge carton of hot fresh ground coffee from a wonderful machine thing. Not by any means a Manor style breakfast, but here, and after the night, fabulous. Siobhán tucked into her sausage and mustard roll with equal gusto while Donald had a bacon and black sausage bap.

'First Irish breakfast?'

June nodded, mouth full.

'Can't fault these places. All organised. I'll just stretch my legs,' and he walked off across the forecourt.

Siobhán took another slurp of coffee. 'We don't always descend to forecourt meals, June, but it suits the occasion.' She looked around. 'If you want a paper or something, please feel free. You're our guest and we're so pleased you could come. It'll be good to have fresh ideas and someone else to talk to.'

'So how long since you were last here?'

'Three months. Then before that, we were out nearly the year. It'll be good to stay in one place for a decent period. The house may need some sorting, so I do have to say in advance it'll be damp.'

'What did you do?'

Siobhán hesitated. 'Donald's a consultant. Tropical medicine, preventable diseases, hygiene, that sort of thing. He doesn't much like to talk about it, June, so please respect that.'

'Of course, whatever you say. But surely, if he's . . .'

'The best,' Siobhán interrupted, 'but we've been at the wrong end of some politician's ideas and . . .'

Donald was coming back and she went quiet. June nodded. 'I think I understand. Thankyou for saying.'

They made good progress, Donald back behind the wheel and unerringly he took them through narrow lanes.

'Better than the main roads up to New Ross,' he'd explained, 'and you'll like the little ferry.'

'Passage East,' Siobhán had added. 'Saves a few miles.'

June could only smile. She hadn't a clue about the geography. Donald was right, she had liked the little ferry, except there was scarce time to take it all in before they were off the flat-decked craft and climbing up the slope.

'We'll bypass Tramore, far too tripperish. Not too far to go now.' Siobhán yawned. 'Despite the few catnaps on the

14

big boat, I'm fair bushed; I don't know about you.'

'I'm not too bad at the moment,' which was truthful enough, 'though an early night might be appreciated.' Her absorption of the different scenery was probably a contributing factor to her wakefulness, other than not having shared any of the driving, and she doubted whether Donald would have considered for one moment offering her the chance to drive his vintage pride and joy.

'You and me both. Have you rung the Manor?'

She hadn't. A twinge of conscience. Far too pre-occupied with this sequence of new experiences.

'Wait 'till we get to the house. Then you can pass on your initial thoughts.'

Siobhán was thinkingly right, for sure Roberta would quiz her, look for reassurance that the new concept was within her disciple's competence. She nodded. 'Good idea. Thanks,' and relapsed into silence.

Donald's route seemed labyrinthly complex, the narrow roads twisting and turning and there were scarce few road signs; if she'd been turfed out of the car for any inconceivable reason she'd have no idea where she was. Then, abruptly, a main road, a turning left and ten minutes later past a sign to Kilmeadan.

Siobhán turned back to her. 'Home stretch. Look, there's the river.' The Suir, broad, slow, glinting ripples in the lazy mid-day sun. 'Another ten kilometres. Then look for the Portlaw turn, not that we're too near there.'

June kept her eyes on the river. 'Wide, isn't it?'

Siobhán nodded but Donald answered. 'Wide and sluggish.' He took a turn and left the main road, climbing upwards towards a timber clad hill. 'You'll be seeing the house in a moment. There!' and he took a hand off the wheel and pointed. 'On the edge, there!'

June heard the suppressed enthusiasm in his voice and thought she saw cream walls under a tile roof. Siobhán laughed. 'Still a couple of kilometres to go.'

Then they came to a wide gate set back between well dressed stone walls, mature trees lining a stone-chipped two minute drive with lawn edges, a fence on the left, pasture to the right, and the car sweeping up to the sight of the house. To a Manor, Irish version. Roberta would have loved this.

THREE

Peter hefted his rucksack onto his shoulder. Yes, it was tatty, creased, and travel worn, but the feel of the strap and the presence of its weight was comforting, familiar and added to the confidence that gave him a lift, a swing and flourish to his walk. A good feel to the day.

The overnight stay hadn't been completely necessary; he could have caught a late train home but really, staying in town became a legitimate and conscience dampening manoeuvre that kept him out of the cast 'n crew thing. Not his scene; he'd been nowhere involved so best out of the falseness of the event, despite a small twist of reluctance at not seeing *les girls* in all their finery. Hazel, his - his?- lovely lass, and Andrea, that smokey smouldering blonde. And Roberta, gorgeous step mum. And sister June, of course. She'd be across in *auld Ireland* by now. Lucky girl. Or was she? Crashing out of her marriage, running home to dad, letting William, stupid arsehole of a bloke, get away with it. She should never have married him. He came to the zebra, ignored the oncoming taxi and made it to the other side, giving the horn blowing driver two fingers. *Try driving in Jo'burg!*

The hotel hadn't been too crappy, he'd sure been in worse. The evening in the bar, over-long despite chatting up a perky girl with a turned-up nose and freckles who giggled. Breakfast not a patch on Mary's. The huge red brick edifice of St Pancras loomed; he glanced at his watch. Half an hour. Back to the Manor to see how Hazel was getting on. First day without Andrea about. Then he remembered, today was

17

Saturday. Not an office day. They'd all be having a great time with the kids, having hot chocolates and sticky croissants in the kitchen; telling stories about last night's do, and dad would be moping over losing Andrea.

Settled into the luxury of the East Midlands express, he bethought of his chat with Richard, the Charity's Director, and the other two guys. How he'd been sifted to the top of their probable pile, how his mum had added her two penny worth, how they'd hung on his quick-fire ideas of checking on volunteer's genuineness. He smiled at Richard's comment over free-loaders, 'cos he'd been one himself, once. Then he'd seen what happened out there in Africa and his life had changed for ever. How one little girl had adopted him, hung round his legs, given him open hearted smiles when she'd only had three days to live, poor mite. So now, here he was, in a pukka job, going to be sending young and keen hopefuls into situations created from over-breeding, under resourced and politically unstable regimes, places from which they'd emerge either seriously grown-up or mentally scarred. He'd grown up after his experiences, that was certain sure. And mentally, a hell of a lot tougher. The train was moving. Heaps better than some he'd been in over the past two years or so.

This was a journey he'd be making a lot over the next few months or even years if the job stayed good. Expensive though. Maybe he should consider a pad in town - step-mum Roberta had hinted at a flat 'in due course' - wonder what she meant? Downside would be the separation from Hazel. The way she'd swum into his life, sheer co-incidence or was it fates conspiring? That evening out in the ultra cool autumn Manor's garden, parked under the old beech when he'd been smitten with her, not just her looks and figure but her whole being, the roundness of her character, the way she worked, spoke, walked, smiled, oh, and the feel of her, warm under his arm. If this was falling in love, then bring it on. He'd have to talk with dad. The train was slowing. Not in Bedford yet, surely? No, this must be Luton Parkway. The airport. Pity they hadn't flown back from Romania to here. Saved the hassle of changes. Wonder how mum was getting on? Donald would look after her. 'Cept she'd been pretty sure about getting him to give the old man her love. Did she regret the divorce? Dad doesn't seem to, but then Roberta's another woman entirely. Sparky, lot more so than mum ever was. And she's hatching again! Hope she'll be all right. How old was she now? Forty?

A West Indian couple had climbed on board, lugging hefty suitcases into the gangway, clattering about, three youngsters - healthy, cheerful, smiley - the two girls with ribboned pigtails, the younger boy with wide brown eyes, all of them full of fun and beaming smiles. How different from the sad vacant drabness of the bulk of the kids he'd seen during those last months in Eastern Europe; made this new job of his so urgent and meaningful. Dad - he would have been okay out there, amongst the orphans, despite mum's scathing comments, 'cos he cared, too. He knew he did, for what he'd done in his own way for both Andrea and, especially, Hazel. Okay, they were both very girly, the bonus, easy on the eye, and living came without hassle, but, mentally, both scarred. Not now. Not after dad.

He looked away, out of the window at the flat boring landscape of brick pits and rubbish dumps that was South Bedfordshire, the piled-up huge box warehouses and sprawled new 'social housing' and the train was slowing down again. Crappy dereliction, symptomatic of the attitude; too much red tape, too little drive, too much thought about profit margins, planning regs, and so like other places but with a different flavour. He grinned at his windowed reflection. The City fathers wouldn't like to have their town compared with one in Leone or Romania, but apart from scale and weather, so many similarities in approach. With a get-up-and-go approach from people who cared, they'd have

19

all this sorted in no time. Give the place a reason for existence. The West Indian family were pulling themselves together again, lugging the cases to the door. He reached up, pulled his travel-worn rucksack down from the rack and eased out of his seat. Would dad have remembered to meet the train?

Andrew met Doc Mac on the front door steps. He liked Mac, old school, grey haired, a 'been there, done that' look, nothing fazed him, not even modern National Health streamlined authoritarian bureaucracy. Patients mattered, not statistics or league tables.

They shook hands. 'Thanks for coming. Sorry to break into your Saturday.'

Mac shook his head. 'For Roberta, anytime. Sorry to hear she's had this problem. Let's go see.'

Andrew left them to it and retreated downstairs, where the twins were now ensconced in their newly raised seats in front of the table. High chairs had been discarded, though one would be needed again before too long. Hazel, saving time and mess, dexterously proportioning cereal into wide-open mouths suggested she'd been at it for years. High time these two fed themselves every meal time. Mary sat in the comfy old basket chair, watching, her lined face showing her evident worry over how they'd cope. He dropped onto a stool.

'Don't forget Peter,' Hazel looked across at him and up at the clock. 'It's half ten now.'

'Oh, lor. I'd clean forgot.' Torn between loyalties, but Mary voiced the commonsense approach he should have taken.

'You go now, lad, soonest gone, soonest back. Doc Mac will stay on, we'll gie him coffee.'

'Unless the train's late,' Hazel added, ever so slightly concerned.

He rummaged in the drawer for the car keys. 'You're right, Mary. Tell Roberta. Be as quick as I can.'

Quarter of an hour passed. As if the twins sensed the strain, they behaved beautifully, and Hazel let them slide to the floor.

'I'll take them outside, Mary. Let them run around. You'll be all right? Give me a shout when . . .,' but there were footsteps on the stairs, a knock, and Doc Mac pushed open the door.

'Ah! Two small terrors. Andrew? Did I hear a car?'

'He's gone to fetch Peter from the rail station, Doctor,' Hazel explained, 'He's coming back from London. They shouldn't be long.'

'Can I get you a coffee?' Mary eased out of the chair. 'Does my lass need ought?'

Doc Mac grinned. 'Just t.l.c. and some adjustment to routines. It's as I suspected. Ladies of her age should know better,' something as a family friend he could say without impropriety.

'As I told 'er.' She reached for the percolator and glanced at Hazel.

Hazel took the hint, shepherded Abby and Chris out into passage and towards the garden.

'Give us a call . . .'

'Aye, lass, ne're fret,' and waited until footsteps had receded. 'So, can 'ee tell us what ails my lass?'

He took a stool. 'Not for me to discuss a patient's situation,' he said, to follow his mild reproof with a grin. 'But she'll tell you anyway.' He sipped at the mug Mary'd pushed his way. 'Pelvic displacement. Happens.'

'Aye. I had it, carrying her.' She nodded upwards. 'Went after she was born.'

'You were lucky, Mary. Nice coffee.'

'Aye. Taylor's. Our Andrew, you ken. Won't have no other.' She frowned. 'I thought that was the problem. What comes of carrying twins and messing about, heaving stuff around in that Barn.'

21

'Speaking of Andrew, how long do you reckon?' He looked at his watch. 'I've another call to make before I get back to my weekend.'

'Twenty minutes or so, if t'train was on time.'

'Then I'll wait. Another mug?'

This was déjà vu, his father meeting him off the train. Not so long ago either, returning home - and the Manor *was* home, now - how life had altered since. New job, a girl friend, family around him after all these years.

'Hiya, dad. Thanks. All well? How did the party go? Heard from June?' He wasn't going to ask after Andrea. That wound would take time to callus over.

His father pulled a face as they walked the hundred yards to the Volvo.

'Party went okay. Not heard from June yet. But we have a problem with Roberta, I'm afraid.'

'Problem? What sort of problem?' Peter's mind went all over the place, crassly wondering if she'd flipped over dad's parting with Andrea.

Andrew flipped the key, opened the passenger door for his son before going round the other side. 'Not exactly sure, but I had to call our Doctor in. We need to get back, sharpish,' he said, sliding into the seat. 'She collapsed after getting out of bed this morning.'

'Dad! No! How come?'

'Pain in her hips. Left her back in bed. We'll see. How was your trip?'

'Fine, thanks. Decent crowd to work with. Nice office. It'll be good.'

They relapsed into silence as Andrew wove through the traffic on the mini roundabouts and headed out of town. A ten minute drive through the outskirts of Trellam and past the new Supermarket, the site where once stood the Brewery, scene of the fateful first meeting with Andrea. Peter watched his father's face turn towards the shiny new façade then quickly look away. He'd miss the bright girl's presence, that he knew.

They left the car on the gravel, alongside Doc Mac's vintage Rover.

'I'll just say 'hello' to Hazel, dad, then . . . '

'Sure. I'll pop upstairs first.'

They went their different ways, Andrew to bound upstairs and Peter across to where Hazel was playing a game of tag with the twins, over by the laurels.

Roberta was propped up on the bedhead, reading. 'Oh, hello darling. Got him back okay? Doc Mac's downstairs. I expect Mary's feeding him.' She put the book down and patted the bed covers alongside her. 'Come and be cosy. It's not all that bad.'

He sat and leant down to her, catching her lips and her arm went round, pulling him close.

'Luv you.'

'I love you too. Now tell me.'

'It's what the jargonese call PGP. And don't I know it. Pelvic Girdle Pain. When bits of you go all soft and out of kilter. The mechanism goes all wobbly, or something. Doc Mac says not to worry, it'll all go away after. . . But I'll have to watch my step, literally. Sorry, love. It was the extra weight of the twins and me being silly on ladders and moving furniture about in the barn. Or so he thinks. Then rolling about with you.' She giggled and he was so, so relieved. 'The sad part is, I might not be as useful to you as I should be . . .'

Her lips were soft, warm and comforting. 'Then I'll just have to go monastic.'

She pushed at him. 'Go and talk to the man. And I'll see how I feel. Oh, and keep an eye on mum, won't you?'

Doc Mac stood up and shook hands.

'Your mother-in-law's been spoiling me. Has she said?'

He indicated they should move out of the kitchen, towards the passageway and the front door. Into the hallway, the one place in the house where Andrew felt most comfortable, with residual overtones of the early days when his association with Roberta had been an illicit, thigh tingling jazz and the build of the flavour of their *affaire* akin to the complex subtleties of a fine wine. As were the components of the space too, warmth, colour, nose redolent of age and grace.

'Tell me.' Here he could come to terms with whatever would befall them, he and his beloved. Strength in association.

'When a woman becomes pregnant, changes occur.' Andrew nodded, the doc didn't need to explain. But Doc Mac went on, knowing he'd have to be forthright. 'Not just facial, and the bulge, but internally. Simplistically, cartilage can soften, ligaments increase elasticity, and hence the components of the pelvic structure are less able to stay in place, especially when subjected to sudden unusual movement.' He raised his eyebrows in query, had his explanation been understood?

Yes, it had. 'You mean, she's falling apart?' His tone was vaguely jocular to lessen his concern.

'She's not a pole dancer, Andrew. She's near forty. Not as muscularly efficient as once. Didn't she ride in the past?'

'Yes, briefly. And fell off.' The day he'd found her, unconscious on the lane's verge, picked her up and fallen for her in turn.

'Ah. All adds up. That said, you mustn't be overly concerned. This could all go away once she's had the child, and likely will.'

'But it could be permanent?'

Mac nodded. 'Occasionally. Let's deal with that if and when. In the meantime, she needs to be constantly aware of what to do and not to do, moving about. I'll let you have a suggestion sheet - I'll e-mail it over if you like. Now, I really must be going. If there's any further pain, I'll prescribe to alleviate it. Otherwise. . .'

'We're extremely grateful, Mac. What else can I say?'

Doc Mac smiled. More of a grin than a smile. 'Good old fashioned patient care, Andrew. Glad I'm one of the 'old school. Get far more satisfaction from seeing practical results than figures on a 'performance' spreadsheet, I can tell you.'

The heavy old door closed behind Doc Mac with its familiar thud. Andrew trod the beautiful red-blue hand woven carpet, smoothed his hand over the polished mahogany centre table, took in the scent of the floral decoration in the centre, Roberta's handiwork of two days ago and looked at the stairs, the broad carpeted stairs up which he'd gone, three plus years ago, to bed this glorious woman of his. And made her pregnant. Not then, true, but since. So his fault. He climbed those stairs, slowly, trying to take it all in, concerned how they'd manage, to bring her through the pregnancy with a child they'd love and without lasting damage.

He'd reached the landing when the static bell from the house phone rang. June?

FOUR

So familiar, or so it seemed. A gravel, well, actually a natural stone chipped drive. Steps. Old oak panelled door. Creeper up the walls. Sash windows (peeling paint), hipped roof. Georgian?

'It's what we know as a 'plantation' house, June. Built in the days when the British Government was keen on piling in the landed gentry to own and run estates - remember the West Indies and so on? Quite a few were burnt during the unrest if the landlords were at all unpopular. This one's a gem. Donald's parent's, then it came down to us. We've held it together, just. Quite a challenge, eh?' Siobhán held the door open as June stepped over the threshold and into history.

She was amazed. Roberta's manor, in a different setting. Not as well furnished though, and it had a musty, unlived-in smell. Siobhán had been right about the damp. Frayed curtains, threadbare carpet. No central hall table. No flower arrangement, obviously. A mess of ash and small fragments of part-burnt logs in the fireplace. Three saggy armchairs. A yellowed newspaper lying under one of them. Goodness me. Donald was behind her with a couple of the cases.

'Soon get the old place warmed up. Anita - she's our salvation - comes in every couple of days or so to keep it aired. God, it's great to be back, eh love?' He turned to Siobhán and uncharacteristically, as June thought, picked her up, one arm round her waist, another under her knees and swung her round in a circle of unrestrained eagerness before she could regain her feet. 'Ritual homecoming. You want the same treatment?' His face creased in a lovely smile, nothing other than a suggestion of huge relief for being back in their own home. Before she'd had time to protest or anything else, she too found herself whirled round in a waft of masculinity.

'There. Now you're officially welcomed. Let's go and get the Aga going. Might take an age. Temperamental old thing. Siobhán'll sort the rooms. Wonder if Anita's left any grub?' He disappeared through a door in the corner of the hall.

Siobhán laughed. 'Boyish enthusiasm. He gets like that. Let me show you upstairs first. Don't be put off by first impressions, dear. Come on.'

She'd been offered a choice of rooms; the one on the front, huge, high ceilinged, enormous bed with eiderdown and carved mahogany head and foot boards, another threadbare carpet. The other, smaller, on the back, looked out over the rising pasture land to the wooded skyline, a smaller bed though still larger than her single one back home - the Manor home - and an inclusive alcove with a wash basin. It also had a far more feminine décor. Somehow this felt much more 'her', and cosier.

'Can I have this one?'

Siobhán laughed. 'I knew which you'd prefer. Was my daughter's.'

'Daughter?'

The Irish auburn hair shook as she nodded. 'Maeve, at the University. She'll come home at the weekend.'

'But . . .'

Another laugh. 'Doesn't sleep here - has a boyfriend in the village. We can't worry, after all, she's over eighteen and we've been out of the country. He's a decent enough fellow, so he is. And Maeve's the making of him. Before her he was a wastrel, now he's up and working all hours at the building. Getting the euros stashed away now. Grand lass, she is, our daughter.'

'What's she studying?'

'Doesn't. Runs the admissions office, so she does. They'd be lost without her. Now, can I get you anything else, or shall I leave you to it? We'll have dinner at eight, provided my man's got the Aga away.'

June smiled at her pronunciation. Not 'Rrr-*gah*', *Ag*-ahh. She'd have to remember that one.

'Can't I help?'

'Not tonight.' and didn't explain. 'Another time. Sort your things now and come on down. We'll open a bottle, so we will.'

She flopped down on the bed as Siobhán's footsteps receded down the corridor, and stretched out. The dinner had better be good, she was starving, but it would also be good to get horizontal, *so it would,* and she giggled. An Irishism but nice. She closed her eyes.

Ten minutes later an arm on its way to pins and needle land woke her and, furious with herself for dozing, she reached out, heaved her suitcase onto the bed alongside and tipped it out, seeking a dress to wear instead of tired, creased and likely smelly jeans. Another few minutes after a swill in the basin over a un-made-up face, the dress making do over bare legs, she trod creaking floorboards under yet more worn rugs towards dinner.

Donald had on a velvet jacket; Siobhán had changed to a rusty red woollen dress that did wonders for her hair. Dinner in the formality of a front room, (mahogany table, balloon back chairs, flock red wallpaper, another tired carpet, a few musty paintings), was a casserole with beef, onions, carrots and large creamy potatoes. Scrumptious, rivalled Mary's best. A potent red wine, full and nicely spiced but not too much so.

'Thank you so much! This is lovely - how did you manage it?' She could scarce keep the surprise out of her voice.

Donald tapped his nose. 'Irish magic,' he said, and, reaching for the now empty plates from each side of him, Siobhán on his right, June on his left, clumped them together. Almost immediately, the door to the corridor opened and a slim woman with apron and a smile appeared.

'Anita, meet June. June, meet our own wonder woman. She's indispensable and proves it. Have you got the pancakes now?'

'I have that. And the sauce, Donald. Will you be wanting me to demonstrate?'

'Why not indeed? Impress our guest.'

Anita took the dirty plates away, to return a moment later with a large platter piled high with *crêpes,* folded into fours, swimming in a gold translucent sauce. This she placed in front of them and, reaching into her apron pocket, produced a long plastic torch lighter, the sort that took lighter fluid, and with a deft flick, lit it and applied the little flame to the pile. Immediately, a whoosh of pale blue fire; it flickered for a second or two and went out.

June hadn't quite expected the drama, but guessed of something along these lines. Anita pocketed the lighter and withdrew. Siobhán passed her a plate with three *crêpe* pancakes.

'Anita's speciality. A homecoming.' She lifted her glass, raised it, Donald copied her and June realised, a toast. 'To a well earnt return, and a welcome guest. June, my dear, may your stay here be pleasant and as useful to you as it will surely be to us!'

After the welcome and three brandy-soaked crêpes, her mind was too relaxed and happy to think, only autopilot got her back to Maeve's room and unconsciousness.

Not until the morning did she find out she'd slept in a dress and forgotten to phone the Manor back home. She struggled up and allowed her thoughts to steady. Ireland. Siobhán and

Donald. Anita's wonderful dinner. Too much alcohol. Not a thumping head but certainly a muzzy one. This dress would need a good iron. Was there a decent shower or did she make do with the hand basin? What time was it? *Oh lor, ten o'clock!*

After a gymnastic and nude manipulation around the basin - thankfully the water was warm - she rustled through what she'd brought, deliberated and chose her warm dark blue skirt and off-white blouse. Comfortable things, something she could wear all day and not feel out of place. The simple silver chain, the small pearl ear-rings, her half-inch heeled black slip-ons. No tights. Her hair needed washing but not today. She brushed it out till it flowed. Now. Breakfast?

She followed her nose, along the corridor, round the corner, across the landing, down the wide staircase into the hall and its tired old carpet. The door in the corner she remembered from yesterday must lead to the kitchen. No one else was about. It creaked, the waft of grilling bacon intensified. Did she imagine voices? The passage floor was bare planked wood with a patina of stains and knot proud. The upper walls peeling pale green paint, a dado rail in stippled varnish, below an anaglyptic effect in the same. Ghastly. A doorway at the end with a semi-circular frosted glass above the only light, another doorway to her left. The kitchen? She tried the ancient brass knob and the door swung open to a huge space.

'Why, hello there! Good morning to you! My, but you're a grand sight the morn. Come in, come in.' Donald, in blue butcher's apron, was in front of the range, the old big cream Aga set into a white tiled alcove, forking over something in a large flat black iron pan.

Siobhán, trouser clad legs resting on a stool, perched on the solid looking wooden centre table, put a book, pages spread, flat onto the raw scrubbed wood. 'Yes, do come in. How was your night?'

June's immediate comparison with the Manor's kitchen didn't do them any favours. Chaotic, in a word. Not unloved, though. A weird contradiction of cosy ambiance and cool indifference. 'Oh, fine, thanks. Totally unconscious, I think.' She wouldn't let on she'd dropped onto the covers, closed her eyes and woken up into grey daylight. Yes, it was raining. Of course, it rains a lot in Ireland. Straight off the Atlantic.

'Than have an Irish breakfast. Donald does a mean fried egg.' Siobhán swung her legs onto the red-tiled floor and stood to stretch. 'Home-cured bacon, though not by us. Anita's father. Black pudding. Soda bread's in there,' and she pointed to a large twin-tone brown glazed crock pot. 'Butter's off the farm, too. As are the eggs. See, we've got the real McCoy here,' and chuckled, 'so we have. You'll get used to the Irish before the week's out.'

Donald reached into the oven, the door swung creakily on its hinges. A tin tray had the bacon laid out. 'Tea or coffee?'

'Whatever's easiest?'

'I have coffee, Siobhán tea.'

'Then coffee, please.'

'Sit yourself down. One egg or two?'

Surprised at her easy absorption of the brilliant breakfast and the so light and fluffy soda bread all washed down with a particularly flavoursome coffee, she began to feel herself. Comfortable, easy in her mind, happy where she was, the light banter from these two so obviously content with each other, she relaxed. 'Lovely breakfast. You spoil me.'

Siobhán eyed her. 'So where do you want to start, June? Or perhaps I should ask, *when* do you want to start. Doesn't have to be today if you'd like time to acclimatise. Walk the estate, soak up the atmosphere - though today's maybe too soft a day for that. We've some unpacking to do, the boxes we've had shipped back. Donald's stuff, things I've collected

- which you may like to see - books, pictures. All remnants of our life abroad. Or you can browse our library? You say.'

'Roberta'll want to know . . .' and she had a pang of conscience. 'I should have rung last night!'

'Then use the phone in the hall. Tell them you're going to stay over Christmas.' She laughed. 'You may not wish to go back to the U.K. at all after a while, my lass.'

'I couldn't!'

'You wait. The place has its own subtle magic. Go on, let them know we've got you here safe and sound.'

FIVE

Andrew turned, to take the call in the hall, but thought better of it and moved swiftly down to reach the office before it stopped ringing. Somehow in all this fuss, he'd not thought of June before, but here she was, all bright and breezy.

'Dad! I'm here! And the place is really atmospheric, full of old world niceness. Siobhán and Donald are different people out here, so full of fun. They say I won't be home before Christmas, but I don't think so. I'll start work tomorrow. Had a lovely breakfast; Donald's a super cook. And the place is so much like the Manor, in its own way. Roberta would love it - but don't tell her! Is she okay?'

'Not really.' He felt his eyes prick. His lovely daughter, so much part of him, babbling on and he had to dampen her evident enthusiasm. 'I've had to call Doc Mac in. She . . .' He took a couple of stomach settling breaths. 'She's got what they call PGP. Means she can't . . .' and stopped again. This was terrible. 'She's got to watch what she does, how she moves, else she mightn't be able to walk properly.' He explained, simplistically, paused and June cut in.

'Dad, oh, how dreadful for her! What's it going to be like for her, what happened? Will she be all right, I mean, as far as the baby is concerned? Should I come home?'

'No, love, you concentrate on what you've gone for, Roberta wouldn't have it any other way. She'd feel terrible if you had to abort before finishing,' realised he'd used the word 'abort' and swallowed. He moved the conversation on. 'Did you have a good trip across?' His own recollection of

33

the ferry, the ports, the Irish roads, gripped him. 'What do you think to Ireland, so far?'

He heard her inhalation, knew she, too, was combating emotion.

'Love it, dad. Peaceful. Quiet. And this place is still in the nineteen fifties. I'll have a lovely time, sorting it all out for them. But it's so like the Manor, it's unbelievable. Even a big old Aga. And they've given me a lovely room, one their daughter used to have. She's called Maeve (and he heard the 'meeve' and knew the spelling in his mind); she 's coming over today some time.' A pause and he stayed quiet. 'Dad, please give Roberta all my love, tell her she's to take every care. Look after her, not that you won't. I know you love her. I love her too. In spite of everything.' Another pause, he could almost hear her thinking. 'Perhaps Peter could ring me, please.' She read the number off the old-fashioned phone's dial. ''Bye, dad. Take care of her. Regards to Hazel and Mary. 'By-eee.'

He replaced the phone on its pad and sat down into the office chair. What wouldn't he do to have Andrea back in this chair? Hazel was his lovely new daughter-in-quasi-adoption and more and more effective in both office role and with the children, but if Roberta couldn't do as much . . . what next? Time to talk to Mary.

She was steadily working on with lunch - good heavens, was that the time?

'I've had a call from June. She's arrived okay, but very concerned about Roberta. Suggested she came home, but I told her to get on with the job. Seems their place is similar to this.'

Mary looked up. ' I ken what's in your mind, lad. 'Nother girl? Or a lad? Summon' who'll take the strain off young Hazel?' She nodded her head at the window and he could

34

see the girl, slim, elegant and lovely, about to pick Abby off the ground, while Peter had Chris by the hand, carefully guiding him across the grass. They were coming back in. His children. His responsibility, and whatever needed to be done, would be done.

He nodded. 'I'd best get back to R. See what she wants to do.' He didn't need to spell it out, Mary knew what was needed. Provided she kept her health and energy.

Roberta was sitting on the edge of the bed, gazing at a chair full of clothes. She smiled at him, a mischievous smile, and he felt the pressure ease, aware now of just how tensed up he'd been these past few hours.

'Help me get dressed, love. Like old times?'

It had been a game then. Serious now. Sharing her weight, adding a helping hand.

'I'll get used to it. Not taking risks, I mean. I may have to use a stick or something. The phone, was that June?'

He nodded. 'Yep. She's okay. Sends you all her love and told me to take care of you. Which I will. The Drivas's place is a carbon copy of this, seemingly, but steeped in nineteen fifties nostalgia. So she says.' He didn't mention the 'not coming back until after Christmas' joke or June's comment about how her step-mum would 'love it'. 'Can you manage the stairs then?

'I should bloody well hope so! Mind you, it might be rather slow. Come on, let's give it a go.'

They managed it. He helped her to the armed chair and she sat like the proper Mistress at the head of the table while Mary passed plates round. By tacit consent, nothing more was said about her condition and the meal progressed uneventfully other than Hazel's battle with Chris over vegetables, as ever. Abby, bless her, got on with her one handed spoon approach and emptied her plate. Peter, unasked, wiped a sticky gravy smeared face without her exercising her right to a mini tantrum as was most often the case. She'd obviously fallen for him.

Andrew watched, mesmerised.

'So, council of war,' said Roberta, clattering her spoon noisily down in her empty pudding dish to attract attention. 'I may be partially knackered because bits of me don't fit together as well as they did, but that is *not* going to stop me from doing what I can. We need another pair of hands. Hazel, you're not going to be able to run the office and the twin's affairs on your own. And I may need you to do some meet and greet jobs if Andrew's not around. We can't rely on June coming back in merely a few days, from my reading of her comments to Andrew. And when she is back, I still don't think we'd manage. The telly programmes go out soon and then all hell will break loose. Peter - I know you'll do what you can at weekends and so on, but we mustn't allow this change in my mobility affect your new job. Mary, I don't want you getting tired out looking after boisterous twins when I can't. Andrew, my love,' and she looked straight at him, 'I know you'd love to call Andrea and sob your heart out to her, get her to come running, but please don't. She deserves a chance to get a fair crack at this girl Friday thing so don't upskittle it. Please?'

He grinned. 'Okay love. But I'd still better tell her, else she'll only be cross when she does find out.'

'Leave it till next week.'

'Okay. We could always ask Hazel to ring.' He looked across the table and saw her smile. 'Oh, and Peter, June asked you to ring her sometime. The number's on the pad in the office. Add double oh three five three and drop the next oh.'

Peter grinned. 'I know.'

'You don't mind me talking to clients, Roberta?' Hazel saw this suggestion as another milestone; it gave her a lovely feeling, to have a chance to add to her given knowledge, and she offered a flicker of a perceptive smile.

'No, love.' Roberta saw the smile. The smile that said '*you made me a woman, taught me all that I needed to know, gave me confidence to explore my sexuality, to be my own person,'* and the responsive emotional jerk went right through her body and in her mind, she felt her baby stir.

The day moved on. A lazy day. Once Mary had the kitchen aspect sorted and their Sunday evening meal organised, she relieved Hazel of her twin's duties and allowed the girl time off. Peter wasted no time and took her out for a walk. Andrew watched them go from the sitting room window, saw hands swing together and hold, felt nothing but joy for them both. He lost sight as they reached the corner of the drive towards the gate, and turned back to Roberta, sitting reading in her easy chair with legs up on the little *petite point* stool.

'We've come a long way, love.' He was in nostalgic mood, having seen in Peter and Hazel echoes of his first love, Samantha. A strange quiver of nostalgia. Where was Sam now, what was she doing, did she ever think back?

Roberta held her thumb in her book. Her steady look, the lovely deep brown eyes, her tentative smile; she knew what he was thinking. Psychic. 'Not going maudlin, are we?'

He moved over to bob down on his heels alongside her. He'd not lie to her, not to this woman who'd completely taken him over. 'Hazel and Peter. She's wearing that skirt. The Irish one. Brings back memories, in more than one way, R, Sam and I in the early days. She had a skirt like that. A see-through one, against the sun. I loved her.'

Roberta carefully placed the book upside down on the small table beside her and reached for a hand. 'You still do, don't you?' Pragmatic, understanding.

'After twenty years together, after having June and Peter? Yes, I suppose I do, in a different way. It doesn't eclipse my love for you.' The hand squeezed. 'And Hazel so much like her then. That day up on the hill in Ireland, in the same skirt. Peter's a lucky guy.'

She knew exactly what he meant, in fact she'd enticed

one or two of her earlier flames in the same way, knowing instinctively how the right dress worn on the appropriate occasion, allowed to drift in an enticingly revealing way, became as an effective weapon in a girl's armoury as any. After all, he'd succumbed, here, on the sitting room rug, when *her* skirt had slipped.

'Hazel's a lucky girl.' She turned it round. 'Peter's a worthy son of his father, love. You should be proud of them both. I just hope our three will be as lucky.' She brooded for a while, and Andrew stayed quiet, his mind away into Ireland, away up on the Sheep's Head peninsular and with a young girl in her prime of life, wondering if he'd then kissed her because she was Hazel or because she was a virtual Sam.

That day. So evocative, blue skies with fluffy white clouds, distant blue sun-sparkling water between the dreamy hills, a girl in a white dress; he'd fallen in love with her. As a daughter. And brought his mind back to the present.

'With you as their mum, R, of course they will. And for the record, I've no regrets about any of this.' He laid his head against her warm thigh. 'I just want you to have this child of ours safe and sound.'

She rumpled his hair with her spare hand. 'Do my best, love. I really will.'

The silence dropped back, merely the old wall clock's pendulum swinging the seconds away to echo the soft rise and fall of her breathing. She'd fallen asleep, bless her, her grip had slackened and her arm dropped. He stayed alongside, as he always would. Always.

Peter and Hazel left the Manor's drive and turned right, towards the village. She walked well, shoulders back, skirt swinging; her hand light and warm in his. They stayed quiet, keeping a gentle pace. The late autumnal afternoon was still warm, the cloud cover thin and untroubling. A small number of the remaining frost bronzed leaves from the horse chestnuts lining the lane drifted down, the tall dried grass fronds showing bleached above the darker green of the verge and the trails of blackberry thorn with a few berries left soft and purple black. A rabbit darted out ahead, stopped, swerved back into the undergrowth. A chaffinch's brief burst of song, the faint blurring noise of a vehicle on the main road a mile away the only sound above the crunch of their feet on the loose gravel on the lane edge.

Without discussion they turned left into the open field gateway and took the track leading up to the wood. Known or not, this was Andrew's accustomed route of his reflective walks. Her skirt caught on an extended briar and she stopped, released her hand and carefully unhooked the thorn.

She frowned. 'Perhaps I should have worn jeans,' she said, catching his hand again.

'I like you as you are, Hazel. Too many girls wear jeans as though they're part of a rag-tag army. Much more refreshing, your kit. Properly girly.'

She laughed. 'Girly! Doesn't alter who I am, what I wear.'

'No, but a picture looks better in a proper frame, a wine tastes better in an elegant glass than an enamel mug. And a girl looks more the woman in a nice dress.'

'My my. Quite the philosopher. Whatever, Peter. Glad you approve. You know where I last wore this?'

They'd reached the top edge of the field and scuffed leaves as they went through the gap under the big sycamore.

'No, should I?'

''Spose not. Ireland. Where I bought it, actually. It's Avoca. Lovely clothes.'

A couple of hundred yards along they came to the bench, half concealed under the sun bleached tall grasses. Neither of them knew of the bench's significance, but Peter trod some of the grasses down, smoothed his hand along the slats.

'How strange! Fancy finding a seat up here! Good view

back down into the valley, though.' He carefully sat down. The slats sagged but held. He patted the space. 'Try it?'

'Doesn't look very safe, Peter,' but nonetheless, she smoothed her skirt behind her and lowered herself, gingerly, alongside him. They sat quiet, taking in the landscape below them, the falling ground across the pasture, the hawthorn hedges growing bronze, the yellowed sycamores.

'I like autumn,' Peter's comment. 'The year on the turn, with all the richness of the colour, the harvest. Despite the oncoming winter.' He slid his arm round her shoulder, just as he had a week or so previously on the evening they'd had the first frost, on the seat round the big beech, back in the garden. Up here, on a warmer day, it wasn't to keep her warm, it was something else.

She leant into his comfort. 'Your father, Peter. He's so in love with Roberta. Don't you mind, I mean, having a step-mum and so on?' Never having met Samantha, she couldn't imagine her or therefore, why Peter's father had abandoned her. She knew about Andrea, of course, and how obviously that girl had affected Andrew's life, and she could see how much more Roberta meant to him, but still that didn't offer a solution to the problem.

Peter withdrew his arm, put his chin into his cupped hands, elbows on his knees.

'Not all that simple, Hazel.'

He stayed silent and she began to feel sorry she'd asked, rather like that time on her walk with his dad in Ireland and she'd asked him if it had been different, holidaying with Roberta before they were married than afterwards. She'd not been answered then, either.

'Sorry,' she said.

He looked sideways at her, at her worried expression, and chuckled. 'For what? Being a nosy little girl?'

Realising he was making fun of her, she stuck an elbow into his side. 'I'm not nosy! Nor am I a *little* girl!'

He'd swayed sideways to avoid her elbow's dig, but now

he came back at her, an arm across her front to reach her shoulder and pull her close.

Eyes closed, her body's reaction one of strange acceptance yet peculiar resistance because she'd not experienced this depth of embrace ever before, the kiss deepened, lips parted, a flick of tongues, her heart beat rose and, and . . . she struggled, running out of air.

'No, you're not a little girl, are you?' She was given another, brief, tender, kiss.

What could she say, aware of her pulse rate and *that* feeling. Like on The Day she'd finally had Roberta's wonderful explanation of *things* and grown up, lost all her worries and gained a uniquely amazing experience, never since repeated. That was way up on the hill above their cottage in Ireland, and here they were, half way up on a hill above the Manor. What was it about hills? Aware she needed to control her emotions, she took his hand away from her front and sat straight.

'We'd best go on, Peter,' she said, not wanting to, more wanting him to kiss her again, and afraid he'd reject her, but no, he was smiling, a different smile.

SIX

June put the old-fashioned phone handset back on its cradle. A museum piece. Dad was worried, she could tell. And she was concerned, being away when it was pretty obvious they'd be struggling. This pelvic pain thing must be awful, especially if you weren't' aware it could happen. Poor Roberta. Should she let on to Siobhán?

The door to the hallway opened. 'Everything all right back home, June?'

Deep breath. 'No, actually, it's not. Roberta's been diagnosed with something called PGP, came on suddenly when she got out of bed. Seems she'll have to take things very carefully, not lift, and maybe use a stick, all that sort of thing.'

'Oh my dear girl, and so soon after you left! Do you need to go home? You can, you know, we can wait. Let's talk to Donald,' and putting a comforting arm round her shoulders, shepherded her back into the room opposite the kitchen where, it seemed, they were likely to live most of the day, judging by the homely clutter. Donald was already ensconced in a huge armchair covered in a tatty multi-coloured woollen throw, reading through a copy of some Irish weekly paper, looking as though he'd never been away a single day.

'Donald, dear, June's had some rather unfortunate news. Roberta's suffering from PGP.'

The paper went down. 'Poor woman.' He pushed a pair of specs up onto his forehead and came over all medical man. 'Affects about one pregnant women in five to a lesser or greater extent. Mostly cures itself postpartum. Uncomfortable, though. Poor girl,' he repeated. 'She's had twins. And I suppose none too careful about pushing furniture about. Does she ride?'

June shook her head. 'Not now. She did, briefly, after her first husband left her, because he left the horse too. After she'd fallen off a time or two, she sold it.'

'Ah. Hmmm. Yes, well. She'd not know. Twisted when she was getting up, or moved too quickly. Seen it happen. She'll have to take it steady. They all right?'

'It'll be a strain on them, I think. I said about going back, but Andrew's adamant I stay and do the job. He said Roberta wouldn't want it otherwise.'

Siobhán patted her on the back. 'I can see that. Well, we can only wish her well. We'll send her a card, Donald.' She touched June's cheek with a light kiss. 'We'd better make the best of your stay, But tomorrow. After lunch, if it stays fine, we'll give you a tour round the estate, if you'd like to, that is.'

Roberta's indisposition wasn't mentioned over lunch. Anita had returned mid morning, cleared up the breakfast things, and put a salad and cold meat meal on the table in the sitting room. June helped and found the 'wonder woman', as Donald had called her, a bright and cheerful person, as welcoming, open and forthright as they came. She guessed at her being in her mid thirties, envied her clear complexion and lovely figure; found, surprisingly, she'd no husband.

'Never found a man to my liking,' Anita explained with a chuckle, hands in the sink, swilling plates about. 'There's many a fella who'd roll me around on the turf but none I'd want to share a lifetime in bed with. More to living with a man than shagging.'

June coughed to cover her confusion. She wasn't used to such straight forward conversations.

'Now yourself, you've had a man, haven't ye? Did he have you every night or jest now and agen? What's he up to while you're away? Or don't you wish to know?'

'He's in the States.' And, she thought, as Anita intimated, probably with another woman. Well, so what. She didn't owe him anything; it had been a big mistake and in Anita with her few inhibitions, found not only an ally but also a receptive listener. 'I wanted children, he didn't. He,' and overcame her reserve to echo Anita's simplicity, 'only shagged me every other Saturday night, sort of routine. As though he needed to remind his prick what it was for. No cuddles. Just open wide and swallow your pride, well, his pride actually. Not mine.'

Anita creased up, a huge laugh, and hands on her hip, bent over in her laughter. 'My oh my. Time ye had a *real* man. Take a lusty Irishman home with ye, there's a few going spare. Try a weekend at Lisdoonvarna,' she said, but didn't elaborate. The plates stacked on the draining board, she dried her hands. 'That's me for now. I'll see you later.'

When Anita'd changed her shoes for the outdoor ones she'd come in, put on her old coat and gone, June wandered back into the sitting room. Donald was asleep, the paper'd slid in a messed-up heap alongside his chair; Siobhán sitting near the window, working quietly away at a crochet frame. She put a finger to her lips, put the frame down and motioned June back out into the corridor.

'Donald always has a nap after lunch. You and me, we'll take a turn round the garden. then we can have a good old natter. *Craik*, it's called over here. A decent chat, about anything and everything. Lovely to have you here, June. I miss my daughter.'

'She's coming tonight?'

'Aye, she is. And that's good. I say it myself but she's a lovely lass. You'll need a coat. I'll wait by the front door.'

The afternoon was turning chilly and June was glad of her jacket, simple thing though it was. Siobhán had a lovely old brown coat, with faux fur round the collar, the edged sleeves and round the big pockets.

'This way.' She led, along the fine gravelled path to the right of the house, into an avenue of quiet tall conifers where the scented silence came muffled down like a cosy blanket. It must have stretched for all of a quarter mile, and at the end, one tree had fallen, remaining uncleared as a forlorn but convenient seat. Siobhán brushed the accumulated drift of pine needles off the rough bark and carefully sat down. She patted the space alongside. 'So peaceful. I love this place, June. Always dream of being here. Our home. Where we belong.' As June sat, Siobhán gently placed an arm round her shoulders. 'Don't you feel the peace, June?'

It didn't seem amiss, this comforting closeness, Siobhán akin to a mother figure and so right in what she'd said. So peaceful. Not a sound, above the gentle murmur of a light breeze in the branches above. Seen from this position, as through a wrong-ended telescope, the old house appeared timeless. 'If I lived here, I wouldn't want to leave.'

'You have a home of your own?'

June laughed. 'A semi-detached box in a hundred others, ten feet of grubby grass, a pavement and a busy road. Yes, I've a home. With an absentee husband. He's in the States on some computer training course. So he says.'

'You don't seem too upset?'

'I was when mum left dad, and he took after another woman. Then I realised how much mum was doing, working for the Charity and really that's what she'd wanted to do; I went to see dad in his new life, saw how relaxed he was, how happy he'd made Roberta, so it was win, win for them both. After that, it didn't matter. Except I was left with a rotten marriage of my own. I went back to dad, he took me as he found me, and well, here I am.'

'Oh June!' Siobhán's arm tightened. 'You poor girl!'

'I'm a lot happier in myself, working with dad and Roberta. William will make his own decision.' She studied her feet, swung them around. 'It's mum I'm concerned about now.'

'Why's that, June?'

'I think she's still in love with dad. And he her, I'm sure, maybe in a different way to Roberta though, but there's still a flame flickering. The odd remark; the way his eyes glaze when her name's mentioned. That sort of thing.'

'Roberta think the same?' Siobhán looked sideways at her, studied the thoughtful profile of this oddly attractive girl.

'Probably. She's very intuitive. And she'd got my dad's passion with Andrea all weighed up so it never really bothered her, not as far as I know.'

'Andrea? Who's she?'

'A girl about my age who fell for dad when they worked together on the old brewery accounts. I think - in fact I'm sure - they had a fling, before dad and Roberta got really serious. Oddly, she got to work as our office manager at the Manor and they were always kissing and hugging, though I don't think it was anything more than a mutual caring thing - dad's a bit like that. Cares for wayward girls. Even me. And Hazel. But dad would never hurt Roberta. She takes it all in her day to day. She's great. I love her.'

'That comes across, June. I like her too, which is one reason why we decided on Smiley designs to help here. Why Smiley when she's a Hailsworthy?'

'Former husband. Business name. Her maiden name was Tower.' She frowned. 'Sad she couldn't be here, she'd love it.'

'I'm sorry she can't come over as well - no disrespect meant to your abilities.'

'None taken.'

A quiet moment, reflective, thoughtful, the two women lost in their own worlds. Then June's distant gaze focused back in to her silent companion, the arm still light across her shoulders.

'Thank you so much, Siobhán, for listening. I shouldn't have burdened you with all this. After all, I'm really only an employee, a sort of contractor. You've treated me like a daughter.'

'That's a compliment, June. You seem like one, too. Let's

go round the block; by the time we get back, Maeve might be here, then you'll see if she measures up.' The arm went, but the loss softened by a gentle kiss on the cheek. 'Come on,' and she slipped off the log, dusting her coat down. The light had begun to fade, a vague promise of mist drifting through the trees. June stood, poised, and looked back at the house.

'I love this view. Timeless. You're so lucky.'

'Yes, we are.' So matter of fact, but simply true. Siobhán tucked her arm into June's and the two women walked on, continued through the trees. A twist in the path took them into the open and on towards a dilapidated rose garden. Cast iron pillars, deep brown with encrusted rust, curved cross beams, a triangulation of stone-flagged paths amidst a tangled strew of un-pruned briars. A few shattered flower heads still showed their yellow colour. At the central intersection stood a small yet fulsome statue of a Grecian draped maiden on a plinth, a patina of orange and yellow lichen adding to her allure.

June fingered the girl's carved tresses. 'Enchanting! How long's she been here?'

'Keela? Ever since I can remember - 'tis a special place, this. I should have warned you though, June. She casts a spell on all who stroke her hair. 'Tis too late the now. You're captive. Ye'll never leave!'

Her expression as June snatched her hand away was half-sincere, a half amused jest.

'An Irish superstition!' she joked, but could feel the pull of the place and a shiver tingled down her back. 'You don't believe it?'

'I came here as a young girl and did exactly that. I'm still here!'

'But you had connections.'

'Not then. I didn't marry Donald until well after. He used to stroke her hair too, as a teenager. Too late now, June.' She laughed. 'You're hooked.'

She couldn't reply. The magic of the place was way too

tangible as they continued down a maze of small paths through overgrown shrubbery, through an archway and into a kitchen garden. Here, some effort had been made to maintain a semblance of cultivation, a few beds hoed, a number of lettuce long gone to seed, onions lying with half rotted leaves on top of the soil, another bed with dahlias, their orange heads a contrast against a mass of dark green leaves. Potato haulms in a heap, turnip tops and beetroot leaves with their red streaked veins. A row of dilapidated glasshouses set against a high whitewashed brick wall opposite added to the tiredness of long-gone horticultural glory. The decaying light of the early evening didn't diminish the air of dereliction.

'Sad, isn't it? When you think this once gave work to a dozen men and kept the big house supplied all year long. Our last gardener retired a year ago, that's his cottage, behind the trees. Empty now, he moved away. We couldn't justify employing another, not as things are. But we've a lot of work to do, June, and you're just the start of it.'

'Roberta's gardener retired last year as well. So she hasn't anyone either. Andrew - dad - might get round to doing a bit now and then. I think he'd quite like to.' She looked around once more. 'Shame to have to let it go. Wouldn't anyone locally like to take it on as an allotment if you don't - can't - maintain things?'

Siobhán looked thoughtful. 'It's an idea. Better than letting the weeds take over. Hmm. I'll have words with Donald. See if he minds other folks around the place. He's quite protective of our privacy.'

Through the opposite archway and they were at the back of the house now in sombre darkness, into a pebble paved courtyard surrounded by outbuildings, a couple of garages. A single small wattage bulb captive in a glass cover on a swan-necked rusting support cast a barely sufficient dim light on the scene.

'That's where Donald keeps the Jaguar,' Siobhán nodded

at the garage on the left hand side. 'We've a little old Landrover as well, in the other garage. You can have the use of it if you want to drive around the place. That's the potting shed, that's full of old junk, and the last one's empty. Just so you know. Our land goes across the road and down to the river, then up to and including the woodland on the other side. Nice walk up to the top of the hill, but let us know if you go, because there's a few traps for the unwary.'

'Oh. Such as?'

'Usual things. Boggy bits, an old quarry rock face, half-fallen trees. We'd like to do some felling and re-planting, but . . .' she trailed off, and June's impression was one of reawakened sadness. Siobhán had become introspective in the last half hour, as though she was re-living better, livelier times. 'Let's have a good cup of tea. Irish tea,' and she led the way through the wide back door, into a flagged passageway, lit by another dim bulb hanging on a twisted cord. They turned the corner and she got her bearings, the corridor past the kitchen. The other door with the half-circle lights over it must lead to the side of the house?

Siobhán guessed her curiosity. 'Internal, the covered wash yard. Drying space and where kitchen servants could take a few minutes off without leaving the house. Rarely used now. Has a funny atmosphere. Stay clear, June, if you've any psychic feelings.'

Curious. With that, the comments about the wood, the Grecian girl - Keela, Siobhán had called her - and the change in her host's demeanour, some of her confidence ebbed away. This place had a history, dark undertones, and despite her initial delight, now she wasn't sure.

SEVEN

M onday morning came like a douche of cold water. The weekend disappeared, as fragmented as the Manor's residents. Peter was first up, had a snatch of a breakfast and cycled into town to catch the quarter past eight train. First day.

Mary was next up, to lay bacon on a tray, whisk a few eggs ready to scramble, and bring the kettle to the hottest plate on the Aga ready for teas and a coffee pot. Then she relaxed into her favourite chair, took up an old Lady magazine and read the short story, waiting for signs of life from the twins.

Hazel lay awake. She'd woken early, tried in vain to catch another hour, and turned to her book but her mind kept going back to yesterday's walk with Peter. So like his father, for whom she'd had a school girlish pash over in Ireland, then accepted it was foolishness when she realised he truly had taken her love on as a daughter. But as regards his son Peter, did her very naiveté in emotional entanglements make her too vulnerable, so her thinking, intelligent mind asked her? The gap in her life, the need for someone's love, mustn't be plugged by the first person to show her affection, so she reasoned. Lovely though, his pulling her close, showing her - *demonstrating* - what a kiss was all about. Triggering that little gem of essential feminine feeling, which meant she'd had to change her knickers. She grinned at the ceiling. Roberta'd been amazed when she'd talked about this effect, consequently she wasn't the *little* girl anymore. Well, she didn't dislike him, far from it, being the son of his father, the man she'd first fallen for, but, and again Roberta's moralistic little lecture came back to her, she'd take it slow and steady. And yes, she could. She was a lot more mature in mind than some.

Time to get up, now the twins would be awake. Sad Roberta couldn't dance down the landing to the nursery any more as she'd taken to doing, ensuring she, mum Roberta, got there before her nursery maid did. Except she wasn't just a nursery maid anymore. She had an office to run.

Roberta stirred, and controlled her urges. Careful girl. No repeat of yesterday. But out of bed she must get. 'Andrew, love?'

'Mmmm?'

'So you are awake?'

'Just. Sleep well?'

'Actually, I did. Feel ever so much better, but thought I'd better ask if you'd stand by when I got out of bed. In case?'

'Sensible girl. Give me a minute.' He stretched, rolled sideways and out of bed to stand up and stretch again. 'Right,' and watched, critically. At least she was being sensible.

She eased to sitting position, flung the duvet aside, swung legs round and down, stood up.

'That's okay. Now,' and aimed at the bathroom door. 'Not so bad. Provided I keep my weight balanced, I think I'll be alright.'

'Clever girl. Does it hurt at all?'

She pulled a face. 'Not like yesterday's fiasco. Sore, and with a kind of imagination, a dodgy bit in here,' feeling a hand between groin and the suggestion of a start of a growing prominence. 'Don't let me think about it. Maybe you'd best keep an eye on me in the shower?'

'Tempting thought, love. I keep an eye on you whenever you're naked, you know that!'

She narrowed her eyes. 'Aye, but this time, my lad, keep

urges under control. Let's get me hatched and back into condition before we go mad again. And after this one, no worries. I'll get them to snip a bit off.'

Then it was just the four of them and two little people round the big table for breakfast.

'I hope June's enjoying her Irish breakfast.' Andrew poured another mug of coffee.

'What was it you reported she'd said, Donald's a good cook?'

'Then she'll put on weight.'

'Best not,' Mary said. 'She's not that skinny a lass. Nay, she'll be canny.'

'Hope so. Wonder if Peter's got to the office yet?' Roberta stared at her mug of tea . 'How strange, to have a London commuter in the house.'

'Hmmm. You commuted.'

'But not every day, and in my own time. Glad I don't do it anymore.'

'Our penthouse flat doesn't get much use now-a-days.'

'Penthouse flat?' Hazel hadn't cottoned-on to that one, and was curious.

'My London home, Hazel, where I was brought up. We had it converted to flats, kept one on the top floor. Very prestigious.'

Hazel frowned. 'Sorry, what's prestigious mean?'

Roberta laughed. 'Grand. Posh, in a nice way. Hey, Abby! No!'

The little girl gurgled. 'Spah! Splah Splat!' and thumped her spoon down in her cereal bowl, sending showers of soggy Weetabix all over the place. Chris approved, and got his spoon ready to copy but Hazel managed to grab it in mid air.

'Well done, Hazel.' Andrew got up, brushing cereal debris from his shirt. 'I need to get on. See you in the office in a while?'

After he'd gone, Roberta suddenly felt alone, isolated in

her precarious state. The children were fine, Hazel was fine, mum Mary, well, seemed okay this morning; it was just her and no back up. The business was her problem. She couldn't ask Andrew to deal with clients' specific needs, good though he was with people, he wasn't into the niceties of colour and texture. June was, but she was in Ireland. Hazel - well, she would be torn between children and the office, her newly acquired territory. She caught herself in time, about to push her chair back and rush off across the yard to the Barn and see who was likely to be on the doorstep today. Instead, she did a graceful stand-up. Imitate dowager duchess, she thought. No repetition of yesterday's pain.

'So, Mary? Can you handle the twins this morning?'

'For a while. Provided they don't get too rumbustious.' She got to her feet. 'Hazel, lass, take them back upstairs for a bit, I'll be up shortly.' She had to let this ache subside and it took longer now.

In a mere five minutes Hazel managed to disorganise Abby and Chris from the breakfast table, clean up the worst of their excess zeal and encourage them to take receipt of a hug and a kiss from their mother. Roberta still experienced the nagging doubt over relinquishing too much parenting chores to Hazel, and to mum Mary, grandmum Mary. The upside was knowing they got as much love and care from her stand-ins and yes, she did still spend quite a lot of time with them in the late afternoons and early evenings before bed. In between it was work, work, work. The Interior Design business was where the money came from, so press on, girl, while you can. As her mum gathered the dishes and cutlery together to start the wash up, she moved her thoughts forward.

'Another pair of hands, Mary? How do you think we should go about it? Advertise, or do you know anyone who wants to dump their daughter on us, like Hazel's mother?'

Mary continued her dishwashing. A contemplative silence.

'Mum?'

'I'm thinking. No lass like our Hazel that I knows of.'

Roberta smiled into her coffee mug. There could never be another Hazel. 'So?'

'Mebbe take one o' them immigrants. Good workers, I hears.'

'Mary! A foreigner?'

'All part of Europe, you ken. There's many that do. Lots o' them about. P'raps one who'd feel wanted, appreciate a decent place.'

Roberta peered more intently into the depths of her mug, as though she sought inspiration, almost akin to reading tea leaves, except there weren't any, only a sludge of coffee grounds. 'I don't know what Andrew will say.'

Mary sniffed. 'So long as she's passably pretty and smiles, he'll tek to 'er.'

'That, mum, is a disparaging remark. As though that's all that matters. And why a 'her', why not a 'him'?'

"Cos I canna see a lad wishing to change nappies and the like, and it wouldna' be fair on our other lass. And they'll mebbe have to share a room.'

'Hmmm. Well, I'll think about it. Can't promise, mum, but I grant you, it is an idea.' She gingerly eased off her stool. 'I'd best go across to the Barn. I'm sure we've got someone booked in this morning.'

'You just take care, now.'

'Don't you fret, mum. I've learnt that lesson.' She rubbed at her tightening waistband. 'Though it's a hard one. I'll be glad when it's all over.'

'You and me both.'

Roberta walked steadily across to the Barn, her sanctuary and her delight. She discovered the knack of swinging her hips that made it easier, as though she was practising a sort of eastern military march. *If I wear a longer skirt, it won't half look like a sexy walk,* she thought, reaching the door without incident. Without June, once more it was all down to her. *This is where the filming took place. This is where we made our name. Where I can be my own girl.* All the little rooms, the unique displays, her concepts - with a touch of the June here and there, which was only right. They'd made her a partner in the business, strengthened the family ties, after she'd demonstrated a natural flair. And what with Peter now living here too, what more could a girl want? In the little space at the end that she'd made her own den, she could doodle and imagine, sketch and innovate, dream and evolve those dreams to reality. She sank down into the cosy chair, tentatively lifted one foot then the other onto the low stool, and relaxed. Then reached for the diary. Ah, yes, half eleven. Cordelia Smith and her partner, Julian what's-his-name. Cordelia and Julian. How absolutely *soouper*! *Frightfully nice* people. Loads of lolly, too. She read her notes. A small country cottage for weekending, about ten miles north. Two bedrooms, co-ordinated, space at the stair head, a living room, a dining area, don't bother with the kitchen (. . .*we neh-vverr eat in, could-n't be doing with cooking smells. . .*). Taking up her pad, she started jotting down ideas, but her thoughts kept swinging back to June. How was she getting on, over in Ireland? Was it raining? How long would she be away? Had she let William know - or was it past the point where the absentee husband would care? Shrugging, she stretched her mind back to the job in hand, listed a number of colours that might suit this classy pair and carried on, grateful that, so far, the day was ticking along. She reached for a new file.

June's Monday breakfast echoed the day before's, understandable given Donald was chief cook and - no, not bottle washer, Anita occupied that role. At least it was quiet, unlike last night's visitation.

Maeve, Siobhán and Donald's daughter, the typical red

haired Irish colleen of legend, had been a delight, a whirlwind in long patchwork coat and tweed skirt, tearing into the house during their teatime relaxation in a wonderfully breezily open manner, unrestrainedly embracing not only her parents but June as well.

'My, but just look at you all, 'tis as if you'd never been away. 'Tis grand to see you looking so well, ma, and pa the picture o' health. And the girl from England who's going to make this poor old place a delight and envy of all the neighbours. Ma, I'll not stay, Brendan's expecting us at the pub, 'tis music night, but I'll pop back mebbe tomorrow. See how we go.' And she'd downed a mug of tea, somehow eaten a scone whilst talking and blown out again.

Today she must concentrate. Do the job she was here for; how long would it take?

'Have we fed you sufficient?'

Her reverie broken, her 'thankyou' type smile achieved a reciprocal grin.

'Then we'll leave you with it, my dear. Donald and I are out for the core of the day, catching up with our neighbours, letting them know we're home. Help yourself to whatever you fancy for lunch - we'll be back around five for tea, and Anita'll be in around then, so she will. Sure you'll be okay on your own?'

'Surely. And it's the two main rooms downstairs?' They'd not got as far as a written brief, which, realistically, should have been completed before she came.

Siobhán looked at her husband, head in the morning's s paper, his domestic chores completed with the last fried egg. 'Donald?'

'Eh? What? Oh - to start with.' The paper went onto the table, his glasses pushed up and June nearly laughed at the expression; a remarkably similar caricature she'd seen in a Sunday paper's cartoon. 'But seeing as you're here, my girl, perhaps some thoughts on what else we should do? The place has been sorely neglected, so it has, for many a year now. See what you think, and pop some notes down, eh?'

'Surely,' she said again, trying to remember not to use the word again. 'Be pleased to. Would you have time to discuss my ideas later tonight?' hoping it would ensure she wouldn't be wasting her time, doing too much too soon.

Donald nodded. 'A good idea. After dinner. Leave the dishes, June, Anita'll do them when she comes in later. Right, my love, shall we sally forth?'

Left on her own, the Jaguar watched from the front window as it purred away down the driveway, the quiet of the house fell over her in a suffocating blanket of silence, apart from the gentle tock, tick,tock of the wall clock. Silence. On her own, in this time-warp of a huge house. Standing still, allowing the atmosphere, the *'spirit of the place'*, to creep insidiously into her soul. Her eyes roamed, wall by wall, across the ceiling, into the crevices, the corners, along the cornices, the dado, around the doors, took in the carpets, the skirtings, the floorboards naked on the carpet's edge.

Last decorated, when, nineteen twenties, or thirties? Before she was born, that was for sure. Would they take her views seriously? She stepped across to the fireplace, its wide gape emphasised by the black fire back plate with its intricate design and stroked the cream veined marble surround. A velvet feel, not as cold as cold. What was that phrase, cold as a marble tomb? The long settee, a four or five seater, covered in a brocade of edged deep cream, and the single cushion sagged as she sank down. How old was it? She wished that she'd had some schooling in interior design fashion, for this was where she could make some horrendous mistakes if she suggested re-covering historic pieces, or replacing priceless fabrics from a bygone period. The enormity of the project came suddenly to grip her. *Oh Roberta, have you chucked me into the deepest of deep ends?*

Ten minutes, or was it a quarter of an hour, later, the conclusion reached her. The thought had come from somewhere, deep inside. It wasn't for her to suggest the despoliation of a classic established concept, more the effective preservation, which, together with subtle enhancements to the existing arrangements and the absorption of historic ideas, would perpetuate the pleasure in the continued use of these rooms. No wholesale desecration. No chucking-out of any old piece of furniture regardless, no stripping of wall paper merely for the hell of it, and the carpet . . . she knelt down and lifted the edge. Not that she knew much about weaving, but this didn't give the impression of being a tatty chunk of mid-wars make-do. Likely a nineteen twenties import from the Far East, maybe Indian, Turkish, or even Kashmir.

A trip back to her room to collect her pad and the newly bought little digital camera; what an inspired thought that had been. Then she set to work, sketching, listing, cataloguing, taking photos. She should have brought a laptop, and that thought engendered a wry smile, a tinge of disappointment but no twinge of concern over an absent computer mad husband. No, none at all. Keela, my silent garden friend, you may be right. Three hours later her tummy rumbled. Breakfast, when was that? Dodging back to the kitchen, she poked around, discovered the bread stash in a huge earthenware crock, used a vicious looking bread knife to saw off two passable slices, applied very genuine farm-house butter from another crock, found a large round of a type of cheese she'd not met before with only one v-notch cut away, read the label - Durrus,- wherever that was - and ate, hungrily.

Reinvigorated, well content with her sampling of this Durrus cheese, she brewed tea, simplistically a teabag (another new-to-her brand) in an interesting hand-thrown mug, polished off three ginger flavoured shortcake biscuits - no doubt made by the multitalented Anita, and returned to her task.

The Jaguar had returned un-noticed, and before the promised advent of Anita.

'June? My dear girl! Still hard at it?' Donald stood at the door, hands on hips. 'Have you had any tea?'

She nearly dropped her pad, being back to the door, and eyes peering up at the way the plasterwork of a dogtooth frieze was showing signs of coming away from the ceiling. She spun round.

'I didn't hear you come back, sorry. Yes, still at it. And I had tea at . . . heavens - is that the time? Glory be.' The pencil tucked behind her ear in true professional fashion, she gave him a 'welcome home' smile. 'Another brew wouldn't come amiss. Did you have a good day?'

'We did, my girl, we did. Time to call a halt now. Don't need to give your brain a headache. Come?' and he disappeared.

She needed a comfort visit, having only just thought about it, and ran lightly up the central staircase to her room. Better that than the Edwardian style heavy ceramics and mahogany of the downstairs loo. Then changing her top for a warmer one - the evenings dropped in cool - she returned to the kitchen, warmth and conversation.

Siobhán had the teapot stirred and was pouring. 'You've been busy?'

June accepted her mug, headed straight into voicing her idea. 'It's restoration to give you back what's been lost, apart from some proportional fabric change, and a careful re-paint; you need a suitable carpet underlay for the existing, re-varnish the floorboards, plasterwork repair and the settee and armchairs need re-upholstering but retention of the covers where possible. And I think, but not having any real knowledge, the paintings may need cleaning. If all that's done, those two front rooms will sparkle and you'll be ever so proud of them. Real gems, they'll be. I couldn't bear to think of changing the style. The house would never forgive you.'

She watched for the reaction. Either a 'go home tomorrow, you're fired' or what?

Siobhán looked at her husband. Seconds passed, even a minute, and she watched his cheeks pucker up, lips purse, eyes narrow. All the signs of an imminent reaction?

'Arrhh. Hmmm. That's what you reckon?' His look was impassive.

Had she blundered? No, she was sure she hadn't. That's what this house was telling her; it deserved appreciative love, not vandalism. They *must* know what it meant, not only to them but to the place it held in the country's history. She'd felt it - did it come from her symbolic touch on Keela's hair?

'Let's walk through.'

She followed the couple, who'd linked hands. They stood in the first room, she'd called it the drawing room. The white and gold wallpaper caught the faint glow of a fleeting glimpse of a setting sun; the light was producing a warmth to the soul. Yes? She watched. Siobhán was leaning into Donald and her arm went round him, her head onto his shoulder. His free hand went up and scratched his chin as his look swivelled round, taking in the whole of the feel of the space. She waited, standing behind them in the doorway. Was she right?

EIGHT

The beautiful couple were early. Cordelia, a drift of gold and white with dark olive eyes and heels she managed beautifully; Julian, corduroy jacket in dark burgundy, open necked pale blue silk shirt, off-white chinos, navy and cream boat shoes; the Porsche bright red with a two letter, two figure number plate. Money, and never talk about it.

They gazed around, polite and intelligent.

She presented her folio binder with its carefully drawn sketches including water-colour highlights, the swatches of fabric fastened neatly in a fan and the wall hanging samples alongside. Her latest little collection of clippings from various up-market magazines to give examples of decorative display pieces had taken quite a while to put together, but a joy to do.

'Roberta, this is a *fascinating* place! How clever you are, putting these rooms together. Oh, how positively *charming*. Isn't it heavenly, Julian, darling?' Cordelia, at her simpering best, holding onto the portfolio.

Don't be churlish, Roberta, she means well even if patronising to a sickly extent. 'I try my best.'

Julian wasn't quite as wet. 'I can see why you have a reputation, Mrs Smiley. Very pleasant.' He took the file binder from his lady friend and opened it. 'Ah yes. Have we somewhere to. . .?'

'This way,' ignoring the forgivable mistake of labelling her *Mrs Smiley*. She showed them towards the end of the barn, where the three chairs were set around an appropriately high table. With them seated, she stood between and elaborated on each made-up set. It took an age. Julian pedantic, Cordelia hanging on his every phrase. She could see the girl had a need for reassurance at every turn, a prayer that her Julian wouldn't desert her. In a less flattering description, she fulfilled the eye-candy role beautifully.

Finally, she got them to a decision, and Julian took out his cheque book. Hoare's Bank; that said it all. She received a limp fish handshake from him, a *mow-ah, mow-ah,* from Cordelia and a flash of gold sparkly hold-ups on thin thighs as the girl dropped into the pale cream leather bucket seat in the Porsche.

The throaty roar departed. The deep breath and the heave of shoulders helped her recover; some of the tenseness eased. At least they'd paid and therefore been committed. Now she had to deliver. She walked determinedly over to the back door, doing her swing hips routine. Andrew would be in the office. Or Hazel? Very close to lunchtime. Good job C and J had been early. She was quite hungry now.

Peter had a vague and fleeting twist of nervousness as he pushed through the swing doors of the building that could well be his place of work for some time. Though confident to a fair degree, engendered from past experiences in tight and messy corners, this was new territory, the world of executive politeness and ultra decision making. Hazel, bless her, had insisted he'd worn a new shirt and tailored jeans. *No tie would be all right,* she'd said, *but polish those brogues of yours. And no, you can't take that old rucksack thingy.* He smiled at the picture of her earnest face, wishing him to be a success and not to get too close to the girls in the office. *What girls,* he'd asked, pulling her leg.

And here he was, smiling at the round-faced receptionist's cheeky grin, her white tee-shirt emblazoned *'I'm a clever girl'* across a well-contoured front.

'Hi, I'm Peter.'

'And I'm Trish. Nice to see you, Pete. Hope you enjoy working here. I do. Loads of dishy blokes. You know where to go?'

He moved close and whispered in her ear. She blushed.

'Sorry, *Peter*.'

'Take you to lunch then?'

Her grin had vanished, but reappeared and broadened. 'Sure, the canteen's downstairs. I'll save you a place,' and giggled. 'Go on with you. I'll tell Richard you're here.'

He got the official welcome, the chatty one from the general office and another somewhat restrained one from a slight girl with mousy hair in a thin pink sweater and tight jeans who, she said, would be his administrative assistant. 'Not secretary; I don't do secretarial. And I'm Angie. Short for Angelina.'

Her hand shake was firm, a good sign and a trace of perfume hovered. 'Been here long?' He'd not met her on his introductory visit last week.

'Three years. Sorry I missed you on Friday. Holiday. Shall I show you the system?'

He liked her. Straightforwardly pleasant, an ever so slightly humorous attitude, no suggestion he was anything but a welcome addition - actually, replacement.

'So my predecessor's been gone a while, then?'

'A couple of months. Gone to Australia, working for a Beach Rescue outfit. Fancied himself in trunks amongst the blonde babes.' She laughed and added, 'doubt he'd have much joy,' but didn't elaborate. 'So you've been committed before?' Was that a rhetorical question, surely she'd know where he'd come from, where he'd been? Apparently not.

Committed? Oh yes, doing a volunteer job out in the field. Sounded painful, but official jargonese for 'being in theatre', another euphemism for working out in the thick of it. He had her sit down opposite his desk - boringly clear of paper, but he liked the computer kit - and gave her a brief résume. His free-loading attitude, his mother's involvement, the way he'd changed, and how the kids out there responded that made it all so worth while. He told her about the little girl who'd tipped the balance, who'd smiled as she died, an unsurvivable victim of lack of care, and Angie cried. He'd had to lend her his handkerchief before she stood up and kissed his cheek.

'Welcome to the power house,' she said, between sniffs, and that was what he would know the office as for the rest of his stay, the Power House.

Hazel wondered how he was getting on, this first day in the office, in the new job. Proud of him, though she knew his feelings towards her weren't as committed as maybe she'd like them to be and she didn't own him, far from it. After that walk up the hill and through the woods and the lovely kiss she'd had, he'd been more reserved. Friendly, but jokey friendly, more brother friendly - not that she'd had a brother to be friendly with - than boyfriend friendly. Not that she'd had any experience of that either, but her girlish instincts were working well. Had she done the wrong thing, pulling away from him after that embrace, the two of them sitting precariously on the rickety old bench? The recall, the thing in Roberta's little lecture, about not giving way, had stuck. She'd even got back home without needing to . . . and blushed at just the thought. Silly girl. Roberta's expression, that, and inwardly, she grinned.

She saw the Porsche go. Not a very practical car, but certainly fast and flashy. The beanpole of a blonde looked drippy, he was overly full of himself, she could see that from her office window. *Her* office window. How things had changed! She was sitting on the chair Andrea had used for two years and the thought amused her. Andrea, Andrew's delight. The girl who'd fluttered her eyelids at him, and probably other bits of her as well. The chair spun round rather well, tipped back, had a sprung seat. Groovy.

'Hoi, miss! That is not what I pay you for, playing fairground rides on that chair. Don't break it, it's expensive. Isn't there anything for you to do, then?'

Andrew was back from wherever he'd been. 'Sorry,' she said, and settled it down properly in front of the desk. 'There's no e-mails worth worrying about, and the invoicing's up to date. I need you to look at the ordering, please. And remind me on how Roberta likes the contract details set out?'

He took his desk seat and spun that round to face her. 'Hazel, before we get involved, can I ask what your feelings are towards Peter?' He nearly said 'my son' but that would have been far too starchy.

She kept her immediate reaction to herself, like 'what's it got to do with you', knowing full well it wouldn't have been right to say so and she'd have felt awful if he'd taken a huff. 'I think he's very much like you, Andrew. So I like him. Very much. That's about it, really.' Then she added, 'we get on well together.'

Andrew had to smile. Clever girl; put him in his place. 'Fine, Hazel, just fine. Just so long as you're not losing your head over him. Girly pash and all that. Give yourself time. Now, these contracts.' He pulled a file out of the bottom drawer and took her through the pro-forma system.

She relaxed as they went through the documentation. Girly pash! What an expression!

Footsteps down the corridor. Roberta pushed open the door. 'Hello you two. How's it going, Hazel?'

She glanced at Andrew. She'd not a lot to do this morning, hardly an auspicious start. Andrew spoke for her.

'She's fine, R. Breaking her in gently.' He closed the file and pushed the chair away from the desk to stand; looked at her, up and down. 'You're not doing too much?'

'Hardly. At least we've got the CJ order. How long their

love nest will be occupied afterwards is another thing.' She didn't normally comment on their clients but these two were weird. 'She's a doll, as per specification. Nods, speaks, smiles, all to order. She's an accessory to his concept of what every successful whizz-kid needs. Nice car though.' She waved his cheque at them. 'Job for you, Hazel. Get a contract away to them; I'll let you have the specification this afternoon. That okay?'

'Sure. I've been going through the format this morning.'

'Then let's go and have lunch. I'm starving. What are you doing this afternoon, dear?'

He had to think. Not much *to* do, surprisingly. Perhaps dig into the accountancy business files to see if there was merit in resurrecting an old client or two. Spot of gardening. Play with the twins. That sort of thing.

She laughed. 'Boring. Why don't you and Mary get your heads together and see about a new girl. Though if you've not got much in mind, maybe we don't need another pair of hands?'

She took his hand and walked off with him down the corridor.

Hazel muttered under her breath. *''Nother pair of hands! Course we'll need someone else - I love those kids but I'm not doing everything on my own!'* She pulled a set of contract forms out of the drawer and started filling them in. *And why don't we have these on the computer? Surprised Andrea hadn't done that already! Andrea - what's she doing today, I wonder?*

That girl was on her own, in a huge office, perspiring gently. She'd been in the new job barely three hours, had run round the studios twice, trying to find people who hadn't answered either mobiles or e-mails; Alain wanted these guys in for a conference at two o'clock and she'd got to produce a brief from cryptic notes he'd given her in the first half hour before vanishing.

'Great to have you on board, Andrea, sort these for me, will you - meeting here at two for these people, make sure they all know, briefing notes copied to all. Contact details in the system. Sorry, Steph's phoned in sick. You'll cope, I'm sure. Be back at one.'

Stephanie, essential girl who she was replacing, sick. Pregnancy catching up with her. And there was supposed to be an overlap of at least two weeks. Contact details, which file would that be under? She found it, typed out a 'Please attend' note, added all the intranet addresses and sent it. Signed *Andrea Chaney, P.A to Alain Perlain*. They'd all wonder about her, the new girl.

And Alain, executive director, Intrepid Productions, now her boss, would he regret wooing her away from Andrew? Would she live up to those Great Expectations? First test, organise a meeting. The briefing notes were easy but she'd put her own stamp on the format. Clear, precise, well laid out, new type font, not Steph's old fashioned Times Roman. Fourteen attendees. Nine prompt replies, including one apology, no sign from the others so that was when she set out on an exploratory tour. Five locations, two in the office block at the other side of the outdoor lot, one in the Special Effects place, another where the story board artists hung out; the last in H & S. Health and Safety, the most demanding, most infuriating, time consuming, money absorbing outfit in the entire Studios, Alain had said. There the diminutive girl who'd taken her note said *'sorry, they're all out but I'll let them know'*, and made no comment about the refusal to answer e-mails.

She wiped her forehead. Unused to all this expenditure of energy, the Manor's environs didn't demand this exercise. Perhaps it wouldn't be a bad idea, keep her in trim. After all, her skirts were a touch tight. Maybe she'd use the private facilities to repair the damage, Alain had said she could. Every Director's office had its own loo. Then a bite of lunch? Then the phone rang. Alain.

'Hi Steph - sorry, Andrea, forgot. All organised? Good. Arrange tea and bickies for half three. Back just before two. Keep them amused if I'm not there in time. Good girl.'

And, of course, he wasn't back at two. So she had to stand her ground, answer personal questions, field the snide remarks, defend her dignity, and actually managed to maintain an air of pleasant attentiveness for all of the half hour he was overdue. The meeting was a lively, interesting, interactive decision making introduction to the world of television programme making. Would an idea work, what would it cost, how long would it take, had they got the resources on tap, who would be the lead presenter, would the broadcaster buy it at the end of the day?

She took notes as fast as she could, wondering if she should brush up her elementary shorthand skills, handed round cups of tea, re-filled the biscuit plate at least twice, and after the last tee-shirted, scruffy jean clad barely shaven guy left the office, collapsed behind her desk and rested on her sprung-back chair.

Alain had remained cool and spruce throughout. He eyed her across his desk and the intervening space. Nearly ten metres away but she could still see the glint in his eye.

'Fun, isn't it?'

What could she say? 'Got me dashing about, haven't you? Was this an initiative test or does it happen every day?'

'Oh, more or less. No chance to paint your nails or tweak your eyebrows, my girl. It is all right to call you *my girl* now, isn't it?'

She returned his grin. 'Provided you don't take liberties, yes. Did I do all right?'

He twiddled a pencil in his fingers. 'Well, the meeting happened. We got a decision, favourably, they all had a well produced brief, no-one made any rude noises, so, yes, you did all right. Next time, use a runner.'

'A runner?'

'Young aspiring hopefuls who'll stand on their heads all day if they think it'll get them a part. Tell Clary what you need and she'll organise. Number's in the book. Now. I'm off, got an evening do. Can't take you on this one, sorry, but there's other jollies in the offing. Go home, Andrea. See you tomorrow.'

On her own again in this vast office, she cleared up, put chairs back in place, got the catering people to collect the debris, having secreted away all the left-over biscuits. The minutes of the meeting were all typed into the system and copies e-mailed out within the next half hour, a hard copy she left on Alain's desk. What more could she do? He'd told her to go home, but it wasn't five o'clock yet. She didn't fancy probing Steph's system any more than she had to, largely because she may come back - it wouldn't be etiquette to disturb any files until the place was entirely hers. She couldn't see herself walking around the Studio lots just for the sake of it either.

Alain's phone stayed quiet - most of his contacts would be e-mailing him, and that was another hurdle to overcome, access to his system. She spun round on her chair, which reminded her of the office - the Manor's office - and she reached for the phone.

It didn't ring above four times.

'The Manor, Hazel speaking. How can I help you?'

My, my, the efficiency of the girl, and what a pleasant voice on the phone.

'It's Andrea, Hazel. How's things?'

'Oh, *Andrea*! How nice to hear you! How's the new job? Is it a breeze?'

'After day one? So far, more of a whirlwind than a breeze.' How clued up was this one, using 'breeze' as an expression? 'Plunged into the deep end, if it isn't mixing metaphors. Had a meeting to organise for fourteen at a moment's notice, took the minutes, all circulated and then he told me to push off home! Didn't think I should, not until normal go-home time, so I rang for a chat. How's your day?'

'Okay. Not a lot to do. Roberta's having to take things easy, 'cos she's been diagnosed with softening pelvic ligaments and she had an awful pain on Saturday, Andrew called the doctor in. June's phoned in, she's found the place rather ancient, from what I've heard. And it's Peter's first day too, but he's not back yet. We're okay,' she repeated. 'We'll manage. At least we've taken quite an expensive order today, so Roberta's happy. That's about it.'

'So you're content with the office as I left it?'

'Of course. Oh, yes, there is one thing. You know the contract forms. There's not one in the memory, is there? One I could fill in on screen so we've got copies and so on?'

Andrea pulled a face. She should have thought of that. 'No, Hazel, love, there isn't. Nothing to stop you doing one,' and she outlined the process. 'So long as you don't save the document on the original format once you've modified it. Give it a new file name?'

'Yes. I think I know what you mean. I'll try; can I ring you with any query?'

''Course you can. Use this number,' and she read it off her phone, 'direct line, so you don't bother the switchboard. Better not stay chatting too long. Give my love to Roberta, and Andrew of course. Tell him my office chair's not *quite* like yours,' and she chuckled. 'He'll know what I mean. Take care, love,' and she put the phone down.

Hazel swung her chair round again. *Not like hers?* What did she mean? Then she heard the shout 'teas -up'. Naturally, at the first opportunity, the question to be asked after being handed her mug, sitting cosily round the kitchen table.

'I had a call from Andrea.' That caught their attention.

Both Roberta's and Andrew's eyes swung her way. 'Asked how things were going. Said she'd had a whirlwind of a day.' She sipped at an over-hot mug. 'Ouch! Passed on her love to you both. Told me to say her office chair's not like mine, and that you'd know what she meant, Andrew.' Another cautious sip, curious eyes looking at him over the rim of the mug.

Roberta raised her eyes. 'Sounds like a euphemistic remark, husband mine. Any particular significance? Ah, are you going pink round the gills?' She leant forward. 'Hazel, my love, go and see if Mary's all right, swop places with her. I'll be up shortly to help with bath time. Take your mug with you.'

She had to obey, but her curiosity was well aroused, to be sent out of the room like that suggested Andrew had some explanation to do. What could Andrea possibly have meant? A chair was a chair, for heaven's sake. She was almost tempted to eavesdrop.

'Andrew, love, I don't much care what ever happened to make an office chair so significant, but let's not arouse our naïve girl's emotions. Andrea should have known better. Tell Hazel something innocuous, please, and make sure it's not mentioned again? Eh?'

'Long time ago, now, R. Not proud of the memory, I can tell you that. *And* I told you. So aqua sub pontum. Water under bridge.'

After Roberta had gone to make slow and careful progress upstairs to ensure Chris and Abby were well on the way to bed, Andrew topped up his mug and reflected. The reported telephone call and the significance of the remark had brought the golden girl back into focus. Not that she figured in his love life to any extent now, but her absence was, nonetheless, still a heartache. She'd been part of him, his life - *their life* - for so long and not to have her brightening the day was going to take time to get over. Good of her to ring, though.

Mary's slow steps heralded her return, and she sagged into her armchair in the corner.

'Not want any tea, Mary?'

'Aye, lad, you can pour us a cup.' She held her hand to her chest and he saw her wince. 'Them youngster's getting a mite too fractious for an old lady. I'll hae a moment afore we gets on with the dinner.' She closed her eyes. This wasn't the Mary they'd come to depend on. She hadn't slumped into her chair at a teatime before. Andrew noticed her normally pink cheeks were lined and grey. He worried. The cup poured, sweetened and stirred, he got up to hand it her.

'Mary? Your tea?' But there was no response and her breathing wasn't right.

NINE

They turned back to her, almost as one. 'You'd not rip the old paper off, paint the ceiling, suggest a visit to the furniture warehouse in Waterford?' Donald's eyes under those shaggy eyebrows were bright and penetrating.

Siobhán had dropped her husband's hand and now stood with arms loose by her sides. 'We've brought you all this way just to tell us all we need to do is renovate?' Her voice had risen and June felt her spirit quail. Her first job and she was about to experience her client's wrath?

She stood her ground. 'It's what the house needs. Appreciation of what it is, the love that it must have had when this - this lovely setting was created. I felt the *spirit of the place,*' - (that phrase again) - 'this morning and it's grown on me. We could re-work all that is here, add our own subtle touches and the room would come alive again. Promise. I'm sure Roberta would agree with me.' She took another gamble. 'The real work would be in the sitting room, the kitchen and the corridors. I've not thought of the bedrooms yet, and that must be a challenge. But these main rooms and the hall should stay in period.' An intake of air, a firming of shoulders. 'I'm positive that's what should happen.' Then she shut up.

Donald returned to view the space of the room again, took a few paces, looked around, almost absentmindedly stroked the brocade on the top of the settee.

'Do you know, Siobhán,' he said, 'I've never thought of the way June's said. But she's right, by God, she's right. It's been under our noses and we've not realised what this house really needs.' He returned to his wife and took her by the shoulders. 'I agree with her. Don't you? Put everything back to where it was in its heyday? Do up the rest of the place, yes, and I can't wait to see what our little miracle girl comes up with - but these two front rooms, yes, she's right,' echoing the phrase, 'I can see exactly what she means.' He leant forward and lightly kissed her full on the lips. 'My darling, let's do it!'

'You're absolutely sure, June? You believe in this place?' Siobhán took Donald's hand once more.

'Yes, I do,' and she threw in her ace card. 'Keela told me.'

For the second time that week, Doc Mac's car was on the drive. It hadn't taken him above half an hour, and in that time Mary had appeared to revive somewhat, but they'd not moved her from her chair. She'd taken a few sips of tea but that was all, and Roberta, summoned with trepidation by her husband from her bedtime routines with Abby and Chris, was being, in his mind, so calm with her it wasn't true.

The old lady's breathing was still shallow and she'd not spoken. Her lips had moved, but no sound. Roberta, kneeling down as best she could, was stroking her mother's hand when the Doc Mac found them in the kitchen. No standing on ceremony here, not when he knew them so well anyway.

Andrew touched Roberta's shoulder. 'Let the doc take a look, R,' and he gently helped her up. 'We'll leave him to it, shall we?'

Doc Mac could see the incipient distress in Roberta's eyes, inwardly felt for her, knowing the bond and the strengths between daughter and mother. He also could sense, from the evident signs, all was not going to be well.

Andrew drew Roberta out of the kitchen and into the sitting room down the corridor, got her down in her favourite chair and crouched in front, holding her hands, seeing the despair in her eyes, the captivating brown eyes of the girl he'd come to love so deeply.

'You know, do you not, my love, that your mother's had a stroke?' He was guessing, true, but the symptoms were easy to read.

Roberta nodded, all she could do. To speak would bring floods of tears and that wouldn't help, not at this moment. She knew her mother hadn't had the energy lately, had seen her fumble at things she'd certainly not before, even heard a slurred or hesitant word, had feared the worst but pushed the worry out of her mind, why, because she couldn't deal with it. Not with her pregnancy, her own medical problem, and the growing pressures of the business.

Andrew knew. His Andrea had lost her father and he'd seen her reaction; how for a while, it had de-stabilised the girl and so grateful he'd been able to care. Roberta was now all the more demanding of the same care, whatever the outcome.

They waited, but not for long. Doc Mac pushed open the door.

'I'm sorry, Roberta. I've asked for an ambulance, it'd be better if she were under observation for a while. I want to check out the heart murmur and her circulation but she's also had a minor stroke, a T I A, and it's affected her speech. And been overdoing things.' His comment was brusque, almost critical. 'I'll follow in so I can ensure she's looked after. You feel all right yourself, or should I have a look at you as well? Not fallen over or had any more creasing pains in your tum, have you?'

She shook her head again. Andrew stood up. 'She's been obeying orders, Doc. Don't worry, I'll keep her in order. Is Mary all right where she is?'

'Aye. Best not move her until the ambulance gets here, shouldn't be long. We may only keep her in a few days - if she's rested and we get her system stabilised her speech could come back without any lasting effect. But we certainly need to consider how to ease the heart problems, and you will have to take the pressure off her, Roberta, without taking it on yourself. Do you understand?'

Once the ambulance had gone, with Doc Mac behind in convoy, Andrew persuaded Roberta back into the sitting room.

'It had to happen, sooner or later, my love, and don't think in saying that means I'm any the less sorry that it has, or that I'm less upset than you are, 'cos we both love her. For all she's done over the years, the worries she's had, the pressure we've put her under these last two years, she's been wonderful. But we all run out of energy sooner or later.'

He was sitting, facing her, she in the self same chair where their relationship had taken off, where she'd seduced him and he'd taken her, given her the love she'd craved, and the lust of the moment had deepened into this unbreakable devotion for her. He'd never have guessed, those years ago, of how that evening would have led him to this.

She turned her head away and he saw the tears trickle. Close to the moment himself, he had to be strong, for her sake.

'Do you want to eat?'

She shook her head.

'You'll have to have something.'

'I'm not hungry. Get something yourself, ask Hazel what she wants.'

'Darling, it's not just for you!'

'I'm not hungry,' she repeated. 'Leave me alone.'

'But . . . '

'*Leave me alone!* Please! Go and ring June, tell her to come home.'

He rose, stood and looked down at her, stooped to offer a kiss but she moved her head into the wing of the chair, so he left her and went to find Hazel.

She was in the kitchen, mixing milky drinks for the twin's bedtime, dry eyed now but he knew she'd cried after he'd gone upstairs to explain. She looked up at him.

'Roberta?'

'Knocked for six. I'm worried, Hazel. I don't want to think it'll affect her pregnancy, but it could. She's told me to ring June and get her to come home.'

'Is that really necessary? I mean, she'll be upset but surely she'll want to finish the job? I know I would. It's not as though Mary's critical or anything, is it? I mean, it's only a slight stroke. Lots of people have them at her age, don't they? Peter's still here.' She finished stirring. 'I'd best take these up.' She looked at the clock. 'And he'll be back soon. Then we'd best get a meal?'

Great girl. What a great girl, with all the unbridled optimistic pragmatism of youth. As she brushed past him, a plastic mug in each hand, he caught an arm round her, stayed her long enough to plant a kiss on her cheek. 'Luv you,' he said, and felt the tears come back.

Half an hour and the clatter of the bike against the wall. Peter, back from his first day in the new job. The back door swung, slammed shut, his son's ebullient whistling indicating a good day. Andrew stood up, stretching, out of the chair where Mary'd collapsed not a couple of hours since. He'd nearly but not quite, fallen asleep in the quiet. Hazel had kept watch over Roberta, now comatose on their bed upstairs.

'Hi dad!' Peter slung his new briefcase onto another chair. Carrying a lap-top around everywhere wasn't going to be his thing. 'How's the day?' then saw his father's face. 'Dad?'

No point in disguising the situation. 'Mary's in hospital.'

Peter slid onto a stool. 'Dad! No! How come?'

'Stroke, coupled with heart murmurs, according to Doc Mac. Slight, but he thought best to get her where she could be kept 'under observation' and a drug regime established.'

'How's Roberta taking it?'

'Badly, underneath. She tried to keep a calm sort of face on it, but . . . ' and he realised her turning away from his attempted kiss had been the first time ever. 'Not good, Peter. But your day?'

'Fine. Very good in fact. Been given an assistant, sort of girl Friday, who's great. I think I'm going to enjoy this,' then sobered up, 'but how are you - we - going to deal with this situation? June'll have to come back. And Hazel, how's she coping?'

'Hazel's fine, well, as far as one can expect. She's upstairs, keeping an eye on Roberta. Abby and Chris have been so good, whereas it could have been . . .' He didn't want to appear emotional, specifically in front of his son, but he was close to giving way.

'Okay dad. What do you want me to do? Dinner? I can cook, you know.'

Andrew managed a wry smile. 'I expect you can, son. Brought up proper. Whatever you fancy. I'll go and let Hazel off, then you two can organise.'

Roberta was asleep, fully dressed, stretched out across their bed, lying on her back, one arm bent over her waist, the other flung across the covers. Hazel, and once more he blessed the decision to bring her into the family, had been quietly reading, seated in one of the tub chairs by the window.

A quiet whisper, 'She's been asleep some time, Andrew. I'm sure she'll be better for it.'

'Bless you, Hazel, you're wonderful. Go and help Peter put a meal together. Something simple, pasta or those better burghers, whatever. I'll wake her and come down in an hour. Twins okay?'

'They're asleep. I'll check again - see you in a bit,' and she'd tip-toed out.

He took the same seat, welcoming her residual warmth in the cushion. The bedroom, cosy and comforting, enfolded its quiet around him, allowing racing thoughts to subside. They both knew the time would arrive when they'd have to meet and manage a change, whenever it came, heralded or no. Now it had come. Unheralded, and at one of the lowest ebbs of their uncertain tides. Six months ago, say, and they'd have coped within the day-to-day. Another six months ahead, having Mary off the strength wouldn't have been the blow it was now, with a new girl to help and Roberta through the birth. The bench marks he'd carved into his mind weren't helping; in fact, he'd no idea where they'd gone.

His wife, this girl who'd been his salvation and he hers, in the full flush of her last pregnancy, now relaxed and peaceful, the tenor of her quiet breathing shown in the rise and fall of her breasts beneath the delicate lacey top. The linen skirt crumpled under her, bare ankles, shoes kicked off but still on the covers. Her hair, still thick and glossy, still the delight to brush, spread across the covered pillow. A few grey hairs amongst the brown. They'd travelled the miles, given each other strength, deep love, understanding. Never part. She stirred, moved an arm, a deep breath and she raised her head.

'Darling?'

'I'm here. How're you feeling? You'd had an hour or two.' He got up and moved to sit on the bed edge alongside her. 'Hazel and Peter are rustling up some supper. Pasta, probably.'

She gave a wan smile. 'She's good at that,' and stretched out a hand to catch his. 'Thank you, my love, for being here. You'll look after me, won't you?'

He raised the hand to his lips. 'Always. We'll survive, you and I.'

Another smile. 'I'll never regret that day,' and he knew exactly what she meant.

'Nor I, my love, nor I.' The memory of the day came as clear as clear, sitting on the old bench, unaware he was watching his future ride into view and tumble off in front of him. 'Do you want to come down? For supper? Then we'll phone?'

Her face clouded as she thought of her dearest mum, lying in some hospital bed, probably all wired up, hating it, wanting to be back in command of her kitchen, enjoying her matriarchal status. 'She'll fight, won't she?'

He nodded, but uncertain. He had to offer some commiseration. 'She'll fight. Unlike some, I don't think she'll give up on us. Though there'll have to be some changes.'

A quiet moment, a consideration, each thinking what was in store.

'Right. Supper it is.' The more determined voice as she swung legs round, pulled on him to sit upright, pecked a cheek and slowly stood up. 'Am I alright as I am?'

He looked up at her. 'Roberta, my love, you're my life.' It didn't answer the question, but it made her eyes water.

'And I yours. I mean, you're mine.' She giggled, irrationally, breaking the fragility of the intense and emotional moment, and wiped her eyes. 'Silly boy. Let's go before we get too overemotional.'

Their appearance at the kitchen coincided with Peter's opening of the door.

'I was just about to shout,' he said. 'We've everything organised. Eating in here, is that okay?'

'Of course it is, Peter.' Roberta released Andrew's hand and sniffed. 'Smells wonderful. I'm starving. What've you done, Hazel?'

The girl, apron on, hair tied back, gave the pan a final stir. 'Pasta, with prawns and sun-dried tomatoes in a basil and chive sauce. That okay?' What she'd done for them in Ireland that time. Possibly her favourite dish?

'Lovely, thankyou so much, Hazel. I don't know what . . .'

'. . . we'd do without you,' Andrew finished for her. 'Peter, uncork one of those reds from up there?' He pointed at the ready-use rack on top of the cupboard where they stayed nicely warm while the Aga was running. 'Earn your keep.'

In the middle of their meal, interrupting Peter's discourse on the events of his day, they heard the phone go.

Andrew looked up at Roberta, their eyes met. She went pale. 'Darling . . .' she started but he had already pushed his chair back.

'Could be anything, R,' and he went out to take the call in the quiet of the hall.

But it wasn't 'anything', it was June.

TEN

'Keela told you?' Siobhán's eyebrows rose. 'Cadhla, as in our little stone colleen who lives amongst the roses?' The smile broke out. 'Our Keela, well, bless me.'

'So you're away with the fairies now, are you just?' Donald grinned at her. 'My my, girl. We'll make an Irish lass of you yet. Well, we'd best get something onto paper afore Keela changes her mind. Come now, into the warmth. 'Tis a mite chilly in here.'

On the kitchen table June spread out her notes and set to copying her thoughts in a far more workmanlike Roberta manner, as she'd been shown. Donald busied himself producing a supper dish as Siobhán sat close to her, chin on an elbow propped up hand, watching.

As June's list and sketches took shape, allied to the pictures on the digital camera's screen, Siobhán could feel a tingling in her scalp, running down her spine, caught up in the mystery of how the house would come alive. Keela, well, folklore it may be, superstition even, but here in Ireland, anything could - and did - happen. She'd not tell June of the origin of the placement or the *being* of the little girl's life or how she'd supposedly appeared there. Not yet anyway.

Donald interrupted them. 'Here, have a bite.' The plates slid in front of them, and June sniffed at the temptation.

'This smells delicious. What is it?'

'Our version of the best of the best. Smoked salmon and scrambled egg, fresh baked crisp bread fried to perfection in extra virgin olive oil. Sun-dried tomatoes.' He went to the fridge and produced a couple of cans, reached into the cupboard for glasses. The 'pop' of a drinks can and the careful pouring before she had a tumbler at her elbow. 'And a glass of the dark stuff to add something to the magic. Ever had Guinness before?'

'No, I haven't,' and she took a cautious sip. 'Umm. 'Spose it goes with the territory?'

'You could say that. If you're going to be friends with Keela then you'd best get used, and to the hard stuff as well. Eat up, now, whilst 'tis still warm.'

Gorgeous. No other word for it. 'Thank you so much,' she said as she pushed her plate to one side and took another swig at her glass, swirling the remnant of the head round. So well matched, meal and drink. 'But you said Anita ... '

'Called in on our way up. Told her not to bother. Donald thought he might treat us. Doesn't always cook, but when he does, perfection. I'm a lucky girl,' Siobhán explained. 'He's better than I am.'

'You have your uses, dear,' he said mildly as he collected the plates and June saw a faint flush of colour rise on his wife's cheek. 'June, have you much more to do?'

She brought her wayward thoughts to heel. No good wishing for something she wasn't going to get, not unless she found another male who would have a better idea of what inspired a lady's emotions, as Donald obviously did his Siobhán's. Lucky girl indeed. She returned to her task with renewed enthusiasm and within another half hour, completed the job.

'There. What Roberta would make of it remains to be seen, but it's how she sets her projects out. This is just the two front rooms. I'll do the service areas tomorrow, if you like. And you mentioned the bedrooms?'

Siobhán nodded. 'I think so, don't you, Donald? While we've got her captured?'

He agreed. The last newly-washed supper plate went back into the rack. 'Another glass, June? The other half?'

'But it'll mean another couple of days.' She moved her glass within reach. Yes, she could take to this 'dark stuff' as he called it. Not sure about the other 'hard stuff', by which she guessed he meant whiskey. 'I'd best ring Roberta and discuss with her. She's the boss.'

'Sure thing, June. Use the phone in the hall.' Then Siobhán added, 'oh, and if you want to and can, stay over Christmas. It'd be good.'

Christmas? Another ten days away. She'd thought she'd be back well in time to help in the Manor's festivities. Her dad had told her all about the big tree in the hall, the planned party, and the way Abby and Chris would be spoilt rotten. No, she'd need to be home for that.

'I can't. I'd love to in one way, but the Manor, the children . . . '

'Of course she must spend Christmas at home, Siobhán, don't tempt the girl. Then she can come back in the New Year and oversee the restoration work. I'll get Declan in.'

The old-fashioned phone suited the place; now she'd accepted what she was all about it wasn't an anachronism, it fitted. She dialled, carefully.

They all looked up at him as he came back in to the kitchen, Roberta especially, taut with nerves, assuming the worst news but praying it wasn't. She ought to have gone to the hospital but knew she couldn't, not to see her mum in a ward of others, looking desperately out of place. No, no, no!

'June,' he said briefly, and she relaxed, though realising that he'd have had to break the news to her, not an easy task. 'On top of things, Roberta, full of it, been asked to stay over

Christmas. Don't worry,' he added, seeing her frown, 'she's not going to. Needs another couple of days, but wanted to cut it short once I'd told her. Said not to, to complete what she can. Wanted to tell you all about it, but I said tomorrow. I've said we'll phone her at eleven. That okay?' He sat down again. 'Seems the place has got to her. Some weird mention of an Irish spirit, a stone creature called Keela, I thought she said. Whatever, our clients have agreed with her it's a restoration job. Perhaps to go back in the New Year once they've organised a contractor.'

Roberta's frown deepened. '*Contractor?* Without a proper specification, and costings?'

'Best wait until you talk with her, love. Don't get uptight.'

'I'm *not* uptight. Just want to make sure it doesn't go wrong. My - our - reputation here.'

'Mum, my sister wouldn't mess things up, I'm sure. She's a bright kiddo, that one.' Peter leant forward. 'and anyway, if she's got an Irish fairy working with her . . .' and he chuckled. 'P'raps I'd best nip over and have a look myself.'

Roberta stared at him. 'You called me *mum*, Peter. That's the nicest thing.' She got up, went behind and putting her arms around him, hugged and bent to kiss his cheek. 'What a lovely son you've got, Andrew. Almost as nice as you. And June.' She turned towards Hazel. 'Don't you think he's nice, Hazel?'

The girl blushed.

'Well, he is. Whether or not he believes in fairies.' She grinned, then Andrew saw the cloud come down. 'I'll ring the hospital. I've got to know how mum is. I can't wait for Doc Mac to report back. What's visiting time, anyone know?'

'Most evenings, I guess. Not sure. But not tonight, R. She'll be in good hands. Tomorrow, love, once we know what the score is. Let the dust settle. Please. Go into the sitting room, put a disc on. I'll wash up.'

Hazel stood up and started collecting plates. 'No, Andrew, you go on through with Roberta. Peter and I'll finish what we started. Was it okay?'

He had to, couldn't help himself, had to lean towards her and give her a kiss, hold her shoulders. 'More than okay, Well done,' kissed her again and followed his wife out.

'You blushed.' Peter, at the sink, starting to run the washing-up water, grinned at her.

'It's you who should have blushed. Being told you're as nice as your dad,' Hazel retorted, trying to avoid a direct answer. 'Don't overfill the bowl. Here,' and she passed the pile of plates.

'Roberta's trying hard to deal with this. It can't be easy for her.'

'Nope.' He plunged the plates into the bowl. 'Just hope she'll be alright. Can't imagine what it would be like for Roberta if she . . .'

'Don't even think like that, Peter. And watch what you're doing. You'll get that shirt soaked and it's a new one!'

'Bossy!'

'Well, someone's got to look after you. You're not out in the sticks now. Come on, shift over. I'll do the rest.'

Obediently, he moved, and then after she'd dropped the cutlery into the water, caught her round the waist, half spun her close and kissed her, hard and longingly. Her arms came up, clasped behind his neck, felt her educated body respond. *'Oh, Peter . . .'*

Roberta listened to the Ward Sister's voice, the reassurance and the warmth in her tone. They cared; it came across even on the phone. *'She's comfortable, we've got her on a drip and stabilised, the dear lady seems to have accepted what's happened to her which is a great step forward. We'll be running more tests tomorrow morning. If you'd like to come in tomorrow afternoon, any time after three? If there's any change, which I'm sure there won't be, other than for the better, we'll ring you. Don't worry, dear.'*

'I'm a dear, apparently.' Roberta gave him a small grin. 'And I'm not to worry, *dear*. We'll go see her tomorrow afternoon. After three.'

'So all's well?'

'Comfortable and stabilised, so they said. Which is something, I suppose.'

Behind them, the phone rang again. Andrew reached past Roberta and picked it up.

'Oh, hi, Doc.' He listened to the brief report. 'Yes, we've just rung the ward. Hmmm, so they said. You're sure? That's very good of you. Yes, I certainly will. Thanks, thanks very much. Goodnight.'

The phone replaced, he ushered her towards the sitting room. 'You need to be comfortable and stabilised as well, my girl. Make the most of it.'

Half protesting, she allowed herself to be propelled towards her chair. 'Will those two manage?' She remained standing.

A quick lift of eyebrows. 'Roberta, dear. Didn't you see the girl blush? Of course she thinks he's nice. I bet they're snogging their heads off in there. Leave them alone.'

Her head turned sharply towards him. 'Snogging? Isn't that what teenagers do? They're adults. What if . . .'

He caught her hand and pulled her close. 'What if what?' Their eyes met. 'Let's go up. Give them space. And tomorrow's . . .'

'Another day. Yes, let's go to bed.' Her eyes had that mystical glow, wide, appealing, luminous, questioning, the reaction from a sense of deep relief her mother's collapse wasn't seen as too bad. Somehow she'd manage, PGP or no. He'd be oh, so gentle with her, that she knew, and her inner girl began to tingle. 'Please?'

The hospital. Where she didn't want to be, and her spirit was ebbing. She tried to remember what had happened. All so indistinct, as if it had been years ago, when she was a little girl. She'd come downstairs, *the Manor's stairs?* so very slowly, afraid of what her parents were going to say.

Funny thing was, she could see her dress now, white, with a small floral pattern, like daisies, the skirt down to her ankles and buttoned shoes. Puffed sleeves, tight on her arms. The collar, too, was tight, fastened so close. Her hair, her lovely long soft brown hair, all in a twist and tied with a ribbon. Had it been a yellow ribbon, or was it pink?

They weren't in the parlour. Why had she been summoned? She hadn't done anything wrong, had she? The kitchen . . .

How old was she? Fourteen? Fifteen? Had she had the sewing basket as her fifteenth birthday present or was it before? Was it still in her cupboard?

Why had her father come home so early? The mill didn't turn out until six o'clock. He'd not been in a good mood for days, scowling at her. And they'd not had a hot Sunday dinner.

Something was going on.

Had she fallen? It had gone all fuzzy. She'd been on a train, that was it. Racketing, smelly, sooty, steamy, noisy. Whistles. Lots of shouting. Being spoken to by a young gentleman, someone was carrying her bag. The bag made from old carpet with the joined-together wooden handles. Her sewing basket as well, she'd not part with that. Tall houses. Too many automobiles.

A beautiful room. She remembered the room, yellow wallpaper and a big mirror on a stand. An iron bedstead with brass balls on the corners. A window that slid up and down. It looked out onto a small park where she'd been allowed to go to walk around. *Push the pram?* Oh, and the new dresses. Pale grey with pink reveals in the skirt. So pretty, so fashionable. But that was for best. When she worked, cleaning the floors, dusting the furniture, polishing the fire-irons, she had that light green wrap-round with the waist tie. So different from the other place.

What other place was that? Her mind wouldn't go back that far. Skivvy, that's all she'd been, at the big Hall. Taken there by her father, being tugged along the village street by her hand, protesting, *'I don't want to go!'* and left there, *why, daddy, why?'* told - oh, what was it she'd been told, in the kitchen, that afternoon?

'Mary, you hae to go tae work, lass. Your da's lost his job, luv, we canna keep you any mair . . . '

In service. Like Betty. Like Mandy. Even like Susan. Sold into another woman's house to skivvy. She did the laundry, didn't she? The smell of carbolic, the caustic soda, the horrible old dolly with a slimy rotten handle, the red tiled floors, the heavy old zinc buckets. The constant odour of gas. Mashed grey potatoes. *Cabbage!*

Did she run away? How did she get on the train? Blanked out. Perhaps she was so naughty the people sold her on. Well, it was like being sold, wasn't it? Highest bidder?

'Works hard, speaks only when spoken to, reads the Bible on Sundays. No, her parents are too far away, she won't want to go home every other Saturday afternoon.'

The nice voice with a strange accent, sort of foreign. *'Mary, you really are a very pretty girl. Here, let me untie your belt. It really is too tight. And if that button were to be undone . . . on your nice new dress,'* after her sixteenth, or was it seventeenth birthday; flattered, she was.

She didn't have to do the floors after that. Or the brasses. Being taught how to look after the master's wife, help her dress, serve afternoon tea. The years - how many years?

'Isn't your maid such a pretty girl? You're so lucky, Henrietta, such a charming help . . . ' No one knew Henrietta slept alone these days, though her husband didn't lack a bed-warmer.

That was after her nineteenth birthday, then the twentieth and the twenty-first. Yet another new dress. And all that went underneath. The Count - *a fashionista,* they called him. A lady's man, who dressed the highest social classes of the day. He flattered. Charmed. She feeling wanted, appreciated. Adored. *Loved.*

The months of uncertainty and nervousness while she'd still been 'upstairs'. Feeling ill. Finding her dresses weren't fitting. Oh yes, she knew. And hadn't minded, because, well, because.

The trip to the south coast. Shown a lovely room, and introduced to a middle-aged woman. Mrs, er, Mrs *Fitz - er no, Florenze. That was it. Italian.* Knew all about birthing. Only a few weeks before, then nursing the wee little scrap. The Count and his wife went abroad, two months it was, so she thought, came home when she'd returned from her confinement.

Henrietta adored her new baby girl. Couldn't do enough for her. *No, Mary, you can't hold her, because, you see, maids don't have babies. I'll pretend she's mine. But you can stay and be the housekeeper. Look after us both. That'll be the way. She's mine now. I'm sure you understand. I'm going to call her Roberta. And the Count is ever so pleased . . .'*

Mary tried to piece the jigsaw together. She'd come downstairs. Sat in a chair. Then a warm fuzzy feeling, slipping into a grey blanket of nothingness. Had Andrew talked to her?

Roberta. Her darling little baby girl. Henrietta's husband's gift of a child to his wife, all she'd ever wanted but couldn't have, so good old Mary had been brood mare. A lovely man, so beautiful, their loving gorgeous, time after time after time . . . What was it they did nowadays? Surrogate motherhood, messing about with implants and all that nausea, all that ridiculous pretend. But she'd got to keep her in the end. Poor Henrietta; that meningitis, so sad. The Count had been devastated. *'Promise you won't tell her you're her mother until I've passed on?'*

She'd loved him. So discreet. Kept him sane. Promised. All for her baby. After all, Roberta was the one who'd benefit. And dear Andrew, he'd always look after her lovely baby girl instead. It didn't matter now. Hazel would help. Shame she'd not see the new baby, but too tired, so tired. Sleep. Dream. Just float away.

Roberta. Roberta. Roberta. Roberta. Rober . . . .

The red alarm light started to flash. The regular pulse display on the screen faltered, picked up, faltered and drifted down to a straight line. The night Staff nurse coming out of the Sluice heard the buzz of the alarm change to its insistent alternate chime, dropped the clipboard on her desk, punched her Team Alert button and ran.

They tried. Tried with all the techniques at their disposal, doing everything within their caring power, until the resuscitation team leader looked around at his colleagues for the never welcomed nods. There'd been no will, no determination to survive, as though she'd wanted to slip away without a fuss.

'T. o. D. 05.35. Thank you, all, I'm sorry.'

Roberta lay on her back, comforted and cosy, mind drifting, vaguely aware her beloved man was asleep; he'd been absolutely wonderful, so tender, she'd lost all sense of anything other than what he could do for her. So it would be all right, whatever came . . .

A surprise; a sharp, stab of needle pain in her brain, gone as quickly as it had come. Her mind cleared and the wounding remembrance that her mother was in hospital came back. And the sad absolute certainty she'd lose her, as she knew she'd have to, one day One of Andrew's spoken benchmarks. Erased.

ELEVEN

Uncomfortable, he woke un-accustomedly early, to wonder why, until he realised the pillow was in the middle of the bed and he'd got his head straight down on the mattress. And the duvet was wrapped tight round his still sleeping wife and precious little around him. No wonder he was cold as well. The time? He blinked at the clock's figures, rubbed his eyes and tried again. Was that six? Had a few hour's sleep then. Despite his low-key arguments, torn between desire, love and concern, they'd spent an incredible hour - hour and a half even - teasing each other's passions to the ultimate. She'd squeaked once and they'd readjusted position; after that, fantastic. Slow, measured, but fantastic. Must have done her ego a power of good, 'cos yes, she'd got there. So had he, naturally, and almost in sync. Wonderful lover, his wife. Very carefully, he tried to straighten out the covers so he could cosy up to her again and snatch another hour or two. Far too early to get up. He'd not heard the other two come to bed, had assumed they'd be sensible. Hazel would be the winner, either way. Peter, well, as his son, he'd keep her safe. No worries.

Hazel stirred, wondered what . . . and sat bolt upright in bed. She felt the flush of colour run up her neck. Oh lor! She had, hadn't she? Her mind skittered all over the place, like a bird dashing its wings against the glass of windows if it were captive in a room. No escape, no return. Done. Past the milestone. Woman. The gamut of emotions to unravel. Her feathers more than ruffled, for one or two were floating loose, twirling around, discarded. Like her virginity.

Peter lay on his back, arms behind his head, staring at the ceiling, doing as analytic an appraisal as he could. Yes, he did love her. Truly, absolutely. No, he shouldn't have let things happen, especially under his father's roof. But. But what? She'd not said 'no', or even tried to discourage him. Why they'd ended up in her room he couldn't - for the life of him - understand.

They had, though. And she'd been a proper tease; eyes alight, egging him on. Almost as if she'd done it before, which, subsequentially, he found she obviously hadn't. So easy, so marvellously soft and enterable. Bloody hell, boy, you've . . . . *No, far too crude, you* loved *her.* Now what? Retribution or reward?

A tap on his door. Was it really her?
'Hazel?'
With pink chenille dressing gown wrapped tight round and tied, she sat on his bed, leant down and offered a tentative kiss.
'Slept well?' Her look was of pure unadulterated mischief, eyes still alight.
'After us? Like a baby.' *Whoops, Peter, old lad, bad choice of words.*
Her eyebrows went up. 'Baby? I hope not,' and giggled. 'Love me?'
'Rhetorical question, my girl. I hope you've no regrets?'
She shook her head and the untidy hair bounced. 'Provided it wasn't merely a one-night stand.'
He eased up to lean on the bedhead and treated her to a narrow-eyed look. 'What do you know about one night stands, Hazel?'
'A little more than I did.'
'Do I need to apologise?'

'Do you think you should?' This verbal sparring, considering how far they'd come together, was surreal.

He considered his reply. This could be a point of no return. How far would they go, together, and was this wise, given who they were, what they were, where they were. But one constant refrain echoed. He loved her.

'I love you, Hazel.'

Still that mischievous look. So she wasn't a coy moonstruck experimental teenager, but a thinking, adult minded woman who'd found a soul mate.

'Sure?' The grin was still in place.

'What do you think?

'What you did to me last night - love or lust?'

'Love.'

'Then I want you to promise me something.'

'What?'

'You'll tell me, straight out, no messing, if you change your mind about me.'

'I won't.'

'What, promise or change your mind?'

'Change my mind.'

'Sure?'

'You're infuriating.'

She grinned. 'I know. Have you had a girl before?'

'That's not a question a girl should ask.'

'Well, I am asking. Have you had a girl before?'

'You're more than infuriating. No. Not really.' Those half-hearted snog sessions in Romania didn't count.

'No?' Did she believe him?

'Surprised?'

Yes, she was. A guy like Peter, floating around half the world, maybe bored, never slept with a girl before? My my. So she was his first? Her heart swelled up. Goodness.

'Pleased?'

'Very. So we've sacrificed our mutual virginity. And, from what I can gather, quite well.'

'Hazel! You sound very er, experienced. Who's told you about these things?'

'Roberta. In Ireland, last September. Awfully glad she did, too. Otherwise I might have screamed the house down and that would *not* have been a good idea.'

'A good teacher.' He didn't want to take this discussion any further because she was starting to embarrass him.

'Mmm Mmm. She was. Did I please you?'

'What do you think?'

'Oh yes. I did. And, if it's of any importance, you pleased me too. Rather well. So ten out of ten. No, perhaps eight out of ten. Make you try better next time.'

'So there will be a 'next time'?'

'Perhaps. Though we'd better not let it get a habit. Nice now and again. And I am *not* going to run the risk of becoming pregnant. Understood?'

'Last night?' knowing now they'd both been desperately foolish.

She went a slight pink colour. 'Three days to period.'

'Ah. You're bright as well as pretty.'

'I know. Brighter than I once used to be.' She stood up, out of reach. 'Remember who I am, Peter. Office admin and twin's nanny. Your father's adopted daughter. Roberta's right hand girl. Don't let's mess things up.'

'I love you, Hazel.'

'I love you too, Peter. Now let's be sane and come downstairs as though nothing's happened.' So adult, so mature, so in love.

'Difficult.'

'Try.'

But then it was so easy, because there was a car on the gravel, a familiar voice, and afterwards their world was never to be the same.

Doc Mac heard direct from the hospital when he made his accustomed early 'how are my patients call,' coincident with the Ward Sister's reach for the phone and, unusually, used as he was to the twists of fate, experienced as great a sense of loss as at any other time. 'I'll tell them,' he told her, put the phone down, heaved a sigh, left a note for his wife, still comatose, got into his car and drove, slowly, towards the most difficult professional call he'd ever wish to make.

Andrew answered the door after the quiet knock.

'Doc! Whatever brings you here at this hour? It's barely seven o'clock,' only to take in the unsmiling face and creases on a worried brow. 'It's not Mary?' for the premonition hadn't left him. That intuitive flash of thought as he'd slipped away from still sleeping Roberta at first light and crept downstairs, ignoring the sound of low voices from down the other corridor, wondering what the day would bring and fearing the worst.

And this was the worst. Over mugs of coffee in the kitchen, postponing the moment he'd have to break the news to his wife. Dearest Roberta, precious, pregnant Roberta.

'Fortunately she's well into the second trimester, Andrew. Chances of an emotionally triggered miscarriage are well reduced. Though it is her state of mind that bothers me, for her mother has been her prop and confidant for so many years, seen her through the worst of her former husband's misdeeds. You've been an excellent help alongside, forgive me for saying. The twins - best thing ever for her - and the new infant will also help. There's an old saying, an old life for a new one. I'm so very sad the way it's been. Not that there's much to be gained, but I know she'll have just quietly slipped away, no pain, no fuss; what she would have wanted. A post-mortem, I'm afraid; I'm guessing it'll show arterial sclerosis, difficult for me to have spotted the severity without tests. Beaten us to it. I think she'd decided it was time to go, rather than be a strain. Some old folks do, you know.'

Andrew twirled his mug round, trying hard to stifle his rising tide of emotion. 'Will you stay put while I tell Roberta? In case . . . '

'Of course.'

As he entered the bedroom, he saw her, knees up, leaning against the bedhead cushions, arms round those knees, staring at him expressionless, almost as though she knew. He sat alongside her, reached for a hand and held it, waiting for the gut-spasm to subside before he could say what needed to be said.

She beat him to it. 'Doc Mac's here. I heard a car, voices in the kitchen.' She was staring at the wall opposite. 'Mum's died.' The pain in her brain, in the early hours. A severed link.

He squeezed her hand, knew his self-control was going and could only nod.

'Poor mum. Not to see her third grand-child. Not to see . . .' and the dam burst. They clung together, tear soaked cheek on cheek, hungry lips on lips, her hand tearing at his hair, his a firm clutch on her breast, as though in the heated climax of a most passionate embrace, seeking solace, comfort, the wildness of togetherness only two people deeply in love can experience.

Cathartic. An incomprehensible joining of two souls, desperately looking for consolation, a pacifier for the tearing loss within her and an outlet for his emotional feeling for that loss.

'Go, Andrew. Go and let Doc Mac go home. I'll be all right, promise. I have you. That's all that matters. Go on. Then we'll tell Hazel, and Peter. Abby and Chris are really too young to know what's happened. And we'll have to let June know. And Andrea. I'll get a shower. Go on,' she repeated, and mopped her cheeks and eyes with the back of a hand. 'I'll be careful.'

He struggled off the crumpled bed and re-dressed, mind churning.

Doc Mac was quietly reading a magazine from the pile. He put it down as Andrew returned to the kitchen and only asked the one question.

'Is she all right?' No mention, no comment over the elapsed half hour.

Andrew nodded. 'I think so. She's tough, underneath. We'll manage. I'll look after her. And ring the surgery if I'm concerned.'

'Do. Or at home if needs be. You've got my number.'

Andrew had, and so grateful that they had a consistent 'family' doctor whose care extended well beyond NHS guidelines.

'Then I'll leave you for now. We'll be in touch about the logistics - maybe tomorrow?'

'Thank you, Doc.' Such an insignificant way of acknowledging what he'd done. 'Very very much.'

They shook hands and the doctor's car purred away down the drive.

Two minutes later and Hazel appeared, still in her pink chenille.

'Andrew? What was the doctor doing here? Roberta's not ill?'

'No, Hazel love. He came to tell us about Mary.'

'Mary?' Her voice rose, with the tremble of uncertainly.

She took the steps towards him and he swept her close, hugging her softness, her pliant young warmth, and loving her.

'I'm so sorry, Hazel,' he mouthed into her hair. 'We've lost her. She passed away early this morning. Her heart gave up. We're on our own, you and I and Roberta.'

Her head came up and as she twisted to look at him, he saw the tears come.

'I . . .' but she couldn't go on; he felt the sobs shake her as he held her, firm and close.

She stood in his embrace for a minute, two, before carefully moving so he could let her go.

'We'll miss her.'

She could only nod, then, 'I'd best get dressed. Abby and Chris will be awake. Shall I bring them down?'

'Do. Roberta'll be down shortly. We'll all have breakfast together - though it's time Peter went. Is he up?'

She glanced at the clock. The world would still revolve, the seconds still ticked away. Eight, just gone. Yes, he should be on his way. The evening and the night, their time together and so meaningful, now pushed down into memory below the crisis of the loss of Mary.

'I'd best see,' and she went; he heard her tripping along the landing, the voices, and Peter's heavier footsteps descending.

Pragmatic, his son. 'Roberta, how's she taking it?'

Andrew shrugged. 'How do you think? You'd better get a move on. Don't let it spoil your day. Grab something on the train.'

A little quick grin. 'Don't worry, pa. I never go hungry. Take care of everyone. See you tonight,' and he'd gone.

Breakfast a routine, but a sombre one. Abby's large luminous eyes caught at her father's emotions, for he could see Roberta in those eyes. Chris behaved, for once, but struggled to be let down before he did his slightly unsteady walk to Roberta's knee for a pick-me-up and a cuddle.

Hazel, now neatly dressed as always, collected them both for a post-breakfast spruce up.

'I can try having them in the office with me if you like, Roberta, but . . .'

'No, thanks, you'd struggle - they can be with me this morning. Then their father can look after them this afternoon. We'll have to see if we can find a nursery place for them.'

'We talked about another pair of hands, Roberta.'

'So we did, Hazel. Ring round the agencies, will you, and let me know what we need to do.'

'I'll do that, R, but not just yet,' Andrew intervened, his job as head of the household. 'No disrespect to Hazel, but better if one of us did it. Sure you'll be okay with the twins?'

'Case of having to be. Life goes on, my love.'

And so it did. It had to. Hazel managed to maintain her equilibrium, Roberta kept a firm grip on her emotions and Andrew undertook a thoughtful reappraisal of how home and business would develop, but as they all realised, each in their own way, their world would never be the same. This was a Tuesday like no other.

TWELVE

Ireland. The grey light and the softness of the rain. She'd awoken peacefully after a dreamless night, eased up, back to the oak veneered headboard, to watch the variation in the cloud cover as a slow procession of shades in slate, granite and undyed sheep's wool. Or, in less decorative terms, simply thicker and thinner chunks of moisture laden air. Whatever, it didn't exactly spur her into doing an early morning jog round the scenery, though the concept of another visit to the rose garden to commune with Keela had emerged during the return to consciousness. Mentioning that feminine statuette's name yesterday had certainly worked the oracle after Siobhán had given every indication of being cross with the concept of restoration rather than renovation. Subtle difference, keep the old, not replace it with similar new. Maybe that's in line with the National Trust philosophy, she thought. Not that she knew much about historic houses, hadn't been her scene. But now, well, it felt more and more her.

Time to get up. She swung pyjama-covered legs out from underneath old fashioned sheets and blankets - ages since she'd last slept in these - and trod the rug covered floorboards to the sash window. Had the rain given up? Maybe she'd have that walk after all. Give her an appetite for Donald's Irish breakfast.

The day smelt fresh, cool, and very gardeney. Dressed warmly and sensibly, she had to let herself quietly out of the front door; no sign or sound from either of her hosts. Even with her stouter shoes, the initial walk across the apron of stone gravel and then a couple of hundred yards of mown lawn dampened her feet and she was glad she'd chosen jeans. Totally quiet. Not a sound, other than the drip, drip from shrubs and overhanging branches and the squelch of her footsteps. She short-circuited, ducking under the rain-drenched rhododendrons towards the edge of the walled garden, followed the brickwork around until she could branch off to where the rose bower lay, lost in its mystery, hidden beyond the overgrown laurels. Her shoes were sopping, the bottom two inches of her jeans dark with damp, and drips had run down her collar to trickle between her breasts. This was a very masochistic exercise though it had an accent of adventure too. She pushed wet hair out of her eyes. Keela, the *Cadhla* girl as Siobhán had named her, stood impervious to her surroundings.

June crouched down in front of the statue, no more than four feet tall, and studied the features. Carved with a faint smile, vaguely imperious, haughty maybe, but an appealing face none the less. Her grey but lichen yellowed tresses reached a naked shoulder, partially covered one pert breast, a lifted hand coyly protected the other. A wrap of fabric, skilfully depicted by the sculptor, caught on the one side clear of hair, flowed into her slender waist, fell across proportioned thighs and drifted down towards shapely legs. Her naked feet, angled in classic poise, stood on a simple base, kept her ever still, forbidden flight or dream of dance. A beauty only poetry could capture. What mortal had carved her thus, given her life from a mass of stone, what former owner of this place had placed her amongst the roses, and what unknown force had brought a mere human to crouch at her feet on a soft winter's morning?

She shivered; the damp brought its own chill, let alone the obscure magic of this place. Foolish to stay and get cold, the warmth of the house's kitchen and the prospect of a decent breakfast had a draw, yet, mysteriously she succumbed to the urge to stroke the stone girl's hair once more. Did it feel soft under her touch? Imagination. Did the blank eyes soften to a sorrowful smile? Stupidity. Did the quiet voice echo in her head, *love this place, give me life in your body?* Totally idiotic. Abruptly, she stood up, looked again at the face. Who was this girl? An artist's wilful imagination or reality frozen from life?

'You've been across to the rose garden?' Rhetorical question from Donald, happy in his breakfast chef's guise.

June nodded. 'Wet out there. And cold. I'll have to change these jeans; they're soaked around the ankles. Won't be a moment,' and went upstairs.

Siobhán caught Donald's look. 'I know. The girl's bewitched by the romance of the place. You'll tell her, or shall I?'

He deftly flipped an egg. 'You spin a better yarn than I. Don't dwell on the past, now.'

'That I won't. She deserves the proper story, so she does. But let's get the job done, now, afore she has to fly back home. 'Tis Christmas in a fortnight.'

June changed into her dark blue skirt and the better sweater, brushed her hair back and caught it in a band, slipped on her comfortable house shoes and trod lightly across the landing, feeling perfectly at home, as though she'd lived here all her life. As the bottom stair tread creaked under her step, as it always seemed to do, the ancient phone's ring brought her to a surprised stop. Should she wait to see if either came from the kitchen? There was a repeater bell in the passage - yes, sound of the door opened and footsteps.

'Oh, June, you can always answer if you're handy, no worries over etiquette, we're all friends around,' but Siobhán lifted the ebonite handset. 'Mor House. Siobhán Drivas.'

The tinny voice echoed, and Siobhán's eyes lifted to look directly at June. 'Yes, of course, I'll put her on,' and held the receiver towards her. 'It's your father, June. I'll be in the kitchen.'

She couldn't tell her it was bad news, that was June's father's job, and not one she envied anyone.

She felt numb. Nothing. No surge of tearfulness, no prickling eyes. Just numb. Though her dad had given her the facts, the simple bald statement of actuality, she instinctively sensed his taut emotion, bottled up. Not his mum, no relation of hers, but Roberta's and the ties between mother and daughter were strong, that she knew. A tragedy, losing Mary, for though she was of an age, could well have had another decade. He'd said, finish what you need to do and come back. Christmas. How could they celebrate Christmas? She walked slowly down the grim corridor, into the kitchen and its enveloping comfort, sat down at the table and buried her head in folded arms. She felt Siobhán's caress and a gentle circling thumb massaging a stiffened neck and shoulders. Not a word spoken, for there was no need.

Mechanically she completed her task, wrote out all her thoughts alongside a schedule of dimensions, cursed the absence of a laptop, took dozens more photos and blessed the camera card's vast memory. She ate a lovely lunch, accepted Anita's commiserations, and was surprised to receive another phone call in the middle of the afternoon, from Peter.

'You were supposed to have rung before, Peter.'

'I know. Sorry. Too much going on. You're coming back?'

'Donald's driving me to Dublin in the morning. I'm not looking forward to it. Not that he's a bad driver or anything, it's just the distance. And the airport. I'd far rather take the ferry.'

'Too long. The drive back from Pembroke, or Holyhead, come to that. No, plane's best. Dad will collect you from Stanstead, or are you flying into Heathrow? Or Luton. Luton would be good. Lot closer.'

'Donald's going to check for me. I'll let dad know.' She sensed he, too, was tensed up. 'You okay?'

'Just wish this hadn't happened. Roberta's fraught with it. Dad's hyped up because she is; Hazel's not a lot better. Be good to have you back. Done your thing?'

She nodded before saying 'yes', and nearly chuckled. Her mood began to lift. 'Haven't you managed to keep Hazel's spirits up, brother dear?'

The pause was too long. 'Er, yes, 'spose so.'

'Ah. She suits, does she?'

'Mmmm mmm. Early days, sis.' Another pause. 'Heard from William?'

That was a bit below the belt. 'No,' she replied, shortly. 'Let him stew.'

'I'd best get on, June. Angie will want to know who I'm chatting to.'

'Angie?'

'My assistant. Must go. See you tomorrow. Take care.'

The dinner wasn't scheduled as an 'event', but it had all the overtones of a wake. Both her hosts seemed as subdued as she felt and conversation faltered. Anita's brighter attempts at enlivening the mood also fell flat and she cleared away the plates with a dour face.

'I'll be off then,' adding to her parting comment, ''tis a shame you're away back to that jammed-up island, now. Come back soon, June, and we'll see what we can do to fix you up with a real man.'

Donald's shaggy eyebrows twitched as the door slammed behind her. 'She's a rare one to speak. It'd be a brave fella who'd take her on. Hope she doesn't offend, June.'

June shook her head. 'Not that one. I like her straight talking.'

'We'll miss you around,' Siobhán drained her glass. 'Selfishly, I wish you'd be able to stay. You will come back?'

'I'd love to,' and she looked around the room, so decidedly familiar now she'd documented its every inch. 'See the job through, though it's more of a personal obligation than a job.

The house deserves it,' then realised she'd implied her hosts had a lack of care, which was certainly not the case. 'Sorry if . . .'

Siobhán's little shake of her hair added to the slow smile. 'June, my love, 'tis as I said, Keela's worked her magic. She'll be the one.'

Donald harrumphed and pushed his chair back. 'I'd best check on those flights, now. You two get yourselves set comfortable in the other room. I won't be long.'

Settled into the saggy comfort of the living room chairs with a mug of instant coffee, a stark contrast to the formality of Anita's superb dinner, June felt as though she belonged. Even the now familiar remembered surroundings of Roberta's Manor hadn't the same attraction and this was a strange thought. She closed her eyes and let those thoughts ramble.

How would Roberta manage without her mother? Her dad would be all she had now. What if something happened to disturb that relationship? What was her own mum up to, and would she visit like she'd told Peter she might? And Peter, he'd better not mess around with Hazel's emotions. That girl was probably far too naïve to realise what it was all about – as she'd been with William, and look where that had got her. Would he come back?

She sighed, unwittingly.

'June, dear, do say?' Siobhán, legs crossed, long maroon cord skirt smoothed down, embroidered waistcoat opened against a lacey top, her auburn hair spread over the chair's back cushion, so much a lovely figure and June trusted her.

'You don't mind?' *It would be reassuring to talk things over, once she'd got them straight.*

'Of course I don't.'

'You've been very kind, considering you employ me – Roberta – to work for you.'

Siobhán did a little headshake. 'I'd like to think it was more a friendship thing and all we do is pay expenses.' She looked up as Donald came back into the room. 'All sorted?'

'Sorted. A flight at half twelve, out of Dublin, gets you

into Luton just before two. Seat's booked and paid for.' He dropped into the remaining large armchair. 'And Maeve's going with you. If you don't mind, that is. She wants to go Christmas shopping in London, so she does.'

'What a nice idea! Company on the flight. Donald, dear, June and I were going to have a little chat.'

'Sure. I've some more things to do,' and he heaved himself up again. 'Don't keep the girl up too late now, early start in the morning.'

'He's happy enough in his little den, June. You don't mind about Maeve?'

'Not at all.' In fact, June thought, a comfort, someone to keep her from brooding. 'She'll be welcome, that she will.'

Siobhán grinned. 'That she will. June, dear, the expressions are catching. Let me tell you about Keela. Mind you, 'tis all hearsay and fairy stories. It is said,' and her voice changed to a low musicality, 'that the one day she wasn't there, the next she was, and no one owned up to her coming. But in the past, the family who owned this place originally had a lovely daughter, a girl who, 'twas told, could weave spells, tell the future, a girl who had a suite of followers. Then, when she was eighteen, her parents wanted to marry her off to a dashing young man from an estate across the valley. So the story goes, the wedding would have taken her away back to England. But her heart was set on another, a local lad with no fortune but who had a way on him enough to turn any girl's passion. There was a stand-up row and she fled, and the young lad with her. Her parents sought her, but the two just vanished. A year or two went by, eventually the old couple died of the fever, though some said of heartbreak, and the house was to be sold. The girl's uncle inherited and he wanted nothing of the responsibility of an estate.'

June's spine tingled. An elopement! How romantic! 'Go on.'

'Well, some days before the sale, the old head gardener

reported to the agent that a young woman had been seen in the policies, but when challenged, ran off. Concerned because the description fitted the young girl who had eloped, a search party was sent out, the woods combed, and they came across a body, in parlous condition, lying at the foot of the rock face above our woods. From the remnants of clothing and a plain brass ring, it was identified as the young lad. Not a trace of the girl, though. The day before the sale, the statue appeared overnight, placed much where it is the now. The remains of the young man are said to have been buried under the centre stone of the rose bower, as a gesture. So it seems she watches over him. Donald's grandparents bought the place and it's been in the family ever since. The odd thing is, only certain yellow roses flourish in the garden. Other varieties and colours tried wither away.'

'And the girl's name . . .'

'Was *Cadhla*. Keela. The beautiful one.'

'But surely someone had the statue carved, and it isn't a lightweight thing.' She couldn't believe Siobhán's explanation, though maybe she wanted to. 'It's a made-up story!'

'June, my dear girl, never challenge Irish folklore. Story it may be, but the statue dates from then. Let me show you something.' She pushed herself out of the depths of the chair, and June followed her, nerves a-quiver.

They went into the front sitting room, where June had spent hours detailing the contents.

'Did you not notice this painting?' Siobhán pointed at the one above the door, tucked into the corner.

A young girl, in a full dark red dress, caught with a brooch on her left shoulder, long hair draped across her right, clutching a bouquet of yellow roses. The background was dark, sombre, as though she was poised on the edge of a wood. June blinked. Yes, she'd seen the painting, thought it familiar but hadn't, until now, realised.

'It's Keela!'

Siobhán nodded. 'It's Keela. Painted a short while before the time of her planned wedding and given to the young man who was to be her fiancé. It was returned to the house after her disappearance. So maybe he had the statue commissioned from the painting, and when it was obvious she was lost to him, he had her placed where she wanted to be, and has been, ever since.'

'What a lovely but tragic story!'

Siobhán turned away, and June followed. As they walked back to the sitting room, Siobhán spoke over her shoulder. 'Yes. With a moral. Don't stand in the way of true love. Keela never was found. Perhaps something happened to her and her beau jumped off the cliff. Perhaps . . . well, who knows. If her parents had accepted him, maybe her descendents would still own this property. Whatever. She's still here, in spirit.'

'So she is. Thank you for telling me the story.'

'Not everyone knows. Folklore it may be, but believable. Now, a nightcap, or straight to bed? A Wednesday early start, as Donald said.'

Maeve kept up an incessant flow of chat, the girl didn't seem to know when to stop. All the way to the airport, in the departure lounge, in the aircraft; only when they emerged into the arrivals area and found Andrew waiting for them did she actually fall quiet, briefly.

Andrew swept June to him, hugged her tight. 'Thank heavens you're back, daughter mine. Good flight?'

She pulled clear, but momentarily kept hold of a hand. 'Dad, this is Maeve, Siobhán and Donald's daughter. She's come over to do some Christmas shopping in town, kept me company. The flight was okay.'

'Grand to meet you, sirrr,' said Maeve, drawing out her 'arrs' and giving him a lovely smile with her handshake.

'And I you.' He offered a query first to June. 'Does she want to come back to the Manor?' then back to the redhead. 'What are your plans, Maeve? Are you going on into London? You can stay overnight if you wish.' He raised his eyebrows at his daughter, an unspoken query.

June hesitated. 'If she doesn't mind sharing.'

Maeve, never one for missing an opportunity, replied. ''T'would be lovely to see June's family, and I've no definite plans. Thanks a million.' She picked up her small case, all she'd brought with her and beamed at him.

'Right-oh. Come on, sooner we get out of this place the better. I can't stand airports.' He led the way out. 'And call me Andrew, Maeve. At least your presence may help lighten the mood, especially with that smile.'

Once in the car, Maeve recommenced her chattering, on what she would buy, where she would go, how her friends would envy her trip, the way she might spend Christmas. June closed half an ear, she'd already heard most of it before on the flight across. Andrew interjected monosyllabic noises at appropriate points until he swept the car into the driveway and stopped by the front steps.

'June! 'Tis jest like mamma's!' Maeve climbed out and spun around on the gravel, the lightweight long tweed skirt flaring. 'Lovely! Jest lovely!'

Andrew couldn't help his smile at the irrepressible girl. 'We think so. Come along in and meet Roberta. She'll be surprised.'

The hallway had its accustomed effect. Maeve gaped, June hid her smile, while Andrew stood, impassive, as their unexpected visitor took it all in.

'Sure, but 'tis lovely, beautiful it is!' Maeve twirled, skirt flaring, soft red hair floating in air as she spun. 'Heaven. Oh, June, can you do this for ma? Please?' She waltzed around, catching Andrew briefly by the waist. 'You're a grand man to

111

have such a clever daughter.' She stopped, gazing up at the paintings. 'The old house needs this. Then Keela'll come home.'

Keela again. What was it about the girl? June's spine tingled and her father's face took on a puzzled look - and she couldn't blame him. The irrepressible Irishness of Maeve would have bowled him over even if reference to the mysterious Keela hadn't.

He coughed, politely. 'I'm so glad you like it. Actually, it had an impression on me, too, when I first came here. But you must meet Roberta. It's her house, her designs.'

Maeve's gaze returned to him. 'Not June's?'

"Fraid not,' and June had to own up. 'I'm a very recent addition to the firm. Dad's right. It's Roberta's place. Though I . . .' and hesitated. Loved it? Knew it to be what she now understood was so right about gracious living; living in harmony with your soul? Contrast little boxes of houses all jammed up together, rushing traffic, jostling people, constant noise - no, this was her future. And all down to her father. If he hadn't met Roberta . . . it didn't warrant consideration. Instinctively she took the steps closer and wrapped arms around, sank her head to his sweater-clad front.

'Hey? June?' He dropped a kiss onto his daughter's hair, felt her taut emotion in the pressure of her clasp. 'Lovely to have you home. We'll talk later.' Ever so gently, he eased her up. Maeve's face offered a surprised look, and then the door in the corner opened and Roberta appeared.

She looked from one to the other, and centred on Maeve. 'Let me guess. Daughter of Siobhán, you share the same colouring. Well now.' She walked across and held out a hand. 'You're very welcome, even if unexpected. What is this, Andrew? I sense an atmosphere?'

'Roberta, you're so right. This is Maeve, who's reacted to the Manor's welcome ambience more so than some.' He'd held onto his daughter's hand. 'And June's expressed her return thoughts of how nice a place it is as well,' which although she hadn't them actually voiced, he intuitively knew.

Maeve's temporary astonishment at June's actions evaporated and she wasn't about to take a back stage role. 'I came over to keep the girl company and do some Christmas shopping, Andrew offered me a chance to come and see the place, and surely, 'tis amazing. I love it, I really do. And so like our own old place, but with a soul. Mor House lost its soul ages ago, though with June here, there's more a chance we'll get it back. Which will be good.'

'It'll be good,' echoed Roberta, uncertain about the 'soul' aspect. 'Shall we get you some lunch? Hazel's doing her thing.'

After a chatty lunch, pork pie and pickles, new bread and salads, a glass or two of cider, Roberta offered Maeve an enthusiastically accepted tour of the Barn, while Andrew shepherded his daughter into the sitting room. Hazel, in her carefully orchestrated balancing act between office maid and nursery maid, took Chris and Abby on their afternoon walk.

Father and daughter sat close on the only settee, overlooking the garden windows. Across the wintry yellowed grass they saw Hazel alternating between remonstration and encouragement, watched her rescue a tumbled Abby, gently scold Chris for smacking her legs. The very essence of family life, except it was Hazel acting as mother, not Roberta.

'She's very good to them.' June held her hands loosely in her lap, feeling an ache.

'The best.'

'You love her?'

'Hazel? Yes, June, I do. As I love you, daughter mine. What's this about a 'Keela'?'

'Maeve's comment?'

'She said Keela, whoever she is, would come back if Mor House was brought back to life. Is the place that bad?'

113

She nodded. 'Abandoned, dad. Not just because Siobhán and Donald have been away so much, but, yes, as Maeve said, it's lost its soul. You can feel it. There's a sadness. There's a sadness here too.' No Mary.

Andrew lifted an arm to pull June close and welcomed her snuggle down. 'She's a great loss to us all. I do believe, however, it was her decision. When she felt her body failing, rather than being the burden and worry, better to switch off. Sad it wasn't here. That's what I regret most of all. But we can't always choose.'

'Roberta?'

'I bless our incipient third child, June. And all of you. It's going to be a difficult time though.'

They sat quiet, listening to the measured tick-tock of the old wall clock.

'This Keela?'

June stirred. She would have cheerfully dozed off. 'The daughter of the people who once owned Mor House. She fell in love with a village lad her parents didn't approve of, ran away with him. A couple of years later his body was found on the estate, she's never been heard of since, but a carved stone likeness appeared in the rose garden; rumour suggests it was commissioned by the man chosen by her parents as ideal husband. He's supposed to have returned her to the garden as a gesture. Her lover's buried in the centre of the garden, so the story goes. The Irish give a lot of credence to such tales.'

'And why not? Very romantic.'

June chuckled. 'Like you? Whatever. But the statue does have a presence. Siobhán said that stroking the girl's hair meant you'd always return.'

'And did you?'

She didn't reply, thinking back to that damp morning.

'June?'

She nodded, foolishly feeling a prickling in her eyes.

He gently tightened his arm. 'Then you must follow your inclinations, my daughter.'

Roberta's reasoned description of her designs silenced Maeve, surprisingly. A hour soon went, with every aspect carefully outlined.

'And we'll be seen on the television soon.'

'I wish I could get my silly head round to think up all this stuff. Me, I've no sense - other than liking what I see. Lovely.'

A word she kept using far too often, apart from 'grand'. And grand it all was. Now she knew why her mum had chosen this Roberta, though June was just right, too.

'Glad you like it, Maeve. Shall we go and find the others?'

Roberta carefully closed the Barn doors and accompanied her guest back across the yard, just as Hazel and the twins reappeared at the gate from round the corner of the lane. Immediately they saw their mother, they scampered towards her, to clutch at legs and stop her in her tracks.

'Oi! Careful, you two!' Hazel advanced, worried that childish enthusiasm might upskittle Roberta; in her present precarious state, not a good idea.

Roberta stood still, reaching down to offer a careful hand to each. 'Maeve, be a dear and hold Abby's hand while I cope with Chris. I'm afraid I have to be rather careful nowadays. In a delicate condition, as they say.'

Maeve beamed. 'To be sure. Abby, is it? Now there's a lovely name!' That word lovely used again. None the less, the little girl was happy to offer a hand to a new friend.

With Chris holding on to his mother, Maeve with his sister, Hazel bringing up the rear, they all returned to the kitchen. June was making an early pot of tea. Andrew, wanting a moment to himself, had retreated to the office.

He sat in her chair. Andrea's chair. It would always be *her* chair. Christmas was almost upon them. What would - should

- they do? Tradition demanded a tree, decorations. Presents had been, in the main, already bought. All the cards had been sent, a Hazel job early last week. Maeve's fortuitous arrival had lifted Roberta's spirit, he could see that. However, it didn't diminish the prospect of a gloomy New Year - they had a funeral to arrange, a little cottage in the village to clear. And he remembered one call not yet made; her number was on the pad, in Hazel's careful script. He picked up the phone.

THIRTEEN

'Alain Perlain's assistant. How can I help?'

'Andrea. It's Andrew.'

He sensed the uplift in her, the change in tone. 'Dear Andrew! How lovely! How's things?'

'Not good, my love.' He could still call her his love, for that she was and would always be, but different. No longer merely a passion, but a deeply loved friend. 'Can you escape, come and spend some little time with us?'

Her response swift, direct, decisive. 'Of course. Tonight? Alain's not here, he's in Spain until at least Friday. Then we break until the New Year. All set for Christmas?'

'Short answer, no. Explain tonight.' His throat caught. 'Thanks,' and listened to her brief words of reply.

'Andrea's coming over tonight.'

Roberta looked up. 'You haven't told her?'

'Not yet. Wanted to talk to her. You don't mind?'

She smiled at him in a sad sort of way. 'Andrew, my love, why should I mind? So long as she doesn't feel she has to come back. We're managing, aren't we?' and he sensed her melancholy.

'So far.' He changed the topic. Maeve and June were sitting in the kitchen. Hazel was, bless her, struggling with the laundry and the twins were 'helping' her. 'Do we have a tree?'

Her brown eyes caught at him. Steady, accepting the

situation. 'Of course. Business as usual. Mum wouldn't have had it any other way. She's with us in spirit, my love.' She picked up her book. 'Do what needs to be done,' she added and went back to her reading.

He spoke to one of his circle of village friends and ordered a tree. 'Of course,' he got from one of his most understanding. 'I'd love to help. Be over late afternoon tomorrow?' Then he tried phoning the hospital, managed ultimately to speak to one of the Coroner's team and was told the results of the post-mortem would be available tomorrow. Tomorrow. Another day.

Relieved, he went to discover how Hazel was managing. Abby, helpful as always, was taking wet washing from Hazel as she pulled it out of the spinner and struggling to fit into the clothes basket. Chris was sorting out pegs.

'Too late to peg that lot out, isn't it?'

Hazel gave him a quick grin. 'I'll hang it over the Aga later on. I think little and often, don't you? Otherwise it'll be calling in the laundry service.'

He pulled a face. 'Not if we can help it. How are you with ironing?'

She grimaced in turn. 'Not my strongest point. Maybe June'll help. I won't ask Roberta.'

'Any thoughts about another girl? What do you think?'

'Leave it for now. Let's see how we get on. After . . .'

He knew what she meant, and the very mature approach she was displaying, given she had stepped partially into Mary's shoes, was heart warming in its own way and he was encouraged.

'Dinner?'

'Simplistic. Supper more like. Fish and chips, that all right?'

He shook his head, amazed. She'd taken over, picked up the essentials of running the house as though she'd be born to it, but it wasn't fair on her.

'Anything I can do?'

Her grin came back. 'Take these two out of my hair. Then I can get on.'

'Andrea's coming over this evening. I wanted to tell her in person rather than over the phone.'

The last of the clothes handed onto an expectant Abby to add to the basket, she closed the spinner's door. "Spose that's best. So long as she doesn't feel she's got to come back.' She straightened up. 'Chris - there are some pegs under the washing machine. Put them back in the box, please.'

Andrew chuckled. 'Roberta's said the same. Don't you trust me?'

'Asking the question suggests the answer, Andrew. I sometimes wish I had her sex appeal,' and felt her face redden. Her own explicit sex appeal had already nearly been her downfall, caught out in the stress of the moment. What was it that made people vulnerable under conditions of stress? Had she been vulnerable? Not that way, fortuitously.

'Hazel, love, you've nothing to worry about on that score, I can assure you. Come on, you two, let's go and see your mother.' He'd seen the blush and wondered, but not sufficient to query her thoughts, for now they had a far greater understanding between them.

The understanding between him and Andrea was another thing. When she tapped on the kitchen door and walked straight into the supper clear-up, it felt as though she'd never left - and given it wasn't all that long ago, not surprising. Andrew greeted her with a social kiss, as did Roberta. Peter part rose from his chair merely to say 'hi' and subside again, Hazel paused in her 'wash-up' role sufficiently to also say 'hi, Andrea.' Maeve and June had gone upstairs to read 'good-night' stories to the twins.

'What's all this then? No Mary?'

Andrew shook his head, took a hand, led the mystified girl through to the sitting room and sat her down. 'Thanks for coming over,' he said, pacing over to the window. The garden was dark and uninspirational; he couldn't even make out the mass of the big old beech tree. He leant back on the windowsill. 'No easy way to tell you. We've lost Mary. She's passed away.'

The surprised exclamation 'Oh! No! Andrew! How - why - I mean, she wasn't ill, was she?' evinced the deep shock she'd felt, given the unveiling of such a sudden and very tragic turn of events in this blunt way.

'Early yesterday morning. She had a mini-stroke or something, the doc came and had her admitted to hospital, but she died in her sleep during the night. Her heart gave up. Thought I'd rather tell you in person than over the phone.'

Andrea leant back on the cushions and rubbed her forehead, then cupped her chin in her hands. 'Poor Roberta! So sudden! What'll you do without her? I mean, she ran this place! And such a lovely old lady. What can I do, Andrew? I could come back?'

'Roberta's adamant you don't upset your new boss, and I agree. We both thought you might offer to return, to take the pressure off, but it wouldn't be right. Not for you, not for Alain, and we couldn't be that selfish. Hazel's risen to the challenge magnificently; it could even be the making of her.'

'So what can I do?'

'I'd thought we might have an evening together, a sort of family gathering - the Manor's family - and wondered if you'd organise it for me. Seeing as that's something you do? Not fully Christmassy, you understand, but . . .'

She held up a hand. 'I understand. Even seen as a celebration for Mary's life? Sort of wake?'

He nodded. 'Say the Friday, New year's Eve?'

'Ah ha. And that as well. Give me food for thought.' She changed the subject. 'How's June getting on with her project?'

'She's back, brought her own Irish colleen with her. They're upstairs, I'll go and see if they've finished the bedtime stories. One moment.'

When he'd gone, she got up and walked round, seeing and

not seeing the room and sucking at its vibes. How she'd attempted to seduce him and failed, here. At his former house, it had been easy and she still cherished the memories of that night in his arms. Then the time in the car, the spin on the office chair, such foolishness; the cast and crew evening when all his pent-up feelings were pressed hard up against her taut thighs, below no more than as soft a dress as the occasion warranted. Despite Alain and his unending innuendos, she couldn't divorce her feelings for this man. He'd taken her virtue, and with it, her soul. Saddened as she was for Mary's demise, for Roberta too, in her loss of a mum and lifetime's companion to boot, she couldn't suppress this rise, this flare-up of exhilaration, yes, that's what it was, exhilaration, at the chance of close contact in party mode when senses would be at susceptible fever pitch. She'd wear the same red dress, and the tiny electric tingles were already beginning to charge her emotions.

Footsteps, voices, a girlish laugh, the door opened.

'Andrea, meet Maeve, daughter of our Irish clients who you've previously met, remember Siobhán and Donald Drivas? She's over, ostensibly, to do some Christmas shopping, or so I understand. Maeve, this is Andrea. Former office paragon and . . .' *A soul mate.* His voice tailed away.

'. . . someone he finds difficult to say 'no' to,' finished June realistically, letting Maeve do the handshake bit.

'Pleased to meet you, I'm sure. How y're doing?' Maeve eyed the blonde girl up and down. 'If I was a man, truly I'd be knocking at the door, that I would.' She turned to Andrew. 'And you let her slip through your fingers. Indeed, a sorry state of affairs, letting her leave.' She might have gone on, but saw June frown.

Andrea laughed. 'Mutual decision, Maeve. Glad to meet you, too. I'd better get home, Andrew. I'll put some ideas together and call you. And confirm the date?' Her eyes caught his, part closed, a slight lift of her head.

'I'll see you out.'

On the top step, the front door part closed behind them, he took her, foolishly, into his arms.

'Are you sure you don't want me back, Andrew?' she whispered when she could draw breath. *'I miss you.'*

Why was it he couldn't resist her? 'I miss you too. Perhaps just as well you went, Andrea. I wouldn't ever wish to hurt Roberta, especially now.'

Her hands went behind his back and clasped, drawing him close, sought and found, pressed, eyes closed; she experienced the same depth of longing as on the night of her leaving party. *'I wish, I wish, I wish,'* she whispered in his ear, then broke free and ran, high heels skittering the gravel.

He watched her little car accelerate down the drive and cursed his foibles.

'She's gone then?' Roberta put down her book and raised her eyebrows at him as he returned to the kitchen, frowning. 'She might have said goodbye. Still afraid of me?'

'Don't be silly, R. No, I think she was too emotionally wound up. Why aren't you with the others?'

'I need some quiet every now and again. Maeve's a little too wearing with her constant chatter. Not that she isn't pleasant with it, but the girl just doesn't know when to stop.'

He laughed. 'Very true. I think she's planning to go into London with Peter in the morning.'

'That'll jazz up his journey.'

'Very true,' he repeated. They were on their own, the others were all in the sitting room, doing what he didn't know. 'I've asked Andrea to arrange a New Year's Eve get-together, love. Only for us Manor dwellers - take our mind off things. Okay with you?'

Roberta leant back in the chair and flexed her shoulders. Her muscles were tightening up, a sure sign she was tired. 'I suppose so. Probably a good thing.' She stood up, carefully. 'I think I'll call it a day. You go and keep the others company. That all right?'

'Sure. See you in a bit.'

The tree came the following afternoon, courtesy of Barry from the hardware store and his pick-up truck, together with a surprising amount of holly foliage. With Roberta's general state of 'delicacy' as she called it, the decoration was left to Hazel and June; Abby and Chris sat on the stairs and issued baubles from the box to each girl in turn, Andrew doing his supervisory role and ultimately holding onto the steps firmly as Hazel climbed to put the fairy on the top.

'Don't look up, Andrew,' she said mischievously, 'I would have worn trousers if I had any. There, is she straight?' She carefully descended and looked up. 'She'll do. Now, where are the lights?'

Half an hour later and the hall looked very different. Christmas was finally on its way.

When Peter returned from London he whistled. 'Smashing stuff. Where's the mistletoe, girls? Can't have Christmas without the mistletoe.'

'A very small piece above the passage door - can't you see it?' Hazel drew him over and stood precociously underneath it, eyes closed and lips pursed, trying hard not to laugh. She got her reward and a whisper. She blushed.

'Hoi, you two. Time to get some tea on the go.' Andrew folded the steps preparatory to returning them to the large cupboard under the stairs. June chased the twins down the corridor.

Roberta had left them to it, spending most of the afternoon with her feet up on the sitting room settee. The remnants of the foliage were strategically placed behind pictures and on the mantlepiece, the few tree decorations that had lost their fastenings laid amongst the greenery. Cards had already started to arrive in quantity and were hanging in strings from the picture rail.

The entire atmosphere of the Manor begun to take on a relaxed and seasonal feel, a winding down. Three days to go.

'Tea in here, I think. Hazel, June, you do the honours. Peter, try and amuse Chris for a while. I'll read to Abby. Where are you going, dear?' Andrew had reached the door; Roberta in her most organising mode could be a tad irritating and he thought to catch up on any e-mails.

'Back in a few moments. Check the office.'

'Oh, all right. Don't be long.' She laid her head back on the cushion. Why did she felt so lethargic? The ache was still there, the physical reminder of her fragility, as well as that dull emptiness that was the loss of her mother. Every now and again she'd look for her, wonder where she was, and have to try once more to suppress the resultant pang after the repetitive realisation she'd not see her ever again. Only having these vibrant people about her, her beautiful children and her constant supportive Andrew kept her going. Without them, where would she be? In a tearful emotionally over-wrought suicidal heap.

Andrew moved the mouse and the screen fired into life. There was an e-mail from Mor House. Siobhán, apologising for her daughter's importuning and hoping it hadn't been an imposition during such a sad period; Donald had spoken to Declan and he would be thrilled to become involved in the project; please would Andrew pass on their heartfelt sympathies to Roberta, and the very best wishes for the future. He acknowledged it, said 'thanks', and wished them too, a pleasant Christmastide.

There was also one from Samantha, giving him a moment's hesitation before opening it. Was Peter's new job to his satisfaction, did he think, for she'd not heard. Was

June's situation with William any better, and it would be nice if she felt she could ring. Her Donald was away - he'd gone to spend some time with his sister in Dorking so she was on her own. What were they doing for Christmas? Andrew frowned at the screen. He hadn't thought to tell her about Mary - somehow it hadn't crossed his mind as important to do so - but here was the opportunity. He pondered. She'd said about visiting, but how strange was that, coming to meet up with former husband and his replacement wife? Well, if he told her of the funeral date . . . and at that moment the phone rang, as if by design.

'The Manor, Andrew Hailsworthy.'

'Andrew. Doctor Macintosh. Thought I'd catch you. P.M results. As we'd thought,' and Andrew listened as Doc Mac went through the clinical conditions, the whys and wherefores.

'I see. So she wouldn't have suffered.'

'Not at all. A peaceful way to go. Don't take it the wrong way if I say she was lucky, though so sad to think that she could have had a few more years if we'd known of her problem earlier. Such an independent old lady. One of the old school. So, the Coroner's released the body. Who'll you use?'

Practicalities. He felt a sudden jerk of emotion, swallowed and fought to regain use of his voice. 'Don't know yet. Let you know. Thanks, Doc.'

He pushed the chair back and went to find Roberta, ignoring the screen and the still open e-mail page.

Abby was contentedly snuggled on Roberta's lap, thumb in her mouth, listening to the adventures of Peter Rabbit for the nth time. Peter and Chris were nowhere to be seen, assumed either upstairs or in the kitchen. The girls must also be in the kitchen, so, other than Abby, she was on her own. He brushed with gentle fingers as he passed behind her to sit on the opposite chair.

'Doc Mac's rung.'

She reached the end of the story and put the little book down. Abby had her eyes closed. Asleep? She lifted her eyes to his. Steady, sad, stoical. 'And?'

'You want the details?'

She shook her head. 'Not now.'

'Perhaps the Thursday after Christmas, if there's a chance.'

'All right, but she wanted to be buried, Andrew, and near where she spent her teen years - Yorkshire. Near Givendale, close to where she once worked. You'd best talk to Robertsons. Perhaps it won't be possible so soon.'

He sensed the reluctance to take action, make decisions - as if doing nothing would prevent this final scene of the last act of a life. 'You'd like me to arrange everything?'

'Please.'

'Do you want me to take Abby upstairs?'

Another little head shake. 'No, I will. In a while.'

The intuition suggested she needed, welcomed, the comfort of her child close to her, the warmth, the softness, the pheromonic companionship of a daughter, and he perfectly understood. 'Right-oh.' Quietly, he returned to the office to find a number and start the wheels turning, saw the still open message page and Samantha's mail. He'd answer it and then ring the undertaker.

'Sorry to have to say, he typed out, 'Roberta's mother died rather unexpectedly two days ago - undiagnosed heart problem - and we're all rather down. Please excuse brevity, can't yet see where we're going. Be in touch. Y. A. E. Andrew' Yours As Ever. Their old signing-off phrase that set him thinking. Was Sam as happy with her Donald now as when she'd first met him? If he'd gone to see his sister without her at this seasonal time? At least she was still keeping tabs on their two. All manner of idle concepts floated around, like if he hadn't seen Roberta fall off her horse, or if Andrea hadn't shown him round the brewery or if Sam hadn't had the urge to do good works abroad - where would they now all be? Hypothetical. No going back now. That was another of those benchmarks. A marker. Now for the next one.

FOURTEEN

Hazel woke. Not quite daylight. The day when, and it tore into her brain, the twins have turned three. Because Christmas Day was their birthday. She listened carefully, and unsurprisingly, there were some background noises. So they had found their early morning surprise gifts - the carefully hung cotton bags put in place last night. Would Roberta go to them, for she ought to, being children's nanny was fine but their mum should still be first in line. She waited; it was still early.

Peter also woke. He'd enjoy the day, first Christmas in civilised surroundings for a couple of years. Yes, it would be less of a festive day but nonetheless, life had to go on. The time? Half six. Another hour or so.

June glanced at her bedside clock. Far too early. She wondered about Maeve, for when she'd left for her London shopping expedition, accompanying Peter on his last day in the office until the New Year, that girl had given the distinct impression she'd gate crash their day. Not that she'd didn't like her, *au contraire*, she was fun, and a connection with Mor House. Oddly, she wished she was back there, and the image of Keela returned. The mysterious Keela. What happened to make the girl vanish and then reappear as a statue?

Andrew knew his wife was awake, and nudged her. 'Roberta, darling, it's nearly seven. The twins will be awake. It's their birthday, remember?'

On her tummy, she murmured something into the pillow.

'Darling. You're their mum. You can't let Hazel be first to see them on their birthday!'

She rolled over, very carefully. 'No, I suppose not. Sorry, love. Didn't sleep all that well.'

'So I gather.' He leant across and kissed her. 'I did cuddle you.'

'I know. And I'm glad you did. Shall we go together? Be nice for them?'

So the twins had a proper start to their Christmas/birthday day, and an hour and a some later, Hazel and June joined the party in the nursery, now to be re-christened 'play room', where new toys were being tested almost to destruction.

'Enough!' for now June was being buffeted with Abby's new puppet doll, Chris was driving a new and larger dump truck all over his recumbent father while Roberta sat back and watched. This was not a day she'd want to commit to memory, for with the present lack of energy and a dullened mind she hadn't been truly able to appreciate the enjoyment her offspring were evincing.

'Breakfast,' she said decisively, getting up with a resolution. 'But I'm going to shower first. Bring them down in half an hour, Hazel, please. June, go and rouse that brother of yours. We're all going to morning service. Three line whip. No slackers. I want you all there. Show the village we have respect.'

During that Christmas morning service, Roberta regained her spirit and the old sparkle returned. Whether it had been the sublime singing, the magical organ music, the ambiance of the ancient church, the cheerful chatter of the congregation afterwards, or maybe even the rector's words, she wasn't sure, but the soul felt all the better for having her immediate family in the one pew with Hazel, June and Peter behind them. She'd felt a tug of emotion once or twice before she got into the carol singing but after that she was fine.

The Rector had been kind. 'I am deeply grieved to hear of your loss, Mrs Hailsworthy, profoundly saddened. Such a dear soul, and an example to us all. I know how much you'll miss her but so will we all. We must take courage from her great fortitude and her grandchildren will be the gift she's left for us. Lovely children, and blessings on the future, too.' He'd shaken hands, patted Abby and Chris on the head and moved on.

'Right. Home for dinner. Christmas dinner. And we've got all afternoon. I feel ready for my sherry. I'll drive back, Andrew. Come on, you lot.'

Cramming five plus two into the big Volvo on the way down had been a real squash and probably against some law or other. 'Peter,' Roberta said, 'you walk Hazel home, do you good. We won't start without you. Promise.' Brooking no argument, with Andrew alongside and the two children with their step sister in charge in the back, she drove smartly off the verge and away. 'I feel heaps better,' she added, 'but I'd have liked to have had mum with us. Never mind, we'll drink a toast.'

Andrew was amazed, but kept his surprise bottled up. If a church service could have that effect on her, then perhaps there was some divine comfort around. Whatever, it definitely helped the day and she was humming the 'Hark the Herald Angels' tune. Glory certainly.

Peter and Hazel watched the Volvo drive away.

'I'd never have thought. My step-mum's back on form. I was getting quite worried about her. Hope it lasts.' He reached for her hand. 'Best foot forward, Hazel. Else we'll be late for lunch.'

'Dinner,' replied Hazel, darkly. '*Christmas* dinner. I'd not have gone to the bother of organising a bird and all the other bits and bobs just for a *lunch*. You're right about Roberta though. Tearing off like that, and with me all set to carry on the cooking. Hope she remembers the bird still needs another hour.'

'Darling Hazel.'

She glanced around. Most of the church-goers had moved away, the Rector nowhere to be seen. 'You haven't given me a proper Christmas snog yet.'

'No mistletoe here.'

'Don't tease me.'

He grinned at her. 'Why not?'

'I thought you loved me.' Her grey eyes widened as she studied his look. 'You do, don't you?'

He took her other hand, pulled her gently towards him and as she softened into his embrace, lips on lips, the world around blurred and time stood still, lost in suspense.

'They're a long time. Shall I take the car back and find them?' Andrew stood, uncertainly, watching Roberta testing the sizeable turkey, the skewer plunged in and withdrawn to check the juices. 'Unlike Hazel not to hurry home, she so wanted to prove herself with all this.' He waved at the array of pans, the two big steamers, one with its stack of vegetable containers, the other with the Christmas pudding, and then the gravy, and the bread sauce. The big Aga was earning its keep.

'She'll be back. You know Peter's properly fallen for her? That's as much the reason I got them to walk back as to relieve the crush in the car.'

'Fairly obvious, I suppose. So long as she's not hurt. I'd never forgive him if he messes around with her emotions, R. She's far too precious and a mite inexperienced. It's not as if she's had a string of boyfriends, is it? He's the first.'

Roberta slowly straightened up and ran her hands down from her waist. 'You'd better put this back, Andrew. I wouldn't want to drop it.' She wiped the skewer and laid it down. 'No he's not.'

His brow creased in a frown. 'Not the first? There's not been anyone else I know of.' He carefully lifted the dish and as she opened the Aga's big oven door, slid it back into the heat.

She grinned at him. 'Silly boy. She had a huge crush on you, Peter's the next best thing. Better, actually, 'cos he's the right age and not as soft as you are.' Then she inhaled, and took the plunge. 'She's lost her virginity to him, which for a girl with her background means a hell of a lot.'

'What! Peter's . . . ' Could he really be as scandalised as he sounded?

She nodded. 'Haven't you seen her eyes? Darling, for a romancer like you, don't say you didn't notice?'

He sat down and wiped his forehead, feeling faint perspiration. 'Women!'

'Maybe I'm to blame. If there is any blame.'

'What do you mean?' The odd rush of concern ebbed. She didn't seem too bothered.

'After Ireland? Remember how she had the hots for you and I took her up the hill to sort her out?'

Up the hill. As he had also taken her up a hill. He nodded, acknowledging that, yes, he had had deep feelings for her, correctly translated into an ongoing fatherly concern.

'Well, I explained,' and she wasn't going to add, *demonstrated,* 'what made us females tick, but she'd already discovered a lot herself . . . ' and broke off. Footsteps on the gravel. 'Just look at her expression, Andrew. But don't let on. Please, darling. It's so right for them. A lovely Christmas present. You gave me two, remember, and - I love you.' Her voice broke and he saw moistened eyes.

She hid her concern well, letting Hazel take over, merely offering little hints here and there, until everything was ready to go. Andrew wanted to do his bit, and Peter hovered. Of June there was no sign, for she wasn't anything like as domesticated, instead occupying the most useful role of twin's butt for play upstairs.

'Go and get some aperitifs organised, you two. I haven't had my sherry yet. Go on, shoo. Another quarter of an hour. Have you got the wine sorted, Andrew?'

They foregathered in the sitting room. Abby and Chris were given little plastic tumblers of orange juice to hold and magically entered into the spirit of the occasion.

'Here's to us,' Roberta lifted her glass. 'And absent friends. Dearest Mary.' Dry eyed, she continued. 'To the best mum a girl ever had.' She sipped.

Glasses clinked, even two little people had their tumblers carefully nudged.

June looked at Peter. *Go on,* she seemed to be saying, *say the right thing.*

'To my step-mum, and my father. To our step-twins,' he added, looking down at them before returning his gaze to his sister. 'And the very best wishes for the next one.'

Roberta beamed at him, caught Hazel's eye and winked. She blushed. Roberta gave an almost imperceptible nod, an encouragement.

'I - ', and Hazel hesitated. All eyes were on her, she had to say something. 'I just - ', gulped, took a deep heaving breath, 'I owe you all. So much. And I'll miss Mary. I really will.'

Peter took two strides. His arm went round her and hugged. 'We all will, Hazel, but she's here. In spirit.' He looked across at his father. 'Without her, without you and Roberta, dad, this wouldn't have happened. Hazel, I mean. Best girl out. Thanks,' he ended simply, and kissed her.

'Hurrah,' said Roberta, grinning, and they all clapped.

'Now let's go eat. Well done, son. Good choice. Treat her well,' and Andrew drained his glass. 'Happy Christmas, everybody.'

They made a proper mess of the turkey, laughed and giggled and drank their way through the demolition of all Hazel's handiwork before stuffing themselves to completion on brandy-flamed Christmas pud and orange custard. The candles flickered over the damask tablecloth, reflected on crystal glasses and caught the shimmer on the edges of the cream Minton plates, the glow of happy faces.

'We've missed the Speech,' said Andrew, laying down his spoon.

'So we have. Nearly tea-time. Anyone want seconds, or is it thirds?' Roberta looked around the table. 'Did you put the mince-pies in the cool oven, Hazel?'

'Of course!' The girl, in her much loved lemon yellow dress, a newly gifted silver and marcasite pendant poised provocatively at the start of the valley between breasts, sparkled, ambition achieved. Proved herself, been loved, declared and fêted.

June pushed her chair back. 'I'll fetch them.'

'No, no, June, in the sitting room, after we've cleared this lot. With a cup of tea. I couldn't eat another bite, my waistband's tight enough as it is.'

Andrew caught Peter's eye. 'Peter and I'll clear. The ladies deserve a rest. You may withdraw, girls.'

'Fair enough. Don't be too long. Abby!' The little girl's eyes were closing and she swayed. It had been a long day. Even Chris had gone quiet.

'I'll take them upstairs, Roberta,' Hazel stood up and lifted an unresisting Abby off her cushioned chair.

'Watch that dress! I'll bring Chris.' Roberta began to rise off her chair. 'Ouch!', and sat down again. 'Oh. I've eaten too much.' She tried again, sideways, slowly, and managed it. 'June, perhaps . . .'

'Of course.' June encouraged Chris to slide off his chair, took him by the hand and led him to the door. 'You go and put your feet up. We'll manage.'

The debris responded to efficient masculine clearance. Plates stacked to slide into the dishwasher, silver cutlery into the bowl, glasses carefully placed on a tray for hand-washing. The worst problem would be the serving dishes and the pans. Oddly, Andrew didn't mind this task, restoring sanity to chaos. Peter rolled up shirt sleeves and donned an apron.

Andrew laughed. 'Three years ago I'd never have dreamt my son would be this capable. Reckon we must have done something right, your mum and I.'

Peter ran the hot tap and squirted a modicum of detergent into the bowl. 'You miss her?'

His father scratched an ear. 'Sometimes. And no, I don't want to back-track, not now.'

'She misses you, dad, in a strange sort of way, at least, I think she does.'

'But she married Donald.'

'That's just it, dad. She didn't. They just said they did, for convention's sake. But she let on, once, maybe in a weak moment. She's still a Hailsworthy.'

Andrew said nothing. Touched, a pang of sudden emotion replaced with surprised disbelief, he started putting plates carefully into the dishwasher's rack.

'Why did you separate, dad?'

'She left me to go on this Charity thing, Peter. You know that.'

'Because she was bored?'

'Something like that.'

'Perhaps you should have gone with her.'

He closed the washer's door and pushed the button. Water started to flow and it broke into the silence.

'Perhaps I should,' he replied, wearily. 'But I'd met Roberta by then. She seemed to need me more than your mother did. I don't regret what's happened, Peter. It's given you Hazel. Roberta thinks you've slept with her. Hope you know what you're doing.'

Peter picked up a handful of knives and forks and slid them into the water. How on earth? It was only the once, and she'd been awfully careful not to give him away, or so he'd thought, so how? Did it matter that they knew?

'She's got a glow on her not seen before, son. She can't disguise that look to another female. In her eyes. A sort of satisfaction, a been there . . .'

'Oh.'

'That all, just 'oh'?'

He wiped his hands down the apron and turned towards his father. 'Mutual, dad, I wouldn't have . . . '

'I know you wouldn't. But girls have a way on them. I know, only too well. It's a dangerous pastime, playing with feminine feelings. Can lead to all sorts of trouble.' *Like Andrea's unstoppable and all-too blatant desires.* 'If you are serious about the girl, then fine. If you're not, or find another pair of eyes flashing at you, then I'll have a few words to say, because I love that girl as much as anyone does, for what she is, and I don't mean physically either. If I'd wanted her, she might have gone along with it, at that time. I didn't, couldn't, wouldn't.'

His son stared at him. 'You'd have slept with her? Despite Roberta?'

'Euphemism, that 'sleeping with someone'.' He used another basic seven lettered word. '. . . . . . an expression of indulging in physical or sexual relief. Not necessarily to be confused with much deeper feelings of attraction between two people who only want to be together and share lives, emotions, challenges. Could you accept Hazel's endless company without needing to take her to bed all the time? Eh?'

Peter ignored the question for the moment. His dad, at his age, may have considered having sex with Hazel? The thought appalled, disgusted him. In his tours abroad with mum, there'd been all sorts of opportunities to experiment, to satisfy masculine urges, but he hadn't, for a number of reasons. His mum's proximity, the chances of catching something nasty, the cheap way a lot of it had been offered, but more so because there'd been no girl who'd even remotely attracted him, in personality or sheer inner sparkle. Hazel had, at very first glance. And had responded, so much so he knew she was the one. Even though she was who she was. He blinked, and considered his reply. Could he keep her out of his bed and still maintain feelings for her?

'Sorry if I've shocked you,' his father said. 'You don't have to answer the question. Just remember who you are, Peter. Come on, we'd best get this lot finished otherwise they'll wonder what we're doing.' He picked up the tea towel and began to polish the newly washed cutlery.

Ten minutes later, Hazel pushed the door open. 'Where are these mince pies then, you two? And the kettle's not boiling. I don't know, *men!*' She advanced into the kitchen, pushed the kettle onto the hottest hob and started to put mugs on a tray. 'Leave the rest, Peter. I'll do the glasses later. Andrew, can you get the small plates down? I don't want crumbs on the carpet. I'll bring the tray through once I've made the tea.'

She was taking over. Mary's true disciple. And lovely.

He looked at his son and winked. 'Peter, she's in charge. Do as she says,' and there was a depth of meaning there. 'Come on, let's rejoin the ladies.'

In the corridor, out of her hearing, Peter said quietly, 'Sorry, dad. I didn't know. You don't mind?'

Before the sitting room door Andrew paused. 'I'm proud of you both. Just don't spoil things. Moderation and all that. And just so you know, I would never have hurt or demeaned her, not one iota.'

'Okay. Thanks,' and let his father precede him into the comfortable room, the lit fire giving its own flickering brilliance to the cosiness.

They played a few silly games, ate too many mince pies, and let time flow. Roberta's eyes began to close. June jerked, an involuntary muscular reaction. Peter had his legs stretched straight out, also beginning to doze. Andrew allowed his head to flop back onto the cushions. A set piece of decadent hedonism. Only Hazel seemed to have any vestige of energy left. She eased out of her chair, very quietly, and headed out towards the downstairs toilet. Needs must.

After her essential visit, she stood silent in the hallway, alone but for the twinkle of the tree's lights and the essence of all that the Manor was, her home. Where would she go from here? This was a perfect place to be, and a benchmark for all she'd ever want. Peaceful and secure. The clock's tick intruded into the otherwise quiet house. She tip-toed across, smoothed her dress beneath her and sat on the second step of the stairs, relaxing. A minute, five, ten, and the Christmas tree's lights flickered, as though the branches had been caught by a playful breeze. She looked up at the fairy, its silver dress sparkled and with imagination, she could pretend it - she - would float across the ceiling, like something from Peter Pan. The witching hour.

A tiny little voice in her mind. *Be loved.* She listened, her senses hyperactive and intense. *Return that love.* Where was this coming from? *Be your own person.* She was her own girl, wasn't she? *Give of your best.* She always did. Had she done right, giving way to the opportunity the other night? *Don't demean yourself.* Had she? Given away her soul? She widened her legs, let the skirt fall in and rested her hands and arms between, lowering her head, letting all her muscles relax. *Be loved.*

The passageway door was opening and she started, broke out of her reverie and sat bolt upright. Who? Peter!

'Hazel? What *are* you doing?' He advanced across the hallway, to lower himself down and sit beside her. 'I missed you. You've been gone a while.'

'Have I? Sorry. Thinking. It's so lovely and peaceful.'

They sat still, together, not touching.

'Did we do right?' she suddenly asked, not looking at him.

He turned his head, sensed her mood, her seriousness. 'It was us,' he replied, simply. 'I love you, Hazel. I want you to be part of my life. If you'll let me be part of yours.'

Now she could look at him, and even in the weird dim and coloured light from the tree, his eyes didn't waver, looked through and into her soul. She stared at him. 'Love me?'

'Love you. All you are, will be. Body and soul. Especially soul.'

A sigh from her, a full expellation, and the way she then had to breath in caused her chest to push breasts out, straining at her top. He longed for her; to caress and kiss and stroke, tease, but knew he should not.

She reached for a hand. 'We'd best go back, my love. Someone will wonder.'

He stood, pulling her up after him, and held her. 'Especially my dad. Did you . . .' and hesitated. How could he ask, to clear his mind? He started again. 'Did you have a girly pash for him?'

A chuckle, and she remembered that night in Ireland when she'd popped blouse buttons and shown her knickers. It started a blush. 'Don't ask,' she said.

'You *did?*' Now he could smile. 'I bet he'd have tanned your backside for you.'

'I've grown up a bit since then,' and tried to release her thoughts into words. 'I think if I'd tried hard enough he'd have . . .' but couldn't go on. Far too silly.

'We talked earlier, over the washing-up. He told me. And they know we've slept together, well, not slept but you know what I mean.'

Alarmed, she pushed at him. 'How? I mean, you never said?'

'Your face, my lovely girl, apparently. Roberta noticed the sparkle, so dad said, and guessed.'

'Oh lor.' She couldn't think past this one and stared

unseeingly past him at the tree, still seeming to move gently as the lights flickered.

He kissed her, lightly, once, twice. 'Don't blush, Hazel. It'll work out. Let's go back.'

FIFTEEN

Robertsons came back to him two days after the rather emotionally draining Christmas Day; yes, they could manage everything provided the local Rector was agreeable, and they expected a confirmatory call at any time.

'I assume it will only be immediate family mourners?' came the question, 'and a simple ceremony at the graveside?'

'Yes,' said Andrew, taking responsibility. He couldn't think of anyone outside the Manor's circle, and intuitively knew Roberta desired no fuss, no elaborate ritual, merely a simple goodbye in a peaceful setting. The New Year's Eve occasion he'd asked Andrea to organise would allow for any slack.

'Very good. Will anyone wish to visit the Chapel of Rest? We have her here.'

He didn't think so. He, for one, wished only to remember her as she'd been, and one particular occasion came to mind, the day when he and Roberta had celebrated their togetherness with Chablis in the Manor's rose garden. Or another, earlier occasion, that very first day after he'd brought Roberta home from her tumble off the big horse. Or there was the day when she'd introduced the younger Hazel as the kitchen help. And when they'd come back from the first trip into London, or the return from Ireland. So many other times. Mary. Now Roberta only had him.

'Thank you. We'll come back to you if necessary,' he replied and put the phone down.

Time appeared to have frozen. Roberta, despite her Christmas day's boost in spirits, had now sunk into a sombre lethargy, spending most of her day in the sitting room with her feet up, reading. Of the remaining Manor denizens, the elders amused themselves playing with the juniors, with board games and with occasional walks. No clients were scheduled and the phone remained stubbornly silent. Even the internet offered little to keep Andrew happy. They all had the one item on their mental agenda, a journey to Yorkshire.

They could do the journey in a day, given an early start, but there was one problem, or rather, two. The twins.

'I can't, Andrew, I just can't take them all the way up there, just for a day. And it wouldn't be right. They don't understand. What am I going to do?' Roberta wailed. 'Why didn't mum think of that when she said where she wanted to go?'

Irrational view on his wife's part, thought Andrew, having an idea. 'June doesn't have to go, not if she doesn't want to. Nor Peter, come to that. Shall I ask?'

'But . . .'

'No buts. I'll ask.'

And he did, tactfully. 'June, have you heard from William?'

'No, dad, I haven't, but then, I don't expect to. He said he'd only get in touch when he was coming back, something about he got on better if he could concentrate.' She shrugged. 'Doesn't faze me. Somehow, I don't think he'll come back. I'm better as a single girl,' and gave him a half smile, 'don't you think?'

'But you get on marvellously with Abby and Chris.' the inherent suggestion that having her own family would suit her well. If only.

'Ah, yes, but I can give 'em back . . .'

He laughed. 'Like pass the parcel. I can't imagine what it would be like if Roberta and I hadn't got you lot around to help out, not withstanding Hazel's input.'

'I love them, dad, they're great kids.'

'Then have them to yourself for a day. You don't have to come north. Peter doesn't have to come either, that is, provided . . .'

She shot him a grateful smile. 'Dad, it's a good idea. I'd wondered how Roberta would manage, but it wasn't my place to ask. Hazel will want to go.'

'Yes, she will. So you'll stay?'

Peter did agree, understandably, to stay as well, so it was just the three of them in the Volvo, Andrew, Roberta and Hazel, setting off into the depths of a dark and fortunately dry early morning.

'Look after them, June. We'll 'phone you when we're there. Be good, you two. Mummy will be back tonight.' She gave them each a hug and a kiss, eased gingerly into the front passenger seat, and waved as the big car edged away.

'Hope she's going to be all right.' Peter watched the tail-lights disappear but June had already turned away with a chubby hand in each of hers. He took one last look and followed. Though Hazel had asked him to change his mind and go with her, funerals weren't his scene, he'd said, and anyway, he didn't think it right to leave his sister on her own. *'Why I know you're the right guy for me,'* she'd replied with a dimpled smile, *'thinking of others,'* and accepted his kiss instead.

'Breakfast?' asked June, watching the twins getting their plastic mugs and bowls from their cupboard. Really, they were coming on in leaps and bounds.

'I fancy bacon and tomatoes. How about you?'

'Fine. You can cook while I dole out cereal to these two.'

It was for all the world as though they were a happy married couple with two adorable children and June heaved a big sigh. What she could have had, and yet she'd told her dad she'd be better off single. Without thinking too deeply she asked an

142

evidently leading question, and got a rather serious reply.

'Marry her? Bit definite, June. I've only known her, what two months, and we're only in our early twenties.' He twisted round to face her and leant back on the Aga's rail. 'Why ask?'

She lifted her shoulders in a Junesque shrug. ''Cos you two seem well suited and there's a light in her eyes. You have, haven't you?' and it wasn't an accusation, for she couldn't blame him. Hazel was that sort of a girl, one who needed loving.

He turned away, not wishing to give the straight answer June obviously sought, thought a moment and then gave in. He owed it to his girl, not to deny her. 'It just happened, June, and I - we - don't regret the evening. Not one iota. And I didn't push her either. Mutual. Do you blame me?'

The twins were now engaged in their morning ritual of spoon banging. She collared both spoons and waited for a reaction. Abby's eyes puckered up, Chris looked mutinous. Time she took them back upstairs for a clean-up.

'Not really. But you've rather nailed your colours, Peter. She'd be distraught if it goes sour on you. And dad would never forgive you, 'cos he dotes on her.'

'He's made that very plain. But, no, the way I feel about her, it ain't likely. Just not sure what to do next.'

'You've discussed her with dad?' Her voice rose, disbelievingly. 'Gosh. You *are* serious,' saw Abby almost in tears from Chris's arm pinching and changed tack. 'I have to look after these two. You do the clear away,' then aligned herself in his favour. 'I'm pleased for you both, Peter, but make sure you look after her. I wouldn't want you to do a William.'

'Never! That bloke's a proper p . . .' but didn't finish the word, for after all, he was still June's husband.

She laughed. 'You're right there,' took hold of two messy hands and ushered them towards the door. 'See you in a bit.'

143

As the car sped quietly and effortlessly northbound up the A1, both Roberta and Hazel dozed. It would be another long hour before dawn and Andrew hoped to get the bulk of the main roads behind them before the line of light would creep over and delineate the horizon. Traffic, with what few cars they'd passed, was inconsequential, unsurprising given it was that odd week between Christmas and the New Year when the world seemed to stand still. He pondered on how the funeral directors organised the logistics so well especially at this time of year, but Robertsons appeared to take the arrangement as a matter of course. Just such a shame they'd lost her at this cross roads in their lives.

Roberta stirred and rubbed her eyes. 'How're we doing, love?'

'Grantham's coming up. Quite well. Are you okay or do you want a breather?'

'When you can stop, dear, so long as it's not too long.'

'Okay.' He took a glance in his mirror. 'Hazel?' No reply. Good, she'll be better for a proper sleep.

Three miles further on and the Grantham Services. Not quite like an Irish forecourt, but it would have to do.

Half an hour later, and for Andrew a bacon sandwich and a quick rinse of face in a hand basin to restore some value to life, on they went. Hazel, alert now to the scenery, sat straight. Roberta continually wriggled, feeling the strain of sitting in the same position. Another thirty miles and some forty minutes later, a change of pace. 'I'll shortcut this bit,' he explained to the girls, having pre-programmed the satnav. 'Then fifteen miles of motorway before we switch to the A614. Should be there well in time.'

'Did you check with that hotel place, near Pocklington, wasn't it?'

'R, of course I did. They've been very good. Said we could have a room from ten o'clock. We'll have a meal after, before we head south again.'

'I'm sorry I don't feel up to driving, love. Maybe on the way back.'

'Whatever.'

'I should really learn to drive, shouldn't I?' came a tentatively voiced comment from the back.

'Hazel, my dear girl, I'm surprised you haven't badgered us before now. Or perhaps I should say I'm sorry I haven't suggested it. Maybe we'll get Peter to teach you?'

A unexpectedly vehement 'No!' surprised him. 'I'd far rather you did, Andrew. Or with a school. Peter might get cross with me, and I wouldn't want that.'

'Wise girl,' said Roberta with a quirky grin.

Andrew laughed. 'I might get even crosser with you.'

'Yes, but I wouldn't mind *you* telling me off.'

He wasn't too sure about the overtones in that reply and lapsed into silence to concentrate on getting through Finningley.

The weather could have been completely against them. He hated to think what would have happened had a low pressure system blown in: the winter, so far, hadn't been at all bad, though a gale or snow showers might well have scuppered the arrangements. As it was, the few early morning clouds had blown away and the weak sun gave dappling shadows from the skeletonised trees as the twisting roads took them towards the Wolds.

'It's very pretty round here,' Hazel offered, gazing through the car's windows. 'Feels clean and tidy. Lot more open than our county, though secretive as well. If that's not a contradiction.'

Roberta smiled round at her. 'I know what you mean. You won't have been here before.'

'Not been anywhere much,' she replied. 'Until you took me to Ireland. That was great.'

Andrew smiled too, taking the left fork towards the

church. They'd had a wonderful welcome from the Hall staff. An inspiration, finding that place - and the way in which the reasons for their visit had been understood; being offered the use of a simply but well furnished bedroom in which to change, given coffee and superb little almond cakes, absolutely right. Yes, of course they'd be very welcome to return for a late afternoon meal, but please understand we're purely vegetarian? That hadn't been a problem, for as Roberta had said, we won't feel like eating much anyway. The very tranquil ambiance had helped sooth down her rising tide of anxiety and concern; the words spoken could have come from a fatalistic viewpoint, but now she understood them as a much wider appreciation of the significance of life - and its end. On returning to the car, she'd reached for his hand, held him back for a brief moment, offered him a kiss, said '*I love you*,' and the very simplicity of her action understandably profound.

And there it was, the little church, nestling amongst the trees, the small group of figures by the door, the hearse parked close by.

'Oh!' The realisation of the inevitability of their journey, the finality.

Left now by themselves, the only sounds the drift of breeze through bare branches, the snatches of bird calls and far distant traffic; holding hands, the tranquillity of Mary's final resting place seeped into the soul. Though born close by in the Midlands, she'd lived her formative early teen years within the nearby estate's working environment, where she'd been taken into service at an early age. Now she'd returned to her long-gone host family's patch. It must have meant something to her, perhaps her decision to be buried here she'd seen as acknowledging her roots.

Nothing spoken, nothing to say, each lost in meaningful thoughts.

Roberta sighed, stooped and laid the bunch of bronze chrysanthemums down.

'I know,' and Andrew *did* unerringly know how much she'd been part of their lives and held them together.

'She'll always be with us.' Hazel had held up well.

Another sigh. 'Yes,' and with that, she turned away.

The Retreat's meal had been excellent, a blessing given on the meaning of their journey but it was time to return. Three hours on the road.

'I wish we could have stayed, Andrew.'

He nodded. 'It would have been good.'

'Perhaps we'll stay here when we come back?'

Another nod. 'Which we will. And bring the children.'

'Of course.' She picked up her bag. 'Let's go.'

At ten o'clock, June thought she'd heard the car, but Peter beat her to it, taking big strides towards the back door. He clicked the outside light switch down just as headlights swept round the corner and there was the big Volvo, pulling round towards the garage. June joined him, arm around her brother's waist.

'Thank goodness,' and Peter heard the same relief in her voice as he felt. It would have been an awfully long and traumatic day for them, Hazel included.

The car's doors opened simultaneously, Roberta easing her legs round and holding onto her door as she cautiously stood up, Hazel far more athletic and shutting her door behind her with a thump.

'Hey, you'll wake the twins!'

'Sorry!' She skipped across and June let her arm slip away as the other girl claimed precedence.

Andrew, more circumspectly, closed his door with a mere clunk and gave his support to a weary Roberta. She leant on him.

'I'm glad to be home. Thanks for being such a steady driver, love. Put the car away tomorrow, come on in, I want my bed.'

'Good journey then, dad?'

'Not bad, Peter.' He aimed the key at the car and heard the locks go. 'Far enough though. My love of long distance motoring has evaporated somewhat. I agree with Roberta, bed sounds wonderful. How was your day?'

'Quiet-ish. Abby and Chris kept us amused.'

'I can imagine.'

The girls had gone into the kitchen, so Peter could ask. 'How's Roberta?'

'Survived. That place I booked not far from the church was ideal. Sort of a mediation centre, nice calm atmosphere. And the church is in a lovely setting. The parish priest handled matters well. So all in all, worked okay.'

'I'm glad. Chapter closed?'

'Chapter closed. And tomorrow's another day.'

Despite Roberta's statement that she wanted her bed, there seemed to be some reluctance to move from the cosiness of hot-chocolate mugs around the kitchen table. They sat in companionable silence, sipping and munching on ginger biscuits from the old stone crock. The Aga burbled away, the shutters creaked in the downdraft from a rising wind, and the wall clock with its station-platform hands ticked the seconds away.

Eventually, Roberta looked up from a reflective study of her mug's emptiness.

'Right. That's it. Bed beckons.'

'You said that earlier, R.'

'So I did.' She eased up. 'June, will you give me a hand

tomorrow? I need to start clearing the cottage. And the room.'

Not 'Mary's' room, June noticed. 'Of course, Roberta.'

Andrew clearly was puzzled. 'You don't want me to help?'

She shook her head. 'Best on my own with June, I think. Then I can concentrate. You have a word with Andrea and confirm the party. Peter, you take Hazel out for the day. We'll have a decent meal at seven.' Back to her organising best.

'But who's going to cook?' Hazel was both delighted and puzzled.

'We'll all go out.' and caught her husband's eye. 'Something else you can do tomorrow first thing, dear, organise a restaurant and a baby sitter. I'm sure Andrea will point you in the right direction. Invite her too. Right,' she repeated. 'Bed. Coming, mate?'

SIXTEEN

She was playing hard to get. 'Out,' said her mother, 'I'm not sure where. Not at work, of that I'm certain. Can I ask her to ring you?'

'Please,' he replied, having tried her mobile and puzzled that it was on voice mail. Unlike her.

He moved on, looked at the dine out options. Not the Royal George, too close to home. Not the Italian either. So maybe the Michelin recommended inn? He phoned. Would they have a table for six? - always assuming he'd manage to contact Andrea.

'Yes, sir, certainly, what time?' A pleasant female voice.

'Sevenish.'

'Thank you for your reservation. We look forward to your visit.'

Baby sitter next. A problem to resolve, before he had a brainwave and phoned Barry.

'The hall looks great with the tree, Barry. Thanks for that. Now, your elder daughter, is she good at baby sitting? - tonight, short notice, I'm afraid. My dear wife's had a brainstorm . . . oh, that's good news. Can you run her up, half sixish? Thanks, great stuff.'

So far, so good. He went to pass the news back to Roberta, and, he admitted, to satisfy his curiosity. The two girls were emptying a cupboard onto the stripped single bed.

Roberta looked up as he pushed the door further open. 'All right?' she asked.

'Table's booked, Barry's daughter Elaine will baby-sit for a tenner. He'll run her up at half six. Can't find Andrea though. You okay with all this?'

An affirmative little head shake. 'So far. Needs to be done. Can't leave it. June'll deal with the wardrobe. Maybe we'll go down to the cottage after lunch. You don't need the car?'

'Nope. It's still out from yesterday. You'd best refuel when you're out, too.' Sensing he wasn't wanted, he withdrew back to the office and went through e-mails. Surprising what came in during holiday periods, as though folk needed something to do to fill their time. Queries, some promotional stuff, some rubbish. And another one from Sam. As he read it, his spine tingled; so Peter's intuition was maybe right.

Rather than beg the use of the car, and given the weather wasn't at all bad for December's dying days, Peter had coerced Hazel into a cycle ride. Mary's old bike wasn't the smartest pair of wheels, but manageable. They made some sandwiches, filled a flask, stuffed some waterproofs into the panniers on his new bike - he'd had to lash out on something decent to get him back and forth to the station.

'Maybe we'll have to get you a better bike?' he grinned at her, 'and put you into jeans. I don't mind the sixties bopper look, Hazel, but it's not very practical, now is it?'

She stuck her tongue out. 'I'm who I am,' then relented, after all, he was only thinking for her. 'We'll see. We won't go too mad, Peter, will we? My cycling skills are about as rusty as this bike. I'm not going up any steep hills either.'

A chuckle. 'No. We'll go down to the Forest Park place. I think there's a visitor centre or something so we might be able to leave the bikes and walk. If you want to?'

She mounted, wriggled, and rested toes on the ground. 'Provided we - I - get there in one piece,' and pushed off, wobbling a trifle unsteadily across the gravel.

Andrea was sitting in her little car in the old dead-ended road that doubled as a lay-by, the place where she and Andrew had sat and talked on the day she'd made up her mind to accept Alain's job offer. At least, that's when she thought she'd decided. It seemed so right at the time, but now, well, she wasn't as sure. In the back of her mind then, she'd had the idea Alain only wanted to make her his p.a. so he'd have more time with her, which might lead to something else. She wouldn't have minded, for he was a decent bloke, fun to be with and maybe there was a spark between them. Or was there?

Her mobile sat on the seat alongside her, switched to voice mail. She was tempted. Phone him, find out what he was really doing. Ask him if he'd like some company. Or was that being pushy, stupid, too bloody obvious? That's what she always seemed to be doing, throwing herself at a male. Andrew, he'd started it. Going back to the story of the horse, why hadn't she ridden, fallen off in front of him, rather than Roberta? Then, hypothetically, he'd be married to her instead, and as it ruefully came clear, she'd likely have become pregnant, had an infant - or two - and they'd be living in Andrew's old house. Not the Manor life style she'd dreamt about but try as she may to dismiss the picture, it kept coming back, that night she'd spent in his arms at the old house.

He'd asked her to call, in order to tell her about Mary. And the consequential old surge of attraction had unsettled her, brought those stupid ideas back into play just when she'd thought she'd got over him. She balled her fists and beat the steering wheel, *oh oh oh!* What was she going to do about the Manor's party? Not that she'd have a problem with the planning, but to try and stay the right side of her runaway feelings? If she weren't so cross with herself, she'd start crying.

The phone bleeped, suddenly, making her start. She picked it up. A message. And from Andrew; her heart jumped and nerves kicked in. So what next, a denial, an acceptance, or what? *Call me, urgent.* Nervously, she pressed 'dial'.

'An! Thank heavens. Where on earth are you? - your mother didn't know? I'd wanted to ask about restaurants, but as I couldn't raise you, made my own decision. Roberta's had a blip, wants to take us all out for dinner tonight, lovely idea, but left me to arrange. Said to ask you to come too. I think she wants some relief from yesterday's pressure. We went up to Yorkshire to bury Mary.'

He's called me An. 'Is it a good idea for me to come, Andrew?'

'Why ever not? You're not infectious, are you? Course you should come, if you're free?'

Oh, I'm free all right. 'Have you booked?'

'Yes - table of six, one of my mate's daughter is baby sitting. The Plough, that okay?'

She knew of it, good reputation, not actually been herself. 'Should be fine,' and made her decision. 'Thank you. I'd be pleased to accept. Should I come to you or go direct?' It was only three miles further on from the Manor.

'Go direct, An, 'cos the Volvo's really only a five seater. See you at half seven?'

'I'll look forward to it. And thank Roberta for me.' She flipped the phone shut. Dinner, with Andrew and Roberta. And, from his comment, June, Hazel and Peter. Her introspective mood duly shattered, she started the car, reversed around and slowly drove down the lane to rejoin the road. Decision on Alain postponed.

She was enjoying this. The combination of exercise, a reasonable day and Peter's close proximity, peddling alongside or behind as traffic and road dictated. Mind you, it was also something of an adventure, for, as she discovered very quickly, skirts had to be severely controlled. She also knew that by rights she should be wearing a helmet, though

153

she had no intention of falling off. The old skills from go-to-school days soon came back; brave, she let go on one side and swept a hand over her hair.

'Hoi! Careful, Miss!' Peter, with infinite control, edged close. 'Just because you look like a schoolgirl there's no need to behave like one. How's your bum?'

She laughed. 'Not sore yet. Too broad a saddle. How much further?'

'Two miles? Ten minutes, perhaps time for a coffee. Enjoying?'

'You bet. Roberta's good idea.' She exerted a little more pressure and surged ahead. 'Last one to the gate buys!'

'Enough. Let's have some lunch. Bring those sacks will you, June?' Roberta looked around. Her mum hadn't had much of her stuff in here, just enough to get her by for a few days; most of her things would be in the end of terrace cottage in the village. True, she'd spent more time here than there of late, for cycling up and down had obviously become a problem, oftentimes either one or the other fetched and carried when she felt she'd had to go back.

She heaved a repetitive sigh. Seemed an age now.

'You don't feel too tired, do you?' June had kept a wary eye on her, wondering how she'd be both on the emotional as well as the physical front. No way did she want Roberta to have another collapse because her pelvic joints were playing up.

'Can't do much more. Thought we'd get to the cottage today but now I'm not sure. Are those children of mine behaving?' They'd been left to play on their own for the last hour.

'I'll pop up and see.'

Two minutes and she was back. 'Andrew's up there. Soup and sandwich time?'

'Yep. Hope the cyclists are okay.'

'Sure they are. Apart from Hazel having to ride an antique.'

Roberta laughed. 'Perhaps Peter'll encourage her to get a new one if today's a success,' then she turned sober. 'Do you think they'll be all right?'

And it wasn't just today's outing Roberta meant, June knew. 'Roberta, Peter'll never have played fast and loose with any girl. I know him - or I think I do - and this affection for Hazel is as genuine as it could be, I'm sure. I know she cares. And . . .'

Roberta laid a hand on June's wrist. 'Don't say it. I know they've rather overstepped the mark, but it's my fault. So long as they behave.' She pulled a face. 'Your father wouldn't be at all pleased if it went pear shaped. Neither would I. Let's just keep a weather eye?'

June grinned. 'I'm not necessarily the best judge, Roberta.'

'Neither am I. Us girls. We all have to learn our lesson. I pray Hazel doesn't find out the hard way. Come along, bring the bags. I'm quite peckish now.'

Sitting at the panoramic windows of the Forest Centre overlooking a rippled lake and the waving reeds on the far bank, they each had a large mug of splendid coffee. Very pastoral and very peaceful, other than the few children chasing around. Other visitors were sat around the place, including couples, a number of very outdoorsy types, some parents obviously trying to do the right thing between Christmas and the New Year and a trio of earnest student types; all taking advantage of what was on offer.

Peter laid a hand over Hazel's, across the table. 'Penny for them.' She'd gone dreamy eyed, staring into the distance.

'Eh? What? Sorry.' She shook her head and her hair rippled and fell over her eyes. Impatiently she brushed it back. She should have brought a scarf. 'It's going to be hard for Roberta, losing her mum. They were great pals. Not sure how we'll manage when she gets so she can't do as much. They - sorry, Peter, your father and step-mum - talked about getting another girl.'

'And?'

She shrugged. 'Up to them. Don't know that I want someone else messing things up.'

'But you can't do everything, Hazel. And June will go back to Ireland soon, I know she will. Pity Andrea left.'

'I think she'll want to come back.'

'Mad if she does. The Manor office isn't exactly the epitome of a successful business position. Sorry, my love, but it isn't.'

'No, I suppose not. I like it though. Suits me. Do you, Peter?'

'What, like the office?'

'No, silly. Love me?'

Her grey eyes across the table had a mysterious yearning look to them. He reached for her other hand. 'I've not met anyone like you, Hazel, ever. I - we've - come a fair way. Yes, I love you.'

'Let's go for a walk.' She pulled her hands away and stood up. 'Come on.'

So Sam was as good as her word. She wanted to visit. How weird was that? But at the same time, mixed feelings of egotism, expectation, dismay and concern. A real fruit salad conglomeration of thoughts. The decision was Roberta's, not his. If she didn't want Sam anywhere near the place, it would be entirely understandable and he'd have to go along with her. On the other hand, she may see it as a challenge. Andrew absent-mindedly moved a couple of Chris's bricks and got a cross swipe from his son. Abby giggled, reached forward and removed a crucial piece. The whole edifice crumbled and she hooted. Chris looked as though he'd burst into tears.

Andrew scrambled to his feet, held out two hands in invitation. 'Let's go and see what we can eat, you two. I'm hungry. You hungry?'

Abby nodded her head enthusiastically. She was a young lady of few words but her facial expressions were magic. Chris sniffed but reached for a hand. At least it was his daddy and not his aunt. She was too slobbery for anything.

While the twins and their aunt were busy with salami sandwiches in the kitchen and out of hearing, Andrew tackled his wife on the problem.

'Sam? Wants to visit? Lordy. Well, if she must, she must.' She noted his serious yet quizzical expression and laughed. 'I'm not afraid of her, Andrew. Are you?'

'Didn't know what you'd think.'

'Well, my love, it's your decision. She's a perfect right to ask, seeing as her children are here. Maybe she's pining. Maybe Donald's not all he's cracked up to be. So long as she's not having second thoughts, 'cos if she is, she's got another think coming. I ain't about to give you up, my love. So there.'

'And I'm not about to be given up, either. So she can come?'

'Don't know where we'll put her,' then saw the obvious. 'Unless we use mum's old room.'

He took a breath. 'You don't mind?'

A brief hesitation. 'Andrew, my love, there's a lot I'm going to have to absorb, but the worst thing I could do is brood. No, we move on. June and I will have sorted most things by tomorrow. It's the cottage I'm more bothered about.'

'We could let Peter have it.'

She stared at him. 'What a brilliant idea!' She wrapt arms around him and hugged. 'Then he can court Hazel in private. Yes, yes, yes!'

157

'You don't mind?'

'Of course not. I think mum would be pleased. She had a soft spot for him, even in the short while she'd known him. Better than letting it out to someone we don't know, and I wouldn't want to sell it. Ask him, Andrew,' and a gleam came into her eye. 'Hazel will say yes. She wants to be a homemaker, that one. We may lose her.'

'Hmmm. You wouldn't want that, not yet, anyway.'

'Oh, I don't mean permanently. She won't want to desert the children, nor the office. If she takes to sleeping down there, she does. We can't prevent that happening, though we may have to re-visit the idea of another girl, darling. You'd like that.' She poked him. 'Wouldn't you?'

'Hmmm,' he said again. 'Depends,' he added, and grinned.

Elaine, long mousy hair restrained in a swinging ponytail, striped sweatshirt, torn jeans, had an open, freckled, happy expression, and the twins took to her.

'Now you won't forget to give us a call if you're in the slightest bit bothered about anything?' Roberta was fussing, but then, this was the first time she'd left them with anyone other than Hazel.

'Sure,' said Elaine, ruffling Chris's hair. 'Don't worry, Mrs Hailsworthy. I've sat for the Bett's kids and you wouldn't want them let loose around this place.' She looked appreciatively around the upstairs children's room, and realised how lucky these two gorgeous kids were. 'So long as you're back this side of midnight. My dad doesn't like me out after. You'll run me home?'

Andrew nodded. 'Of course. And the best telly is the one in the sitting room. Don't use the computer. Please.'

She shook the ponytail. 'Naw. I've brought me book. Homework. I'll be fine. When do I put the lights out?'

'Just after seven, no later. Don't stand any nonsense.'

'Naw,' she said again and carefully released Chris's grip on her jeans. 'I won't.'

June sat on the edge of her bed and looked at her skimpy collection of dresses. She hadn't had anything new for ages, and the pink thing was really way past its best worn before date. She sighed and nearly opted for the long navy skirt last worn in Ireland and that tugged at her thoughts. Dad, Roberta, this Manor, all now very much lovely parts of her life, but Mor House had her hooked. Either the house or that strange romantic story and the lovely *Cadhla*. Another week or so and she must go back. Must. She stood up, dropped her flimsy work-a-day striped skirt and pulled off her old sweater. It wouldn't do to be the last one ready.

Hazel, feeling decidedly windblown and, to be truthful, rather tired, looked at her reflection in the wall mirror and pulled a face. Red-cheeked, very untidy hair. She didn't really fancy a shower but it was a best dress evening so needs must. And Peter was right; she'd have to invest in jeans or something. He'd been awfully nice to her all day, very gentlemanly, kissed and hugged but nothing more, which suited her mood fine. They'd walked, quite slowly, all the way round the Maulden woods, seen lots of interesting things, met a fair few pleasant people and on the whole, it had been a thoroughly enjoyable day. She changed her mind. She'd strip wash.

Peter lay flat out on his bed, going back over the day. Been good. Hadn't overcooked things, hadn't encouraged her, taken it as it came. Reckoned she'd enjoyed it, he had. That little exchange in the café place, she'd asked if he loved her. Yep, sure. A solid gut feeling she was absolutely right. Staying under the same roof might prove difficult, not that he'd seek to push, but that sudden rush of emotion before their irrevocable mutuality might reoccur when least expected.

He didn't want their relationship to be purely based on sexy sex. Time to get cleaned up. Roberta's evening, and he understood the reason. He felt for her, he really did.

'You think she'll be alright?' Roberta's query inevitable.

'I should think so. Barry's a steady sort of guy; she takes after him. You'd best hurry up, R. Time's pressing.'

Roberta stepped into her slinky pale blue dress and Andrew tried to bring the zip together. There was a moment's pregnant pause. 'That's a shame. It'll have to be the other one,' and she let the discard fall round her ankles, picked it up and slung it onto the bed. 'Hope it'll fit in another six or seven months. Pass me the pale grey - yes, the flirty-skirted one. That won't show the bump.'

Ten minutes later and they'd gathered the troops together at the back door where Andrew had the big Volvo waiting.

'My, we are a smart looking bunch. Hazel, you're lovely, and June, well, beautiful. Come on. Peter, who's the lucky one, sandwiched between those two?' Roberta, now much more practiced at the art of moving in line with weak pelvic muscles, sat into her seat and swung legs slowly on board. 'Right love. Let's go stun 'em.'

The restaurant cum pub was set back from the road, a gem of oldie-worldliness brought back from near dereliction by a trio devoted to good food well prepared. The click of the latch brought pleasant attention from the hostess and seats shown near a flaming log fire with menus readily to hand. Aperitif drinks were ordered. Andrew looked around. No Andrea? He raised the query.

Their welcomer shook her head. 'No, sorry, no-one has mentioned your party. There's still plenty of time, please don't feel under any pressure.'

They concentrated on the splendid choice. Peter took a swift look and made an instant decision. Hazel ummed and aahed. June had her head on one side, saw the Irish stew and thought, why not? Andrew couldn't focus, and Roberta pointed a finger.

'You always fancy that, love?' her finger under the venison dish, ''cos that's what I'm having.'

He laid his menu down. 'Why not? But I wish . . . '

Roberta laid a hand on his knee. 'She said she'd come, so she'll come.'

And come she did, ten minutes later, in her flame red clinging dress that did everything for her figure and nothing for Andrew's peace of mind. The silver pendant necklace sparkled and her eternity ring was there. The long, carefully coiffured blonde hair turned to gold in the candle lit low beamed room and her slender ankles rose on four-inch heels. He kissed her.

'You look charming,' said Roberta, initially gracious, 'I feel sorry for my husband, having to pretend I look better than you do. But then, I'm pregnant and you're not, which says it all.'

Andrea writhed inwardly. Trust this woman to jam a sharp sliver of old jealousy into a weak spot and twist. She kept her smile in place. 'One day, Roberta. And when I am, I hope I carry my infant as well as you do.' There, that should calm the waters. 'Thank you so much for inviting me. I really do appreciate your allowing me to be part of the Manor party again. Alain's not into office parties, not unless he can gain some mileage out of specific invites. He's still abroad, Spain, I think. His time off, so he doesn't have to tell me.' She turned to Peter. 'How's the London job, Peter? And Hazel, I hope the office isn't too boring for you.' To June she offered the most genuine smile, for she truly felt for her, being saddled with a drip of a husband. 'You had a good time in Ireland?'

The conversation spun round. Ireland, London, pregnancies, television programmes, and inevitably, the gap in the Manor's line up. As they were invited to take their table, Andrea managed an adroit nudge-up against Andrew. 'How's she managing?' she whispered.

'I worry, An. I think she's got grief bottled up. Don't rile her, there's a love.' He'd seen the way the two women's minds were working and wasn't impressed.

Roberta eased herself down, took her serviette and fluffed it out. 'I know we're having a sort of party in three day's time, but this was my idea of a more formal occasion.' The others quietened down and looked at her. 'An opportunity to offer my thank-you's to you all. Four years ago it was just me and my Mary. I had a divorce, a slow sort of business, and not much to live for. Oh yes, and I had a horse.' She laughed a slightly high-pitched forced laugh. 'Fortunately for me, he threw me off. Even more fortunately, I was picked up. After that, life was never the same. June, Peter, dear people, I have to say, I'd have never have met you if it wasn't for your father, and that would have been a shame. I think you're both great kids. Hazel, love, I'd never have forgiven you if you hadn't shrugged off that stupid stupidness. Truly, I don't know how I'd have coped without you.' She stopped and looked around, at them, their intent faces in the candles' flickering light. 'Andrea, you and I may fight a few more battles yet, and though I could hate you for what you mean to my beloved husband, I don't. I believe you make him who he is, and I can live with that. In a strange way, I think I love you too; for all that you are, a cuddly sexy girl who really ought to find someone else to go to bed with. Now, let's drink a toast. To my mum Mary, who I always knew was someone special. Rest in peace, mum,' and she raised her glass, 'To Mary!'

Truly an emotive moment. Glasses clinked. 'To Mary' echoed around and as Roberta's glass went down she looked round at him and Andrew saw the tears. What could he do or say? Nothing, except lay his hand on hers and curse the way his thoughts were running.

SEVENTEEN

Andrea stood for some few minutes, gazing at her reflection in the long mirror. It had been, on balance, a lovely evening with so much easy chat over beautifully prepared meals. Oddly, she managed to keep her inner girl under control, even though their knees touched a few times under the table. She should have been sat opposite him, not alongside, but that had been Roberta's choosing. Maybe she'd been testing him. Whatever, when it was time to break up the party and come home she'd had another proper kiss and his hand had been round her bum, fingers spread. Nothing to come between him and her warmth other than the dress. The dress. Now she had to take it off herself, wishing otherwise wouldn't alter the fact. Still single, still without a lover.

Hazel kept Peter on the threshold. '*No*, Peter. It's not that I wouldn't love you to love me, but it won't work. Not here, not now the others know. Thanks for being so nice.' She waited.

He looked at her, and a slow grin appeared. 'You're the nicest thing that's happened to me, Hazel, but you're a hard lady underneath that lovely soft exterior. Tough, you are, girl, but I don't hold it against you. Come on, give us a goodnight kiss, then I'll let you alone.'

June kicked off her heels and collapsed inelegantly into the bedroom chair. Beside that Andrea she felt a frump. Old married woman with no love life. All right for Roberta, and Hazel, come to that, though she felt for Andrea. If ever there was a girl with an '*I want it*' smell to her, it was that one. Poor dad, having to pretend he didn't fancy her. Which was only right and proper, but she knew what she knew. An embarrassment for Roberta, who'd done a very good job of looking after them all tonight. The whole evening had worked rather well. Meals lovely, a decent wine, and an occasion they'd all remember; well done, Roberta.

She ran fingers through her hair. Another week, ten days maximum, and she'd be off again. Tonight, in a lull in the chat, Roberta'd said she'd need three days to get the specifications finished for Mor House, then if she, June, wanted to go back and supervise, then fine. Goody good goody. Back to Ireland. Back to see *Cadhla*. Her cheeks puckered in an incipient grin. Maybe, just maybe, something would happen. She pushed out of the chair, reached for the hem of this old thing and pulled it over her head. About time she treated herself to some decent new dresses.

Roberta lay back on the bed head and watched her husband strip. Without doubt, he was still, what did they say, finely tuned? No excess flab, no potbelly, and still had a decent head of hair. Other bits were in good order too.

He caught her glance and grinned. 'Just checking?'

She smiled back. 'At least we share the same lack of modesty. Did you enjoy the evening?'

'Yes, I did. And I thought you said all the right things, R. Made the girls pleased.' He laid his divested clothing on the chair and added, 'even Andrea.'

'Ah, yes. The Andrea. She's still in the frame, isn't she? I can tell. And *that* dress. I think I've seen it before. Perhaps she believes it's her lucky charm.' She wriggled to get comfortable and watched his mood change. She'd test the waters and have a little fun at his expense. 'Why do I put up with her?'

He frowned. 'You don't have to. We could cross her off the welcome list.'

'You'd hate me if I said yes.' She took a calculated gamble. 'And then you'd only find somewhere secretively cosy and shag her.' Almost immediately she regretted the facile and stupid suggestion as his lips tightened.

'Roberta!' and the way he called her, it sounded like a verbal slap. 'I can't alter the way she behaves, but I am doing my damnedest to block stupid thoughts about her. Really, I am. And I wouldn't. I don't need to, don't want to.'

'Liar! You do. You would, too. If I was in your shoes, I'd also get a hard-on if I knew she wasn't wearing her pants,' and her eyes couldn't avoid the visible reaction. 'Go on, admit it.'

Suddenly he grinned, catching on. 'You women! Are you jealous, R, because of this?' He lifted the duvet cover and slid in alongside her. 'I dare you to ask her.'

'Ask her what?' Roberta knew it wouldn't stop at this and shifted further down.

'If she wants me to . . .,' and not wanting to be as direct as his wife, euphemistically said 'to take her to bed.'

Roberta giggled. 'Oh, how sweet of you. *Take the darling girl to bed!* You've shagged her in the past, so if you want to repeat the exercise, for that's all it would be, an exercise, what's going to stop you? Me, is it me? You wouldn't because of what I'd do, or think? Or because your conscience won't let you? Or because you've finally realised all she wants is to ape our lifestyle, and she envies me our beautiful kids? Come on, darling, she's the jealous one,' but maybe her jocular comments were getting a tinge serious. No smoke without a smouldering little bit of passion.

He ignored her coarseness. 'I'm not so sure. There's more to her than that. She may, just may, explain if, *if,* you ask her. Woman to woman. I can't. Ask her, I mean, now how can I?'

She giggled again. 'No you couldn't - well, not unless you were prepared to do the gentlemanly thing and fulfil her

165

expectations. Not that a gentleman with a sexy wife like me should want to shag another girl unless . . .' She stopped, and her narrowed eyed look betrayed a deeper thought. 'Go on. Take her to bed, shag her. I'll let you, provided you take suitable precautions. I don't want any by-blown half-sister or brother for our three, thank you very much. No way.' Then she added, very prosaically, 'and if you're sure she's not h.i.v. positive. No-one else been there since you last visited, I hope?'

'R! You're not serious!' This, coming from the woman he loved in every way, was totally unreal. 'I thought you were teasing me. Weren't you?'

The idea had found a sensitive and fertile patch in which to germinate. 'No, I'm not. I'd even say I'd watch,' not believing her words, 'to make sure you did the job -her, properly. *Then,*' she added emphatically, 'with a modicum of success, she'll be satisfied and we can get back to normal.'

'She might come back for seconds.'

'You egotist!'

'You do.'

She gave up. Half in banter, pulling his leg, half-serious in that she didn't otherwise know how to cap the other girl's flirtatiousness, she didn't expect any other reaction, though wondered if she'd gone too far, debating that if what she'd suggested happened, what she'd actually think, let alone do. Sling him out? No way, especially feeling as she did. Was this a set of jesting remarks too far?

'Go to sleep.' He switched the light out. 'I'm going to forget this conversation. Thank you a lovely evening, darling.'

And that was that.

Sam would be delighted to accept their invitation. She'd come up on the train, would that be all right? She'd only be able to stay the two nights because Donald would be back in the New Year.

She sounded sort of resigned.

Andrew took a risk. 'Are you okay with things, the two of you?'

She didn't give a direct answer, said something like 'you know how it is,' and confirmed the train time. 'See you then,' she said, and the phone went down.

'I'll fetch her mid morning,' he told Roberta. 'She says she'll stay the two nights. So, yes, she'll be here for the party.'

'That'll be lovely, dear. Have you spoken to An?'

'I'll ring her next,' not showing his surprise at her use of his abbreviation for the girl. Neither had referred to their previous late night conversation. 'How's it going?' The Mor House plans were taking shape on the Barn computer's large screen.

'Fine. June did a very good job, didn't miss a trick.' She reached for his hand. 'So glad she's joined us,' and smiled up at him. 'Hidden talents, your daughter has.'

'Tell Sam. She'll be pleased.' He saw the smile fade.

'I hope we'll get on.'

'So do I. No reason why not. We're all sane, thinking people. Decisions were taken, and time has moved on.' He leant down, pecked her cheek and relinquished her hand. 'I'll be in the office. Coming in for a break?'

'Half an hour. Where is everyone?'

'Peter and Hazel are out with the twins, June's in the sitting room, mugging up on eighteenth century Irish houses.'

Roberta laughed. 'Takes her responsibilities seriously. See you in a while.'

Andrea answered her office phone number. 'So you are at work?' he said, rather obviously.

'Thought I'd better see what was happening. Then I can start the New Year with a clear desk. Alain's still gallivanting.'

He sensed her disapproval in her flat tone of voice. 'You are okay with him, An? Not regretting the move?'

The pause suggested her reply wasn't all that honest. 'Of course I am, Andrew. Why shouldn't I be?'

'I'll leave that question on the table, An. Have you sorted our party?'

Another 'of course'. 'Caterers booked, I've some of our people to do the décor, Tim - remember Tim? - he'll provide the music. And I've arranged to borrow space heaters. It'll cost you, but nothing like the full whack. The van will be up on Thursday. That sound okay?'

'There's only us lot, An, not the entire village! Oh, and Samantha.'

'Sam?' she sounded surprised, maybe forgivably. 'You invited *her*?'

'She invited herself. After all, June and Peter . . . '

'Of course. Her children, not that they're children. Should keep you on your toes, Andrew.'

'As you do, An. Please, my love, restrain that desire.' Now that was an egotistical remark! Would she take offence?

A gurgling chuckle came back at him. 'Am I that obvious, Andrew? Well, you know me. In every which way,' and added another couple of phrases that didn't help his *sang-froid*. 'so there. On tap. Just say the word, darling man,' and the phone went down.

Using the kitchen table as conference facilities at coffee time was normal and today as normal a day as they could make it.

'I'll have finished the Mor House specification sometime tomorrow, June. As I told your father, because you did such a super job, it's been a lot easier than I thought. Your comment about a laptop was right. You should have had one. Take mine with you when you return, I'll get another. Perhaps you'd like to ring them and arrange a date to go back.' Roberta sipped at her coffee mug. 'And get an idea of how much time this Declan of theirs has got to spend on the project?'

'What about my time, Roberta? Do you charge them by the day or is it an inclusive cost on the contract? I feel they go out of their way to make me feel part of the family. It doesn't seem right to charge them for me having a good time.'

'True. We'll make it all inclusive. Hazel will sort out the next stage of the contract, won't you dear? Perhaps they'll be so good as to sign and e-mail it back.'

'And the CJ one?' Andrew asked. 'How's that going?'

'Clear in my mind, love. Next onto the virtual drawing board. My turn for a query. What about a new girl?' she asked, turning her gaze to Hazel and seeing the frown. 'Don't pull a face, my girl. We need to apply common sense, and, just in case you're concerned, there's another idea on the table. Peter,' and he looked up from his magazine, 'your father and I wondered whether you'd like to do us a favour?'

The magazine went down. 'Sure, mum. Whatever,' not appreciating how much a favour this was.

She liked the 'mum', and that encouraged her. 'Take over Mary's old cottage. We need someone to look after it, live in it, so we don't have to let it or even consider selling the place. Would you mind, moving out from here? Then we'd be able to offer your room to the new girl. And, of course, if Hazel could keep an eye on you down there, to make sure you kept the place clean and so on?' She watched the idea take root, the way the two young people's eyes met, and felt all warm inside. A dream come true for the girl. Lovely.

'You mean it? What about rent and so on? I couldn't expect to live there for free! I wanted to pay my whack here once I got my first proper salary cheque. I mean it, dad, Roberta. Days of sponging are long gone. But I'd love to do what you asked.' The way Roberta had put the idea forward was clever, he knew it was her way, making it look as though he was doing them the favour, whereas, in reality, they were doing him - and Hazel - the huge favour.

'Good. Then that's settled. Once we've sorted the place out. Andrew, love, do ring that agency. A nice blond haired

Polish lass. About eighteen, five foot six, good sense of humour, not afraid of hard work, reasonable English, gets on well with little people. You know the . . .'

'Roberta!'

She chuckled. 'Or maybe an old square faced woman with a forty forty forty-five figure from a country that breeds serious minded people with no sense of humour? I'll be on the interview panel, never fret. Right. We'd best finish the room down the corridor, June, if you don't mind, for Samantha's use tomorrow. Then I'll go back to the Mor House job with a clear conscience. You rang Andrea?' addressing a final question to her husband.

'All done. Caterers, disco, décor, all there. Shame it's only us lot. Sounds as though we should have sold tickets.'

'Then get the new girl sorted for tomorrow. So she can come too. Good introduction and we can watch her behaviour. Hazel, are Abby and Chris all right up there?'

'Peter and I'll go and see. Come on, Peter, stir yourself,' and she heaved him up from the big old chair. 'Thanks for the super cottage idea, Roberta. That's really great.'

The troops departed, Peter and Hazel to the play room, June to the final task of emptying the wardrobe of Mary's things. Andrew stood up.

'We talked about using the little barn for something, R, maybe we should let it as a function room for small parties; if Friday night's do works, we'll get an idea?'

Roberta shook her head. 'Not sure about that. Could get out of hand. We'll see. You go and ring the agency, I'll help June,' something she felt she had to do, albeit a agonizing experience.

The girl, woman more like, at the Agency sounded pleasantly helpful. 'Thank you for ringing. I'll have a look through our files and ring you back, if that's all right? About half an hour?'

And almost exactly half an hour later, she did. 'I've two

girls who may be suitable, both already in this country. We have other names but they're still in their home countries. The one, as you suggest, is Polish, the other Latvian. May I forward their details - if you have an e-mail address?'

Sounded promising. He gave the address and put the phone down. Things were dropping into place. Another quarter of an hour at the desk, and in came the promised e-mail, with attachments. Pictures as well, which, on reflection, was a sensible action.

Having read through both the four hundred over-wordy descriptions, checked over the qualifications offered, scrutinised the portraits, he made a choice. Roberta might not agree, but . . . his choice. Back to the phone.

'Thanks for the info. From what I've seen, maybe Kasia would . . .'

She interrupted him. 'Katarzyna. You know the name means 'pure' when translated? Kasia is the shortened from. She comes from a good family, is here to make friends and all reports coming back have been favourable, as you will have read, and it's a shame she's available, but I won't expand on that.' and the slight pause could be interpreted as 'meaningful'. 'A good choice - provided there's a degree of mutuality. So would you like to see her?'

'I'll check with my wife, the answer is likely 'yes', and in the meantime, would she be free on Friday night?'

'New Year's Eve?' The lift in her voice was understandable, the query no surprise.

'Mmm. We're having a family and friends party here, a good as time as any for an introduction, so everyone could meet a prospect. We're like that, all working together,' and he wondered what Andrea's reaction would be.

'I'll enquire. She may be booked for a party herself. In the meantime?'

'I'll confirm with you later, or tomorrow morning latest. Thank you.'

Roberta had retreated, left June with the vestiges of the clearance. She'd struggled, put on a brave face, but enough was enough. Andrew found her back in the sitting room nursing an unaccustomed glass of gin and tonic.

'Darling!' He perched on the chair arm alongside and took the glass away from an unresisting hand. 'I'm sorry, my love. Maybe I should have helped - have you finished?'

She let her head sag back onto the cushion and briefly closed her eyes. 'Clear. So Sam can come. How have you been getting on?'

He stroked a cheek. 'Okay. They had a couple of girls - I've picked one out - Kasia, she's Polish - and asked if she could come to the party as you suggested. Would that be alright? This is her,' and he held the print-out for her to see.

She peered at the photo and scanned the précised life history, where she'd been, what she'd done, the explanation of why she wanted to be at someone else's beck and call in a foreign country.

'What was the other girl like? You said two?'

'Nothing like the experience, only here to earn money. This girl,' and he tapped the paper, 'as you see, wants to make friends and improve her 'cultural experience'.' Anyway, she's prettier.'

The smile was a tired one. 'That's all that mattered?'

He shook his head. 'We'll see. Can I confirm the party invite?'

'If you like.' Her eyes closed again. 'Let me have a half-hour, then we'll have supper. Early night.'

'Sure.' He stroked her hair, touched his fingers to her lips. 'Love you.'

'Mmmm,' and before he closed the door quietly behind him, she was asleep in the chair.

EIGHTEEN

At half past nine, the phone rang, a minute later and he'd have gone. That Irish lilt he'd recognise anywhere; Maeve, at her irrepressible best. Could she possibly, because they were such dear people, come and see them again, I mean, she said, just to get her away from the temptations of the City because, well, there was this man . . .

He sighed. He couldn't say no, far too churlish, anyway she was fun to have around. What time did she say? Well, as luck would have it, as he was meeting someone else, perhaps they'd be on the same train? One or two errands to run in town first, but yes, she could come, he'd be at the rail station at half eleven. Thanks a million she'd said, and rung off.

He counted fingers. June, Hazel, Sam, all resident, then Andrea of course, the potential new girl, Kasia (who'd apparently been very pleased to accept the invite) and now Maeve. She'd need a bed as well. Himself, Roberta, Peter, so nine of them. Two blokes, seven women. Had all the makings of a brilliant party, so with that happy thought, whistling, he slammed the office door shut, shouted 'I'm off,' and went, completely forgetting to mention to Hazel - Roberta still being in bed, an allowably lazy woman - that Maeve was coming back. It came to him as he entered the paper shop and saw Tricia's untidy red ringlets behind the counter, so, with the 'Times' tucked under his arm, he dug out his mobile and managed to catch June, explained the situation to her and pulled a face at her caustic remark. He'd buy her some earplugs for a laugh, recognising that sharing a room with someone as free spirited and vibrant as celtic-haired Maeve might be construed as a psychological punishment. Next stop the supermarket, his own self-inflicted penalty; then on to the station and one of those decisive points when he'd either welcome Sam as a casual visitor or, as like the moment one draws curtains or opens blinds in the morning, there'd be a upsurge of life energy at seeing the familiar in a new day's dawning.

And there she was. An encapsulation of former times, with an open smile on the oh, so familiar face, now wind and travel tanned, disguising lines that care and concern had etched. Slim, taut, and hungry for his kiss within a tight embrace.

No animosity. No suggestion of guilt, retribution. No 'I wish' in the silence between them as she caught his hand and they walked out into the wintry sun.

In the car she settled herself, tugged her skirtline down. Before he started the car their heads turned and eyes met. The years, the eroding trivia that had etched away the brilliance of their early love, rolled away and he saw, felt, the tear she brushed away. Her thigh he touched briefly before he eased away from the station forecourt. Forgotten Maeve watched the car go, *'well, now would you believe it!'* and dug out her mobile phone.

He pulled the car into that blind layby, the old road to nowhere; the familiar spot, the place where he'd chosen to say 'no' to Andrea; and to Roberta another 'no' against any thought they'd conspire to kill a womb-borne child conceived in such spontaneous and frenetic love on a peat-stained gardener's bench. She looked across at him, puzzled; Samantha, his wife and bed-companion for twenty changeable years.

'Andrew?'

174

'Have we changed so much? Since then?'

And she knew the time to which he referred, those last few months before she'd secretly accepted the position with the Charity. Since then - yes, they had changed. She the more focussed, more aware of what life was all about, the horror, chagrin, starvation, need, oh, all aspects of deprivation people in their cosy comfortable existence knew nothing, *nothing*, about. Her erstwhile husband now the more alert, more lively, more aware of his responsibilities and his support for their two children - grown-up, but still demanding children. Their love, their passion, the cementation of their partnership had cooled, embrittled, and hence the dissolution of the essential fabric of their lives.

She sat still, hands in her lap, wondering and beginning to wish. To wish she could wind the clock back. To wish she'd not been so self-centred, more conscious of his needs for her, that perhaps some other external factor should have brought them to this dissolution. Too late. The shrug of her shoulders, did that signify no suggestion of a chance of any reconciliation within her?

'Roberta will wonder where we are.'

He restarted the car and immediately his mobile bleeped. Samantha recognised the voice even second hand and distorted. June. He was pulling a wry face as he snapped the phone shut.

'I forgot Maeve,' and grinned at her. 'Because all I saw was a former wife. Back to the station, sorry, Sam.'

Maeve had no inhibitions. 'Took his mind off the promise did you now? Well, there's the man for you. P'raps I should be the jealous one and me with the flaming hair an' all.'

Samantha had to return the infectious smile that took the sting from Maeve's words, and proffered a hand over the seat back. 'I did live with him for twenty years,' she said, mildly. 'And we've not seen each other for a while.'

175

'Three years,' Andrew added.

'So why'd you leave the gorgeous man?'

Andrew coughed. 'Flattery to get you a bed for the night, is that it, Maeve?'

'Are you offering? Sure and Roberta might have something to say about that!'

Sam laughed. 'Shows how he's altered, Maeve. He and I were a very faithful couple. Times have a-changed!'

'Not as much as all that, Sam,' glad he'd not offered Maeve an answer and changed the subject. ' So how was your Christmas?'

'Too boozy for words, and my memory's got a conscience. At least I didn't get laid which sure is a blessing. Mind you, the man was persistent enough. I'd near lost my knickers before the cramp got him, thank the Lord. Mamma'd never forgive me if I took a bastard home.'

'Haven't you a man back in Ireland?' Andrew recalled June's comment, wondering about how free this outspoken Maeve was with her favours. Sam sat quiet.

'Sure, and a grand lad he is too, but you know how 't is. The party spirit and all that. Still, past history. His lovely wife found out, so it'll be a pilgrimage for him come Easter.' She lapsed into a welcome silence as Andrew, inwardly smiling, wondered how June would cope tonight, and whether Maeve's presence at tomorrow night's party might prove rather interesting.

The driveway, the gravel, the sweep round, the steps and the solid wooden front door. The hallway, the flashback and another world away. June was there, and Peter, and tears to be shed while Andrew went to salve his conscience and Maeve went looking for two young people she'd come to adore.

The diffident smile and the deep brown eyes he loved with a curious lift of eyebrows asked an unspoken question. He hugged her to him and whispered in her hair.

176

'Really?' She felt his nod and heard another affirmation, sufficient to be able to go and greet this previous woman of his without malice or worry. She kept close hold of his hand and stayed under his arm as they returned to the hall.

Samantha released June to greet her successor with a calmness belying her inward emotions. The last time she'd been in this place she'd just resigned her interest in this woman's husband, having accepted the folly that had driven her to abandon him, but now, after Sierra Leone and Romania and all the other places inbetween she'd give the world away to return to her former status. Not for passion, but for the companionship, the laughter and the beaten challenges she and Andrew, her once chosen husband, had shared across the years. Donald came nowhere near.

'Roberta.'

'Sam.' They shook hands, formally, rigidly, aware of the sudden stillness of the other three who'd suffered equally through the changes she'd wrought.

'How's Donald?'

'I'm not sure, Roberta. He went off to stay with his sister. Allowed me the chance to invite myself here. I hope it's not a burden for you.'

'Burden, Lord no. We're glad you felt you could. Come through. We'll sort some lunch out, hope you didn't have too early a start.' Then she added, 'You'll know I've lost my mum.'

'I haven't had the chance to say, Roberta, how desperately sorry I am. She was a lovely lady, so very sad, especially . . . ' and she trailed off. Especially what, because it was Christmas, or because of Roberta's now visible pregnant state?

'I know,' and that was all she was prepared to say. 'Thank you, Sam. Shall we go through?'

Hazel was in the kitchen, arranging rolls and sandwiches on the large round Denby service platter, the purpley one with the stripes. 'Buffet style,' she said, giving Sam a welcoming smile. 'I'm Hazel. Roberta's spare girl. Nice to see you. Would you like tea, coffee or something else?'

'Hi,' said Sam, wondering about the 'spare girl' cachet. 'Coffee would be good.'

'You lot can help yourselves,' Hazel said, 'I'm off up to see to Abby and Chris, let Maeve off. Shall I bring them down, Roberta?'

'Do. Then Sam can be introduced. My, but it is getting crowded. Nice, though. Do you folk mind if I take the big chair?'

They sorted themselves out, small people were introduced, conversation ebbed as lunch took preference, then Peter, strategically placed, saw a vehicle on the driveway.

'Dad - there's a van outside. Were we expecting someone?'

Andrew got up and dumped his crumb laden plate on the table, mouth still half full. 'Andrea. Or at least someone from her place. Party kit, I expect. 'Scuse me,' and went.

She was driving, on her own, and in jeans, hair tied back, close fitting sweater and looking a very sexy sixties-ish girl. The smile, the invitation for a greeting on glossed lips, the closed eyes and the arm that pulled him close. The kiss lingered.

'Sam's here,' he said, easing free from her arm. 'And Maeve. Girls ad nauseum. I'm spoilt for choice.'

The eyes swept his face and held. 'Choose me,' she said. 'Just the once.' Her hunger was so very demonstratively clear. He gave a little head shake, not wishing to say 'no' in quite that way, and she shrugged and walked ahead of him toward the little barn's new door. The place renovated by the film company she now worked for, part of the deal for the programme going on air in the New Year. He followed her inside.

'Andrew's been gone a fair while,' Hazel suddenly announced, breaking into the silence of Roberta's post lunch doze in the big chair. Maeve had taken Abby and Chris back to the upstairs playroom, June and Peter were now in the sitting room with their mother, catching up.

'Eh? What? Oh. Sorry, Hazel. I shouldn't really be dozing like this or I won't sleep tonight,' and re-adjusted her position. 'Put the kettle across, love, so we can make a pot of tea. I expect he's getting the barn all sorted for tomorrow night.' She noticed, gratefully, that everything from the scattered lunch had been tidied, the washing up done, and from the book she held, Hazel had obviously kept her silent company, reading something. 'Then perhaps you'd go and have a look? See what you think?'

'Sure.'

Behind the Manor, the van was tucked into the little barn's access track, the rear doors open but otherwise no sign of life. Hazel walked steadily onwards, and a silly, silly thought went through her mind. She coughed, scuffed her toes on the gravel, slapped the van's side panel as she passed it, and went through the open door into the gloom of the barn. Andrew was standing on one side of the near wall, holding up a backcloth as Andrea, on a small pair of steps, was pinning it into place. Another backdrop, with some woodland scene, was already in place on the far wall. Artificial grass had been laid, strewn unevenly, across its front. A tree trunk had come from somewhere and she wondered if it was real or film-set plastic.

'Oh, hi, Hazel. Come to spy?' Andrea stepped down, picked up the steps and moved across towards Andrew. 'Just this one to pin up, then you can say what you think?'

Hazel felt her cheeks going red. Spy? Her thoughts and Andrea's remark were too close together. 'Just came to see how you were getting on. Heading towards teatime. Do you need anymore help?'

The last pin went into place. 'Nope. Reckon this is it.' She put a hand on Andrew's shoulder and used him as a prop to jump down. 'I think I've achieved my aim,' she said and the hand swept down. 'What say you, Andrew?'

'Fairy glade, Hazel,' he said, not answering the question. 'Midsummer Night's Dream and all that. There's some lights to put up. Then it should do, I guess. All courtesy of the film studio. Good, eh?'

She nodded. The effect was pretty good, all things considered. She had memories of this Shakespeare stuff from school, dressed as a fairy in the end of year play.

'Do we dress up, then, fancy costumes?' Andrew asked a jokey question.

Andrea looked at him and her eyes danced. 'You'd look good in tights.'

'Come off it, Andrea, this is New Year's Eve, not a Summer Ball!'

'Think 'Masquerade', darling,' Andrea said, and Hazel froze. "Darling", Andrea'd said, perhaps unwittingly. Oh, no, Andrew, *please, no!*

New Year's Eve had come. Tomorrow, for them, reality. Today, unreality. A dry day, and Maeve could not be separated from the twins, not they from her, so together they scampered about on the lawn under a cool watery sun. Roberta spent a couple of hours at her desk in the big Barn, putting finishing touches to the *Mor House* renovation specification, Andrew a similar time in the office, where Hazel joined him later in the morning. Peter, June and their mother had gone off up the hill for a walk. She had him on his own.

'Hi, love,' he said in an absent-minded sort of way as she pushed open the door. 'Just seeing what's what before the new week kicks in. How's you?' He spun the chair round and faced her. 'You look serious?'

She sat in the other chair, his, because he was sitting on hers. *Hers*, not Andrea's. She took a breath, and plunged.

'Andrea. She's still after you, isn't she?'

'What? Hazel, is this really anything to do with you?' His chair went half round and back again. 'How we conduct ourselves together isn't your concern, my girl. Is it?'

'It is if it's likely to hurt Roberta. And now you've got Samantha trailing after you as well. When Roberta's pregnant and suffering and low and not being able to go to Ireland, and you play around with these other women as though they were toys? Like you nearly played around with me?' Her voice had gone up a notch or two and she knew it, but couldn't stop. 'Why can't you just send them packing so Roberta *really* knows you *really* only love her? And what's going to happen when this other girl turns up? Will you want to see what colour knickers she's wearing? Oh Andrew! Please, please, . . . ' and inevitably, she could feel her muscles tightening, the tears came and the last 'please' turned into a wet and eye blinding sob.

He sat still, finally to put his head in his hands, elbows resting on his knees. A moment passed, the silence broken only by another hic-cupping sob and a sniff from the girl and a scrabble in her skirt to find a handkerchief. Finally he looked up.

'Is it that obvious?'

'You and *she*,' the *she* in a distasteful tone, 'in the barn, yesterday. She'd got you cornered, hadn't she? You and her, in *that* barn, where Roberta's first husband . . . ' she couldn't say 'fucked' because it wasn't a word she wanted to use, 'did his secretary! I know you did. It showed. Her face. Smug. And her zip was undone. Is it Sam's turn next or are you going to see if this Kasia will spread her legs?' She stood up and walked towards the door. 'And are you going to try and persuade me too, now I'm no longer a virgin? Poor poor Roberta. If it weren't for the twins I'd leave. And I'm going to tell Roberta unless you promise to keep your trousers zipped.'

She folded her arms and lent against the door frame. Her blood was up, the adrenalin racing and suddenly she didn't care. Peter would never treat her like his father seemed to treat the women around him. Roberta had promised them Mary's cottage. She'd get a part time job in the village, they'd manage. Andrew could stuff his job. She'd still care for the twins though, unless this Polish import ousted her.

'Sit down, Hazel. Please, *sit down!*'

'Why should I? Unless you're going to confess.'

'*Sit Down!*'

Now he sounded rather fierce. She obeyed, but kept her legs tight under her. No peeking.

'I'm only going to say this once.' He was looking at her, but she dropped her eyes to her hands, twisting nervously in her lap. 'Whether you believe me is your decision. Perhaps you'll understand, perhaps you won't. Up to you. But for a girl who's allowed herself to be ravished by my son, under my roof, you've got a nerve. I could have lost my temper and thumped you. Chucked you out.' He pushed the chair back to give himself some space. 'Andrea. She's a nymphomaniac - as least as far as I'm concerned. I know what she wants, it's bloody obvious. Yes, she flirts, no, she doesn't wear underclothes, yes, she tries to get me wound up. Which admittedly she has, in the past. *In the past, Hazel. IN THE PAST!* Do you understand? Past. P. A. S. T. Yesterday, yes, she tried it on. Yes, I could have had her, on the floor, exactly where Michael fucked that sad little Fiona girl. That red dress of Andrea's? Never worn with underclothes. Warm, soft, cuddly, and I agree my manhood has a superb time rising to the occasion. But, I have not once taken it any further, not since before Roberta. Do you understand? Never! There's a need in that girl for loving, I know that. And I care for her, very very much, I'll even say I love her, but not in the way you think. And as for Sam, I do not believe she'd want to cheapen herself by applying the same sort of techniques

Andrea does. The Polish girl - well, Hazel, I'd run the risk of some pretty hefty legal action if I tried anything on with her - *even if I wanted to!* I've only seen her photo. And as for you I'd never, ever, wish to spoil our relationship. I've loved you for a long time, Hazel, but as a daughter and I thought that was clear since Ireland and our trig point walk. I still do, despite you doing your level best to wreck things today. All I can say is, I admire your pluck, and your bloody obvious devotion to my wife, and, not least, the way in which you've faced up to what you consider as a problem. Have I missed anything?'

She sat silent, still twisting her handkerchief.

'Tonight, Hazel, we're going to have a party. As a token of our - Roberta's and me - feeling that we've got the best and nicest bunch of people around us anyone could wish to have. Andrea will be here. In her red dress with nothing underneath it, I can guarantee that. Do you want a challenge? Go up to her and ask? Say *'Andrew knows you want him and that's why you've got no panties on?'* Only, if you do, she's likely to run off and do something stupid. Then she'll be on *your* conscience, not mine. Except that I'd never forgive you if she maimed or killed herself merely because she didn't get another chance of being loved! Which is what she wants. What you wanted. What Roberta wanted. What Sam still wants, and it's very sad that her Donald obviously doesn't fulfil the same role as I once did. And now my June has the same problem. Gaps in lives, Hazel, gaps in lives. We try and fill them. Sometimes it works, sometimes it doesn't. I could no more hurt Roberta than I could you. Than, I hope, my Peter could you. He seems to have properly fallen for you, my girl, and I'm extremely happy that he has. That you've skipped over some of the best bits of a courtship and landed in bed together too soon is a modern trait and I'm a mite sorry you've done so this early on. If a relationship is going to be worthwhile then don't rush it. Put one block in place at a time, and cement it in. That way it won't fall apart. Marriage isn't just pure passion, Hazel, not even a series of non-productive cuddles, it's a tolerance, an understanding, a partnership in everything you do and love together. I had a thought about benchmarks a week or so back, you know, those little arrow and level marks surveyors use to establish points of reference? We've got these in our lives too. Standards. I've got standards, Hazel, despite what you seem to think. And caring for people is one of them, even lustful beautiful creatures like Andrea. I cared for Mary too, for lots of reasons, and I'm going to miss her, a lot. She was a benchmark. A rock solid level on which Roberta based her life. I've got to be that benchmark now. Peter will be yours. I've a sneaking feeling June will find hers in Ireland. Sam I don't know about, yet. The twins - and number three - will have us. Without the *two* of us, their world would be lop-sided. Another good reason for cementing a partnership together, for if children are part of it, then God forbid you should abandon it merely because one wants, as you so succinctly put it, to find out what colour knickers another girl is wearing. Or in a girl's case, whether one bloke's thingy works the same as another's.'

Despite herself, she had to smile. He had a point. Several, actually. She'd never known him so serious, so talkative, or so straight with her.

'Thank you,' she said simply, letting her tension slacken. 'I'm sorry. I didn't understand. I think I do now. You mean you have to guard Andrea's feelings in case she does something stupid? Like I might have done if Mary, and then you and Roberta, hadn't taken me on? Is that what caring is all about? Giving people what they think they need?'

He grinned at her, and she relaxed another notch. 'Up to a point.' Then he went serious again. 'Andrea wants a child, to love and care for, but I'm not going to be the one who gives it to her. Far too dangerous. And she shouldn't go through a pregnancy and child care without someone who *loves* both her and the child at her side. Kids born without full and proper care are often desperately sad little people who are, mundanely, a drain on society and no joy to themselves, poor mites. Let alone contributing to the world's excess carbon dioxide heap. Ask Sam. She's seen it all, out in Africa, and Eastern Europe.'

She'd giggled, but now he wasn't smiling. It was so true. She took refuge in the Andrea situation.

'So you let her *think* she'll get lucky to stop her from brooding?'

'You've got a wiser head on you than some, young lady. Except you needed a bit of guidance. Yes, in a word.'

'Dodgy,' she replied.

He laughed. 'Very. And Roberta knows. We do work together, despite what you may think. So will you ask Andrea if she's got her pants on?'

Hazel shook her head vehemently. 'No way!' She got up. 'Am I forgiven for being so rude and forward?'

He stood up as well and held out his arms. 'Of course you are, you silly girl,' he said as she took comfort in his hug. 'But please, my darling daughter-in-lieu, talk to me? If you've any doubts? Don't store up imagined problems up, talk to me - or Peter. He's a far better son than I thought he'd turn out to be, thanks to his mum. Now, are you going to wear a decent dress for this party?'

She lifted her head from nestling into his sweater, and grinned up at him. 'I might even have my knickers on, too.'

'So you should, my girl, so you should. And . . . ' but he didn't have to finish he sentence, she did.

'Keep 'em on?'

'Please. He'll think the more of you, you know.'

'Okay, dad-in-lieu,' she said, and they were friends again.

Strange how the walk away from the Manor and up the hill always took the walkers past the bench.

'What's that doing here?'

'No idea, mum,' replied June. 'Except it's part of dad's

routines. He sits up here and thinks. Roberta told me about it. They've had a session up here not a while ago.'

'And I brought Hazel up here too. It's a little suspect, been in place a long time.' Peter prodded at the slats again, but they still held.

'Then I'll sample it as well.' Samantha sat down, gingerly, on the least mildewed end. 'You can see the valley lane and the Manor roof!'

June knew the tale, wondered if her mother did. 'This is where dad was sitting when he saw Roberta come off her horse.'

'Oh,' said her mother, and stared down the hillside. 'So I'm back where I started to lose him.'

'Mum, don't be maudlin. You've both led fuller lives since then. You can't turn the clock back.'

'Can't I?'

'No, you can't!' Peter rounded on her. 'Mum, dad and Roberta, they're great pals, super parents, except she relies too heavily on Hazel, and if you made owl eyes at dad he'd get all stewed up, not good for anyone. Okay, he still loves you, that's clear enough, but you can't get back in bed together!'

'Hmmm,' was all she said in reply.

'Mum? No! Don't even think it!' Now June added her weight. 'It's bad enough watching Andrea making sheep's eyes at dad without you starting. She's a poor sex-starved gal who can't get our dad out of her system, more's the pity. Roberta's all he wants, their relationship is something very special and I'd give anything to have a husband like our dad is to her. So what's happened to Donald, then? I thought he was everything?'

Sam looked up at her two grown-up children and pulled a wry face. 'Owl eyes, sheep's eyes, make up your minds. Donald, my June, gave me a wonderful time for a while. Very good at bonking. But too many sweeties gives you tummy ache. He hasn't got that *je ne sais quoi* your father had. Has. Shame.'

'Yes, mum, a shame. And I'm not going to say it was your fault, because it wasn't. It was boredom. You both needed a refurb and didn't realise it. So it happened anyway. Someone said you have to re-invent yourself every ten years. You managed twenty. Not bad. But you cannot go back. Think memories but go forward. I am.'

'Oh?'

'I've fallen in love again, mum.'

Peter stared at her. 'You never said? Who with, for heaven's sake?'

June chuckled. 'Blame Ireland. And a girl called Keela, or more accurately,' and she did a passable job at the Irish, '*Cadhla.*'

'You're daft, girl!' Her mother was also staring.

'Maybe. All I know is, I can't wait to get back.'

'But the Manor, the twins, the job you're doing? And what's happening about William?'

June tossed her head. 'Oh, *him*. Don't know, don't care. Well, I do, because of the house. If he isn't coming back, I'll let it - or sell it.'

'Bit drastic, isn't it?'

'You should never have let me marry him, mum.'

Samantha snorted. 'If we'd have said 'no', you'd only have gone your own way. Headstrong, the pair of you. Learnt your lesson the hard way. Well, at least you've done all right, Peter, if nothing goes awry. Hazel's a lovely girl.' She got up. 'We'd best get on. I've got cold, sitting here.' She patted the bench's back. 'Good old bench. Made its mark. First Andrew, now me. I've decided. Come on, children.'

'Decided?'

'Yes. June, if you'll let me, I'll move into your house on a temporary basis. Donald can get lost. I'll find myself a new man, when the right one comes along.' She seized a hand in each and swung them. 'New Year resolution. And I'm going to enjoy this party, you see if I don't.'

NINETEEN

In the grey hours of an indifferently grey day, the New Year rolled into their lives. Quiet, in a sort of sagging, sad light to creep over a subdued garden, a patient timeless beech spread protective naked arms over the lawn, the shrubs, the entity that was the Manor's estate, the place where life was reluctantly beginning to stir.

Different minds gave diverse starts to the day. The children the more active, creating their own eddies of noise to impinge on the somnolence around them. Hazel stirred. Her mind began to clear like the drifts of early morning mist had given way to the reluctant dawn. The party! The noisy, jazzy, fun-filled let-your-hair down party. The whirling, dizzying dance with no determined steps, Peter crashing her into the corner so she tumbled down on top and he'd kissed her hard. Her lips bruised even now. The deliberate slower and accurate lovely waltz Roberta and Andrew had demonstrated, he with the care, she with the elegance she still possessed, even twenty weeks pregnant. Maeve throwing her skirts around in a gamBorlinng Irish jig of a thing, she and Andrea together not much better in their attempt at a tango. The country style dance rounds, orchestrated by the guy Andrea'd imported to provide the music, was where June seemed to score. Hilarity and good-natured ragging. Too much to eat from the tempting yummy buffet, and far too much to drink. But she'd survived, apart from the little dull ache in her head that would soon go after a large glass of orange juice. Another day, another year.

Samantha couldn't work out where she was at first, as the insidious grey light crept through strange curtains, touched the floral patterned wallpaper, the panelled cream painted door and a tall dark brown chest of drawers. A thick head, too much red wine. Oh, yes, the party, the Manor's New Year party and all that rumbustious dancing and silly games. She'd slept well though, like the proverbial. As the past hours recollection became clearer, so came an almost physical pain of loss, the loss of what at one time she'd been an essential part. A family, a solid band of people who together loved, depended, existed all under the same caring roof. And due to her own stupidity, she'd allowed hers to fragment. Or had she? Under this, another woman's roof, a woman who'd stolen her husband, lay her two children, each a newly re-invented persona. She should be proud of them. Certainly sad that June's marriage hadn't worked out, and, looking back, maybe she and Andrew should have foreseen it wouldn't last. They may have subsequentially lost a daughter's love if they'd said 'no', tried to persuade her against him. But here she was, in a different world and blossoming, a lovely woman. And Peter, clearly at peace with himself, happy in the new position in the Charity she'd worked so hard for him to get and this girl Hazel - so absolutely right together. She wiped the trickled tears away, threw back the duvet, stood up, stretched, and, with the New Year upon her, made the first resolution.

Peter's wakening thoughts, a hasty reappraisal of where he was, were rather like his mother's, not that he was aware; his subsequent actions were more in tune with Kasia's, an efficient get-up and get the day started, and he wouldn't have known that either. His years out in the 'field' with different places, different tasks, had provided good training, so being unexpectedly evicted from 'his' room in the Manor in order that the young Polish girl could have a bed wasn't too much a difficulty, especially as this place was apparently soon to be his anyway. And, a nice warm feeling, where he and Hazel might begin to establish a working partnership. The occasional kiss'n'cuddle was fine, but if they were going to discover each other's foibles, this was the way. He didn't envisage a problem. She knew what was what, and so did he. They'd be fine and this was a great opportunity for which he owed his dad and step-mum. And that dear old lady who'd been so much a part of their lives, how desperately sad that she'd died when she had. Bless you, Mary.

As his thoughts rambled on, he methodically straightened the place out, gathered up his things and put them into the duffle bag, slung it over his shoulder, and went out into the cool dampness of the first morning of the New Year. A brisk quarter of an hour's cycle ride back to the Manor and breakfast.

Kasia woke suddenly, alert and clear minded, as was her wont. Trained, after a few years wandering around Europe and so often changing homes and places to sleep, not to waste time but to get on with the day. She used the basin in the room - so civilised - and the nice soap, to refresh her essential bits and keep her feminity odour-free before a vigorous towel-over to encourage the blood to circulate. She dressed efficiently, quickly, with clean underwear and the shorter skirt, drew the curtains back and put them back into their ties, remade the bed, dried the hand-basin and straightened the towel on its rail. There. Tidy, clean, and ready to face the day. This place was good, the feel of joy and friendship, clean and full of nice things. The little people a delight if exuberant, their mother a 'full' person even if she had a feeling of sadness, but with the loss of a dear mother upon her, that she understood. Her husband, the man she'd been told to call 'Andrew', he liked the ladies, that was obvious, though she had no reason to believe it a problem, for his concern and care for 'Roberta' was also apparent.

She shook her head at these thoughts, saw her fine hair wisp up, smiled at the reflection in the mirror and combed it out. She'd not tie it in the bun this morning.

June, much earlier, had also stirred, straightened her arms and cautiously lifted her head. Maeve, red hair strewn carelessly across the pillow, an arm flung wide, still fast asleep. Thankfully. The last thing she could cope with at this hour was a Maeve style reprise of last night. Carefully, she eased feet to floor and padded across to the window. The garden below sombre in its winter garb, sadly no sun to lighten the corners, and her mind swam across to Mor House and the vast avenue of pines, the rose garden, the statuette and quiet, the quiet she'd absorbed and come to love. Hands on the sill, she stretched, filled her lungs, turned, swept a bundle of clothes from the chair, and as silent as silent, left the room to the sleeping Maeve.

She dressed downstairs; the kitchen not cold, she moved the still-full kettle onto the warmest Aga hob and, barefoot, went out into a damp-aired morning. Across the dewed grass, and cool-toed over to the beech and its bench. Here she sat, hands flat beneath her thighs, and wondered on the new day, the New Year. Wondered where she was, where she was going, what she would achieve. Become her own person, true, but still within the wrap of her father and dear Roberta. And a tie, in legality alone, to a uncaring male lost in his colourless two-dimensional world of flat screened monotony. She gazed down at her toes, still cared for, still with neat coloured nails. The rest of her echoed the same care, nothing to despise, nothing to get upset about, a body to love. Or to be loved, given the right inspiration. A pigeon flapped into the tree above, sending droplets of overnight moisture scattering down and she brushed the wet off her hair. The bird flew away, startled at her sudden movement.

Last night. A boisterous evening, but good. Country dancing more in her line than Andrea's tango. The girl had

191

been brilliant, putting both décor and the party all together; pity it was going to disappear and leave them with an empty space. Memories. Pity there hadn't been another couple of nice uncomplicated men to share around. Never mind, it all went well. Even dad's little speech, with Roberta tucked under his arm, happiest she'd seen her since coming back from Ireland. Such a pity Mary hadn't been there. Poor Roberta. Then she thought of how her father had pulled them all together, and really, that was the lovely part of where they were. Together. Her mum, who'd laughed and danced with the best of them, her brother and his new love; the over-active Maeve and the new, polite, reticent to a degree, slim blonde, Kasia, the potential new au-pair.

Kasia dropped off by taxi just before six; skirted down to her ankles, a blouse-style coat over a colourful hand knit sweater, sensible shoes, the fullness of her soft blonde hair carefully pinned into a stylish bun. A small hold-all gripped in gloved hands. Her English, intriguingly stilted with the unmistakeable accent was simple and clear. Her blue-grey eyes smiled, her cheeks dimpled and her handshake firm. Dad had liked her, that was evidently clear. So did the most important people, Abby and Chris. Most of the evening she'd sat and watched, demure and silent, getting up to help serve the buffet supper without the asking, taking part in the country dances with precise and flowing steps. Asked when she had to return, had seemed surprised and a little nervously replied '*I thought I was here to stay?*'.

That had meant some hasty reorganisation, with Peter sent off into the village just after midnight to doss down in Mary's old cottage while Kasia had his re-made bed. Lucky girl.

Would they keep her? It would be surprising if they didn't. How could one not like a girl like that? Provided she worked. But the Polish mainly did, didn't they?

Now she was getting cold. Sitting still for too long. Breakfast beckoned. As she unfolded herself, the gravel rattled under cycle wheels and Peter hove into view. She waved and he skidded the bike to a sideways halt.

'Hiya, sis. Happy New Year! You're about early, Anyone else alive?'

'Happy new Year. Thought it was actually New Year when you left, Peter. How was your night?'

'Not so bad. Cosy little pad. Couldn't you sleep?'

'Oh, yes, I slept. Rather well. But escaped before Maeve could get into gear. I like these quiet times. Ready for breakfast?`

The kitchen lights were on. Hazel, with a youngster parked each side of her, was reading yet another Beatrice Potter book.

' . . . and they all lived happily ever after.' She looked up. 'Morning.' The twins slid down and ran across to each take a June hand. 'Good. Now you're here I'll be able to get on with breakfast. Slept well, Peter?'

Their eyes met.

June noticed and the element of déjà vu hit her. There had been a brief time when that happened to her. Not now. 'I'll take these two back upstairs, shall I? See if I can get Maeve into the act. Breakfast in what, half an hour?'

'Sure.' Hazel's eyes hadn't left Peter, and June knew there'd be a celebratory New Year cuddle once she'd left the room.

In the master bedroom, the lights were also on, making the room sparkling and bright. Roberta was warm and satiated. It had been a lovely night after a superb evening, but now life had to resume. She ruffled his hair.

'Darling?'

'Happy New Year, love. You okay?'

'Absolutely. Marvellous time, both during and after. Thankyou, my love.' With extreme care she half turned to offer lips and a tip of tongue. 'Did it come up to expectations?'

193

He turned on his side to let her relax onto her back, met her embrace, returned her salutation and smiled. 'Which do you mean, the party or the afters?'

Her contented pussy cat smile returned. 'I know which I prefer.' Then came the serious question. 'Kasia. What do you think?'

'I like her, R, she seems uncomplicated and so far, fits in well, but I wasn't expecting her to ask to stay. Poor Peter, getting turfed out of his bed for a stray girl. What do we do?'

'Don't suppose we'll be able to contact the agency today, bank holiday and all that. See what she says. Plenty for her to do,' and she changed topic. 'Maeve. You don't think she'll extend her stay?'

Hands behind his head, Andrew contemplated the ceiling. ' I suspect she'll want to go back with June. She has a job, you know. Perhaps June will find out. I'll ask. And when do we move Peter? Permanently, I mean.'

'I'll go down today. Perhaps I'll take Kasia then we can get to know each other. Right,' and she pushed the duvet back. 'Breakfast beckons. Oh, and thank Andrea for last night. Came up trumps, she did. No problems?'

And he knew what she meant. After the unexpected diatribe from Hazel and his responsive verbal rationale of where Andrea stood in his scheme of things, keeping her at arms length somehow seemed a whole lot easier.

Roberta drew back the curtains and gazing out across the lawn, saw June walking back across the lawn like a wayward maiden returning from an assignation, hair free, barelegged, and arms in tune with her jaunty step. Peter was pushing his bike alongside her.

'Your children are up early.' She turned back to her husband. 'How's your head?'

He blinked a few times. 'Okay. I didn't think I'd overdone it. A few glasses of water helped. You were very good, my love.'

'Yep. No alcohol for me. Don't want Tertiary to be born with a hangover.'

He laughed. 'Well done, you.' He bounced out and reached for his clothes. 'I'll have a shower later. Get the show on the road first. Lots of houseguests. You want a hand?'

She considered. 'I think I'm okay. You get the twins underway, if one of the girls hasn't beaten you to it. See you in a bit.'

Three quarters of an hour later and they had a job to squeeze everyone around the big table in the kitchen, so much so the twins had to have a little table of their own. The orange juice jug took a pasting, Hazel had a job to keep pace with the demand for bacon, tomatoes, fried and scrambled egg and another loaf had be dug out of the freezer. Kasia, quiet, unbidden and with the coy smile a permanent fixture, managed to help smooth out the chaos remarkably well, and both Roberta and Andrew noticed.

At a suitable moment, Roberta, unbidden, asked the question. 'Kasia?'

The girl froze in her action of taking dirty plates towards the sink and, with a slight sideways upward movement of her head that later became a recognised Kasia trait, returned an open, uncomplicated smile. 'Yes, Miss Roberta?'

'Would you like to stay, now that you've met everyone and seen what happens around here?'

The group fell silent, embarrassingly so, and the girl looked around at each, finally catching Hazel's eye. Kasia knew it was this girl she was replacing, even possibly evicting her from a cherished role. Hazel nodded, almost imperceptibly. She'd be okay.

'Thank you, Miss Roberta. I would very much like to stay and work here. I feel, is it *cherished* feelings?' and her expression altered to include a mischievous, vaguely cheeky grin.

'Cherished is as good a phrase as any, Kasia. Not *quite* right, but it will do. I hope you'll find it more appropriate as time moves on. Don't drop those plates!'

Maeve, her irrepressibility having to find expression, clapped. 'Well done, now. Mind you, they'll likely work your fingers to the bone, but never mind that. They're decent people, so they are.' She pushed her chair back and stood up. 'I'll give you a hand with the washing up, then I must be on my way. I've taken too much of your hospitality, Roberta, Andrew. It's been great.'

June was surprised. 'But I thought you'd come back with me? End of the week, wasn't it?'

A phone conversation in a spare moment yesterday to her Irish clients after agreeing matters with Roberta had confirmed the details and she relished the thought of her return.

'Would have been a grand idea, now, but duty calls. I've a job, sad though it is at times. And a man who misses his cuddles. I'll take a train down to Luton later, if that's agreeable, Andrew?'

'If you must, Maeve. You'll need some more supplies, I think, Hazel?'

She looked up from sponging breakfast smeared faces. 'And do we need to collect any more of your things, Kasia?'

The world was spinning. Roberta caught Samantha's look and returned the smile. She eased up, and slid carefully off her stool; she found it was a better sit than in a chair,. 'Come and talk to me, Sam. We'll leave this lot to sort out their day. Andrew, dear, I'll catch up with you after your run into town. A later lunch, Hazel?'

Roberta led Samantha into the sitting room, away from the melee. The two women sat facing each other across the hearthrug, the fire newly lit by an ever-thoughtful Hazel.

'This is cosy.' Samantha had lost her unease over this near impossible-to-imagine scenario, and now reinforced by the brief moment of considered thought post-waking. 'Before you say anything, Roberta, please let me explain what's in my mind.' Did Roberta look nervous? 'I've not had an opportunity to properly offer my congratulations about number three,' and she nodded at Roberta's lap. 'We stopped at two. I'd had enough of waddling about.'

Roberta settled into her chair. 'It wasn't planned, Sam.'

Samantha raised her eyebrows. 'Oh?'

'He's quite a passionate man at times. We got carried away.'

'You're very frank, Roberta. Don't you feel this is strange, us together, discussing a common man?'

She shrugged. 'It was a reasonably amicable affair. You had your reasons to do what you did. I seem to have benefited. In retrospect, would you have changed things?'

Sam considered her reply. So many times had she asked herself just this question, and given herself different answers. Sometimes yes, sometimes no. Now she could see where her former husband had gone, what he'd achieved, how a number of people now depended on him and his relationship with this dark haired brown-eyed Italianate girl - woman - she had to be pleased for them. And both her grown-up children were the better for what had happened. Was she the one who'd lost out - another repetitive question. On balance, not really. Again, both June and Peter were well on the way towards a more fulfilled role in life, once their own relationships had been sorted. Certainly, Andrew was a different person. Her relationship with Donald she dismissed as a rebound affair not worth pursuing. She had to find a more meaningful partnership somewhere; the job would continue for as long as she wanted - or for which she retained the stamina.

'Hypothetical, Roberta. Don't let's go down that road. Suffice to say I bear no grudges. What I did, I did. I think I've made a difference to a lot of young disadvantaged lives. Re-invented myself. No, no grudges. You happy?'

Roberta nodded. 'I fell in love with a guy who's given me the world. Without him, and my much-missed mum, I'd have gone suicidal. And we wouldn't have discovered and -

using your phrase - reinvented a Hazel. She's the winner. And Peter,' she added reflectively. 'I should say I owe you, Sam. Can we stay friends? Good friends?'

'I'd like that. Can I come and stay again?'

'Of course you can. Anytime.' She reached out to drop another log on the fire and yelped.

'Aahhh! Oh, silly me,' and sagged back, putting a hand on her hipbone. 'Oh, Sam, sorry, forgive me. I should have known better.'

'What is it? Can I help?'

'Bits of me aren't as strong as they should be. You didn't have the problem when you carried Peter? Softened ligaments or something? I nearly passed out once. It's okay if I'm careful about moving. Put that log on, there's a dear.'

Alone in her single state, Andrea tossed and turned. She'd managed to drive home, maybe stupidly, having had far more to drink than was sane. She should have left her car at the Manor and called a taxi. Her red woollen dress lay discarded over the chair with a stain down the front of the bodice. Red wine, white wine, it made no difference. She'd not wear it again. He'd made it so very obvious she was no longer the beloved siren and that thought had kept her awake, as all the stupid thoughts went eddying around her brain, chased around like moths against a lampshade. What had gone wrong? Was it the new girl, Casey, Kassy, whatever her name was? Was it Roberta, keeping too close an eye on him? She rolled over once more and buried her face in the pillow. If only she could drift away, let him mourn her and then he'd know what he'd missed. Everything she'd dreamt about, yearned for, schemed over, let her femininity work for, her sex, and all now as though it had never happened. Yes, he'd said thanks at the end of the party, but so had Roberta. He'd told her how efficient she'd been, how inventive, how well organised, given her a peck on the cheek when what she'd hoped for was a deep, smoochy long lasting kiss as his hand slipped under the softness of her dress, a feel for her nakedness, fingers to run, to stroke and feel for her yearning. No, it hadn't happened.

Oh yes, then she'd made herself happen, merely to lessen the tension, and that in itself had been momentarily great, but nothing like what she'd have felt in the true old fashioned way, the proper get-up and go-for it. Which wouldn't have taken very long at all, not even outside, standing up against the barn wall in the dark as she'd planned.

Once more she rolled, onto her back and let nature take over. Was this all that she was going to have to expect in the future, regular sticky fingered self-indulgence? Not if she could help it, and in a sudden fit of resolve, flung off the bed and straight into the bathroom.

Her mother heard the shower go and glanced at the clock. Gone ten. Well, it had been a late evening - she'd hadn't heard her come in, and the last time she'd glanced at the red-numbered clock face, it was twenty past twelve, so sometime after that. So her girl wouldn't have seen the message - it was still on the table.

'Andrea!' she shouted up the stairs as soon as the shower stopped. 'There's a message for you. Best get a move on!'

Her girl, her one and only quirky, man-mad daughter, came slowly down the stairs, sweatered and jeaned. 'What's up, mum? What message?'

She pointed at the old envelope where she'd written it down in pencil. Good news and bad. The bad, sad bit was it would see her with an empty house, she'd be alone with her memories until whenever. The good bit, her lovely daughter would take a long overdue turning in her life.

The day rolled on. Hazel spent far too long in the filling station grocery shop, and they'd had to drive rapid miles down the A6 to take Maeve direct to the airport, fortunately Kasia's scant remaining belongings didn't take long to collect from the back street lodgings in Luton. Andrew had the girl sit in the front passenger seat on the way home, and glanced, surreptitiously, at her expression from time to time. Composed, intelligent, quick eyes, hands still, not fidgeting, an occasional smile when she did catch his look. What a happy way circumstances had landed her with them, unless there was some hidden vice, yet to be unearthed. Hazel chattered on but he scarce heard her, as his mind had drifted back to last night, to Andrea's pouting obvious dismay when he'd said no, he wouldn't take her outside. Too cold, his excuse, I'll keep you warm, her reply, and he'd guessed at her ploy. Well, though he loved her for what she was, he'd passed the point where he felt physical yearnings for her possession. Once, maybe. Not now. He hoped she was all right.

Back in time for the late lunch. Left-overs and stir-fry vegetables. The twins chattered on about their play time with Uncle Peter (Uncle?, asked Andrew, yes, said Roberta, and why not? They wouldn't understand 'brother', not with the age difference . . .) Then June took herself off for an hour's walk with her mother and Kasia familiarised herself with the washing machine. Domesticity, Manor Style.

TWENTY

A lain fretted, unusually for him, as he mentally admitted. On the cusp of something impossibly great, impatience came with the territory. He got up from behind the desk, stalked to the window to look unseeingly towards the winter sparsity of the landscaped shrubs and the lead grey stillness of the small lake. Another month and they would be in the thick of it, the heat, all the frenetic buzz and hustle and adrenaline tear and rush of full-scale production. And she would be there. The phone trilled, to generate a pulse jerk and a hoarse answering 'Perlain' , but it wasn't her, merely a simple request from the dining room staff, was he in for lunch. New Year 's Day didn't see many in the Studios so they'd be watching quantities. Yes, he'd be there, please make it as late as they could, yes, he hoped he'd have someone with him. He sat down, in her chair, spun it round. This was what he'd hoped for, and now it had happened. Like so many of these things, a minute's conversation, a chance comment, a chance to pass over the photo he'd kept in his wallet and then watching the lift of eyebrows, the nod of appreciation. And it had gone on from there, and she wouldn't know why he'd absented himself from the office during the festive - hah - season. You had to take the opportunity whenever it showed. Where was she, why hadn't she rung in? Tomorrow she'd have been in anyway, but the opportunity was now. Now. Not tomorrow, and the Bond phrase swung back in, tomorrow never comes.

'You enjoyed your trip to Ireland?'

They'd walked on down the road, a gentle saunter, a companionable undemanding stroll.

Her mother's attitude appeared to have softened since last night, and maybe it was the time she and Roberta had spent together this morning.

'Very much so, mum. And I'm looking forward to going back. Lovely people and a beautiful old house. It'll be a thrill to see it brought out of its slumber. Maybe you should come over. Sinead and Donald are very welcoming. I'm sure they'd love to meet you.'

Samantha gave a startled sideways glance at her daughter. 'Not another Donald!'

June laughed. 'I haven't met your Donald, but my guess he's chalk to the one I know's cheese. Think Maeve.'

'Ah. That girl's father?'

'The very one. Though Maeve's more Siobhán, her mum. Same colour hair, sort of.' They did another hundred yards in silence, then 'you've made peace with Roberta, mum?'

'Peace with myself, June. I take comfort in what you two have become and how your father has - changed.' The pause wasn't lost on June.

'Yes, he has. For the better. He's even cooled down over Andrea. And Kasia won't come under any pressure either, which is what I'd worried over. Maybe Mary's death brought things more into focus.' She sighed. 'Such a shame, not seeing her third grandchild.'

'Roberta's different.'

'You've noticed? Yes, she is. More reserved, quieter. Bound to have an effect, mum. And worrying about her ongoing pregnancy, with the dodgy hips. I'm glad we've found another girl.'

They reached the bend in the road and June stopped. 'Shall we go back?'

'If you like. What do you think about Peter's falling for Hazel?'

June smiled, a cheerful grin, and linked arms with her mother. 'She's lovely. And my theory, for what it's worth, is that she'd already seen dad as an ideal, so Peter's the next best thing. Better actually. They'll be okay, mum. She won't stand any nonsense, and I reckon Peter's seen more of what makes the world tick than many, hasn't he?'

Samantha nodded. 'So long as they're sensible. Keep an eye, June?'

'As far as I'm able, I will. And you find yourself a decent stand-in for dad. Don't lose his friendship, will you?'

'June, I could never do that. And now I've made my peace with Roberta, as you said, I'm a good deal happier. Things will work out. Home for a cup of tea?'

Andrea's mother handed her the scrappy envelope with the scrawled message. *'Ring me soonest, I need you - something's come up, Alain.'*

'He also sent his love, An. Give her my love, he said before he rang off. I'd say he sounded excited. Will you ring him?'

'Yes. Yes, I will,' and she added an aside she'd never ever have thought possible. 'Andrew's dumped me.'

Her mother blinked. 'Dumped? But he never . . . ' then realised. Her girl had been pursuing this earlier flame far longer than was realistic, let alone practical. 'I'd say sense prevails, my girl. You and he? Not a chance while he has a decent wife and kids. If he's as good as told you to leave him alone, then you just accept it. Otherwise you'll get your fingers burnt. Think yourself lucky you didn't get yourself pregnant by him, An.'

But yes, if she'd had her way last night, that's just what she'd have hoped for. But now? She blushed. 'Sorry, mum.'

'I should think so! What ever would your father have said? Now ring this Alain. It sounded important.'

Kasia hefted her much-travelled large holdall out of the Volvo's capacious back and dumped it on the gravel, then reached in for the pile of clothes wrapped up in the vintage faux-fur edged coat. Her new employer, Andrew, he with the crinkled-eye smile, shut the car's rear door and picked up the holdall.

'Come. Kasia, I do hope you'll like working here, with us. We're a happy bunch, in the main, if a little scatterbrained at times. You okay with that lot?'

She couldn't help her smile. Scatterbrained? *postrzelony* the nearest equivalent. How happy was that? Scarcely managing to see her toes under the mass of clothes clutched firmly in hand-joined arms, she followed him across the gravel.

Upstairs, a careful tread at a time, and into the room where she'd slept last night.

'But this is your son's room, I think?'

Andrew placed the holdall carefully down by the window and relieved her of the bundle, laying the assorted dresses, coats, jeans onto the bed. 'He's moving into our cottage in the village, Kasia. That was decided before you came. If you can allow him to clear the wardrobe before you put this lot away?'

She stood still, hands by her sides. 'You are very kind people, I think. I hope I will give - satisfaction - in what I do. You will say?'

He nodded gravely at her earnest expression. 'We will say. Please feel 'at home', Kasia. You too must say if there is anything that concerns you. I am going to ask Hazel to tell you what needs to be done, if that's going to be all right with you?' How stilted that sounded; perhaps in a day or two they'd be easier with each other. He was conscious of how delightful a person she was, and how easy it would be to become overly familiar. Not in way to be construed as a sexual thing, more a 'happy family' touch, as he was with Hazel, but, now-a-days, the pleasantry of undemanding, un-assertive casual intimacy with no overtones of anything other than long-established human need to express care for each other had been savaged and ruined by this growing blight of political and social 'correctness'. Hah! Correctness!

'Kasia. *Katarzyna,*' and he watched her mischievous smile at his pronunciation, 'I think we're going to love you - sorry - like having you here.' His stumbled words became an embarrassment and he moved to the door. 'Come down to the kitchen when you've unpacked.'

'Mr Hailsworthy,' and she caught at his arm, 'please, do not feel concerned. I understand what you mean, and what you say. If I have - *concerns* - I will say, truly. You are all *good* people. Not like my last place. I will say, later. Thank you for your help.' She gestured at the pile. 'Too many clothes, I think,' and her dimpled smile was a delight, 'but then, I am girl,' and laughed, the light and different laugh that would be her trademark in the months ahead.

His office wall clock's second's hand appeared to have slowed down. It hadn't, but was a fair measure of his impatience that would shortly explode into action. He'd call her again, send the stand-by car for her, drag her here by a handful of that glorious golden hair. Anything to demonstrate his promise to put her in front of the lens. They'd asked for a preview tape and he'd sent one. Then when they'd asked where she'd trained he'd laughed and said '*in a Brewery*'.

He thumbed through the script outline again and immediately envisioned her. Then the phone rang and the vision clarified into sound. 'Andrea! Where the hell have you been? Get yourself into that matchbox on wheels and down here. With an overnight bag. We've a 'plane to catch. . . . No buts, no excuses, just do as you're told. Else I'll come and abduct you. . . . No, I'm not sure how long, it's only a screen test on location. . . . To hell with the office. Plenty more women to staff the phone. This is us, my girl. *Us!*'

She'd sounded surprised, and he grinned. She'd be even more surprised when she found out the role and who she'd be working with, let alone the location - and the money. Made, she was, provided she didn't screw up the screen test, and that unlikely. After, he'd take her for a drive along the Med's coast, park up; they'd go skinny dipping as a prelude, then the al fresco meal under the date palms, the evening at the casino and . . .

'Yes!' He punched at the air, shoved his chair back and strode out of the office, *en route* for the reception hall. Barely six months down the line and his intuition had been proved right. A discovery. His discovery. And his personal feelings in line. Lucky, he and her. They'd make it, together.

A far more muted evening, almost an anti-climax. Roberta had woken up to her responsibilities and held a logistics discussion with both Hazel and her newly appointed additional house-keeping resource. Kasia, as it turned out, had received training as a pastry chef before deciding to widen her horizons, or, she'd added with that now familiar dimpled grin, to get away from younger siblings. 'So I've had experience at managing younger ones. Perhaps not as young as yours, Mrs Hailsworthy.'

'Please, Kasia, you may call me 'Roberta' like everyone else. And my husband is 'Andrew'. Now, I don't want to be too formal about this, but normally, Hazel gets the children up and brings them down to breakfast. If, sorry, when, she moves into the cottage, then it will become your job. And until we find a suitable place in a nursery school, you'll have to keep an eye on them during the morning, and afternoons if I've too much to do in the Barn. Oh, yes, and I'll explain what it is we do tomorrow. Your evenings will be free once the twins are asleep, except when we say otherwise. You can drive?' So the girl's CV had said, but she needed reassurance.

Kasia nodded. 'I had a Polish certificate to drive, but I thought to have some lessons and took your United Kingdom driving test eight months ago. It is a 'clean' licence,' and the emphasis on the 'clean' was proudly said.

Hazel looked envious, as well she may. 'I've still to learn. I'm hoping Andrew will teach me, but the Volvo is ever so big.'

'Then we'll buy a small car for you both. Nothing swish, but large enough to take the children. Andrew!' she called across the room to where he'd got his head in a book. He didn't read all that much, but when he found something to his liking, it was difficult to tear him away.

'Eh? What?' He put the book upside down on the floor alongside him and stood up to stretch. 'Sorry, I didn't hear. What were you on about?'

'A car for the girls, my love. Kasia can drive and we need something for Hazel to learn in, you won't want her putting the Volvo at risk.'

Coming across the room, he put hands on the back of their chairs. 'True. So what did you drive in your last place, Kasia?'

'I think it was what you call 'a heap,' she replied, and her little laugh said it all.

'Then we have a choice. We'll go shopping tomorrow.' He glanced at the clock. 'Time we all gave it away. Earlier night, make up for yesterday. Hope the others won't be too long.'

'Shouldn't think so. Sam's going back tomorrow?'

'So she says. Been good to have her here, hasn't it?'

Roberta merely nodded. Not for these two girls to be party to her thoughts - they'd keep until later. 'Right, you two. Bed. I'll check on the twins. Breakfast at eight, working day tomorrow.'

Samantha and her two adult children had gone down into the village to inspect Peter's new abode.

'You're very lucky, Peter,' said an envious June as he unlocked the door. 'With your own place and no mortgage to pay. I hope you realise how lucky.'

'I'm sure he does, June,' Samantha's comment as she ducked into the low-ceilinged front room. 'Except he'll have to remember to keep his head down.'

Peter grinned. 'I'll remember. I've thumped it already. Don't forget I'm going to pay a rent.' He moved a pile of magazines off a chair so his mother could sit down. 'It still needs to be cleared of Mary's things. That's the sad bit. It's still very much hers.'

Samantha sank into the armchair. 'I suppose it is.' She looked around, at the two landscape paintings - prints - and the ornaments on the mantelshelf and on top of the old oak sideboard. 'A life's recollections, memories, all bound up in a few objects. We all do it. Preserve keepsakes, I mean. What we are.' She lent her head onto the chair back. 'I left most of mine with your father when I quit the family home. Wonder what he did with them?'

June, still standing, looked down on her mother. 'You didn't seem much bothered, mum. I think most things got boxed up, and they're in the Manor's attics. The furniture went with the house in the main, as I understand.' She peered around. 'Have you looked into drawers and cupboards, Peter?'

'Nope, not yet. When I got back last night I was pretty well bushed. Just crashed out.' He looked round the kitchen. 'Doesn't seem right, to start moving things around. Not until Roberta gives me the say-so,' and came back into the small front room. 'Did Mary realise what would happen to her things, I wonder? I mean, was there a will?'

'Dunno.'

'That's a very cryptic answer, daughter mine. But there should be a will, Peter's right. Best ask. Let's finish the tour of inspection, then get back for a meal. I've actually worked up my appetite.' Sam heaved up out of the chair and followed her son and daughter up the short flight of stairs.

Mary's former bedroom was, as anticipated, neat, clean and very straight forward. A four foot six bed, a bedside cabinet, a comfy armchair, a chest, the built in wardrobe over the stairwell, two prints on the wall, one of the Thames and Tower Bridge, the other a landscape. Four ornaments, two each side of the simple clock. Peter had slept in the adjoining room, where the single bed was sandwiched between the same style cabinet and a straight-backed chair.

June had poked her nose into the miniscule bathroom. 'No shower. And the bath's a little on the short side. Still, it's not too old fashioned. Has Hazel been here yet?'

'I think so, but weeks and weeks ago.' He bounced on the double bed. 'Mattress seems okay.'

Samantha opened the wardrobe door, to see the dozen or so dresses and skirts. 'Oh, how sad. And these shoes.' She picked a pair up. 'Good quality. Not my size,' and dropped them back. 'I'd hate anyone having to do this for me.' She shivered. 'Let's go. Before I get too maudlin. Just so sad,' she repeated, re-fastening the doors.

As they walked back up the road, June reached for Peter's hand. Their mother strode on, seemingly unaware, lost in a reverie.

'She wants to stay at my house, Peter. Donald's obviously past history. Is that a good thing, do you think?'

He glanced sideways at his sister and then forward at his mother, twenty paces in front.

209

'I didn't think Donald would last, so that's no surprise. Staying at your place is a reasonable idea, if you're happy, so long as William doesn't suddenly come home. She needs another project abroad, somewhere not too demanding. Or . . . ' and he stopped abruptly. 'I've had an idea. I'll speak to Richard. No, I won't explain, not at the moment,' seeing his sister's puzzled look. 'Leave it with me, sis,' and quickened his pace. 'Come on, else they'll be wondering where we are.'

Andrea shot into her car parking space, grabbed her holdall and her favourite coat, locked the car, suddenly thought, unlocked it again and reached for her dress shoes. Thus burdened, she struggled towards the reception door, only to have it open miraculously in front her. Alain, smiling all over that travel-lined face of his.

'What's all this panic, then? You've had my mum frantic.' She dumped the bag down as he relieved her of her coat and shoes.

'Spain, in a word. You and me. Six o'clock out of Heathrow. Studio driver'll take us. Come up to the office and I'll explain.' He picked up her bag, slung the coat over and handed her the shoes. 'From these I guess you've come prepared?'

'Guess - that's what I had to do! No prior warning, drop things and run, what would you have done if I'd gone away?'

'Found you,' he replied abruptly as the lift whirred to a stop. 'This, my girl, is your lucky break. I told you I'd show your pics around.' The doors opened and he ushered her in. 'Screen test on location to get the colouration right. Tomorrow at noon. If it works, and there's no reason in my view why it shouldn't, then it's the big screen.' The bag thumped onto the lift floor, the coat on top. And as the lift came to its gliding halt on the first floor, she discovered just how nice it was to have a film producer boss who knew how to treat a girl, yessss sirrr, even if she had a pair of heels clutched in a wildly waving arm as the other went round his neck. Andrew's indolent lack of interest didn't seem to matter any more.

TWENTY ONE

'You're sure you have everything?'

June nodded. 'I think so.' She hefted the laptop in its padded bag. 'Thank Roberta so much for this.' The boarding lights were up. 'I'll probably spend half a day in Waterford and get some new clothes. I expect they have Sales over there like we do. Give you a call as soon as I'm back. Keep my step-mum in good order, won't you?'

Andrew grinned at her. 'Think I won't? Though I'm glad we've got an extra pair of hands.' Then, as their eyes met, he leant forward and kissed her, cheek on cheek. 'Keep yourself in good order too, darling daughter. I'll miss you.'

Her head dropped, and she had to wipe her eyes. 'I'll miss you too, dad. And Abby and Chris. And the others,' and she turned and walked towards the barrier.

He watched her go, head high, straight back, positive, confident, lovely; and wiped his own eyes. When would she be back? There was a intuitive feeling she was heading towards her own private benchmark, her destiny. At least she was very much her own person now, thanks to his Roberta and the comfortable ambiance of the Manor.

Once he'd sorted the accumulation of e-mails, Peter spent an hour with Angie, his right hand girl.

'Good Christmas?'

'Yep. And not too drunk neither. You?'

'Very much a family affair. Bit on the sombre side,' and he explained.

'Oh, poor old you. Did you know her?'

'Briefly. Very much my step mum's support line. Rather an intriguing history - I'll tell you sometime. Now, what's the most important project?' and focusing onto the top-most need, they began to put a list of candidates together. This was the part of the job he most enjoyed, matching personalities to requirements, looking forward to the subsequent reports and how well his assessments had worked. Volunteers became personally identifiable characters.

Lunchtime came, and conversation returned to matters closer to home. Angie eyed him across the canteen table. 'You seem less edgy, Peter. Settled in, have you?'

'Yes, I think I have. Working in the Power House is very satisfying, as I think you know.'

She held her coffee mug in both hands and slurped before nodding. 'My old man wants me to shift into his empire, but I turned him down. I might have gone though, if you hadn't turned up.'

'Angie! Why's that?'

''Cos you know what you're doing, pleasant with it, don't ogle me bra and give a girl a nice smile. Got a girlfriend, have you?'

Leading question, he thought, and actually her bra-line was well worth an ogle. 'I have, Angie. My step-mum's au pair. Name's Hazel.'

'Lucky girl.' Her questioning look begged an answer he wasn't going to give, and changed the subject.

'You know my mum. She and I were in Romania?'

'And did a good job, as I understand. So?'

'She's at a loose end, but the system won't want to send her out again for a while. I reckon she'll get bored - and get all introvert. I had an idea.'

Angie drained her mug. 'And?'

'She'd be good at running a home. You know, derelict kids in transit. Don't know of anything?'

'I don't. You'll have to ask Richard.'

'What I thought. Oh, and your cleavage is great.' He ducked as she aimed a swipe at him.

'I'll wear a roll top sweater tomorra!', but her open grin removed the sting. She was okay.

He caught Susan, Richard's secretary, as she went on some errand down the corridor and begged audience. 'Personal, really, 'bout me mum?'

'See what I can do,' she said, and within twenty minutes, he got a call.

After the usual post-Christmas pleasantries, he explained to the boss. 'She came to the Manor after Christmas, a brave thing really, but got on well with Roberta after all this time. But the bloke she's shacked up with ain't a patch on dad and it shows, how she misses him. Can't be helped now, of course, she knows that and I reckon she's come to terms with it, but she needs a challenge. I had an idea she ought to run a home, or hostel, or something, unless we can get her out into theatre again.'

Richard pitched his fingers together and ran his face across them. 'Ummm,' he said, and smiled a wry smile. 'First she pleads your case; now you're pleading hers. At least you look after each other. I reckon,' and he paused, 'she could do well in social services. Better than some I know. She's got the right attitude. Heart in the right place and all that, not a textbook career warrior like one or two I could name. Be as shame to lose her off the strength though. Leave it with me, Peter. And thanks,' adding, as Peter rose from the chair, 'as *a by the way*', I've no regrets about taking you on. Good approach. Angie speaks highly of you too, and that's no mean achievement. She was pretty scathing about the last guy.'

'Thanks,' was all Peter could think of saying in turn. Compliments didn't sit well on his shoulders. He gave a sort of half wave as he went out of the office. Good approach?

Mmm. Thanks, mum. And dad. And Hazel. Thinking of her added a smile to his face as he got back behind his desk.

'So you managed an audience?' asked Angie. 'Did it work?'

'I hope it might. He's going to have a think.' Peter reached for his next file and grinned. Her untidy blouse had slipped, revealingly so. 'A roll top sweater, Angie, and I'll ask for a new assistant. Got to have something to brighten the day!'

She smirked, breathed in and brought her shoulders back. 'That better?' and they both laughed. A fine working understanding, that was what it was all about, and his spirits lifted. The Power House. What they were good at. Helping the less fortunate. Brilliant job.

The plane touched down with a slight lurch and the strange feeling of de-acceleration. Wheels that screamed weren't necessarily a sign of a bad landing, merely of a very dry surface. Ten minutes and they were in the jostle to reach the access tunnel, hands linked.

Alain's squeeze brought her glance round to his. 'Enjoy the flight, Andrea?'

Having explained that this was her very first flight, and understandably had shown her nervousness, he'd been solicitous in the extreme, and not at all arrogant. The whole experience had been mind-boggling, from the moment he'd soundly kissed her in the lift, to the exquisite buffet style lunch, and the walk round the back lots as he'd explained what was in store. Then him showing her the script laid out on his desk while his hand explored from her skirt band upwards, massaging her spine, her shoulder blades. Finally, unable to stop themselves, buttons had gone, then straps, and she was back to that first night at Andrew's place when she had but hadn't. Only this time she had, and it was as though a curtain of mist had lifted. Clarity, pure crystal clarity, and inwardly she laughed at her thought of an executive desk being a casting couch. Tonight, he'd said, it's the best hotel in town, and her spine tingled as they walked across still-warm tarmac into the reddening sky of a Mediterranean dusk. The Manor was a world away. *This would be her new life,* so it was a good few hours after a successful screen test the following day when she'd thought to ring and dutifully thank Roberta and Andrew, perhaps a trifle spitefully, for how they'd pushed her into the limelight.

The two Manor house girls were having an exhausting morning. Now that the house guests had all gone and, as Hazel said, life was returning to normal, they'd stripped beds, collected towels and behaved like a couple of hotel chamber maids. Down in the little utility room behind the kitchen, the washing machine was doing its thing. Hazel lent back on the dryer and folded her arms, eyeing Kasia in her newly acquired pinafore style apron.

'So what - where - were you before, Kasia?'

The girl, standing straight and relaxed, watched the big washer rock about on its feet. 'My last position you are asking about?'

'Hmm mmm.'

Kasia gave Hazel an old-fashioned look, as if to suggest it wasn't what she wanted to discuss. Then she gave that characteristic little shrug. 'Large family. Impolite kids. Impatient mother. And the man, he had a different thought of what an au pair should do.' Her eyes took on a distant look, introspective. 'Because I am blonde, am a Polish girl, he think I am, what is said, a 'loose' girl. Not so. I have morals, standards, and I expect *respect.* Your Mr Andrew, he has respect?'

'Kasia, I don't quite know what to tell you, other than I am so very, *very,* lucky to have found a home here, so I won't have anything said against him; please understand that. But

216

he is who he is, enjoys having us women around him, flirts maybe, and . . .' What else could she say, knowing something, though probably not all, of his relationship with her predecessor in the office. She'd seen her, leaning up against him on party night, her beseeching look, sex oozing out of every pore. But something had gone wrong, for Andrea's demeanour later on hadn't suggested she'd been successful in whatever had been her idea. Serve her right.

The Polish girl was poised, elegant and still curious. 'Yes?'

Hazel shrugged. 'He's a man, Kasia. A lovely, caring man who adores his wife. And he loves me too, I know that. And I love him too.'

'*Love him?*'

'Yes. They - he and Roberta - have taken me into their home as a daughter, Kasia. They didn't have to, but they did. So never, *never,* think he'll harm you, in any way. You'll be okay here, I promise you. Any worries, you say.'

'But his other woman, June and Peter's mother - this Samantha?'

'She left him, Kasia. Sort of. Their marriage drifted apart, from what I gather. Then Roberta fell off her horse in front of him, so he picked her up, and *the rest* - we have this English expression - as we say, *is history.*'

'Ah, so.' Kasia's bewitching smile appeared. 'Then I flirt with him so I become daughter too?'

'You dare!'

'Hah! This Manor, it is an interesting place.' The washing machine had run its cycle and stopped rattling. Kasia reached down to open the door. 'I think I will enjoy my stay here. And those two little people are a challenge.'

'They are that. And another one to come around June time. You'll stay?'

'I stay. And flirt,' and laughed, not meaning it, as she reached in for the newly washed sheets.

❧

Roberta looked up from her book. She was doing a lot of reading, with the necessity to keep her feet up for far longer than she was used to.

'She got off okay?'

'I left her at the barrier. I don't like those places. An inhumane way to travel.'

'And very un-green.'

He chuckled. 'Quicker,' and changed the subject. Losing June back to Ireland after upsetting Andrea and seeing Sam off to an uncertain immediate future meant he was feeling emotionally sore. 'The other girls?'

'Being very domesticated. You think we'll be pleased with our new Polish girl? Something upset her at her last place. Gives me the impression she's slightly nervous.'

'She'll get used to us. Hazel likes her, which is the main thing. Sam also liked her.'

'Ah. Sam.' Roberta dropped the bookmark into place, closed the book and placed it on the little table. 'She's not the happiest bunny, is she? Any feelings, my love, or shouldn't I ask?'

He sat down opposite. 'Difficult. There's a fair few angles to this, R.' Legs crossed, he leant back and contemplated the ceiling. 'Reassuringly, we parted friends. As you did. And we've all agreed she can come and visit again, so it's been a useful reunion in that respect. My main worry is whether breaking up with the Donald guy will upset her more than she realises. Not a girl who can survive without some t.l.c. '

'Ha!' Roberta gave a tiny cough. 'Then you had something in common! No yen to fill the gap?' She moved on. 'And Andrea? Did she leave in a huff? Certainly didn't look too happy towards the end of the party.'

He shook his head. 'My darling Roberta. There's been so much change these last couple of months, we've all matured. You've steadied down, I've been very much concerned about the next stage and fooling about with Andrea isn't what I want to do. Okay, I brought her back into the frame, thinking I needed to tell her personally about your mum, then you invited her to the dinner, then the party. She must have thought she was back in favour.' The soft warmth of her under the red dress and the depth of those eyes, the pressure of her thighs against his feel for her had been an intoxication. And their history. He'd seen her go, stiff and hurt, and the pain of that parting was still with him. 'I hurt her, Roberta.'

Brown eyes caught him. A small, sorrowful shake of her dense gloss dark hair. 'Oh, my love, I'm so sorry.'

'Had to happen. Otherwise I'd have hurt you and that I will never, ever do. Not if I can avoid it.' He'd made his final choice, and Andrea had gone. He still loved her, for what she'd been, what she was. Who she was. But no longer in the carnal way of the past. 'I'll ring her, see if I can gauge her mood. If you don't mind?'

Roberta shook her head again. 'Darling, the last thing I'd want is to lose her friendship, for either of us.' A smile broke out, and a tiny chuckle. 'You talked of benchmarks. I reckon she's one. You measure your passion for me against hers. So if she's no longer accessible as a yardstick, where do we go next?'

His reaction, which slightly alarmed her, was to get up from his chair and advance, hands outstretched, reaching for hers. Then she was pulled, firmly yet gently, into his arms, and . . .

The door opened. 'Oh, I'm sorry,' and Hazel backed out, grinning. Just as well she'd gone to see what they wanted for lunch, not Kasia. Then, having given them a minute, tapped on the door and tried again.

Like two errant teenagers caught by strict parents, Roberta and Andrew stood side by side in slight disarray.

'Yes?'

Knowing she now had pink embarrassed cheeks, Hazel did her best. 'Kasia's doing well with the twins. I'd like to prepare lunch. Wondered if there was anything you'd like in particular?'

'Hazel, whatever you feel like.' Roberta flung her hair back and smoothed her sweater out. 'I'm sure it'll be appreciated. Then after lunch, I'll show Kasia what we do in the Barn. Can you and Andrew take the twins for a decent walk this afternoon? It looks dry enough. And tomorrow, we'll spend some time sorting the cottage?' Her way of regaining her equanimity, organising. Having her instincts woken up before lunch was lovely, but embarrassing; on another earlier occasion they'd have taken themselves upstairs. Not any more. Sad, but a function of their maturity. At least she'd not have to worry about the competition anymore.

Donald was waiting for her, tweed jacket, cords, well polished brogues, every inch the Irish gentleman. June handed over her holdall but kept tight grip of the padded laptop bag. Precious.

'Sure and it's a delight to see the bright young lass again. Good flight?'

She reached up and pecked a slightly bristly cheek, scenting the masculinity and the hint of Brut, or something. 'Good to be back in Ireland. Yes, good flight. How's Siobhán?'

'She's grand. Looking forward to your visit. As we all are. Maeve speaks well of her stay at Roberta's Manor. Grand party ye had.'

'You heard about the party?'

'Nothing will escape Maeve's attention like a party. She's a wild thing, now, when it comes to a knees-up. Pity ye hadn't more men about the place.' Together they walked down the long wide corridor towards the exit. 'The car's over there,' and he pointed across to the Jaguar. 'How are your folk?'

'Fine, thanks. Well, Roberta's rather subdued, but only to

be expected. We had a knock with Mary's loss - Roberta's mum. Unexpected.'

'Aye, sad that.' He unlocked the car and June slid into the evocative depths of leather.

'Have you thought any more about what you want done?'

He glanced across. 'You'll be telling us, that I'm sure. But we have a wee surprise for ye. I'll say no more. Just you enjoy the ride, now,' and the big car slid graciously away.

Of course she enjoyed the ride. Donald drove efficiently and carefully out onto the new motorway and pushed the car to the steady sixty. In no time they were back onto the narrower roads of the county and she recognised the terrain. The Suir still flowed, the wooded skyline appeared, and the fleeting glimpse of the Mor House roof before they turned into the driveway. She relaxed; the uncanny feel that she was coming home yet it wasn't her home, merely where she'd felt at peace with herself for the first time for ages.

'A wee bite of a late lunch, or would ye rather the wait for Anita's offerings later?

Donald had her holdall from the back as she stepped down onto the gravel. The House's impressive frontage so reminded her of Roberta's place, yet she knew it wasn't the same.

'Maybe a sandwich or something to tide me over?' She saw his smile and wondered.

'Come and let's see what can be done. Siobhán's awaiting ye.' He led the way, dropping her bag at the foot of the stairs in passing.

The hallway hadn't changed. The kitchen passage hadn't changed. But the kitchen! From the tattered homeliness and ancient echoes had sprung a beautiful renovation, in cream and golden brown, new stone tiled floor, a massive centre workstation with slung lights above a solid slab of granite. The Aga was the same, the settee recovered, but new stools and a set of new prints on the plain lighter cream walls. It gleamed, amazed her, though with no suggestion it was done with anything other than care for the *ambiance*. Siobhán stood, back to the Aga, hands on the rail behind her, with a smile she couldn't disguise before advancing; those hands now outspread in welcome.

'June, my dearest girl, welcome back. Tis lovely to have you back under the Mor House roof.' She offered cheeks to kiss and an arm to hug her tight before holding her back at arm's length, searching for the reaction she knew would come.

June's swivelled gaze took it all in, amazed, not only at the effective way the renovation had been done to maintain the right feel, but the speed! In Ireland? She'd only been away, what, less than three weeks?

'I'm stunned! On this evidence, you don't need me. Who did this for you?'

Donald's quiet satisfaction was evident. 'Declan. Remember I said I'd get the man in? Gave him a challenge. Told him all about this wee slip of an English girl who'd knock spots off his eye for a decent bit of decoration. That she'd not take him on as contractor unless he could demonstrate his ability. So what d'you think, eh, lass?'

Released from Siobhán's clasp, she wandered round the centre block, feeling the surface, opened a couple of cupboard doors, peered up at the little spotlights, and prodded the settee's arms.

'Amazing! What does Anita think to all this?'

Siobhán's face dimpled into her smile. 'She helped. After all, she has to work in it. So you think it works?'

'Oh, it works. Wait 'till I tell Roberta. To get a man to do all this within a couple of weeks! Amazing,' she repeated, and flopped down on the settee. Still comfortable and cosy, but the new fabric gave it such a lovely pleasant touch.

'So we can get the man in to do the rest?' Siobhán joined her, alongside.

'If you're happy and his price is right, then how can I argue otherwise? Who is he, anyway?'

'Maeve's partner's brother. And the two of them work together. Declan's the brains and the tidy man; Fergal, Maeve's man, is the energetic one, once he's wound up and not after a night at the jars. They'll be up in the morning to have a wee peek at ye.' Donald had taken Siobhán's place in front of the Aga. 'Now, a sandwich, did you say? Sure ye'll not have something more?'

Roberta honoured her promise, and took a curious Kasia across the yard to show her the Barn.

She could tell the girl was intrigued, and fairly sure she'd also be appreciative of what they did. Their new au-pair seemed to be that sort of girl, intelligent, an active mind and ready to absorb anything of interest. And her two children had taken to her; their judgement was nigh on impeccable so it looked as though Andrew's intuitive choice had been a good one.

She unlocked the door, stood aside and let the girl enter.

A moment's hesitation, a gaze around, and 'wspanialy - wonderful,' she added in English. Lapsing into Polish was something Roberta realised was akin to a compliment. 'All these little spaces!' and she wandered from one to the other, occasionally touching fabric, the surface of pieces of furniture. 'So this is, what we say, mily pomieszcjenia - lovely rooms?'

'I change them from time to time. It allows my clients to visual what can be done in their own homes. From these ideas we can agree what needs to be done on an individual basis.' Seeing Kasia's brow crease in a slight frown, she tried again. 'My customers decide what they want from here,' and watched the forehead's furrows disappear.

'Ah, I understand! A demon-stration!'

Roberta grinned. Not quite what she'd say, but certainly demons were apt to appear from time to time. Well, gremlins, perhaps. She took the girl from one bay to another and pointed out the highlights and what she'd set out to achieve. It went down well, that was quite clear, and the hour she'd planned to spend soon went. Finally, she shepherded her out, locked the door, and they returned to the kitchen and a possible tea break.

It was during the companionable chat over mugs of tea and slices of chocolate cake that the phone went. Andrew and Hazel were still out with the children, so it was down to her, but, she thought, Kasia would need to answer the phone sometimes so now a good a time as any to start.

She nodded towards the little mobile, sitting in its holder on the far worktop. 'Kasia - you may answer that. Show me how?'

The blonde girl slid off her stool, reached for the phone, hesitated, pressed the right button, and answered.

'The Manor. Kasia speaking. How may I help you?'

Perfect. Roberta relaxed, and then watched as the girl's face took on the same puzzled expression she'd seen earlier.

'Please hold the line. Mr Hailsworthy is not available. I will ask Mrs Hailsworthy if she will talk with you.' Kasia put a hand over the phone's front. 'It is the girl Andrea. Calling from abroad. Wished to speak with your husband. Will you speak with her?'

Roberta held out her hand for the phone. Abroad? What, since the party night? 'Hi, Andrea. Where are you? *Spain?*' She couldn't keep the surprise out of her voice. 'What *are* you doing out there?'

The conversation didn't last long. Roberta handed the phone back to Kasia to replace on its pad. 'That's a turn up.' She didn't elaborate, but congratulated her new au pair on her approach.

'Well done, Kasia. That was excellent,' and knew this girl's help would be invaluable; more so now than before this call.

Later that evening, once they were alone, she told Andrew. 'We had a call from Andrea,' and watched his face.

224

Startled, he tried to maintain composure. Her departure on a sour note still rankled.

'And?'

'She's in Spain.'

'*Spain?*'

'On location, with Alain.'

He shrugged. Her job, he supposed. Lucky her, getting away from prospective chill mornings.

'She's starring. Well, in a minor role, but still in front of the camera. And, lover boy, she was quite frank. Embarrassingly so.'

'Oh?'

'Perhaps I shouldn't say, 'cos it may have been one girl to another, especially as we had something - sorry - *someone* - in common. She didn't mince her words. Maybe she had to pay for the call.'

His face was a picture. She took the plunge. 'Spent the night with Alain in the hotel. Said to say 'thankyou' for the opportunity to re-invent herself. That she'd never forget you - us - and that the red dress had been given to a charity shop.'

'Oh.'

She laughed. 'Oh, *Andrew!* If you could see your face! Your dolly bird has finally found another man. So what with Sam being straight about her way forward, Andrea now out of reach, and you're certainly toeing the line with our Kasia, I reckon I can relax and enjoy my pregnancy even more.' She nestled into him. 'And my hips seem to want to stay in place. Wouldn't you like to experiment just a little?' His fashionable expression came to mind again, so she added, 'see if I can come up to your benchmark standard?' as she carefully lifted her slip over her head.

TWENTY TWO

Of course she had to. It was the only thing to do, even if the rain clouds were low and ever so slightly threatening, but at least she was prepared. New hi-tech anorak over jeans, sweater, woolly socks, stout shoes, headscarf (she couldn't abide hats, they made her head sweat), little digital camera in her pocket, and off she went, following the well-remembered route across gravel, lawn, path, through the shrubs in their winter garb, and into the rose garden. Keela was still there, waiting with all the time in the world on her side, patient, a frozen enigma.

June stroked the little girl's hair again. She'd come back, as she'd promised, as, if the Irishism was to be believed, she'd been put under a spell so to do. *'Keela, my love, I'm here, and we'll see just what we can do.'*

She remembered all Siobhán's revelations. If true, deep under the triangular sectioned stones, centred before her, lay the remains of a girl's lover. *Cadhla's* lover. The portrait - deep burgundy dress, a bunch of yellow roses, auburn hair flung in a flowing tress over a left shoulder. What had happened to the girl after the couple had eloped? Had she, too, become victim of mischance, so was lying, a mouldered forgotten ruination of a life, somewhere deep in the woods of this estate? Or had she found a new life in some other's arms? A girl whose affectations were so easily diverted that her original intended had committed a macabre suicide? If only she could discover the truth, allow this likeness to smile again. 'Silly girl,' she added aloud to her otherwise unspoken thoughts. A statue cannot change its appearance, other than

226

become weathered as this Keela certainly was, though that wistful, rather sad, expression might be all the better for some lichen removal.

The dull light eliminated shadows; the morning light just sufficient and in winter mode, the surrounding trees cast no shade. The photographs were fine; she took several from different angles. Then she heard a distant call, muffled but enough. *'Breakfast!'*

Lovely. No disrespect to Hazel's effective management of breakfasts at the Manor, but Donald had a knack and she doubted whether she'd be able to do justice to a lunch after the third slice of Aga toast. And this new kitchen, how had they managed it after all that was said about the Irish contractors' reputed indolence?

'Ah,' said Donald at her query. 'Ye've not met the Declan, now have ye?'

And where did this 'ye' come from? She'd not noticed it before. Perhaps he was slipping into more traditional colloquialisms. 'You say he's Maeve's Fergal's brother?'

'The same, and he'll be up afore lunch to give ye the once-over. Your reputation has travelled, my lass. Now, what have ye to show us?'

She'd brought the laptop down from her bedroom and left it plugged in. Opened and switched on, the screen sprung to life. Her photographs were all loaded, carefully edited.

'Good Lord!' Donald peered at the display. 'Is that our drawing room?'

She moved gentle fingers across the pad, as though stroking the textures of the room, sliding from one aspect to another, showing the design in all its complexity. The furniture, the carpet, the detail of dado and cornice, then the paintings, and *Cadhla* appeared.

Siobhán tittered. 'Bet she'd be amazed at all this. Being painted is one thing, having a statue carved another. But this. Captured in technology. You've worked hard on all this, June.'

'Not me. Roberta. She's a wizard at these programmes. You should see the things she can do on the computer back in the Barn. There was a young couple who came before Christmas, properly posh people; money didn't enter their heads. What they wanted, they had. Roberta showed them a few schemes on her screen and she had a cheque there and then. She couldn't have clinched the deal without it 'cos they were that sort - mesmerised by anything technophobic. Me, I much prefer to see and touch.' She moved into pictures of the next room at the shift of fingers. 'But this does save a lot of time, I do admit. I've got some samples for new materials and the specifications for the cleaning and floor treatments here,' and reached down for the files lodged in the back of the laptop bag. 'Then there's the schedules. We've also done some schemes for the sitting room, the corridors and the bedrooms.'

Donald put his arm round his wife. 'Siobhán, my lovely, we've surely made a good choice in this girl's boss. That Roberta knows what she's on with, and we're the winners here. Now all we want is Declan to say he can fix the place.'

'Is he the right man, I mean, has the qualifications for this? It's historical accuracy and some sort of finesse that's needed in here. Not a tear and shunt merchant.' June could hardly believe herself, saying these things. Six months ago and she'd have proverbially gone and hid in a corner rather than become involved. However, after time spent in her father's shadow and with the constant reassurance from Roberta, she'd changed. Watch out William, I'll be after getting shot of you once this project's done.

Her hosts - and clients - looked at each other, the smile and the twinkled eyes must have meant something, as Donald reassured her.

'Oh he's the man,' and as he spoke, they heard the back door slam and a tuneless whistle preceded the entry of a round featured fairly broad chap with a mop of brown curly hair.

'How y're doing?' He advanced into the kitchen, peered at the screen, caught June's eye and grinned, a wide, uncomplicated huge smile of a grin. 'Ye'll be the wonder girl, June.' He grabbed a hand and shook. ''Tis a lovely woman ye are. And what do think to Siobhán's new kitchen then? She said I'd never do it in time for ye, and so that's a challenge a man just has to meet, so he does. Fergal and me, now we're miracle workers when we have the right inspiration, eh, Donald?'

June, feeling rather faint in front of this excessively energetic apparition, was lost for words.

Donald rescued her. 'Declan, man, remember she's English, not one of your broad beamed, broad minded Kerry girls. And our guest.'

'Then it is my apologies you have.' He stood back a step and surveyed her. 'English, is it? Well, now, I'd take you for a fair maid out of Tralee any day. Not that Tralee's the place to aspire to nowadays. Well, now, you have the magic box?'

She had to chuckle. He'd brought a warmth with him that was difficult to deny and instinctively she responded. 'Sure and if 'tis the magic you're after I'll be the telling of it. Watch now,' and she rolled the control around to fly back through the catalogue of pictures, stopping at Cadhla. 'She's the one.'

Declan sobered. 'The *colleen* who spurned the O'Farrell's lad. I remember the tale. And what is your knowledge of this one, my lovely June?'

'Only what Siobhán's told me. How she ran off with a local lad and disappeared. And her statue's in the rose garden?'

'Ah, yes, the enigmatic Keela. Well, if you have that one's blessing, we'll not be far out of the way. So tell me, is this kitchen to your liking?' bringing the question back into focus.

'It's lovely. You must have worked hard, Declan.'

'Me and me brother. Sure and it's to prove we can do a good job. And you'll favour us with the rest of the work?'

June looked at her employers. True, she would have a say, and Roberta would look to her to make the right choice, but the Drivas couple had to pay the bill and agree with what was done. They had to live with it; she'd be able to walk away, hopefully with head held high and a reputation intact.

'Just have a look at the papers, Declan, and give us your opinion.' Donald lifted them off the table and handed them on. Declan sat down on a new stool and to June's surprise, took a pair of spectacles out of his top pocket. Silence, other than the burbling Aga and the rustle as papers were turned. Siobhán retreated to the little sofa and sat down.

Finally, he looked up. 'I don't see that there is anything that we cannot accomplish,' and his voice was on a far more serious level. 'I can see your worries, June. I'll have the Duchas people ring you. We did a job for them over Jervaulx way, and we got the million thanks. And if Fergus fu. . . . .,' he hesitated, grinned and rephrased his comment, 'messed things up, he'd have Maeve to answer to and she's no woman to cross. So what d'you say?'

'Subject to that reference, Declan, and June's employer's agreement, it's fine by us, eh, Siobhán?'

'It would be nice to keep it in the family, so to speak, Declan. You won't seek to overcharge us merely because of being sole contender?'

He looked pained. 'Sure and aren't you the suspicious one! Get another company in to quote and we'll do it for ten percent less, so we will, if it's any higher than what we say.'

'Fair enough.' Donald offered a hand, and that appeared to be that.

Not what she'd expected, but then, this wasn't England. 'Can I ring Roberta?' June asked.

'That you may. She - or your father - will want to know you're safe and sound. Then we'll have lunch. Declan, you'll stay?'

'Ah! Peter! Glad I caught you. Spare a minute? Got something I think might suit your mum.' Richard in his most suave *director* manner couldn't be denied, and Peter followed him into the office. 'Sit down, my boy, sit down. Had a coffee yet this morning? No? Then I'll rustle some up,' and he reached for the phone.

Peter sat and waited as Richard sorted papers, specs pulled down off his forehead. Would this be good news? His mum had phoned, on the erstwhile pretext of letting him know she'd got back to June's house and had, in her words, *'done a fair amount of de-lousing'*. He'd not responded, let her ramble on, and, as anticipated, had explained how she'd had words with her Donald.

'So you've given him the heave-ho, mum?' he'd asked, knowing it could be a rhetorical question. Yes, she'd responded, and added that her clothes and things were, as she spoke, on there way on to June's by carrier, in assorted cardboard boxes. He'd sympathised, but from her tone of voice, guessed there wasn't too much regret. 'He'd had his day,' was her comment, and the final observation on that subject was pithy and rather embarrassingly rude. How she'd changed!

The specs got pushed back. 'How is she?'

Peter came out of his reverie, back to the present. 'Fine, thanks. We had a good chat on the phone last night. She's staying at my sister's house.'

'Then the Kent thing didn't work?'

He shook his head and attempted to drift away from the personal side of things. 'She'll be better once there's something to do.'

Richard picked up one sheet of A4. 'New initiative,' he said and Peter got the steely look over the glasses. 'There's always a 'new initiative' that someone's dug out of a twenty-year old report and re-hashed to make it look like their fresh idea,' he commented in a scathing voice, but carried on. 'There's this idea of taking the brighter teenagers out of remand centres, giving them some outdoor vocational training and assessing their ability to work on VSO. Residential, two or three weeks at a go. Under strict supervision, of course, and has to be voluntary - but the incentives would be better accommodation, good reports, maybe even a fresh look at their conviction. I'm not convinced they'd be right for us to deploy, but maybe it's worth a try.'

'And you thought Samantha has a role?' In a professional way, she was always 'Sam', not 'mum'.

'She's tough, yet still got the caring streak. And she knows what we need, and a very good organiser. Leading a team. I'm not asking you, Peter, whether you think she's right or not; I'm saying it's a job she might be very good at and I'm going to ask her. Just so you know I've considered your request. Okay?'

The audience was at an end, but he managed to start one question. 'Where . . .' but Richard cut him off with a tight smile and one phrase. 'Just outside Bedford.'

Roberta began her working day in ebullient mood. She felt fine, her hips weren't troubling her half as much, she'd had a blissful time last night and new girl Kasia was a dream come true. Even Hazel agreed, over a confidential second mug of post breakfast coffee (was this much caffeine good for embryonic development, she'd wondered, and used the de-caff jar instead), that Kasia's presence was 'good news'. And now June had reported in and explained that the contractor Siobhán and Donald had organised seemed to be well aware of his responsibilities, the New Year had started well. Even Andrew was whistling, she could hear him away down the office corridor, no doubt catching up on accountancy clients before Hazel took possession of the computer. Abby and Chris had certainly latched on to their new nanny and were giving her a challenge. It wouldn't be long before the twin's vocabulary would rival her own, and high time she considered that nursery school. After Easter, she thought, before I get too large. Later today the new little car was due to arrive; they'd be back to a two car family again, even if the girls would have the benefit. How Andrew would get on with teaching Hazel to drive was another thing, but he'd got far more patience with the girl than she might have, even if it were sensible for her to climb into a small car.

The Barn greeted her with the usual lovely atmosphere. Maybe it was all her creation, her designs, but every time she opened the door came that feeling of pride. Not long now before their television series would be screened. What a change that had wrought! Hazel's restoration to sanity, Andrea's 'discovery', June's decision to accept the offer to join the firm. Then Peter coming home, falling for Hazel (lucky girl) and finally, even Samantha's restoration to the circle.

She walked to the end, into her little design office, settled down into the comfy chair and switched on the system. Time to do the detail for C & J's country retreat. How much was it they were paying her? Ten grand? And now she'd had a call from one of their cronies - talk about Jonesmanship. Just that one sad, never to be forgotten gap in her life. Dear Mary. And as she thought and moved to adjust the chair's tilt, she felt it. Another tiny little movement; immediately, she knew. Another girl. Another Mary; and then she couldn't prevent her tears.

At the end of the first full day, June was far more comfortable with this Declan. They'd gone over the whole house, almost inch by proverbial inch, specifications in hand, scribbling notes on margins, taking more photographs, taking ideas back to either Siobhán or Donald, until finally she was exhausted.

'Go home, Declan,' she'd said, around six o'clock and after the seventh or eighth mug of tea of the day. 'It's dark, cold and wet out there. And I'm bushed. Haven't you a wife to go home to and a lovely roaring fire?'

He'd laughed, encircled her waist with an arm and swung her round as though she was no more than fifty kilos. 'Did they not tell you? I live over the pub. No wife would put up with that, now. Still, I do spend some time with Fergal when he's not got Maeve warming the place. The pub's got the fire, though, and I swear 'tis a grand one, even if it gets through the turf like there's spare tons of it drying up on the bog side.'

When he'd gone, roaring off on an old motorcycle, she'd retreated to her room, washed, and changed before coming back down to find another of Anita's superb suppers laid out in the sitting room, and yes, the fire was lovely.

'Turf?' she'd queried, 'is that peat?'

Siobhán put down her crochet work. 'It is that. Turves have a wonderful scent to them in the burning. But 'tis hard work, the cutting and the turning, the stacking and the fetching. There's many who've abandoned the old peat digging in favour of the oil or the gas. We still have our hags above the timber - and an old friend who's a master at the cutting.' She looked hard at June, seeing the tired eyes and the drooping shoulders. 'You've had a long day. And Declan, has he been a help?'

Donald peered over the top of his paper. 'From what I could see - and hear - of the two you, I'd say you were having a fine old time.'

June had to agree; one reason why now she felt frayed around the edges was because they'd put life and soul into the discussions. 'He's been a great help, and yes, we got on very well. Another day or two and we'll have it all worked out. New Year, new house.'

Siobhán wondered. Wondered if putting the two youngsters - yes, youngsters, given she could give them both at least twenty years - together wasn't putting June's known problem relationship under strain, then did a mental shrug.

So what if they did produce the odd spark between them? Could only be fun, and heaven knows, perhaps they both needed it. Maybe Mor House and its protective spirit would be the making of them.

TWENTY THREE

The days went by. The New Year brought its changes, as Samantha found when she was summoned for an interview. The concept of becoming a supervisor at what she initially described as an 'up-market Borstal' taxed her imagination somewhat, so the first instinct was to turn the job offer down flat. However, the invitation to pay a visit to an establishment already considered as a 'step in the right direction' couldn't be ignored, not unless she was going to be seen as churlish. So she went and was surprised, both in what she discovered and in her instinctive reaction. And that reaction? To see how much better a job she could make of it; to rise to the challenge.

Three weeks later and she moved into the accommodation provided; let June have back the spare key to the now abandoned Essex house and began to re-build her social life, though careful to resist the temptation to include the Manor's residents until she could be confident she wouldn't intrude. Sensible as she was to Roberta's acceptance of their relative positions, she knew how too close an involvement might bring its own complications. Her former husband deserved his space, and she wouldn't wish to upset the status quo; however she might regret her stupidity in abandoning him. Maybe time would bring its own solution.

June meantime had seen the Mor House project under way and returned, albeit reluctantly, to the Manor and her role as deputy to Roberta. She'd left a verbal promise to return and check progress when the opportunity presented and given Declan a parting kiss.

'Come back soon,' he'd said, wrapping a muscular arm around and trapping her in the embrace. 'I'll be a' missing you now, my wee English colleen, so I will. You and I have unfinished business, d'ye hear?'

She'd mused on that comment more than once, the more so when the Christmas card she'd sent to William came back, unopened. The query when that happened was whether the total absence of feeling was a reflection on her or on an absentee husband. She took her concerns to her father.

Andrew felt for her. 'What can I say, June? That your mother and I were at fault, letting the wedding happen, even though we had concerns? Difficult, you know, 'cos you could have shut the door on us and we'd have lost a daughter.' He wrapped an arm round her as they stood, looking out of the sitting room window at a grey, damp day. 'And I would not have wished that. Bad enough when you reacted to Roberta.'

She nestled her head down on his shoulder. 'Sorry about that, dad.'

He gave her a little squeeze. 'Just so very pleased that we now have you here and part of the firm. And as far as William's concerned, may I suggest we get Marjorie to write to him, put him on notice?'

She jerked away and stared at him. 'Marjorie? Roberta's solicitor?'

'You can't avoid the inevitable, my lass. She's very good.'

Divorce. That very act she'd been so scathing about when her father had taken to Roberta. Well, if she was going to take her life forward . . . and if her father had suggested it, then so be it.

'Okay,' and changed the subject to try to push the thought of it all away. 'Kasia - will she stay on, do you think?' The Polish girl had fitted so smoothly into the Manor's way of life it would be difficult to imagine it without her.

Andrew recognised her ploy, and understood. Marjorie would be commissioned, the wheels would be put in motion and nothing more said. Kasia he wasn't sure about, for sometimes the girl looked spaced out, as if she was in another world.

'I'd like to think she will. You like her?'

'She works so well. Abby and Chris dote on her. She gets on well with Hazel.'

'That's the important bit, June.' Hazel spent most nights down at the cottage with Peter, which was fine in one way but concerning in another. 'Have you any thoughts about your brother's relationship with her?'

'Dad!' She pulled a face at him. 'Peter's a different guy. So's she - she loves keeping house for him. Don't knock it!'

'I'm not - just wondering . . .'

'Well don't,' she interrupted him. 'All in good time. Either it'll work or it won't. Remember *me*?'

The wry grin said it all. 'If she says anything . . .'

'I'll tell you - if I'm allowed. Now, I'd better get back to my job. Can't have the staff slacking.'

Roberta looked up from her table where she was engaged in an endless game of pushing fabric samples around. 'You look serious.'

June humped her shoulders. 'Dad's suggested that Marjorie sends William a letter. Telling him I'm suing for divorce.' She sat down in the lumpy chair in front of the desk. 'I suppose I needed a shove. The Christmas card coming back was the final straw. Stupid man.' She thought back to Ireland. 'When do you think I should check on what's going on at Mor House?'

Roberta's deep brown eyes caught June's own troubled ones. 'You want to go back, don't you? More than the job?'

'I'm sorry, Roberta.' The image of the garden, the little stone statuette, Siobhán's comment *you'll never leave* and

Declan's parting remark returned. 'Something draws me back. It's a magical place.'

'So it seems. I've had my own moments out there, remember.' She carefully stretched and flexed her back. 'If it wasn't for this one,' and she rubbed her waistband, 'I'd be out there with you. All your father's fault.'

'Yes. And no one else's, I hope! Does it worry you, the thought of giving birth again?'

A slow shake of her head. 'Not really. I'll be in good hands. It'll be another girl, I'm sure of it. Last one. One for mum,' and June saw the glistening tear. 'Oh, June!'

June slipped her hand across the desk and laid it over Roberta's. Nothing needed to be said; they had that feminine rapport.

January slipped away. June contained her impatience within a flurry of small jobs, a single room makeover, a holiday cottage, a distant medical practice deciding it needed a better waiting room ambiance and an odd one, an Old Folks' Home lounge. Roberta was still involved with the C&J project where expense was no object and the clients had changed their minds three times so far. She didn't work above four hours a day though, and began to feel tired after the early afternoon. Andrew fretted.

'You shouldn't be quite so involved, R. Can't June do more for you?'

Roberta shook her head. 'She's a busy girl in her own right, my love. And still has her mind elsewhere. I'll have to turn jobs away. I'm frightened about the telly programme now.'

'As I am too. Should we think about employing another pair of hands?'

'For the business? Probably more hassle than a help.' Then she thought, with a sudden ray of inspirational light. 'I'll have a word with an old mate of mine. Girl called Freddie. Used to do the odd thing for me in London, ages ago. We used to get on okay. Wonder what she's doing?' She rummaged in the bottom filing drawer of the two-drawer cabinet alongside the desk and produced a tatty red and black address book, rubbed at her waist to relieve the pressure. 'Bending over isn't a good idea.' She flicked the pages over. 'Freddie. Surname's Ransome,' and reached for the phone.

Andrew stopped the hand. 'Sure about this, R? I mean, it was only a comment.'

She gently released herself. 'And a sensible one. She can only say no.'

'Or yes. Strange name, Freddie,'

A smile back. 'Frederica. Tall, willowy, speaks posh. Wears odd clothes. Or used to. Not your taste, fortunately.' The ringing tone he could hear went on and on. 'Maybe she's moved,' then abruptly he heard the answering '*Hi there, this is Freddie's place. Say your piece.*' An answer machine.

'Hi Freddie. Roberta Smiley. Fancy calling me?' Roberta added the number and dropped the handset. 'Tea time. Time to put my feet up. Where are the twins?'

'Kasia's got them upstairs. I think June's with them as well. Shall we go?'

They walked, hand in hand, across the yard, the Barn securely locked behind them. The February dark was cold and shivery, the threat of snow ever present.

'Not a nice time of year.' Roberta felt the pressure of his fingers.

'No.'

'Spring'll soon be here.' She knew what he meant. April, then May. Her due date.

'I love you.' He turned her gently round as they reached the back door, held her face in both hands, cool hands, and kissed her. 'I want you to take the greatest care of yourself, R. You're the most precious thing in my life.'

She reached up and took his hands in her own, brought them down to her swelling belly.

'Thing, Andrew? Am I merely a *thing?*' and smiled a gentle smile. The warmth of her tummy; her gift to him, the fulfilment of their loving and the filling of the gap in her life left by her mum, here, within her. 'I'll take as much care as I possibly can, my love.'

⁂

Freddie returned her call, jumped at the chance of renewing her association with Smiley Designs, even if it was a short-term contract.

'Love to, darling,' she'd said. 'And so opportune. Thought I'd have to go on the game or something to make ends meet. Such a bore when the money runs out.'

Andrew had winced at Roberta's reporting of the conversation. 'She sounds frightfully Knightsbridge.'

Roberta laughed, relieved and hence light-hearted. 'Beneath that shocking frontage, my love, she's all gold and generous. And rather free with her favours as I recall, but she'll respect my territory, never fret.'

Within two weeks, Freddie was installed in the downstairs bedroom - Mary's old room - and as she took over the basic running of the day-to-day Andrew saw the difference in his wife. Less tired, more sparkle, she spent lots more time with the children when they weren't at the playgroup in the village and he blessed the day they'd made that instant decision to ask her to come. And June could see the benefit too, as she could concentrate on the quirky individual contracts she loved, let alone bringing the chance to escape back to Ireland that much closer.

He caught Freddie alone in the Barn one afternoon after the third week. 'Why didn't Roberta ask you to join us before, Freddie?' He loved the way she narrowed her eyes and wrinkled her nose. 'You've made a heck of a difference.'

'Have I, darling?' Everybody was a darling. 'So glad. Love being here.' She lifted a slender fingered hand and stroked his cheek. 'Especially when there's a gorgeous male to drool over. Don't worry,' she added, sensing his concern, 'I'm not about to ravish you. Far too dangerous.' Her smile was all invitation and longing. 'Unless . . .' and left the phrase hanging in the air.

He backed off, grinning at her. 'There was a time,' he replied.

'I can imagine. Lucky Roberta. Or not so lucky. Don't think I'd like three kids. Sorreee,' she added, seeing his frown. 'Your two are cute, but I'm glad I didn't hatch 'em.' She bent down to pick up a sweet paper a client's errant child had dropped and he was treated to the smooth expanse of bra-less bosom as her lacey blouse front opened. Returning upright she caught his eye. 'Tits wouldn't be the same afterwards.'

He turned away. Once there was a time, and his mind flicked back to Andrea. She was still in Spain as far as he knew, and out of reach. A chapter in life now ended. At the Barn door, he looked back to her. 'Don't stay out here too long, Freddie. Dedication to the job is fine, but I doubt any more clients'll come today. I've got to - like to -see Hazel before she goes home.'

How times had altered. Once it was just him and Roberta. Then Andrea, with Hazel in the background. Then June. They'd taken Kasia on, and now Freddie in her assorted long skirts hand made from fabric samples. And still the business grew, with the telly programme scheduled for early next month. Each step with its attendant pressures and concerns. His own accountancy business keeping him mentally active and out of the girls' hair. Two children, a third imminent. He stood for a moment, holding the outline of the Manor in his view, dark against a less dark sky. Not brooding, nor menacing, but a sturdy fortress encompassing all Roberta's desires. He'd defend them all. Not even a glimpse of Freddie's availability would tempt him. His benchmarks had changed.

Hazel was closing the system down, a quick tapping of keys, a push of the mouse and she swung round on her chair with an incautious flash of thigh as he opened the door. An infectious burst of a smile greeted him.

'Hi,' she said, and stood up, straightening her skirt. 'I've just finished. Was there something you wanted?'

He shook his head. 'Not specifically. Other than to ask how life was in the cottage. I miss you at breakfast - and supper. Kasia's all very well, but she's not the same.' How naïve was that comment? 'Sorry,' he added.

'Cottage life is fine, Andrew. I enjoy playing the housewife,' then unexpectedly, blushed. The wife bit was too obvious. 'Sometimes I think back and feel a bit sad. But then, nothing stays the same, as you said.'

They stood, looking at each other. He saw her on the Sheep's Head, that glorious day in Ireland; she saw him standing tall alongside Roberta at Mary's funeral. Nothing stayed static, but there had to be some stability. She was part of him, and always would be. Andrea had been, but now was another's - or at least, that was how he read her silence, her absence, and there was the nagging sense of loss.

'You're looking pensive.'

He clenched his lips, wondering why he'd dropped into maudlin mood. No reason, essentially, given the pressures had eased. Maybe that was it; the adrenalin rush had ebbed away and left a vacuum. He needed something, an urge to *do* something. He asked a silly question. 'When's Peter back?'

'Late, tonight. Office monthly meal out. I think they go for a Chinese. Saves me cooking.'

'Then stay and have supper with us.'

She closed her eyes, briefly, as if to consider, and nodded. 'Okay. I'd like that,' knowing Kasia, with that calm absorptive capacity of a well brought up Polish girl, had slipped into her domestic shoes without a tremor of a hiccup. Even the role of smoothing out overnight childish disasters into streamlined, clean-smelling offspring ready for Roberta's approval she'd taken in that same measured stride, so an extra for supper wouldn't faze her, and Hazel momentarily experienced a mixed sense of pride in her tuition and a sadness the role wasn't hers any longer. At least, not here.

They left the office together. In the bright lights of the kitchen, there was the warmth and the comfort of a well-ordered familiarity, with two children already at the table and a competent Kasia clearly in control. She looked up from her dexterous plate clearing and smiled, the open uncomplicated smile of a girl who knew exactly where she wanted to be.

'Supper in half an hour, Andrew,' she said. 'And Hazel is with us?' Intuitive accuracy.

'Yes.' He ruffled Abby's hair and she responded by grabbing his hand and holding it to her cheek. A sudden rush of love for these two brought an unexpected tear. Chris wouldn't be left out and reached out for another hand. A simplistic conversation ended as Roberta came in from her usual afternoon sojourn in the sitting room.

'Do I scent conviviality?' she asked, putting an arm round her husband. 'You all seem to be in happy mood. These two ready for bed?'

'Let me,' Hazel begged, 'so I can earn my supper. Give you a breather, Kasia.'

'Breather?' Kasia occasionally had to have idiomatic words and phrases explained.

'A small amount of free space or time, so you can catch your breath,' Andrew explained.

'Ah, yes. Thank you, Hazel. I think they will like the opportunity to play with their old friend. I will carry on with the supper. You will like my recipe, I hope.'

'Come along, kids. I'll race you upstairs,' and scarcely reached the door before the two were off their chairs and pushing past her in their eagerness to score points. 'Nighty night!' they chorused as they disappeared.

'No problem there. Hazel's still got the knack.' Andrew kept Roberta's arm pinned so he could slip his own around her. 'Where's June?'

'She went out quarter of an hour ago, Andrew.' Kasia grinned. 'For a *breather*. I think she took her mobile phone with her.'

'Ah. Talking to Ireland, I guess.'

'I think so,' Kasia replied as she took a heavy frying pan down, added a splash of olive oil and reached for the prepared bowl of chunky vegetables. 'A Polish stir -fry I do. This accept -table?'

'Anything you do is accept*able*, Kasia.' He let Roberta go and pulled out a chair. 'Are you happy here?' he asked, wondering if she'd take the opportunity to reveal the cause of her occasional introspective moods, given there were just the three of them in the kitchen.

Kasia shook the pan to toss the oil through the added vegetables. 'I am verree happy here. I hope I give you good feelings in what I do. And the children also.' She turned and stood facing them, hands by her side. She never slouched, never lent on the furniture. 'Please, I also hope to stay while the new child is born. This I would like *verree* much.'

As she spoke, Roberta noticed the misting eyes. 'Kasia, my dear girl, nothing would please me more. I - we - love having you work for - with - us. Are you sure your family do not miss you?'

'My family wish the best for me. I tell them, I think I am lucky to live with *nice* people.'

The hesitancy wasn't lost on Andrew. 'But there is something else, Kasia?' He saw the extra breath lift her breasts, charming girl. Her eyes dropped, her right foot sketched a circle on the tiles.

'I wish a husband to love me and give me charming children like the ones I care for here, before I become, I think you say, *wrinkled.*'

Roberta caught Andrew's eyes. She understood, perfectly.

'Dear girl, you've a year or two before you even need to worry. I'm sure there is a wonderful man out there. Don't be in a rush. I rushed and regretted it. Then another man crossed my path, and look at me. Ungainly and unsteady.' She grinned. 'Never rush. Take your time. Choose wisely.' Abruptly, she changed topic. Too much of this pontificating would bring out the emotions and that she didn't need. 'What seasoning will you use in that, Kasia?'

The moment had passed. At least they knew it wasn't anything else other than a desire to replicate what they all knew, that they had a way of life many another would envy. One to be guarded, as Andrew had already determined. The markers were in place.

TWENTY FOUR

June stopped half-way along the lane, dragged out her mobile phone and, leaning against the bole of an old horse-chestnut tree very near where Roberta had come such a significant cropper those years ago, rang the Mor House number in Ireland. Now Freddie was well entrenched, there was no reason why she shouldn't return. Cadhla's spirit beckoned and she yearned to discover the truth.

'Siobhán? It's June. How's things?'

The warmth in the reply, the lovely Irish lilt, was evident despite the antiquated phone; June could see the picture clear as clear, Siobhán leaning against the mellow woodwork of the stair rails, the mahogany table with its stains and light-damaged veneers, the ragged edges of the red and blue Kashmir rug, the smell of aged panelling. They hadn't got to change anything in the hallway yet, or were they still working in the drawing room? Declan would be making their lives a constant battle.

'June, my lovely girl, 'tis good to hear ye. We're grand, now. Real grand. Apart from keeping yon Declan firmly into the supervision and out of the kitchen. You'll be truly amazed, you truly will. When do we see ye back here? The man's pining for the sight of you, for sure.'

June laughed, she couldn't help it. A blackbird flew out of the hedge alongside, its scolding call echoing. She stirred the relict, bronzed, fragments of leaves around with a foot. 'Tell the man I'll have him re-do anything that isn't perfect. And he's to keep his eyes away from the Cadhla portrait.' She made up her mind. 'I'll come over on Saturday, provided there's a flight. I'll call you. Donald'll meet me?'

'That he will, or 'twill be myself. Should I let on, or would you spring the surprise?'

She laughed again, instantly happy in herself now the die was cast. 'I'll surprise him. Oh, it will be so good to be back. How's Maeve?'

'That girl? She's a constant mischief. Can I tell her?'

'If you wish. Will she ever be an honest woman?'

Siobhán's voice dropped a notch. 'Mebbe. Maybe too much the free spirit. Takes after the Keela girl. Come back, June. We'll take you out to the cottage. Then you'll really see our Ireland. Call us.'

June folded the phone and slid it back into her pocket. Ireland. Ireland, where her heart had taken root. Cottage? Oh, yes, away down the Borlinn valley. Her spine tingled. She couldn't wait.

Peter worked steadily through the possibles list. Though this was a tricky assignment, there was no shortage of prospective volunteers - indeed he'd fancy a go himself. Office bound was all very well, and he'd been at it for over three months now, but he could feel the itch. The buzz of travel into odd places, the sense of adventure and the kick of adrenaline when life became complicated, as it often did. He couldn't quite understand how mum Samantha had settled so well into her new role, but settled she had. He enjoyed the chats over the phone every week or so; keeping in touch like that was fine, but he wondered what she'd say if he owned up to becoming bored.

'Angie? Spare a moment?' His girl Friday as he called her lifted her head from the strange left-handed pose she had when she drafted reports before typing them into the system.

'Yep?' A very down-to-earth girl, stood no nonsense from anyone, he'd grown quite fond of her, in her weird tee shirts and scruffy denim skirts.

'How does this grab you?' He passed over the list.

She leant back on her chair and stuck her brown-stockinged legs with fashion-booted feet onto the desk and read his offering. A minute, two, and he waited.

'Hey! What's this?' The feet came off the desk and she sat bolt upright. 'You can't go - Richard would slay you!'

'Why not? Good experience - and it's only for a couple of months. You'd be okay on your own for a while - probably better, actually.'

'Hmmph.' She read the list again. 'That's dodgy. Too many females. Take her off - she came back last time to an abortion. He's okay. So's he. Don't know these two.' She flung it back at him. 'You can't be serious about this? Can you?' She knew him rather well now and once he'd made up his mind, stood firm, even obdurate. Moreover they got on well together and the idea of seeing an empty desk opposite for however long didn't appeal. She knew he'd got something serious going with a girl back home - lived with her - but she had a gut feeling it wasn't quite the same sweetness and light it once had been, so maybe such an absence might show them the way forward.

He got off his chair and stretched, picked up the list and made for the door. 'No time like the present. I'll see what Richard says.'

'On your head be it.' She returned to her scribbling, but her mind wasn't in it and she flung the pencil across the room. 'Bloody bloke!'

Half an hour later he was back, and from his smile she feared the worst. 'Well?'

'He said okay. Appreciated the point, agreed I'd keep the thing on the right lines, but added two provisos. One, you agree, and two, that I come back and don't stray again.'

She shrugged. She'd managed for a while before he came; she'd manage again. 'What's the girl friend going to say?'

'Hazel? She won't mind, I'm sure. Dad'll look after her. She's plenty to do anyway.'

'When does it kick off?'

'Ten days, flight out to Dar es Salaam. Trek from there. Should be fun.'

'Check your medical kit then. Don't want you back with malaria, or yellow fever. And avoid the women.'

'You care?'

'Yes Peter, I do.'

His father wasn't amused. *'Two whole months! Leaving Hazel on her own?'* He could tell he was concerned, but whether it was more for his sake or the girl's was doubtful.

'I needed a new challenge, dad. Staying behind a desk for three months gets boring. She won't mind, will she? I mean, it's not as if we're married or anything. And she's got you lot, her job and all that. See what we're like when I come back.'

'Have you told her?'

'Not yet. Thought I'd tell you first.'

'I think you're mad. And if Hazel becomes upset I won't be amused. You fall in love with a girl, you look after her.'

'Dad, if she loves me, she'll know it's what I do. Works both ways.'

'Hmmph. Well, go and explain. Don't be surprised if she cries.'

Cry she did. Thumped his chest, clung to him, sobbed and sobbed and he felt terrible, but he wouldn't give way. 'It's me, Hazel, it's what I do. Go and help where no one else will. If you were stuck in a desert with precious little food and scarce any water even if it was mucky, and had a clutch of kids dying of some disease or other, wouldn't you be grateful if some guy came along in a Landrover and tried to help?'

Then she saw, realised that there were those who cared. Like Peter's father who had cared enough to offer her a place in a full time family and to take her out of a situation where she could, heaven help her, eventually have become merely another wasted uncaringly pregnant girl, dependant on drugs and prostitution to pay for them.

'Sorry Peter.' She sniffed, and he pulled a clean handkerchief out of his pocket and wiped her eyes.

'Just because I'm taking this on doesn't mean I don't care for you too, but these guys out there need a helping hand. You could come out as well - but I don't think it's your scene. Not this one. We could try something else less desertey later on if you like.'

Under her tears she had to smile. 'Desertey? Whatever sort of a word is that?' Taking the handkerchief from him she blew her nose. 'After Roberta's had her baby. Then we'll see.' She disengaged herself from his comforting arms. 'When do you go?'

'Ten days time. And I'll keep in touch.'

'What, even out in the desert?'

'Satellite phones, love. Better than e-mails, though I'll do that when I can.'

Roberta saw what he'd done, and recognised the twin strands of being his own guy and one who shared his good fortune. 'You should be proud of him, Andrew,' she said later on that night as they prepared for bed. 'Chip off the old block.' She'd heard all about it from Hazel herself, and sympathised. *Men do these things*, she'd said, *because they need to prove who they are; don't worry about it - because if they come back to you it shows they care about you too.* And the girl had cried on her shoulder again, but more from relief than from a feeling of anger. *You've not been spurned*, she'd added, *far from it. You wait and see.*

They all seemed to be drifting away. Andrew ferried June down to the airport and held her tight before he let her go.

'Take care of yourself, daughter. Mind the Irish faeries don't bewitch you. Give us a ring. Give our regards to Siobhán and Donald. Take plenty of photos. You can e-mail them back, keep Roberta happy. Bye, my lovely girl.'

His throat caught as he watched her disappear through the security system and into the departure lounge. There was that strange feeling, that he wouldn't see her again for some while, and he'd miss her. He heaved a meaningful sigh and returned to the car. Andrea had gone, June had gone, Peter would be away before the end of the week. Thank heavens for Hazel. And Kasia. And, though she was a strange phenomena, Freddie.

Roberta, understandably, was in sombre mood. Kasia had taken the small car and gone out for the evening, something about which they were relatively relaxed, for she was never late and as a declared teetotal girl, as safe as any. Hazel was down in the cottage with Peter. Freddie had also gone out, goodness knows where. They were on their own, and retreated to the sitting room where the fire thoughtfully lit by Hazel earlier gave the room its nice homely feel.

Andrew drew the curtains and switched on the table lamp.

Roberta sat in the same chair. The chair where she'd sat all that long time ago.

'Get me a drink please, Andrew.'

He raised his eyebrows. 'You sure?' They both understood alcohol and pregnancy wasn't a sensible mix.

She nodded. 'Just this once. Brandy and soda.'

He poured the drinks; a clear sense of déjà vu, when it all came back, sweeping floods of poignant recall and a surge of emotion. Where they'd started, where she'd let her defences down, offered him her soul, her body, and he'd taken her, literally and figuratively. Taken a step into the dark that became light.

'Remember?' He passed her glass down.

'I remember. Always will, my love. Were we very naughty?'

'You were. Showed me your knickers.'

'You took them off.'

'You let me.'

She grinned. The imp was still in her. 'I'd do a reprise if I could. It was - great. You did things to me I'd longed for for ages.'

'Three times that evening, as I recall. Was the third time for luck?'

She took a sip and put the glass down. Luck didn't come into it. 'I'd never been *loved* before. Not as you loved me that night. Kiss me?'

He knelt down on the fireside rug, exactly as he had those years ago, leant forward and kissed her. Her bulging pregnancy forbade any further relapse into a significant action, their kiss sufficient.

'No regrets?'

She shook her head. The dark hair swirled, her amber flecked dark eyes sparkled. 'Never.

Andrew, my love, never leave me?'

He curled up at her feet. 'Never. I'd die first.'

'And so would I.'

Those words.

TWENTY FIVE

No worries this time round. Siobhán greeted her like a mother and in no time had her bundled into the Jaguar and on the road towards the Suir valley. Siobhán handled the old car with the same professional aplomb as her husband, even perhaps with a more appreciative touch. She'd smiled as June raised the query.

'Oh, I do get to drive the old girl from time to time. When he's got other things on his mind. And anyway, I told him I wanted to get you on your own,' and June was treated to a smiling sideways glance. 'Tell you about Declan.'

'Oh?'

'He's a great one for the ladies, that one. So I wondered whether perhaps I should give you the low-down before you two get mixed up together in what's going on at Mor. Of course you can make up your own mind, but I'd feel very conscience smitten if I hadn't explained.'

'Explained? Siobhán, I not sure I'm that attached to the man. He's good fun and certainly a great one to work with, but I've no specific feelings - he's not the reason I've longed to come back. The house, the ambiance, the history, the way you make me feel so at home, the garden - run down though it may be - and, naturally, the Cadhla story. Declan's just a pleasant man to work with, and good at what he does, or so we - Roberta and I - hope. That's the case, isn't it?'

June's earnestness calmed Siobhán's worries.

'Donald and I are well pleased with progress, June. Still a way to go - and the work doesn't carry on day after day.

Some times we don't see him or any of his staff for two or three days on the trot. We're in no specific hurry, for it would be better to take matters slowly, I think.'

'So long as it doesn't leave you in a mess. Roberta wouldn't be happy with the laid back approach, though. She likes to see her jobs completed smoothly, and to time. It's what she is.' She paused and thought as Siobhán took them through the next little village with its multi-coloured pastel painted houses. Perhaps she'd drive the conversation away from Declan. She'd make up her own mind about him, if she needed to. 'We've got another member on the team. A rather bohemian old friend of Roberta's from her London days. Wears home-made clothes most of the time, drives an old VW Beetle and lives in London, on her own, in an old coach-house alongside Regents Canal. Christened Frederica; we call her Freddie. Great fun. Good with the clients, too. Takes the strain off Roberta. She's not got long to go now.'

'Is she well?'

'I think so. My father is very much into looking after her.' Her gaze moved from windscreen view to the sideways vista opening up of the tree clad valley. 'He's more in love with her than ever. She's a very lucky girl.'

'And your husband?'

June closed her eyes and a dull vision appeared, of him with his specs and unkempt hair peering at a screen, and - her assumption - the equally untidy woman who had taken him to an untidy messed-up bed in some New York tenement. 'I've sued him for a divorce, courtesy of Roberta's solicitor girl. Marjorie, who dealt with Roberta's divorce, and then my father's from Sam.'

'Oh dear. Sorry, June. Shouldn't have asked.'

'No problem. We married too early. Too immature. Didn't think. Glad I didn't have any kids. I don't care if I never see him again. I'll put the house on the market as soon as I can.'

255

'Will you stay with your father and Roberta?'

June took a breath. 'I'd like to move here, to Ireland.'

Reaching the old house was like arriving home - an odd feeling, given that technically her home was an anonymous semi in an equally anonymous outlying suburb of Chelmsford and her present address was her father and step-mother's Manor in Bedfordshire. And this only her third visit. Donald greeted her with his customary bear hug and a smacking cheek kiss.

'Splendid lass. Good to have ye here again. Will you have some supper, now? Anita's done us a grand spread - come along through.'

She shook her head. 'If I may, can I have a peek at what's been done, first?' The brief hesitation wasn't lost on her, nor the exchange of glance betwixt her two hosts. 'If that's okay?' she added, easing off her coat.

'Best seen in good daylight, my dear girl,' Donald suggested, putting an arm round her once more and drawing her towards the kitchen corridor. 'Leave it until the morrow. Plenty of time.'

So she had to behave, act as the dutiful guest, enjoy the mix of cold meats, spicy fried vegetables, Irish bread and bottled Guinness, engage in good as she got repartee of Irish *craik* and absorb the sense of belonging until her eyelids grew heavy and the languor took her to a dreamless bed.

In these, the first days of March with its proverbial lamb-like start, her glimpse of the Mor garden in early morning sunlight was a sight June hoped would last. The prospect of the dew dampened lawns and the scent of freshly washed shrubs from the late evening shower was heavenly - even the dark row of conifers against the immediate skyline was a delight. The mantlepiece clock had ticked its way past eight o'clock and breakfast would be on its way. A Donald breakfast -

what more could she ask? On with the warm things - it would still be cool - and she'd wend her way along the familiar path, renew her acquaintanceship with the *spirit of the place*. Keela was still there, as enigmatic as ever.

'I've come back, Keela. As you knew I would.' June spoke out loud, stroking the little girl's stone-still tresses. 'And maybe I'll stay. Who knows?'

A five minute stay, all she needed before continuing on and returning to the back of the house, duty done. Now she was officially back in residence.

Comfortable with the traditional Irish breakfast inside her, warmed by two mugs of decent coffee and in anticipatory mood, she followed Donald and Siobhán out of the kitchen, along the corridor and through into the hallway. In the dim light of last evening she'd not seen much, but now? The woodwork shone, the tired dullness of unloved wainscoting gone. The carpet sat on its new underlay, the centre table's grime replaced with a burnished gloss of newly applied polish; the fireplace metalwork now a crisp jet black and the brass fire irons gleamed. The fire grate displayed a collection of decent logs and a new wickerwork basket alongside held further supplies. Two armed chairs placed either side of the fireplace - she couldn't remember them from her last visit - were in what looked like old blackened oak, with upholstered seats and backs in a heavy cream floral patterned fabric. She let her gaze swivel round, amazed at the transformation. The tapestries were straight, hanging without creases and clean; the few paintings she'd remembered cataloguing were still in place, unchanged, but the overall effect was impressive.

'And that's not all,' Siobhán said, eyes shining at June's evident awe at what had been achieved. 'Come this way,' and preceded them into the drawing room. 'It's the pictures that we aren't sure about. Declan won't touch them as he says it's a specialist job - and we have to agree. Do you, or Roberta, know of anyone?'

June wasn't listening. The effect she'd imagined was here, in reality. Woodwork cleaned and given a coat of protective polish, the brocade hangings had lost their dust, as had the ceiling and plasterwork no longer with cracks and missing parts. The chandelier sparkled, the windows cleaned, new blinds hung half drawn against the light, and the carpet, yes, it too had a new wool underlay. But the chairs and the settee were missing.

'The furniture?' she asked.

'Not yet back from the specialists in Dublin. Any day, so they say.'

Cadhla's picture was still in place. June looked up at her, at now what she recognised as a wistful expression. 'I wonder if she ever was happy?'

It was Donald who voiced an opinion. 'Doubt it. From living a sheltered life here, running the risk of being discovered if she did manage to get out, to finally risking all by running away, how could she? No feather-bedded marital bliss for her - leastways not that was ever recorded. Poor girl.'

'How did she meet the village lad, do you think?'

'Probably because he was a gardener. She'd be allowed to walk the grounds - likely sat in the rose bower where the statue is - and she's holding that bunch of roses,' was Siobhán's suggestion. 'Talking of which - you suggested we let others have use of the old kitchen garden. Which we have - and there's three of our neighbours without too much ground of their own who've been up and started work already. Didn't you notice this morning, when you were out?'

She hadn't; her eyes and thoughts had been elsewhere, but she'd certainly go and have a look later. In the meantime . . . 'I think this looks splendid - aren't you pleased?'

Donald linked hands with his wife. 'We are that. And our thanks to you, my girl, for pointing out we had a jewel of a place under our noses. And the other room?'

They moved across the hall. In the dining room, much the

same treatment had also produced a cared-for ambiance.

'It's great. The lads must have worked well. I'm sure it took a lot of patience and elbow grease to achieve this polish. And the chandeliers!' June was impressed.

'Four thousand separate pieces of glass, so they said. And it takes hours to dust the fabrics down as per the true conservation specification. Declan took it to his heart, so he did. Looked it all up and wouldn't short cut. Now we have it back under control, we'll keep it up. And Anita's quite keen to become involved too, happily.' Donald ran his hand over the table's shine. 'So no massive change of style. No lavish use of new paint. But the place has responded, don't you think?'

June nodded. 'I'm glad. Very glad.' She spun round, with an inwardly glowing feeling it had all come right. 'I wish Roberta could see this. Photos won't do it justice.'

'Then she'll have to come over once she can travel. And bring the children. We'd love to have them all here, wouldn't we, Donald?'

'Surely. What the place needs, a family to bring it to life. We'll have to wait awhile afore Maeve offers us a chance o' that.'

They returned to the back quarters and to warming mugs of coffee with Anita's ginger cookies. June was a very happy girl. Her ideas had worked, Declan had proved he was the right man for the job, her - Roberta's - clients were satisfied, all that remained now was picture restoration and, mundanely, the upstairs rooms where historical accuracy was of far less importance, giving way to modernity, a euphemism for comfort.

'You're pleased with what you've seen then, June? Ready for the next challenge?'

'Very pleased. And I can't wait to see what restoration does to the pictures. Shall I ask Roberta for guidance on that? I'm sure she'll know where they ought to go, as well an idea on costings.' She sipped at her mug. 'What's the next challenge you mentioned?'

Siobhán looked at Donald. 'Shall we?'

He nodded. 'I'm game. Time we went out there.' He glanced out of the window. 'Provided the weather holds,' and grinned at June's quizzical expression. 'Recall the cottage we mentioned? Our retreat - where we can hide away. Rather neglected, sadly. Fancy a trip into the wilds of west Cork?'

'I thought this was as good a retreat as any?'

'Ah, wait until you see this one. 'Tis miles from anywhere, with stunning views. Mebbe the weekend after next, or whenever. After we've got our next phase under way, provided our man's in the mood. No doubt he'll be up afore long.'

And true to prophesy, he was.

'June, my lovely lass! How're keeping? My, 'tis good to see ye!' She suffered a bear hugging embrace and a smacking kiss on both cheeks. 'And what d'you think to our Siobhán's newly awakened décor then? And Donald's, of course,' seeing the shaggy eyebrows twitch.

'It's grand,' she said, lapsing into the vernacular. 'Thanks a million for a super job.'

His grin stayed well in place as he let her go and turned to offer Siobhán a similar greeting. 'This one'll be an Irish lassie yet - will she stay a while now?'

'I hope so, Declan. At least until we've finished the upstairs and the passages.' She wasn't going to mention the Borlinn valley trip - Declan was unaware, as far as she knew, about that hideaway. 'Tea?'

'Thought you'd never ask. Then me and the lady here will have a look around for the next phase, it that's in order.'

During the course of the next ten days, June managed to put the 'next phase in order' as Declan had said, spending the best part of a day and a half sketching ideas, taking more photographs and maintaining a steady exchange of internet ideas betwixt her and Roberta, with some of Freddie's' input as well. Freddie, with her web of well-placed cronies in London, trumped Roberta's suggested picture restorers with one of her own. 'She's done a lot of work for the Trust,' she'd said, passing on the name and contact details, 'as well as lots of lesser country house stuff; does it for the love rather than the loot. Her daddy's well heeled and supports her, you see. Give Bett a bell and tell her Freddie wants a good job done.'

So June rang her, with some small trepidation, not ever being in that world, but found a pleasantly voiced rather young-sounding girl respond with enthusiasm.

'I'll nip over tomorrow,' she was told. 'No time like the present and it's ages since I was in Ireland. Don't worry about meeting me, I'll hire a car. Can I stay in the house or do I need to book an hotel? Where did you say you were?'

Another phone call came late in the afternoon of the following day. 'Bett here. I'm in some place called . . . ' and she did a passable job of the pronunciation. 'Can you guide me in?'

An hour later and a silver grey BMW estate rolled up to the front door. Donald, who'd done the navigation after June had handed over both task and phone, met and greeted her with uncharacteristic politeness. Maybe it was the thought of having a London art expert at his door, or that he welcomed the idea of yet another young lady here to help them recover - restore - their lost heritage; whatever, she deserved her welcome. Smart in a grey costume suit, skirt pleated and flared, plain pale red blouse, a neat bob of brown hair, Bett had a ready smile. She advanced across the gravel, took his outstretched hand.

'Mr Drivas, thank you so much for the instructions, Ireland's a wonderful place but not noted for its signposting. And thank you - or your consultant - for the invite. I do so love these unknown challenges. You never know what's in store.'

June loved her. So open, so friendly, not at all disparaging; and she blessed Freddie for the introduction, moreover she was sure this girl would be sympathetic towards the Mor collection; underneath the easy-going attitude she detected a steely resolve. Over an Anita style chicken and potato casserole served round the kitchen table, Bett explained her background.

'Boarding school girl, me, then off to Switzerland; you know, what every well bred gal has to go through to satisfy doting parents she's good for the marriage stakes. Picture in Country Life at twenty-one or a heritage planned engagement. Daddy's a banker,' she added, as if that said it all. 'Provided I come up with the sensible chappy to wed before I'm thirty, I can do as I please without being starved of funds. Love this job though,' and she paused to take another serving spoonful of casserole without being asked, 'especially if I get to eat in places like this.' She gave June another of her speciality beaming smiles. 'You're a lucky gal, too, roaming around on assignments like this. Who did Freddie say you worked for?'

Siobhán and Donald stayed quiet, content to let the two young people prattle on, so it was June who explained. 'You know Smiley Designs? Roberta Smiley - she used to be London based until about four years ago. Her husband at the time fled to Austria with his secretary, only to rather fatally drive his Audi off an alpine road, fortunately alone. Then she met and married my father. I rather fell into this job more by accident but I love it.'

'And does it rather well,' added Siobhán. 'Wait till you see the house in the morning.'

Bett leaned forward, wiping her chin with the linen napkin. 'Smiley? Michael Smiley?'

'Mmm. Think that was his name. Did you know him - them?'

'Oh yes, I knew him,' though her face exhibited no emotion and she changed the subject. 'You've found a good local guy for your restoration work then. Unusual for this part of the world. Has he done other work in the locality? I mean, are there other houses with decent art collections?'

'There's Naylor's place across the valley. Once upon a time the two estates could have been linked, but we don't have much to do with the current owners. Lottery types.'

'Ah,' said Bettina. 'I see. Well, there may still be paintings.'

'There was a sculpture,' June interjected, using the chance to bring Keela into the conversation. 'Which came from there ages ago. Modelled from one of their paintings, now in our drawing room. Girl called *Cadhla*. Lovely romantic story,' and she launched into her version of the tale, as learnt from Siobhán. 'I'd love to know what happened to her.'

'Wouldn't we all?' and Donald summed it up. 'Irish folklore. Lost in the mists of time. Right, anyone for coffee and liqueurs? We'll shift to the sitting room.'

Around eleven o'clock both Bettina and June had succumbed to the indulgences of warmth, good conversation and Donald's liberal application of alcohol.

'Girls,' said Siobhán, rising to her feet, 'I think it's time for your beds. Sorry you're in a front room, Bett, but it's all we have with a decent bed. Breakfast at nine. June, you'll show her?'

Bettina collected her small case from the hallway and the two girls made their way up the wide staircase. At the top, Bett turned and surveyed the hall from above.

'You know, June, if this was your inspiration, then it's exactly what I'd look for. And once we get those landscapes out from under their grimy varnish, even better. But that's tomorrow. Bed beckons with a loud voice.'

June laughed. 'Funny expression, that, but I know what you mean.' Then she frowned, remembering an earlier comment. 'You mentioned you knew Roberta's former husband? That's rather a coincidence, surely?' She was curious, intrigued even.

Bettina produced her own frown. 'June, you don't want to know. Sufficient to say I was a silly and stupidly naïve girl who got lured by charms that guy should have kept for his wife.' She turned towards the corridor. 'Where's this room?'

In the morning, after another decent breakfast that sadly Bettina couldn't completely absorb, the two girls were left alone for the day.

'We're going to see one of Donald's former colleagues in Cork, June. You'll be all right on your own? I doubt Declan will be up today. Anita'll do lunch for you. Back at five-ish,' and the Jaguar purred out of sight down the drive.

'Nice car.' Bett stared after it. 'If I was a car freak - which I'm not - I might fancy that. Well, best get started. You have a list?'

June produced her list. 'Twenty five in total, but maybe not all need cleaning. Begin in here?' and they moved into the drawing room.

Bett stared round. 'You *have* done a good job. Good as an NT house. But you are right. Some of these are in pretty poor shape. Too much exposure to coal fires, and probably cigar smoke as well. Not to mention damp. Can you give me a hand, we'll take them down and look at the backs. And, by the way, it's not *cleaning,* it's 'restoration'. Just in case someone thinks we're throwing surgical spirit or meths at them.'

'Can you manage any 'restoration' here, or do you take them away?'

'Depends. Cost of proper transportation back to the studio adds up, certainly, but to stay here and set somewhere up locally would be equally expensive, though better for security and for the paintings. We could control the humidity as near correct then.'

'I'm here for as long as it takes, Bett. I could help, and I'd love to learn.'

Bett stared at her. 'So you like rural Ireland?'

June nodded. 'I've come to love the place, the pace of life, the way folks have time for each other. So different to what I was used to, back in Essex. Mind you, the Manor's okay. Roberta has a lovely calming attitude.'

'And your father, how does he fit into things?'

'It's a nice story in its own right, Roberta falling off a horse and he picking her up. They do seem right for each other, though it's a shame my mum suffered a divorce.' How many times had she recounted this tale now? At least she could retell it without feeling as emotional as once she had.

'You've no one in your life, Bett?'

'Not at present. Once bit, as they say. Though I'm not twice shy. How about you?'

And so it went on, as they took one picture down after another and Bett made notes. Before the end of the morning, not only had they explored each other's life story, but they had become firm friends.

When Siobhán and Donald came home as promised, shortly after five and as the March evening was beginning to draw in, the catalogue of damage and action was complete. All that remained was a decision, and the sitting room took on an air of a board room.

Bett explained. Total cost, excluding transportation. Timescale, excluding transportation.

Or an alternative. Set aside a space for her, possibly let her to take in other work, allow June to work with her, and within a year, all would be pristine.

'A *year?*' Donald looked down his nose at her. 'Surely it wouldn't take that long!'

'Have you ever seen a restorer at work, Mr Drivas?'

'Donald, please. No, I haven't.'

'Or seen the results?'

'Now I think on, no.'

'Well, it's not a thing you rush. And some of your paintings here are valuable, which means they'd have to be assessed. I won't work on anything unless it has a value and is insured. Sorry.'

Siobhán laid a hand on his arm. 'Donald, dear, I believe we have an opportunity here.' She turned to Bettina. 'We'll discuss your recommendations, Bett, and let you know tomorrow. Now,' and softened her mothering-like order with a smile, 'you girls get yourselves to bed. You've had a busy day. Breakfast at the same time. Now go on, shoo.'

After the girls had gone, and she and Donald had moved to their respective comfy armchairs by the fire, she gave him a couple of minutes before explaining her ideas.

'Donald, dear, we've got a wonderful opportunity here. Both June and this Bettina seem to have fallen under the same spell. If they want to stay and work here, why not let them? Why not use some of the spare buildings to start a little business like Roberta's, but in restoration rather than pure design? I believe it would be just right for the old place, and certainly a talking point. We can benefit, the girls would love it, and Mor house comes back to a life it deserves. What do you think?'

Pursed hands, a reflective upward glance at the ceiling and an 'hmmm' the only sign he'd taken her ideas on board. She waited, her hands folded in her lap, wondering if these changes wrought since their return weren't too great. The last few traumatic months abroad had taken their toll, endeavouring to combat the differing aspects of tropical medicine with associated politics, and the last thing she wanted was a stressed husband.

'Hmmm,' he said again.

'Don't you like the idea of having these girls about the place?'

That made him both snort and then smile. 'Tempting me?'

'Maybe. Though I can't see you succumbing, Donald dear. Not while I keep a decent figure,' and their eyes met. They both knew what they knew.

'Then I'll go with it. Where had you thought? It'll need light, and heating. And do the girls live in?'

'Maybe,' then hesitated. 'No, I'll not ask them to share in the house. Perhaps the cottage? And as far as a work area -

266

the old wash yard, though it'll need a bit of work. Unless we give up the dairy.'

The dairy - a long, stone floored room, slate benched, still with a few relics from the old days, abandoned to damp and cobwebs. 'Let's ask the girls in the morning. And we can sleep on the idea. Actually, dear,' and he eased out of the comfort of the chair to offer her a hand and a warming smile, 'I'm rather taken with this concept. Come. Time for bed. Justify your existence,' and though the remark may have been misconstrued elsewhere, she could feel the glow within her. Mor House was coming alive.

TWENTY SIX

'The wash yard? You said it was spooky.'

'Not spooky. I said it had a funny atmosphere, and you should stay clear if you had any psychic feelings. Now you've met Keela and survived, I guess there's not a problem.'

'You mean I've passed the test?'

Siobhán smiled. 'You came back. Now, shall we have a look? Go and find Bettina.'

The door creaked open. It hadn't been used for some time and the immediate whiff of stale damp stone and brick wafted through. The overhead glazing was patched with green mildew, the brick walls had spalled in places, the flags were uneven.

Bettina was appalled. 'We can't use this! Far too damp!'

'Only because it's not been used, Bett,' Siobhán mildly responded. 'My main query is whether it's large enough. We can get the glass cleaned, another floor laid and the walls dry-lined. And it is secure.'

Bett walked the length, glanced up. 'It's big enough. Are you sure it'll dry out? It'll take ages!'

'It was a drying area for the laundry.'

Bett heaved what might have been a sigh. 'Nowhere else?'

'Only the old dairy, but that's outside and loads of windows. Not as secure, and probably just as humid when it rains. Which it does.'

'Which it does,' Bett had to agree there. 'Okay then, if you're sure you don't mind us using the space?'

'Not at all, Bett. We wouldn't use it ourselves. Can I ask

Declan to liaise with you two and sort it? We'll stand the cost, but expect our work done at reasonable rates in return.' Siobhán grinned at her. 'When you start making a profit you can pay us rent.'

Bett grinned back. 'You know, I think I'm enjoying this. A real proper challenge. Far better than mooching round London, even though I had a decent studio there.' She lent across and pecked at Siobhán's cheek. 'Thanks.'

Two weeks later and the wash yard was transformed. Declan, probably with a vested interest, responded with enthusiasm, brought in two extra pairs of hands and even worked late into the evenings. June watched with wry amusement at his amateur attempts to brush up against Bettina as she offered instructions, and her adroit sway and sidestepping out of reach, almost like a ballet.

Eventually they collided, and though his muscular arm was nearly round the girl, she trod on his foot, accidentally of course.

'My, but you're a lively kitten and no mistake,' said he, hopping on one foot. 'Can't a man get within a whisker before he's ripe for the hospital?'

Bett had her hands on her hips. 'Kitten, is it? I'll show you a wild cat and a scratcher if you don't keep those paws to yourself, *mister* Declan. Now, let's have those racks in and then you can go home to your lady friend.'

He turned to June. 'This one's a right English minx and no mistake. I think I'll go afore she spits at me.'

They all laughed. No malice in him and the girls took it in good part. '*No mistake,*' Bett copied him. 'Make up your mind. Minx or kitten. I prefer kitten - and no, don't get ideas. Go home, Declan, and thanks.'

The workshop was complete, now with overhead glass lights

clean and sparkling, new lighting, fresh smooth new walls of painted plaster and a proper screeded and plain carpeted floor. It even smelt bright and business like. Bettina twirled round, her work-a-day grey calf length dress swirled.

'June, love, I like this place.'

'Even though you turned up that snub nose of yours at first?'

Bett grinned. 'Even though.' She sprung backwards onto a bench, smoothing dress below her and swung legs, all in one concerted action. 'Tomorrow, we get to work. Mor House, this is just the start.' Then she suddenly jumped down. 'Come on, let's go celebrate.'

They took Bett's BMW into the village and aimed at the pub. June had been in there a time or three so the landlord knew her and though his eyebrows lifted at Bett, true Irish politeness took it no further. After an hour and a half, two Guinness and a home-made pie later, they left, the wave and the 'cheerio now' perfectly natural.

'Decent bunch.'

'Yes. It's where Declan hangs out most nights.'

Bett twitched her eyebrows. 'So why not tonight, I wonder? We'd have stood him a drink.'

'To be sure.' June's Irishisms were growing on her. 'He's probably tucking into a steak with Fergal.'

'Ah, yes. Well, let's see if there's any afters left at the House.'

Donald peered at them from below the bushy eyebrows. 'Pub not lively enough?'

'It was fine, Donald, thanks. Is there any cheese cake left?'

He laughed. 'So that's it. Anita's magic cheesecake brought you back. Sure, and there's a piece or two left. Help yourselves, then join us in the sitting room. There's coffee there if you'd like it.'

'Happy now, you two?' Siobhán put down her crochet

work as they pushed open the door, each holding a plate and a mug of steaming coffee. 'You didn't have to go to the pub, unless there was an ulterior motive?' The incipient grin broke out. 'Perhaps a glimpse of the men folk, now?'

June shook her head. 'Bett's had enough of Declan's antics. No offence, Siobhán, but it made a change.' She sipped at her mug. 'Ow! That's hot. But the workshop's finished, so tomorrow we start work, eh, Bett?'

'Studio, please, June. And yes, tomorrow it is. So early night for an early start. I much prefer working fresh.' Bett remained standing. 'And the sooner we get on top of the Mor collection, the sooner I can advertise for more work and start paying for my keep. You've been so good to me, Siobhán - and Donald, of course.'

'No problem at all, girls,' Donald recrossed his legs and settled into his chair. 'It's nice to have you around, and our house has taken on a happy feel once more. And there's no worry over the rent, not at all, eh, Siobhán, dear?'

Siobhán was grinning at them. 'You're all using 'mor' like a common habit. No worry over rent, Bett, we'll take it out of your bill,' and the grin dispelled any feelings of wanting to score points. 'You really like it here, Bett?'

The girl nodded enthusiastically and nearly spilt her coffee. 'Love it.'

'And June, how about you? Surely you hanker after the Manor? Don't you?'

June put her mug down. 'Sometimes. More because of the twins - and the prospect of Roberta's third. And my father, of course. And Peter - oh yes, I suppose I miss them. But it's so peaceful and serene here, and I've got this strange yen to discover more about Keela. Attached to the place 'cos I stroked her hair!'

'There you go again. Said 'mor' twice.' Siobhán didn't want to say it in as many words, but once the restoration contract was finished, June would have to find alternative employment. Lovely girl though she was, they couldn't house and feed her indefinitely. 'So what will you want to do once Mor House is finished?'

'I'm not sure.'

Bett wrinkled her nose in reflection. She loved working with June; they got on so well together, almost kindred spirits. 'Let's sleep on it, June,' and she pushed herself upright from her lean on the doorframe. 'Come on. Bed beckons.'

Once the girls had gone, Siobhán resumed her crochet and Donald picked up his book again. Silence then, apart from the dull crackle of burning logs from the fireplace. Ten minutes passed, the only other sound the clock and the faint murmur of a breeze in the nearby trees. The peace and serenity June had mentioned enveloped them.

'Can we afford to keep her?'

Donald put his marker into his book, put it down on the table and stretched. 'Which girl are you referring to, dear? I assume you mean June. Bett's sorted, even if it was rather a *fait accompli*. Would they wish to continue working together? And if they do, they'll want to stay in the cottage.'

'Why not? No one else wants it. Maeve won't need to come back here, and I love having them about. Makes me feel young.'

'Ah, so that's it!' He chuckled. 'I love having them about too, pretty young things as they are. Bett doesn't always wear a bra.'

Siobhán scowled at him, good-naturedly. He'd never stray, and if *les girls* did dress flirtatiously, there'd never be any harm done. All part of the joys of living. She had her moments as well. 'Time we went up, my love. Tomorrow let's think about the trip across to *our* cottage.'

So come Saturday morning, the start of the weekend, a small holdall of clothes and walking boots for all four were safely stowed in the Jaguar's boot. Donald drove them across and into Cork county, through Macroom and the narrow streets of Bantry, on down the coast road through Balllickey and towards the hidden turning for the cross-border road to Kerry. With the rain holding off despite grey skies, the back seat passengers had a good view of Bantry Bay, stretching away towards the mist-shrouded hills of the Sheep's Head and the Beara. The pewter coloured waters of the bay seemed to swallow Whiddey Island and the fringes of the Glengariff woods, an air of timelessness June found hard to believe. Donald spun the car to the right, right again, and across the old bridge.

'You'd never guess this road goes all the way across the hills towards Kenmare. Such a beautiful drive. Wonderful views. Far better than the Healey Pass road. Lot quieter, too.' Siobhán had turned towards them in the back to explain. 'We only came across the place by accident, many years ago. It's got a lot of history wrapped up. Bags of atmosphere.' She smiled at June's face. 'You're quite a sensitive soul, aren't you, June? You'll both love it, you see,' and she faced the front again.

Bett looked as though she was in a trance, perhaps bemused by the variation in the scenery.

June nudged her. 'Am I a sensitive soul, Bett? You look rather reflective.'

'Such a change from town. I'd never have thought what was in store when I took the job on. So different. Wondering what my gang would be up to.'

'You miss them?'

A vehement shake of the head. *'No way!* Imagining what they'd think - and say - if they could see all this.'

'What about the boys?'

Bett gave June an odd look. 'When you've experienced what some of them have on offer, you'd enjoy a sabbatical from sex as well. No, I'm fine. For a while, anyway,' and lapsed back in to introspective mood.

The tunnel of trees seemed endless, mile after mile, virtually straight, the road like a shelf between hill and the river on their left. Then the car slowed.

'Nearly there.' He swung the Jaguar to the left, to cross another narrow bridge and the road narrowed down still further, began to twist and turn. Glimpses of the high hills and skyline between the trees, the sense of the enclosure of the valley and the feel of driving back into former times.

Then the road dipped towards a gate opposite some old stone barns on the right. A field track veered to the left, and ahead, a solid cream-washed cottage standing foursquare with the stone walled garden. Journey's end.

'Hop out and open the gate, someone.'

June had the door open before Bett had come alive. Gate open, the car rolled through. She closed it behind them, sniffed the air. Damp, yes, but clean. Clean, with subtle hints of shrubs, grass and the overwhelming sense of ageless country. Wonderful. Above the roof of the house the outline of the hills, miles away and up the valley, and now the clouds dispersal gave the first sight of sun, a tinge of blue, a herald of a better day. She walked slowly down the track towards where Donald had parked the car; the boot opened and he was handing out luggage.

'Well, June? What do you think?'

'It's lovely. And so quiet.' True, there was scarce a sound; the distant burble of the stream, the whisper of a light stir of wind in the trees, a few snatches of suppressed birdsong. No traffic. No hustle of people. 'Remote.'

He laughed. ''Tis that all right. Imagine spending all your days out here?'

She pulled a face. 'Perhaps a mite lonely for some. All right for a while. Good place to find one's soul. Maybe write a book, compose some music.' She looked at Bett's expression. 'Or perhaps a honeymoon?'

Siobhán chuckled. 'Now now, girls. We'll lend it to you, as and when. In the meantime, you've to earn your keep. Get the stove going, open up the windows and give the place an airing. I'll put lunch together in a while. Then, if the weather holds, a short walk about the place this afternoon?'

They explored. Three bedrooms, two with double beds, the last with twin singles. A decent sized bathroom with both bath *and* shower. The main room downstairs did double duty as lounge and diner, with a sizeable kitchen and separate walk-in larder. A further, somewhat cold and dismal, space acted as a utility area, with washing machine and what looked like a big chest freezer, and beyond that, another toilet.

Bett did her nose wrinkling exercise. 'Bit basic,' her immediate comment. 'Could do with a makeover. And some decent rugs about the place. Don't like all these bare floors. Can't stand clumping feet, especially on the stairs. Wouldn't suit some. No telly. Probably no broadband either.'

'Do you *mind*?'

'Me? No, not really. Well, perhaps a telly. Evenings might drag, else. Can't cosy up in bed every night,' then she blushed. 'Sorry, June, train of thought. We'd best see what Siobhán's doing.'

Donald had the wood burning stove going. Sitting against the back wall of the kitchen, it looked like the only form of heating. As the girls returned from their exploration, Siobhán looked up from her chopping board, where a neat stack of assorted vegetables was growing.

'Irish stew. My version. Warming and filling. Lunch cum dinner. I'm not as inventive as Anita is, I'm afraid. Basic but wholesome.'

'She does all right, girls. You can have a go at the catering whenever you like, but we'll need to go shopping. We don't keep much here, for obvious reasons. It's ages since we were last here, so we'll have to air beds and use hot water bottles. Damp, else. Mind you, this monster does very well, though it has a voracious appetite for timber. The stockpile's in the barn across the road. Basket is over there.'

Bett looked at June. 'I think he's dropping hints, June. And Irish stew sounds lovely.'

Two hours later, after a tummy warming stew and additional boiled potatoes, washing up done, they took advantage of the better afternoon. With most clouds gone, the sun had brought brightness and warmth to the valley. Donald led the way.

'You can actually follow this path all the way up to the valley head, and then it splits, one path climbs up there,' and he pointed to where the angled scar showed the line of the Kenmare road as it climbed obliquely up the valley side, 'the other goes into the re-entrant valley over to our left. We've never actually been right up into the hill, not yet. And, no, not today,' he added as June started to open her mouth. 'It's a fair old hike and we'd run out of time yet alone puff. Another day.'

She swallowed her disappointment as they played follow-my-leader across the rough pasture towards the gentler slopes of the northern side of the valley. Once onto the hill proper, he led them along sheep tracks and through gorse and heather, heading west. With the spring sunshine coming in from their left it was pleasant going, not as taxing as she'd thought.

'You okay, Bett?'

'Sure. Great. Look,' and she pointed. 'Isn't that the sea?'

Donald had slowed down and waited for them, Siobhán at his side. 'Not the sea. Well, not quite. Bantry Bay, then the Atlantic. Nothing between us and America. Good, eh?'

'When were we last up here, Donald?' Siobhán asked a rhetorical question, shading her eyes. 'We didn't get out to the cottage last time, so it must have been nearly a year and a half. Good to be back.'

'Hasn't changed.'

She laughed. 'The view's the same. Like it, girls?'

'Beautiful.' June spoke for them both. Life in Essex - or

276

Bedfordshire - didn't allow for this sort of jaunt very often. Here, it was marvellous. The distant water had changed colour to the azure tinted deeper navy, the blurred outlines of the Beara framing the view. 'I could stay here all day.'

'Me too,' added Bett, 'except when it rains. Are we going on or back?'

'On,' replied Donald. 'A wee bit further, then slant down and find the road. Home for tea,' and he strode off, Siobhán ambling in his wake. The girls brought up the rear, picking their way carefully between prickly gorse.

Half an hour later and they were back on the tarmac, two strips between the grassed centre, and judging from the rippling noise, the river - stream - wasn't far away, down to the right. The cottage wouldn't be more than a mile further on. Bett had moved on ahead, catching up with Donald. June fell in with Siobhán.

'Thank you so much, Siobhán. For everything. The job, the welcome. The support. It's been great, really great.' She was treated to a sideways glance, a smile.

'June, love, you've been just what we needed. A refreshing addition to the place. After the stultifying existence we've had over the past few years Donald nearly closed in on himself - if we hadn't come home when we did, I believe he'd have gone into depression. You can, you know, if you don't see it coming. Bringing Mor House back to life has been exactly the tonic he - we - needed. And you've done it, and Bett's work will be exactly right to complete the task. So we owe you. Thanks a million, as we say,' and the smile came back once more. 'Have you decided what you want to do next?'

'We, that is, Bett and I, had a discussion last night. She wants to stay here, if she can find enough work and you're happy to let her remain.' June felt a heave of emotion and wondered what it was that made her go silly like this. 'I'd love to stay as well, start an Irish version of what Roberta does. I'm sure it would work, but I don't know how she'd

277

feel, or dad, and it depends on what you think as well.'

'Leave the Manor?'

She nodded, and the tears began to build. 'Dad would feel it most. He and I . . . ' and she couldn't go on.

'Formed a bond?'

June nodded. She swallowed, took a breath, waited until her tummy muscles had relaxed and went on, carefully. 'Since his divorce, and Roberta, and the twins. And Andrea going, I think I've been a sort of support for him. I know Peter's there now, and with his attachment to Hazel it'll have helped.'

As she paused in her explanation, her own attempt at voicing her rationale, Siobhán interrupted. 'But he's got Roberta?'

'She's been preoccupied. And not all that great in herself. I hope she'll be all right. I think he used Andrea as a sort of foil, but she's gone, and as he loved her in his own way - not to disparage Roberta, of course, - he misses her. As he missed mum, too, though she's not far away and they're still good friends. Even Roberta's got to like her.'

They weren't far from the gateway now, and could see Donald and Bett slipping their boots off in front of the cottage door. Siobhán put a hand on June's arm, stayed her and caught her eyes.

'Are you saying you're worried about him?'

The tears came back. She nodded, all she could do. She knew he was inwardly very stressed, something he'd not show, but it couldn't be good for him.

'It'll be better once Roberta's had her child, June. Perhaps he's more worried about her than is obvious. You'll have to be there. Don't worry about us. He's more important.' She hesitated. 'It may seem silly, June, but take the thought of Keela with you.'

'What do you mean?'

'Keela lost her love, but stayed as a symbol in that statue. Think of something as a symbol that he can hang on to. An anchor point. A benchmark - you know, a permanent level.'

'Keela's statue is a *benchmark?*'

'A point of reference. How a love can endure. I believe, from what you've said, your father hasn't had that fixture. His point of reference has kept on changing. Lucky people find a soul mate and then each person uses the other as a reference. A benchmark. If you don't have one, your life becomes unstable. I am right?'

'You mean, because my mother went out of his life, he got mixed up with both Roberta and Andrea, and then,' and she couldn't believe this, 'Hazel, so he's not been able to find that fixed point? Even though he and Roberta seem so close?'

Siobhán's look said it all, with the little nod.

'Gosh.'

Siobhán laughed. 'How old fashioned! Last time I heard that expression was from a real old public school guy in Singapore. Find him a Keela, June. She's become your benchmark.'

June thought. Maybe she was right. 'But Keela lost her love.'

'Not really. I had a dream once. I won't tell you now, but believe me, she found her happiness, I'm sure of it. So will you.'

'And you, Siobhán?'

She caught June's hands. 'Donald,' she said, and leant forward to offer a cheek kiss. 'There's never been anyone else. Not a masculine version of Roberta, nor an Andrea, not even a Hazel. Just he and I. We've been lucky, June. So you go home and look after your father. Make sure he's found his benchmark. Then, and I can't wait, you come back here and Keela - *Cadhla* - will find you a proper man who'll cherish you as you deserve to be cherished.'

TWENTY SEVEN

Kasia giggled. These two kids were a proper delight, especially when they were in a good mood. Chris was tickling her feet, Abby weaving fingers in her hair. Okay, not the most comfortable of positions, spread-eagled on the playroom carpet, but at least it proved they loved her, and that was all that mattered. Time they were tucked up. She struggled, sat up, hands propping her as the twins joined forces to try and push her flat again.

'Finish!' she cried. 'Finish! That is enough! Abby, you take Chris to shower,' and that did the trick. Abby, becoming quite the little madam, loved to boss her brother around. Happily, Chris was the more placid and largely enjoyed his sister's push and shove. With the prospect of a shower and all its attendant fun, they started tearing clothes off, just as their mum pushed open the door.

'Ah, just in time. Kasia, I'll shower with these two if you like, so long as you stay within shouting distance? It may be the last chance for a while.' The way her bump had moved progressively downwards it could only be a matter of a few days. 'Get them ready - I'll only be a moment.'

March had moved into April, April into May. The Manor's fame had spread, the television programme had fulfilled all their expectations and she'd struggled to keep pace, even with Freddie now a permanent fixture. June had flown in for another three week spell and that had been great, but tomorrow she was due to go back; tonight she was spending the last night with her mother at the Hostel. The Mor House

280

project, completed to everyone's satisfaction, had been a prelude to the launch of an Irish arm of her business, totally beyond her wildest imagination. The girl Bettina with all her conservation skills had become another asset, though the niggle was there, still unresolved, where exactly she'd figured in the London scene. Freddie wasn't all that forthcoming - and as the disparate constituents of the team appeared to work well, should she really be bothered?

Andrew was in the bedroom; he wouldn't let her out of his sight now. 'Darling,' she told him, 'I'm showering with the twins. Kasia will stay within reach. Don't worry, I'll be careful.'

'Sure you'll be all right? They can be quite boisterous . . .'

She cut him off. 'I know. But as their mum, I need to.' She began to peel clothes off. 'Give me a hand?'

Minutes later and as he wrapped her in the large bath sheet, had to make the inevitable comment. 'Be glad when you're back to size, my love. Maternity is all very well, but . . .'

'I know. Me will be glad too. At least I've kept everything together. So far. Right, I'll waddle on. See you in a little while.'

The shower was lovely, a gentle, relaxing stream, and the two little people, very understanding now they'd become aware of all that was involved in their mum's strange shape, gently soaped and sponged. Maybe not every mother would go through this routine, but to her it was a wonderful way of bonding the family. They knew there was a little sister in their mum's tum and took great care. She in turn did her best to lather them without shoving soap in eyes or ears, and then it was time to call it a day.

'Kasia!' she called, 'can you take them? And let Andrew know?'

The lithe blond-haired girl slid the shower doors apart, reached in and took a small hand, then another. 'Come, please. Then I will dry you with a rub-a-dub dub. Come. You are okay, Roberta?'

Roberta swung a hand and caught her hair behind her, took another proffered towel, and stepped out. Then, and it had to be then, she knew. 'Oh. Oh. I think . . . ', and felt the pain.

'Andrew! Darling!' and sagged onto the bathroom stool to watch the pool of wet that wasn't shower damp spread across the mat.

The well rehearsed wheels swung into action. Phone calls, a timing of surges of pain, another phone call to bring their proficient own doctor into the picture because the peripatetic midwife was otherwise engaged the other side of town, another delay, more anxious moments, and then it was too late. Far too late. She didn't want to go anywhere, not now.

'Sorry,' she said, and gasped. 'Oh. Ohh - arrh - ohhh!'

The tyres on the gravel. The Hall door banged, the run of feet on the stairs. 'All right, Roberta. Not a problem. You'll be fine. Andrew, you take one arm, we'll have to use your bed. Sheets, anyone?' Doc Mac was in control.

Then Kasia was there too. 'Doctor - I have helped my mother before, if you would allow . . .'

Doc Mac smiled at her. 'One odd benefit of your problem, Roberta. Easy when you know how, or have relaxed ligaments like yours. She's beautiful, isn't she?' He gathered the rest of his things together and made one last check. She was fine, and knowing that being in her own home with its familiarity and with all her family and friends around her had made her delivery so much the better - hardly any trauma or stress. He'd get the midwife to pop in later, for reassurance. 'I'm away. Might manage a few hour's kip before breakfast. Take a nap in turn, you three,' he suggested as a parting shot.

'Evening deliveries are all very well, but I wish you'd showered earlier.' He grinned, waved, and went.

Hazel answered the phone when Andrew rang the cottage just after dawn.

'Just thought I'd let you know. Did Peter come back last night? No? Oh well. He's got another step sister. Six and a half pounds, or three kilos if you prefer metric. MaryAnn.' He heard the gasp, the intake of breath, and then the worried question.

'She's fine, Hazel. So far, anyway. And no-one's more relieved than I, I can tell you. . . .yes, a home birth. Too fast by far. Moral of story, don't have a hot shower with your twins.' He heard her laugh and suddenly his bottled-up tense emotions gave way. 'Hazel, I'm sorry . . .' was all he managed before he had to drop the phone. All too much.

Hazel sensed that he'd broken down. Since she'd become virtually independent, with most of March and all of April on her own, she'd grown up. Though a competent girl generally she'd still have weaker moments, flash-backs to her dumb days, but these had become fewer and fewer. As the demands of the business had increased, so had her confidence. The days of her girlish crushes had long gone. Even Peter - and she smiled in her recollection - had to watch his p's and q's. But now, Andrew needed her. She scribbled a note for Peter in case, left it on the table, grabbed her bike and took off for the Manor.

As she pedalled, fast but not furious, she bethought of the birth of the twins, that Christmas Day. What a change! This was a beautiful May morning; the early clouds were shading into a pinkish light as they caught the rising sun, the trees and hedges were that gorgeous light green of freshly opened buds, a snatch of birdsong echoed. MaryAnn. Always a Mary. How Roberta would love the new infant! Thank heavens for Kasia, too. What would June say? Would Andrew manage to contact Andrea, to tell her? And another thought. She and Peter. Would she have an easy first pregnancy? He hadn't suggested a date, but they would get married, he'd promised. After all, he'd had to ask several times before she'd said yes! Roberta and Andrew had been so pleased. How lucky was she? All down to Mary. And now there was a new Mary. She nearly skidded on the driveway gravel, slowed up, dumped the bike against the warm stone wall by the ceanothus bush and ran diagonally, lightly, across the steps, across the hall, up the stairs. Voices, laughter, a lovely sound.

'Oh *Hazel!* Dear girl. Look - my brand new Mary.' Roberta, pale but happy, tousled hair, infant at her breast, Andrew on the bedside chair, holding a hand. His smile, and their eyes met.

That time, when, last year? On the hill in Ireland. When they'd climbed up to the strange triangulation point. When she'd become as a daughter to him. A flashback - something about three people?

'Roberta, may I hold her?'

'Of course, Hazel, love.' and the somnolent infant was carefully transferred into Hazel's infinitely careful arms. A pair of brilliant brown eyes with amber flecks briefly opened and closed, almost like a wink. Hazel felt the surge of feeling, knew what Roberta had said was true. She, too, would be a mother, a loving mother, in due course. She looked across the bed at her inherited father figure.

'Remember the trig point, Andrew? It was you, and me, and now this little girl makes the three. Isn't that right?'

'Spot on, lass. Well thought.' He rose, came round the side of the bed, held her shoulder briefly, paused at the door. 'I'll make some more phone calls. Then we'll have breakfast?'

Kasia was looking after the twins, trying to restrain them. Andrew looked in at them on his way downstairs. 'You were a marvellous help last night, Kasia. Saying 'thankyou' doesn't seem adequate.' He caught Abby to him and swung her up. 'You've got a beautiful new tiny sister,' he said to her solemn little face. 'When Kasia's got you dressed you can go and see her. Chris as well,' he added as he put her back on her feet.

'I am happy I could be of help, Andrew,' Kasia smiled at him. 'This was my third time. I have two much younger brothers I see - *saw* - born. This, my first girl. I think it must be good to be a *midwife*. Tough though. I stay with children. Especially happy children.' She almost bobbed a curtsey, to acknowledge his position, a father with a good wife and nice children. 'I make breakfast with twins. Quarter of an hour.'

He sat in front of the office desk, a blank computer screen staring at him. Who to contact first? June, of course. She should have been here. And Sam. The Hostel's number was in the phone memory now.

'Could I speak to Mrs Hailsworthy please?' This was always a surreal moment, asking to speak to a woman who still owned his name. A minute, probably less, then Sam's voice.

'Good morning, Samantha speaking. How can I help?'

The odd feeling again. 'Sam, it's Andrew. Don't mind me ringing this early?'

'Andrew! Of course not, but what's brought this on? Do you want to speak to June - she's about to leave to come across to you?'

'In a moment. Thought I'd let you know, Roberta gave birth last night, at home. MaryAnn.'

Silence, momentarily, before he heard the suck in of breath and the congratulatory words. Okay, he knew it was difficult. Did she envy him, or Roberta?

'I'm pleased for you both, Andrew. Really, I am. Can I pop over later - or maybe tomorrow? Should I tell June, or do you want to?'

'You can tell her - you are her mum after all.' He paused. 'It'd be good to see you again, Sam. Do come,' and he ended the call. Mixed feelings. Yes, he still cared for her - but then, he cared for Andrea too, but hadn't had contact with her since she went to Spain. Maybe she was back. Should he try?

Her old personal number was still there, in the phone. He dialled.

'Mr Perlain's office. Mandy speaking. Can I ask who's calling?'

So she wasn't back in her old job. Not surprising. 'It's Andrew Hailsworthy. I'm looking for Andrea - Miss Chaney.'

'Oh, right. She's about somewhere. Can I ask her to call you?'

'That would be kind. Thank you. Is Mr Perlain at the Studios today?'

'I'm expecting him later on. Shall I say you called?'

'Please do. Thank you again.'

Time for breakfast. Before he left the office, he sat and let the feel of the day wash over him. Roberta, safely delivered. A new Mary. An overall, overwhelming sense of relief. Okay, more hurdles to overcome, but the concerning one now behind him, thank heavens.

June arrived in a flurry of enthusiasm. 'And I missed all the excitement! Dad, you should have rung me!'

'I'm sorry, June, but we were rather preoccupied. She didn't give us much option. In the end it was just the Doc, Kasia and me. Better than a trip to the hospital.'

'She's all right?'

'Go and see.'

Next came a call from the Film Studios. Andrea, and oh, how good it was to hear her voice again after all this time. 'Come and see us, please, Andrea. If your new lifestyle allows. Bring Alain if you want. We've a lot of catching up to do.'

That gurgle of a laugh, sending shivers down his spine. 'Love to, darling, but it'll have to be later on. I've got some cut-away shots to do, and a little thing for the next film. You know how it is. Give my best regards to the new mum. Tell her she's a lucky girl. Be in touch.'

She'd changed. Become more, what was the expression, brassy? Maybe superficial? More confident, certainly. Well, he shouldn't begrudge her the success, even if it had been her position at the Manor that had provided the trigger point. These things happened. At least she returned his call. Some newly discovered celebs would have spurned a humble guy like him in their rush for the big lights.

Nothing from Peter, yet. 'Hazel? When did you say Peter was coming back?'

'Later today, he said. He'll call once he's back in the country. I'll be glad to have him safely home.' She was back behind the desk, catching up. 'There's another e-mail from Bettina. Something about the Cadhla painting?'

'Oh, that'll be for June. I'll ask her to come down.'

June was reluctant to drag herself away from the bedroom and the sight of contented maternalism. Deep inside she knew it was envy, envy of not only Roberta's obvious pleasure in her achievement, but the very fact it was her father who'd succeeded in making this woman happy, whereas the guy she'd been foolish enough to marry - and now divorced - hadn't had a clue. She was going to be very careful about any new relationship, very very careful. Once bit, as Bettina had said.

Hazel vacated the chair. 'Take your time, June. I'm just nipping to the loo.'

June sat down on a warm seat. The e-mail was open, ready for her.

'Hi June, thought I'd let you know I've discovered a name on the Cadhla painting. Probably the artist. From what I can make out, it's Dufaigh, there may be an 'O' in front. Siobhán says the English version is Duffy. Are you coming back tomorrow? Best, Bett.

So? Did that mean anything? And now Roberta had hatched, did she want to go straight back? Perhaps she'd take another day or two. Bett wouldn't mind, she'd have the cottage to herself. And she remembered Siobhán's considered analysis of her father's worry, and how she should endeavour to find him his Keela.

In the course of chatty conversation over coffee, June elaborated on the e-mail from Ireland, and the query over when she was going back. 'I'll stay another day or two, if that's okay, dad, 'cos I can't miss seeing MaryAnn after her birth wrinkles have gone. Bett was quite sure I'd want to know the name of the *Cadhla* artist. She's good, you know. Takes so much care.'

'Rather a change, staying out in rural Ireland after a London highlife. P'raps she's lying low after a failed relationship.' Andrew's romantic mind sketched possibilities. 'You say she's got a rich daddy?'

'She has,' and June remembered. Roberta's first husband had been involved. Should she say? 'I think she knew Michael, Roberta's . . .'

Andrew cut her off. 'Enough, June. Let sleeping dogs stay put.' He changed tack. 'So who was the artist? Anyone we know? Joshua Reynolds perhaps?'

'Dad! You're showing off! No, the name was Duffy, or at least the Irish version.'

'Duffy? That rings a bell. Hang on a mo',' and he disappeared upstairs, obviously to talk to Roberta. Under medical advice, she'd been advised to rest up for at least forty-eight hours to allow muscles to settle back into place, with Kasia acting as efficient, and disciplined, nursemaid.

Hazel's puckered brow suggested she too had an idea, recognising the name, or thought she did. She also left the table and vanished. June was left wondering, but not for long. Hazel was back, clutching the painting taken from the office, of her and the trig point, the one Sheila had done last year.

'What's that say?' she queried, holding it out for June to see, just as Andrew returned.

'Remember the girl who . . .' he was saying, to stop as he saw what Hazel held. 'You . . .'

'Yes,' she said. 'Duffy. I wondered what it said, given her signature is all up and down. But it is Duffy. Isn't it?' looking at June for confirmation.

'As good as. I'd say this is the Irish version. I'll get the e-mail, to check the spelling,' and she wasn't gone above half a minute. Ó'Dufaigh, as copied out onto a slip of paper.

'Could be. Roberta's confirmed her idea of Sheila's surname. Coincidence or what?'

'There'll be plenty of people with that sort of name, dad.'

'Painters?' queried Hazel.

'Whoever painted *Cadhla* is long dead. We're talking a couple of hundred years here.'

'Painting runs in families.'

'Send a copy over to Bett, June. Let her romanticise.'

'I'll do it,' and Hazel jumped up. 'Won't take long.'

The following morning Hazel settled herself back behind the desk as normal. Peter had come home after his expedition and they'd had a lovely evening together, somehow he'd seemed far more settled in himself, they'd even allowed themselves to go just that little bit more like 'married couple', and the aftermath was still with her. Dreamy eyed, Peter called it, which was nice. It'd be better when they could *really* be properly married. Like Roberta. With a lovely little cuddly baby, giggling and kicking chubby little legs.

'Oi! Daydreaming, are we? Have we had a reply, Hazel?' Andrew had crept in, unseen.

'Sorry.' She pulled herself up and scanned the in-box. 'bettinaknows@ art.com. That's her.'

She clicked. '*Duffy. Same family. Only the girls painted. Yours must be great granddaughter. Remarkable similarity in brushwork. Well done you. She's got quite a following but no-one seems to know where she lives. Sells thru a Dublin gallery. Hang on to what you've got. Valuable. Best, Bett.'*

'We don't know where she lives either. But we know which pub she - and her partner - go to. So your portrait has been done by a Duffy. Same as June's Cadhla. Well now. Weird, as you would say.' He pushed himself upright, away from the leaning position on the door frame. 'If you want me, I'm upstairs for a bit, then I must see how Freddie's going to spend her day. Roberta will want a minute by minute update, and rather that then see her struggle up too soon. Oh, and if Andrea rings . . .'

She didn't give him a chance to finish. 'I'll call you, don't fret,' and turned back to the screen. Him and Andrea! She thought that flame had been extinguished months ago, but here she was, emerging out of the mists of time like the proverbial ghost, but when she glanced round again, he'd gone.

The new mum was feeding. Kasia hovered, then fled when a scream echoed down the passageway from the twin's room. It was high time she got them dressed and delivered to the playschool anyway, and she didn't want to find the lively pair locked in combat.

Andrew settled himself down on the bed end to watch in strange fascination as MaryAnn guzzled away. 'She's a little glutton.'

Roberta scowled. 'Too enthusiastic, certainly. I'll be glad when I can get her onto a bottle.'

'Isn't breast feeding better?'

'Maybe.' Then she relented, for after all, it was her last one. 'We'll see. But you didn't come to discuss pros and cons of baby feeding, Andrew. Or did you?'

He laughed. 'No, not really, though it's a nice picture, R. Which reminds me. The painting, last night's query? Bettina's replied. She reckons our 'Hazel and the Trig Point' painting is a proper Duffy, and the artist is a relative of June's Keela portrait painter. Says it runs down the family, but only on the female side. Which suggests either a concerted attempt to retain the family name or none of the women married, the more unlikely given the strong belief in marriage in Ireland. So our Sheila herself can't be married.'

MaryAnn was transhipped from left nipple to right, and Roberta waited until she was settled before answering. 'A professional name, Andrew, I mean she must be married. No, if she's that good and selling well, then that's what I'd do, retain a name.' The infant stopped sucking; Roberta did the approved action, moved her over her shoulder, patted, and MaryAnn burped beautifully. 'Amazing coincidence. I'm not all that psychic, Andrew, but this coincidence gives me the shivers. Pop her back in the cot, love. Saves me getting out.'

'You're getting lazy, R,' he said, taking the swaddled, well-satisfied bundle and carefully laying her back into the cot. Baby eyes stared at him and he got a lovely smile. 'June wants to postpone her return for a few days. Step sister attraction.' He leant down and gently tickled a chin. 'Understandable. So are you going to get up, dear?'

'In a bit. Make sure Abby and Chris are okay. Kasia . . .'

'Is taking them to playschool. High time you started moving about, my love.'

Roberta waited until Kasia returned from her taxi run before getting up, but she did make it down before lunchtime. Freddie was alone in the kitchen, making herself a sandwich.

'Roberta! How's it going?'

'So so. I'll be all right once everything's back in place.' She eased onto a stool. 'Can't you wait for a proper lunch?'

'Nope. Still got some drawings to do, and another client at two o'clock.'

'I'm very grateful, Freddie. I don't know what I'd have done otherwise.'

'Roberta, you've done me a favour. I'd only have got stuck in a job in a second-hand clothes shop or something.

No, I enjoy being here. Great clients you've got. Quite like old times.'

Roberta thought of Cordelia and Julian, settled into their cosy cottage with a design concept that had brought her the best part of twelve and a half thousand in consultancy fees on top of the extravagant purchase price they must have paid. And there were a few others in the same bracket now, so Freddie's commission was a justifiable expense. Perhaps . . .Andrew wouldn't mind, she was sure, and given June would spend a lot more time in Ireland . . . .

'Freddie, dear, would you like to make this a permanent job?'

TWENTY EIGHT

MaryAnn was thriving. Roberta had followed all the instructions and, with a highly critical self-assessment every morning, was trying hard to regain her shape and muscle tone. After a rigorous and rather intimate session at the hospital with the gynae consultant she spent a day in a private clinic in London and came out with a mixture of strange feelings, maternal loss diluted with one of relief. At least she'd been reassured that her pelmet ligaments - as she called her pelvic regions - wouldn't cause her any more grief, provided she did the exercises and didn't attempt to move heavy objects on her own. Fat chance. Freddie had all but taken over on the day-to-day; she was relegated to the design side, not that she regretted her decision. Andrew, bless him, had endorsed her choice of extra staff wholeheartedly, though occasionally she wondered if she shouldn't have a word with Freddie on the quiet to tell her a bra was de rigueur. Chesty females and her husband didn't mix too well.

Hazel and Peter - well, apart from the occasional tearful girl when she discovered the path of true love had occasional trip-wires in the way - managed to give the impression they were happy in their unconventional state. The girl was going to have to revert - and probably happily - to joint role of nanny and office maid for a while, for Kasia had announced she'd like to go back to Poland for a month. They couldn't deny her, but simply and sincerely hope that she'd come back. She'd said she would, but anything might upset even her avowed intent.

Sam, engrossed in her matronly duties at the Hostel the

other side of the town, came over every now and again. The friendship had developed over the months; Roberta welcomed her visits and so did Andrew, or so she thought, despite the flutter of eyelids and the pursed cheek-on-cheek kiss. And Andrea; she'd changed. Become hard, superficial, less *friendly* in a peculiar way. Which was a shame. She much preferred the old Andrea, the flirty, happy-go-lucky sexy wench, even if she'd set Andrew's pulse racing and gave him the occasional bulge in his trousers. The time she'd come over to say 'howdy' to MaryAnn, she'd not stayed long, flashed her cleavage at them all and gone without seeing Hazel. Poor girl, she'd taken that to heart. So too had Andrew, in so far that he'd moped for the best part of a day. Oh well.

Roberta sighed and put her book down. She'd not absorbed the last chapter in any depth and she'd have to read it again. Her mind couldn't stay still. June, having gone back to Ireland this morning with another copy of the trig point painting, one they'd had done by the *proper* process, what was it called? *Gicleè?* had left a gap, and she knew Andrew would miss her, probably why he'd gone out for a walk.

June. Her mind had been elsewhere most of the time she'd been 'home'. The magic of Ireland had certainly gripped her. Roberta sighed again, as the mental image of that special morning a year or two ago when she'd done a runner from their holiday cottage with the car, sat in the layby up on the Castletown Berehaven road and wished. Wished what? That they could escape from the self-imposed drudgery of a business and revert to being their own people? Or that she hadn't got to worry continuously that her Andrew might stray away? Foolishness, she said inwardly. Total foolishness. Every indication nowadays suggested his roving eye had settled down. Had she worried? He perhaps had. Andrew - now where was he?

'Kasia dear, have you seen my husband?' The slim girl

had emerged with a tea tray, bless her, and placed it carefully down on the little table.

'No, Roberta. Not since he went out after lunch.'

'He took his stick?'

'Yes, and his old coat, the one with the funny smell.'

Roberta laughed. 'The old Barbour. Yes, it has that strange odour. It's the wax coating, Kasia. But he loves it.' She remembered it well, for he'd been wearing that coat when he'd first appeared, miraculously, in her life, to pick her up from her fall off old Bouncer. How the mind flew back to that crucial day!

'He has been away some time now.'

'Oh, he does that sometimes. Goes up the hill to think. I don't mind. After all, we women must get on top of him some times.'

Kasia gave her a funny look, and she twigged. 'Oh!', and blushed. The girl grinned at her, understandingly. 'Sorry, Kasia.'

'Not a problem. I think he is a lucky man, Roberta. Maybe I am jealous, no?'

'Now then girl. Don't get ideas!'

'That is not in my - how do you say - make up?'

'Then that's all right. Do you want to have your tea here, with me?'

'Thank you, but no. I have Abby and Chris in the kitchen. But I think MaryAnn will be awake now.'

'You're right. I'll just drink my tea then go up. Thank you, Kasia.'

The girl nodded and left the room. How good she was! Almost as good as Hazel. Roberta put her cup back on the tray. She walked across to the window. Out there, way up on the hill - his hill - he'd be there, thinking of her. Wondering about their future, the lives of their three children. Dreaming perhaps. The lives they'd influenced, the impact they'd had on so many, clients, friends, employees even, She was blessed, truly blessed. She turned, longing for his return and the comfort of their companionship. Now MaryAnn needed her; the pressure of her milk was there.

On a May evening, the sky stayed light until gone nine. The breeze of the day had dropped, the garden was still, the vague scents rising from the border and the grass just beginning to dampen as the cool of the night set in. A solitary blackbird was serenading the oncoming twilight. He still hadn't returned.

Roberta was phoning the cottage.

'Peter, your father's not come back from his afternoon walk. His mobile's not answering, I'm sure he recharged it. He's not done this before. I'm worried. Can you come up?'

Peter had already sensed her emotive state from the tone of her voice, let alone what she'd told him. Hazel, who'd initially answered the phone, stood there, hand to her mouth, eyes wide.

'Of course. Hazel will come too. Be with you shortly. Perhaps he's sprained an ankle or something. Has he gone onto the hill?'

'I - I think so. After lunch, mid afternoon. It's,' and he felt she was close to tears, 'it's over five hours now. At most he's away only three, maybe four.'

'We're on our way.' and as he replaced the phone on its cradle his spine chilled. Not like his father. Not with Roberta. 'Bring that torch, Hazel. And find the big sweaters. It'll turn cooler, especially if we have to go looking.'

Roberta was on the front door step, huddled into her woollen cardigan, arms wrapped around her, a taut and anxious figure with a drawn face. 'We'd best go up the hill, past the bench, you know the way I mean. It'll be getting dark in the wood. Oh, Peter!', and she fell into his opened arms. 'It's not like him!'

No, it wasn't, Peter knew, and his thoughts were not helping. 'You shouldn't come, Roberta, not yet, too soon after MaryAnn. Hazel and I will go. I have my mobile, you stay with Kasia,' he suggested as he saw the outline of the Polish girl in the hall behind. 'I'm sure it'll be something simple.' He gently disengaged her, turned her round and saw her back into Kasia's care. Then, with Hazel's steady hand in his, they went off across the lawn, to the stile over the stone wall and the path up towards the wood on the rise and crest of the hill, losing its outline as the light began to fade.

After his turn round the village, calling in at the old church to spend some time in quiet reflection before taking the path through the ancient avenue of chestnuts, then dropping down to the lakeside, across the pastureland towards the farm, he'd thought of having an early half at the Horse and Jockey. Convivial banter, an exchange of light-hearted gossip, an appreciated offer of congratulations once he'd admitted to their third child, then it was time to get on. He still hadn't been round the normal loop; if he got a move on perhaps there was just enough time before getting back for an early evening meal.

'Thanks, Dave,' and he replaced his glass on the bar, gave a half wave and left.

It had been the usual steady pull up the slope, the initial ease giving way to the deeper breaths as he climbed, unusually he had a bit of a stitch in his side. Normally he should be able to take this in his stride, even after a couple of hours steady walking and an hour in the pub. Twenty minutes to the old bench and he promised himself a breather. First time he'd been up here since before MaryAnn's birth - even a week or two before. He really should do this walk more often.

He missed the challenge of the Irish weeks, given Roberta

had gone maternal again they hadn't had the chance. June had, though, lucky girl, and he thought of her, comfortably lodged with that other girl Bett at Siobhán's place. So if she did make it her home? Did he mind? Yes and no. She'd come back into his life and given him support, fallen on her feet with Roberta and the business. Taken the pressure off. To lose her would leave a gap. Freddie was all very well, but not the same. Even her rampant availability as a woman didn't stir him, unlike Andrea. Now she was out of reach too. The picture of her, abandonedly naked amongst the debris of his ex-marital bed after that fight over Sam's discarded pants, did stir him. And Hazel - but he tried to push that picture of her, spread across the sun-warmed grass on the Sheeps Head, poised on the cusp of her virgin sexuality, out of his mind. Roberta - his *wife* - she who had seduced him with a glimpse of *her* underwear and a desperate cry for help - *she* was his lover. *Roberta!* The gardener's shed, her skirt all rucked up and around, backed up against the potting bench, eyes alight with mischief and desire, pulling at him. What a furious little shagging that had been! And now they had MaryAnn, a gift to treasure, to love and guard, like the other two. How precious!

He reached the bench and sat, carefully, onto the decaying woodwork, and massaged his side to lessen the stitch. He really must get these slats renewed. Okay, it technically wasn't their property, but what the heck. Someone had put it here, ages ago, and how many travellers had rested here awhile? He had, four years ago, and seen his life change before him. Was it about to change again? Was sitting here a sort of magic thing, like June's Keela in Ireland, something to pull at the deeper, unconscious inner soul? How daft was that! His mind skated around, twirling, twisting, and as he tried to focus on the glimpse of the Manor below him, the last vestiges of the sun dipping below the trees across the valley and giving them a transient golden halo, it seemed as though the early evening light was fading far too soon into night, soft, velvet suffocating night. It was getting cold, very cold. He tried to get up, to move, to return to Roberta. *Roberta . . .*

✿

From the Manor, it took Hazel and Peter fifteen minutes to reach him.

As Hazel, fresh from her sessions on First Aid, swallowed her emotions as best she could and set to work, Peter was on the mobile, not wanting to take in the reality, holding his own feelings in suspense. This just wasn't true. It couldn't be true. The message given, the location explained as best he could, he knelt down and tapped Hazel on the shoulder. 'Between us?'

They worked on, hoping, praying, desperate and yet solidly convinced they'd win.

The twin tones echoed, stopped, yellow jacketed figures moving up the path, reassurance and measured questions, an appraisal, then an anonymous recumbent figure on a blanketed stretcher taken down to the care of the box-like capacity of the ambulance.

They could only wait while the paramedics worked on in quiet desperation.

Finally, 'you want to come?' The mature guy with the pleasant face, experience and concern mirrored, asked the question.

Hazel looked at Peter. 'You go,' he said. 'I'll go back to Roberta. Phone me,' and he passed her his mobile. They couldn't admit the reality, not yet.

As Peter watched the vehicle accelerate away, heard the siren sound as it reached the main road, he had to face up to the task ahead. Numb. As chilled as his father's body, all life drained away. The unreal reality. Fleetingly, he thought how calm his girl had been. Hazel, calm under a situation she'd

299

never had to deal with before, concerning someone who, he knew, she loved desperately. How would she be once she'd finally been told? They never gave up, did they, these paramedics. Not while there's a chance. Only the hospital A & È staff would say, but he knew. Roberta. Sam, his mother. June, Andrea, the village, all to tell. How? Why? *Why!!* Why had his father gone, at the best time of his life, with everything in place, a new little girl, oh, *God!* He'd seen tragedy abroad, felt the pain as that little girl had given up on her life and died in his arms. This was different; deeply despairingly different.

He stood alone in the road; ironically, not that he knew, in the very same place where his father had first discovered Roberta, where, but for a lucky chance, she might also have died. Looked up at the first twinkle of a star in a cushioned deep blue, at the sliver of a moon, at the hole in his universe.

Footsteps on the gravel. She'd automatically turned the drive lights on, as an encouragement, but she was petrified. Something deep inside had twisted in her soul and she experienced a sheer ice cold inner pain. She brushed her skirt behind her and sat on the top step, the chill of the stone unfelt. Kasia was up with the children. Peter was coming back, alone.

She looked down at him facing her, an expressionless face.

'Peter?'

'Hazel's with him.'

A surge of hope, then dismay, then another douche of worry. 'With him? Where?'

'Yes. We found him. By the bench.' How could he express his frozen feelings, when he didn't know them himself? I'm sorry? Too simple, too crass. Instead, he found himself reaching for her as she rose and all but fell into his outstretched arms. Together, crushed tight, he felt her wracking, heaving tide of emotion and his own self control went.

Kasia, all-controlled but stony faced, probably guarding her own feelings, with a meal on the go and now abandoned, made them some strong tea and encouraged Roberta to rest in the sitting room. Peter could only wait, mind churning, for Hazel's call. Eventually, it came. After the 'it's me' came the silence, the sob, another silence, and the words he'd dreaded. Too late. Too late. He took a deep breath, quelled the stomach muscle's rise and endeavoured to bring rationality forward.

'Darling. I need to know. And come and fetch you?'

He knew she was trying. After another pause, she whispered 'they think it was an aneurism. If . . .' and again the pause. 'Roberta - will she . . .'

'I'll see.' He tried to stay calm. 'You're a very brave girl. I love you,' but then he had to give up, and he knew she'd switched off too.

Roberta looked up, staring eyes, the question in them. He shook his head, all he could do.

She got up, hesitated, took a few steps across the room and sat in the fireside chair.

'It was here, Peter. In this chair. He sat on the rug at my feet, and I made him love me. My world. My entire world. Gave me the children, love, support, strength. I've lost my mum, now I've lost the only other person who I ever properly loved. He loved *me*. The other girls didn't matter.'

He waited, aware that once she talked, the initial pain would ease.

'Your father still loved Sam. I knew that. He tried - wouldn't let it show, but he did. A measure of how much I mattered to him. All we did.' A moment's pause. 'Did I destroy his marriage, Peter? Was I responsible? I'd hate that. I never wanted to hurt him, never. Why did he leave me?

What have I done? I should have taken more care. Peter. Peter, what do I do now? He shouldn't have gone up the hill. He never saw a doctor. What was wrong? Why did he die? Why up there? Why not in my arms? He's only fifty. Fifty!' Her voice had risen, gone falsetto, and the last words were like a scream.

This was his father she was taking about. His father, the person he was only just beginning to understand, to re-learn all the joys of comradeship, the way he'd been guided so recently in his love for Hazel. And Roberta had been his life, at least for the last four years or so. He'd known how happy his father had been with her, more so perhaps than with mum, though that had been different. And she'd need to know. He wondered how to comfort his step-mum, to quell this rising tide of hysteria in her, but Kasia beat him to it. The door opened and baby MaryAnn was in her arms.

He drove, carefully and slowly, to the hospital and found Hazel in the mortuary waiting room.

They asked, did you want to see him, sympathy as part of the caring, but he shook his head. Not now. Perhaps tomorrow, in a day a so, maybe if Roberta wanted to see him. Hazel held his hand, her presence a tremendous help.

'There'll have to be a post-mortem.'

'Of course.'

'We'll be in touch. Your family doctor?'

Hazel knew and was able to say. She wondered how Doc Mac would take it, given he'd seen them lose Mary, and so recently looked after Roberta during MaryAnn's birth. Thank heavens she'd been born. So Andrew had at least seen her, held her. Now there were the others to tell and she'd do it, if Peter wanted her to. Anything to share or diminish the anguish that it was. Deep down, the hurt from the loss of his love, the knowledge that she had been loved, even in the platonic way it was, though, a wry strange smile, it might once have even got physical. That triangulation point in Ireland, the painting, the mysterious power it appeared to have. Now June was ferreting about around there, looking for answers.

'We'd best get home, love,' he said, and led her back to the car. The little shopping, run the children to playschool car. Not the Volvo. Not Andrew's car. Would Roberta sell it?

'Yes.'

They drove home in silence, each lost in thought. How nicely the day had started, how tragically it had ended. As he went to sit with Roberta, Hazel went into the office, switched on all the lights, sat in the swing chair, spun round and picked up the phone.

TWENTY NINE

She pushed open the cottage door. The late afternoon light streamed through the sitting room windows, giving the room a warmth beyond the mellowness of the day. Good to be back.

'Bett! I'm back!'

The girl emerged from the kitchen at the back, tea towel in hand, polishing a mug she'd obviously just washed up. 'You're early, didn't expect you so soon. Good flight? Tea?'

'Sure thing. And no delays. Sorry if I'm a day or two behind schedule.'

'No worries. How's the new mum - and dad? Another step sister!'

'And the last. Roberta's seen to that. Between you and me, I think they were a bit scared of things going wrong. You know she had this problem?'

'You said. So all went well in the end. I'll get you a mug,' and she disappeared into the bijou kitchen. June followed her.

'How's the restoration going?'

Bett dropped a teabag into June's mug. 'Not so bad. Donald's always popping into the studio to have a look. What do you think to the provenance?'

'The *Duffy* thing?'

Bett nodded, handed June her mug. 'The milk's in that jug,' and she pointed at the table. 'I'm sure I'm right. I read it up. The Duffy girls specialised in these romantic stories; some say there was always an undercurrent of bad luck if you had a Duffy painting done. That wouldn't have helped their business!' She chuckled. 'Only on portraits, of course.'

June cautiously tried her tea for temperature. She didn't care for a scalded mouth. 'And the Irish believe in luck, good and bad. So if the *Keela* painting *was* a Duffy, the *bad* luck suggested she'd lose her lover?'

Bettina's eye's narrowed down. 'Just let's say I wouldn't like to have a *Duffy* portrait painted.'

'Oh.' June put her mug down and folded her arms. 'So, if the one that Andrew and Roberta were given over in Glengarrif was done by a . . .' Her arms went down to her side. 'There's something of a superstitious problem.'

'Uh huh. You brought it?'

'Oh yes. Sorry. In my case. I'll fetch it.'

The print, fresh and pristine in its roll, was brought out; June carefully slid it out of the tube.

'Wow!' Bettina studied, turned it to the light. 'You say this was on hardboard?'

'I think so.'

'She did a super job. And this is?' she asked, pointing at the figure they had assumed was Hazel.

'Hazel. At least, the clothes are what she wears sometimes.'

'Hmmm. How old?'

''Bout twenty.'

'This girl -woman - looks older to me. See, the lines, the waist. More mature.'

'But the hair colour?'

'Luscious brown.

June hesitated, took the curl-stiff roll and took a critical look. 'I don't know. So it could be Roberta in a different guise.'

Bett shrugged. 'You know them, I don't. A painting will speak to you - dependant on what you want it to say. Like a book. Or a poem. Means different things to different people. Show me a painting that *everyone* likes. Or a book *everyone* enjoys reading. Does everyone enjoy a strong curry? Do you like wearing tatty jeans? So subjective.' She eyed June with a quizzical expression. 'And if I fancied Declan, it doesn't mean you have to.'

'Bett, you've drifting away from the problem. Does this painting mean bad luck for us?'

'Just remember that *Keela* lost her lover. And there's a record of another Duffy painted girl seeing her lover commit suicide 'cos he couldn't . . .' she mused, 'at least, that's how the story goes.'

'Enough. This is making me feel all funny.' She picked up her now cold tea mug and drained it. 'Yurgh. Let's see if we can beg supper.'

Over the supper table, Bett re-ran her theory. 'So, if the *Cadhla* girl's suitor had her portrait painted, he was sealing her paramour's fate. Which, by legend or no, seemed to be what happened.'

Siobhán looked across the table at Donald. 'You'd better not have my portrait painted then, my love. I don't want you falling off a cliff or whatever he did.'

'I couldn't afford a Duffy anyway. How come you came by this one, June?' The print lay on the sideboard, pinned down by four books.

'Oh, it's not mine. Given to my father - or Roberta - or to Hazel, we don't know who, by Sheila Duffy, a year ago. We thought the girl was Hazel, by the clothes, though Bett thinks she's too old, and the hair colour's not right for Hazel.'

'Um.' Donald got up from the table and went to take a closer look. 'Could be Roberta; I don't know much about the Hazel girl. Whichever. Coffee, anyone? In the other room? I'll break out the liqueurs if you like.'

The evening drew on, and June felt sleepy. 'I'll call it a night,' she said. 'Coming, Bett? Back to work in the morning?'

Bett stretched her back and rose to her feet. ''Spose so.

Thank you ever so much, Siobhán, Donald. Somehow didn't fancy cottage cooking tonight.'

'Just as well we had lashings. Glad you felt you could ask. Night night.'

The two girls made their way across the yard to the stables cottage, now a home from home. Overhead, the new moon was just showing its fine crescent against the evening sky, the only sound a faint rustle of a breeze. June stopped and looked up.

'I wonder if the Manor's sky is like this?'

'Probably. Do you miss it? Your father?'

'Bett, he's been marvellous. Of course I miss him, but I can't live in his shoes, or Roberta's. They've a new family. I'm best out of it, and anyway, as Roberta's found this old friend of hers to take over what I used to do, then there's no problem. I'll manage. You've left your circle.'

'True.' She hesitated. 'Will you ever think of re-marrying, June?'

June laughed. 'Maybe. If the right guy appears. A younger clone of dad perhaps. What about you?'

'I'm not ruling it out. I quite like Declan.'

'Ah ha! Just as well I can take him or leave him!' and she moved on towards the cottage. 'We'll get cold, mooning about.' As they reached the door, she added, 'I fancy living by the sea. Though somewhere like this would do. With three kids and a husband who can stay sober!'

They'd been indoors for half an hour, just about to go to bed when there were footsteps across the yard and a knock on the door. 'June,' and she heard Siobhán's voice, taut and strained. 'I've Hazel on the phone. Do come, quickly,' and the footsteps receded.

'Hazel? Why should she ring this late? Bett, I don't like the sound of this.' June looked around for her sweater. 'Will you come with me?'

307

'Of course, love,' and she too found something warm. Together the two girls hurried back into the dim light of the house's rear passage.

Donald and Siobhán were standing by the kitchen door. 'The phone's off the hook in the hall, June.'

'Thanks,' and she went into the even dimmer hall and picked up the handset on its tangled cord. 'Hazel?'

The anxiously waiting three heard her '*Oh NOoooo!*' and the '*How? Why?*' then the strange comment, '*You've done well, Hazel, very well. Thank you, for being so efficient,*' and the clatter as the handset dropped back onto its cradle. Slow footsteps.

June's pinched face was white even in the dim light. 'It's dad. They found him up by the old bench,' and as Siobhán started towards her, fell into her outstretched arms.

Samantha sat in front of the unheard television, staring at an uncomprehended screen. Hazel's call had come immediately after she'd returned to her flat after a visit to the cinema, something she did every now and again to take her out of the mundane. A hollowness, an empty feeling. She couldn't cry, for the emotive side was stunned, frozen. Her mind drifted; through the past, the children's upbringing, the years on their own, the drift into separation and the past few months when they'd regained something of the old comradeship during the few times they'd met, mostly at the Manor. Having Peter and June so close had helped. But now, what? How would Roberta manage? She didn't seem the one to shrug and carry on, and with a new child?

The programme droned on. Sam suddenly reached for the remote and switched the thing off. The silence closed down around, and the appalling suddenness of this newly created emptiness shook her. She shivered, not from cold, but from a combination of shock and a profound deep, deep sense of loss. *'Stupid, stupid, stupid woman!'*

The message reached Andrea via the Studio's night-time security. *'Please call . . .'* and the number was the Manor's, instantly memorable. She looked at her little gold watch, another present from Alain. He was always finding something new to give her, trying to drive away the old links from her time with Andrew. Was he that jealous? No reason, or was there? She'd never felt anything quite like the jazz electric buzz Andrew had given her that time. Eleven o'clock. Should she ring now, or leave it until the morning? Perhaps he needed to talk to her? She took out her all-singing, all-dancing brand new phone. Another Alain gift.

'Hi, it's Andrea? *Hazel?* What are you doing at this hour?' then she listened to a clipped, tight young voice relaying the necessary minimal information. *'No! no! no! no-ooh,'* dropped the phone on the floor and screamed. She tore at her dress, at her hair, flung herself flat down on the couch and beat the cushions until her hands bled. She howled as if the devils were after her until her throat became sore, and falling off the couch, stumbled to the sideboard to splash brandy into a glass, to gulp it down and nearly choke. Then she collapsed into an untidy heap on the floor and sobbed, sobbed and sobbed.

After half an hour she was drained, drained of energy, of emotion, of any sane thought other than that she had lost the only man she'd ever wanted, and now she knew, positively and definitely, she'd *never* marry, not now, not Alain, not ever. Her spirit had died within her.

Hazel retreated to bed in the Manor, in the room that had once been Mary's. Peter had gone back to the cottage in the village, but they agreed she should stay with Roberta. Kasia, with all the dignity of her race, had stated categorically she would stay on to look after the children for however long, and had phoned her folk back home in Poland to explain.

Roberta, after a late night visit from Dr Mac, was under a mild sedative and sleeping.

After the telephone calls she'd made, with the different reactions she'd had, Hazel was drained, feeling as though she was a shell, a hollow shell with nothing inside her. The voices stayed in her head, swinging round and round. June's response, after the initial shock reaction, had been calm to the point of unbelievability, rational, understanding, praising her for what she'd done. Samantha, not understanding, not believing her, before it sunk in and she'd merely said *'oh, goodness, poor Roberta,'* and put the phone down. Andrea, after returning her call, screaming *'No No No No'* before she, too, had dropped the phone. Hazel worried for the girl, wondering if she'd get so hysterical she'd do herself harm. Now she had to try and empty her mind and get some sleep, for tomorrow she'd need all the strength she possessed.

'I loved him, I loved him, I loved him,' That wasn't emptying her mind, that was trying to fill a void. A void she'd have to fill with her love for Peter. That was what she needed; Peter's love would be his - Andrew's - gift to her.

Roberta woke, cold and uncomfortable, in the early hours, her mind asking an immediate question, wondering why Andrew wasn't alongside her, before the tidal rush of a wave of total anguish rushed in to drown her senses in black despair. Never again. An empty bed, a lonely waking, solitary dressing, showering, single play with the children. No more happy expeditions to the London flat, to the theatre, dining out, shopping for extravagant dresses for him to admire and strip off her late in the evening. She felt stripped of her very soul, a shattered fragment of a disjointed skeletonised woman. Alone.

She lay on her back, shivering despite the warmth of the room, listening to her mind's rush of thoughts. Images of the past. His tentative approach, then his acceptance of her wants, her desire. His lust for her which grew so quickly into care. The Irish trip. Her broken arm, silly girl. The other girl's crush - and how he owned up to sleeping with her. Samantha's reluctant divorce. Mary's thoughts. June, and how she'd looked after them. And then Hazel, how close she'd been to a foolish de-flowering. The television thing, Alain, the mattress in the barn, Andrew taking her in the gardener's shed, MaryAnn's birth . . ..

It was then that her mind cleared, as though he was talking to her. She listened to her mind as the flickering grey demons weakened away, skirled into nothingness and . . .

Dawn.

This was a bright May morning, curtains flicked gently from the part open window, sunlight danced across the carpet; somewhere out there, from the branches of the beech, a thrush was greeting the day. She pushed the duvet aside, slipped naked limbs out, stood, threw a nightdress away and tiptoed into the shower. So now she was a single girl, but still a girl, with a life, a business, three children, staff and years of life ahead of her. Andrew had been her life for a while, but she'd lived thirty plus years without him. She would again, but with his guidance and support at her side, coming from wherever he'd gone. Bless him.

Showered, she dressed carefully and in her favourite things. No going back. No sobbing, grieving widow. Yes, she'd miss him, yes, she'd be seen to do the 'right thing', but after that?

The phone rang for quite a while before Siobhán's greeting, 'Mor House.'

311

'Siobhán, dear, can I have a word with June?'

'*Roberta! Oh, my dear girl, I am* so, so sorry *to hear of your tragic loss!*'

'Thank you.' She paused, wondering about other folk's reaction to her avowed calm state. 'June?'

'She'll still be in the cottage. Will you hold on, or shall I ask her to ring you back?'

Roberta sensed Siobhán's curiosity, on how she could be so cool less than a day after Andrew's demise, and allowed a faint smile. 'I'll hold, thankyou.'

June was panting, she'd run, silly girl, and her greeting was subtly phrased.

'Roberta, I didn't expect you to ring so soon; how are you taking my father's loss - it's been a shock to us all. I still can't take it in.'

'We've both lost the physical presence of a very dear, dear person, June. I know that, as you do, and everyone will miss him, but life goes on. I want you to do something for me.'

'Anything, Roberta.'

'Find somewhere in Ireland for me to stay with the children for a while. Somewhere not too far away from you, but preferably on the Cork side. Please?'

Silence meant June's mind was in free fall.

'June?'

'Oh. Yes. When? How long for?'

Roberta nearly chuckled. *Ever?* 'Oh, for a few weeks.'

'*Weeks?*'

'Maybe longer. We'll see. Call me when you've had some thoughts, there's a dear. Now, I've got some logistics to deal with. My regards to Bettina.'

THIRTY

The initial presumption had been proven correct.

'It happens,' said Doc Mac, a day later when he'd dropped by as a sort of courtesy call and to check on MaryAnn's progress. 'A great shame he was away up the hill. If he'd collapsed at home and you'd dialled triple nine we'd have saved him. How are things?'

How are you taking it, Roberta knew he meant. Well, since that first night and her getting a grip on her situation, she'd done pretty well. Oh, yes, she'd had her moments, private floods of tears and the occasional heave of tummy muscles, but on the whole . . .

'Coping, thanks, Doc. I can't afford the luxury of brooding on what might have been. Life goes on; I've three little ones and a business.'

Doc Mac looked at her. A steady gaze. An intake of breath, and a knowledgeable understanding. A strong woman, Roberta. 'So now what?'

'I'm going to Ireland. Hazel and Peter will move back into the Manor. I'm letting Freddie run the design side of the business here, with Hazel doing the commercial bit. She's proved herself very competent. I'm best out of it.'

'I can understand, Roberta, but isn't it rather a quick decision? And you'll be moving away from your friends, your support. How will you manage, if it isn't rather forward of me to ask - but then, I've known you a long while.'

'There's a lot of friendly people out there, Mac, and June will be nearby. I'm sure something will turn up. And I shall sell the London property; it'll fetch good money.' Her eyes pricked and she could feel the emotion swelling. 'I can't stay here, Mac. Too many very happy memories, very strong ones. And I need to make the break now. Once . . .' she tailed off, unable to say more, and she could sense his perceptive feeling. He'd understand. Once the formalities had been gone through, she'd feel better. 'I'll take his ashes with me,' she went on, as a spur of the moment thought. 'He'd like that. Up on the Sheeps Head. Where he was happy. Then he'll be in Ireland, like he always said he'd like to be.' The tears rolled, unstoppable, as the mental scenario played out. 'Why did he have to die on me, just when we were in the full swing of things!' Her voice rose, and Doc Mac opened his comforting arms for her. Maybe way beyond the call of duty but she was a friend, and one in dire need of his friendship.

Thus it was. Weeks later, as the summer brought its warmth to the deep greens and distant blues of the magical isle, Roberta, with a small box and with Hazel as guide, took the path past the black stone seat and its inscription *'Water and Ground in their Extremity'*, up towards the skyline and the point where she could say her last goodbyes.

'Here?'

Hazel nodded. 'Here.'

He was gone. She'd walked his contours, reached his trig point, now she understood his benchmarks and was content. Her three children would grow and become worthy of their father. She would always love the treasured moments, the joys and hurts, the foibles and fancies. Her English business would flourish in Freddie's care, the Irish one would grow with June and Bett's help. Peter and Hazel's marriage was planned. June seemed to have captured Declan's heart, despite Bett's best endeavours. Sam - dear Samantha - was

314

understandably going abroad again for a while. And Andrea? As the two woman stood, arms around each other, looking at an eternal view of distant waters and protective hills in the mid-day haze, Roberta chuckled.

'She had her fling, Hazel. He loved her too, so I can't begrudge her that joy. Maybe she'll come to her senses one day. He'll look after her, from wherever he is.'

Hazel nodded. 'He was always good at looking after us girls. Every single one of us.'

Roberta turned her head. 'You know, you're right. Every single one of us. Gave us each what we needed, whether we knew it or not. Shall we go?'

POSTSCRIPT

By a strange quirk of fate, the Naylor's house, where Cadhla's suitor had once lived, came onto the market not many weeks after Roberta had undertaken her final duty for her late husband. With the substantial proceeds of the sale of the London house burning a hole in her financial pocket, Roberta bought it.

For some four months or so afterwards there was a flurry of activity as the house underwent a full restoration, and with all the splendid resources at her disposal, Roberta ensured it would be an absolute gem, a superb example of not only her talents, but also June and Declan's.

And in early October she held a house-warming.

Siobhán and Donald were the first guests to arrive, but then, they only had to come across the valley. The rest of Roberta's family had already foregathered, Hazel's clear tones somewhere in the back quarters.

'We've brought you a present,' said Siobhán, carefully holding out a rather large flat parcel. 'After all, we really only were looking after it for you. Bettina's brought her back to life.'

Roberta's eyes were shining. The local love story never dimmed in its retelling, and she unwrapped the brown paper with care and fascination. As the sheets fell away to the floor of the hall, the hall refurbished to be so like the Manor's one, back in Bedfordshire, *Cadhla* was revealed once more in her original setting.

- - - *The girl in her full dark red dress, caught with a brooch on*

316

her left shoulder, long hair draped across her right, the naked
shoulder, a hand clutching a bouquet of yellow roses partially
covering a pert breast. The background was dark, sombre, as though
she was poised on the edge of a wood - - -

'Keela!'

Siobhán nodded. 'Keela. Back where she belongs. Painted by an ancestor of your own paintress. Bett is sure it was you Sheila painted, up there on the Sheeps Head. Whatever bad luck went with the painting, bringing Keela - *Cadhla* - back here will complete the circle and inspire good luck instead. I'm sure of it, Roberta, so she comes home with all our blessings.'

'She was a lovely girl.' Roberta held the painting out at both arm's length, gazing at the faint smile, vaguely imperious, haughty maybe, but an appealing face none the less.

'Is,' said Donald. '*Cadhla* is yourself, sure she is. You've come back, lass, and we're all the better for your return.'

He was grinning at her, but Roberta could feel her spine tingling. She could hear Andrew's chuckle, see his mischievous smile, feel his arms around her. He would be here with her and the children - she could hear their laughs as Kasia got them dressed for the party - he'd be here with his love and all his care. She had found them all a home, and *Cadhla* would be her own comforting benchmark, a girl who had wandered, who had loved and lost but eventually had came home too.

May 2010

ACKNOWLEDGEMENTS

Every aspect of delivering a story requires support or inspiration.

It is not possible to list everyone involved - for they are many and various - but especial thanks to Helen Dixon (and Jess) for being so encouraging, to an Ordnance Survey representative at the LBF who suggested the title, to Stephen & Nicky at Creative Iglu who do magical things for the cover, to all the staff at Waterstones who help promote the series and, of course, to the professional production team at Troubador. Not forgetting (as is often the case) the guys who turn an electronic file into a very nice book - well done, TJ International and the team at Padstow.

Thanks also to the devoted readers, so I do hope you enjoy this, the final (perhaps) episode in the Manor series.